Concealed in Myths
Book I

VEILED

Dirty Talk
PUBLISHING

Ruby Smoke

COPYRIGHT

Veiled

Ruby Smoke

First published in Great Britain in [2023] by

DIRTY TALK PUBLISHING LIMITED

First published Great Britain in [2023] by [Ruby Smoke]

This edition published in [2023] by

DIRTY TALK PUBLISHING LIMITED

ISBN: **[**978-1-916521-69-8**]**

Edited by: **Ruby Smoke**

Cover Design: Ruby Smoke

Published by **DIRTY TALK PUBLISHING LTD**

Dirty Talk

PUBLISHING

For all of those who almost lost the will to live, to keep going, and are still here.
To those who found that reading was their life's pulse.
&
Finally, to those who realized that the power of ink on a page can literally become the air in your lungs.

Keep going. *The fight may hurt, you may feel lost, but we are still here. As a survivor who struggles everyday,* **I am here with you.**

"In a world with Faeries, man does not sit nicely atop the food chain."

-Theresa Bane

THE OTHERWORDLY

The World of Faerie has never been an easy one, nor has it been a difficult one. In fact, it is both one of the most complex, yet simplest worlds one can encounter. The world of Fae and those who inhabit it are a paradox. A paradox that both intrigues, and should, rightfully so, fill you with an unsettling amount of fear. It's not simply a city or a town, rather it is Otherworldly for a reason. It is an entire world with both safe and dangerous places, Fae and non-Fae. The mistake, often made, is believing that one can discern one danger from the other.

Though, for the sake of this novel, we will focus on the Fae. Throughout history, we have seen, read, and heard various depictions of "the good folk," a force too propitiated and protected against. But those tales are for mere mortals. For those who seek knowledge that can both tantalize and wither the senses, enslave you to a deep well of unattainable knowledge, and leave you drowning and gasping for breath. A breath that you'll never catch, for the Fae will not let you come up for air. So, heed the warning of many researchers before you and do not seek what you are not truly ready to find, and if you believe yourself ready, it is quite simple... you are not.

Descendants of Gods.

For thousands of years, the Fae have held a hierarchy of Queens, whether those Queens were benevolent or cruel was up for debate at the time of the rule. However, what has always held true was the tenuous balance within the realms, good and evil, natural versus unnatural. Whenever that balance is destroyed, the Fae will war. Those wars can bring down the Veil between the Fae and Mortal realms, casualties on both sides causing dismay and destruction.

What you hold in your hand can either educate you, intrigue you, or destroy you, depending on how much information you wish to seek and how much faith you plan to place in an author who may or may not be a Fae, wishing to ensnare you.

Reader Beware.

> *"Stand I at the crossroads at the place between night*
> *and day.*
> *With my witch's finger, open the Faery way.*
> *Stand I at the crossroads, at the place between life and death.*
> *And bless I all who read this book,*
> *With my witch's breath!"*
> *Storm Faerywolf*

"COMMON" TYPES OF FAERIES

Baobhan Sith- In Scottish lore, the "woman of the fairies" was a vampire-like Fae. It took the form of a beautiful woman and would drain hunters or men walking alone at night of their blood.

Brownie- A species of domestic fairy, or house-spirit from Scottish lore, short in stature. Nocturnal and love to do housework. When offended or mistreated, said brownie turns into a boggart.

Changeling- An ugly fairy child put in place of a kidnapped human child.

Dark Man- In Irish lore, he is the physical and solid embodiment of death. Only serving the fairy queens.

Dragons- Existing in almost all cultures, they are also tied to fairy lore.

Dryad- One of the twelve species of nymphs, they are of the forest and the trees, particularly oak trees. They have the power to punish those who harm trees and reward those who actively extend and protect their trees. Life of the dryad is tied to its tree.

Djinn- Race of demons, immortal.

Dwarf- Short, but powerfully built, are beneficent and will assist those who treat them with respect. They prefer the night and because they are isolationists, they are said to be members of the Unseelie court; however, the lore varies on these creatures.

Elemental Fairy- Fae linked to the primal power of the elemental forces of nature, air, earth, fire, and water. Each was its own species. Air- Sylph, Earth- Gnomes, Fire- Salamanders, Water- Nereids.

Fairy King/Queen- Individual fairy beings who rule over a court of subjects, as much as Fae can be ruled. In Scotland, the royal Fairy King and Queen are recognized by ancient law.

Fairy Triad- In the Celtic fairy tradition, a fairy triad is a place where ash, oak, and thorn trees are all growing together; where this occurs, the area is considered to be a sacred grove, and a place inhabited by the Dryads.

Fairy Land- The homeland of the Fae, described as being an enchanted place where happiness abounds, no illness or death, where time stands still. Although the entryways into the realm of the Fae are located here on Earth, Fairy Land is said to be attainable underground or underwater, while other times it is described as being in a nearby dimension or in-between place, invisible to the human eye.

The Fates- Depicted as three sisters who guide over the fate of man rather than control or determine it. In many accounts, they are more powerful than Gods.

Furies- Primary concern is the retribution for the killing of family members. We link them with darkness, death, night, and the Underworld. In fact, we also know them to drink the blood of mortals.

Gnomes- Shy and cautious by nature, they seek the company of their own kind.

Goblin- A fairy with injurious or malicious intent.

Grindylow- Water fairy who lives at the bottom of pits, ponds, and wells that grabs small children and holds them underwater until they drown.

Grundels- Found in the homes of larger elves/Fae, they have a symbiotic relationship where they will work for elves in exchange for a safe and happy home.

Kelpies- Associated with water and believed to be carnivorous and cannibalistic. Male kelpies can shift and lure young women into the water to consume them.

Trooping Fairies- Small, benevolent, and kind, freely helping humans.

Seelie Court- Light elves

Solitary Fairies- Tend to be injurious and if they chose to assist, it will be at a price.

Unseelie Court- Dark Elves, avoid light and can be intimidating when provoked.

THE PROPHECY OF THE FAERIE QUEEN

There sits an imposter, a Queen of old
Frozen in time, without the touch of Gaia,
for Gaia has left long ago, leaving the throne without guidance.
Nature weeps, the breeze has abandoned the Fae as Darkness takes over
The Dark Fae, the Unseelie, will draw a line against the very core of nature
The cold will take over the hearts of those Fae,
for as Gaia creates, Gaia will also freeze to preserve.

The Light Fae will thrive and flee into the safety of the heart of Gaia, led by loyal warriors.
The vines beyond the Veil will run deep with blood in every death; every slight against the very nature of who we are.
Nature will twist and churn until the Unseelie are as unfeeling as the coldness in their hearts.
Until one worthy is born to unfreeze the hearts of those shrouded in darkness.

In two hundred years' time, there will be a true Queen born of Gaia, one who will unite the Fae, both the Dark, who can be saved, and the Light, who may still need saving themselves.
Twenty years a child; twenty years running wild
Come, heart, for there is the mystical brotherhood.

Queen.
Not everyone is as they seem, despite their greatest of intentions, be wary.
The nights will be long, the darkness will soon creep within every shadow.
Travel in the light, travel within the path of Gaia. For the night is full of secrets, but the breeze will guide you with song.
Caution. For while secrets can destroy, they will also be the guiding force of the future.
Your future.
There will be significant loss, great pain, destruction, betrayal, scorn, and anger.
There will be death.
There will be blood.
There will be tears.
All ingredients for a brighter future, if wielded correctly.
Do not lose yourself to your pain.
For your pain, your humanity is your greatest strength, not the blade you wield.
Queen be wary, **Níl aon ghrá ann go dtí go mbeidh teaghlach ann.**
Níl aon anró anam ann go dtí go mbeidh leanaí ag duine.

PROLOGUE

Unseelie Queen

I paced back and forth within my chambers, which were adorned in all black with obsidian walls, and the only color was the sun shining through the window. It's been one hundred years since I snatched the power from that ridiculous sham of a Queen and her intended heir. Sure, it took countless amounts of sweet talk, amazing sex, which admittedly, I wouldn't mind partaking in again, but when I finally killed the Queen while her daughter slept, I felt victorious. There is something to be said for a well thought out plan and takeover. But now, there is talk about a prophecy being spoken across the kingdom, *MY* kingdom. No, after years of planning and then years of breaking the Seelie people, a silly prophecy will not stop me from keeping control of the Fae.

I smoothed my black dress down and looked out the window, sipping from my goblet of fairy wine mixed with blood. More specifically, the blood of a Seelie caught trying to escape the kingdom. There have been talks of an uprising, people leaving the kingdom, and rebuilding the Seelie court elsewhere. I scoffed. They could try. I had eyes everywhere. If there was one thing I learned, it was that no one was ever as they seem, so trust no one and at the same time, trust everyone, as that gives your enemies the confidence they needed to act out. Bold people are easy to destroy. It was the quiet ones who needed to be weeded out. This blood belonged to one of the quieter ones.

"You may enter," I said softly as a knock echoed throughout the room, from the door.

"My Queen, if I may?" I waved the soldier in and he bowed.

"Yes, what is the word?"

I swirled my goblet, I relished the feeling of taking the life of a subject, however loyal. Bad news was rewarded with death, good news with death. In death, there was power and if power was food, I was ravenous.

I frowned at the handsome dead Fae on my floor and sighed. He was good in bed. What a pity. Still, I guess I should have waited until he finished pleasing me, but news of the prophecy was whispered, and I was upset. Ah well, someone else will finish what he couldn't.

"Well?" I asked softly.

"Queen, the prophetess did indeed have a vision. She said that in two hundred years' time, there will be a Queen born to challenge your reign." He stood at attention, his black gossamer wings tight against his back. He was one of my favorite soldiers, having been with me since the start of the rebellion, one hundred years ago. I sighed.

"I see," I said quietly. "Read me this prophecy," I seethed, staring at my goblet in silence, until he was done. Overall it was an intriguing narrative; 'Twenty years young, twenty years freed.' The idea of a twenty-year-old taking my power was comical. I didn't go through years of careful planning, having to fake sympathy and emotions, I shuddered thinking of all the emotions, reflecting on the infiltration, murder, and leading a coop, only to be put in any position where I would lose my power.

"I have a portion of the prophecy for you to keep," he continued. "It will be a young Queen of noble blood born, but part of the prophecy was cut off, the prophetess murdered so she wouldn't repeat her words," he stated.

My eyes shot to him. "I see. Who, pray tell, killed this crone and took the prophecy?"

"Oberon," he finished. I cackled, oh that's rich. Oberon? It was almost poetic, an old Fae King and Queen going head-to-head. Intriguing almost, if I wasn't certain that this particular King was equal to me in power. This wouldn't do. There had to be a reason why he had come out of hiding and took a portion of the prophecy. He must have been close this entire time, in order to get there before my men, which was problematic.

"We'll need to increase sentry watches. There should be no one in my kingdom I'm not aware of. Whatever hope this silly crone has brought must be met with force. Spread the word that I'll relish in the death of anyone who leaves my court. And anyone who thinks that even two hundred years from now they can take it from me? I will hang their very wings from my throne room."

The eyes of my soldier bore into me, and I knew he was shocked I would go so far. Ripping the wings from a Fae was the ultimate punishment. Not only did they not grow back, but the back never healed, so their wounds eventually festered until they begged for death. For only death from another Fae could actually kill a Fae. We were immortal but could be slain nonetheless.

"What else?" I snapped.

"The old Queen, her daughter, she lives," he finished. I thought her dead, falling upon her own sword after realizing she had been betrayed, her mother slain, and then letting whatever ideations of love she may have had, stop her from fighting for her rightful place. Her lack of action further solidified my hold, I had many thanks for her. Whatever hope she would have provided dwindled immediately. I smiled slowly, not ideal, but this will work to my advantage.

"Interesting indeed. Well, that is your task then. Find her and gain her trust. I imagine it will be easy for you." He nodded and walked out of the room at my command. I stared out the window and overlooked my kingdom. Hope is a fickle thing. Enough of it can bring just enough faith for change. Too much of it can cause false bravado. The facts will not change, I now lead both the Unseelie and the Seelie, the attempted deserters can live in their false sense of hope, but the loyal will know who will come out on top. I now have two hundred years to plan, siege, and destroy. Two hundred years to gain allies within the realm of Fae. Still, humanity? Who would be as foolish to possibly conceive a child out in the mortal realm where my hold still reaches? Who was brave enough to take me on?

The corners of my lips tilted. *No one.*

Prince Shea. *Two hundred years later*

It was supposed to be a missionary expedition to find allies to continue strengthening the new Seelie court. I didn't expect to find a beautiful, raven-haired Goddess, and, in my confusion, I didn't realize that she was more than a mere mortal. It wasn't my intention to conceive. I laughed darkly, how many men have said that? Gaia, I was pitiful.

I hung around for days, creeping into the nursery window. Each time, I looked down and my breath caught. She was gorgeous. A beautiful, perfect baby girl with dark hair, as dark as the midnight sky. I shed a tear knowing that her hair would soon be as white as snow. The timing was just right, and I had helped conceive the child the Seelie court had been waiting two hundred years for and I had to make sure she would always be protected.

I couldn't imagine giving up so much, just to lose more. I tentatively reached in to caress her face. Her mother named her Hudson and somehow, the name was rather perfect. *My dear, sweet Hudson, beyond the veil you will be safe. I'll do everything I can to ensure it, with protectors in the shadows, and protectors in your very own heart. You'll never be alone, I swear it. Little Riona of Fheall, you'll be the strongest, I'll see to it.*

I looked at her one more time before disappearing into the night. This will be the last time I see her in person for a long time; but in my heart, I knew that my daughter would be the sunshine, moon, water, and the fire. She will hold within herself two opposing explosive forces and she will bring evil to its knees; for only those who understand the darkness, but choose the light, are able to lead.

"Hush, little baby, don't say a word. Daddy's gonna hide you in the mortal realm. When it's time for you to be Queen, hush, little baby, it's all been foreseen."

PART I

20 Years a Child, 20 Years Running Wild

"Standing at the edge of dreams
Beneath my feet, they shine
eyes cold and beautiful
bathed in storm and moon
Inhuman eyes that draw me near
I rise
Against my own free will
A pit in my stomach
Aches as if poisoned.
I am drawn,
Against my trembling fear
A sound in my ears
Deafens all reason.
I cannot move
I cannot speak
My soul is snared
My power faltered
Seized by fear and gripped with malice
A trap is set, and I am captured"

Storm Faerywolf

CHAPTER ONE

"Fuck no! When you said I could choose my college, I wasn't under the impression I would be disowned by doing so." I'm furious, beyond, actually. X, my cat, snarled next to me. She always got upset when I did. I honestly think she would've eaten dear old dad had I given her the chance. Okay, cat was a loose term, she was actually an all-white mountain lion. She had followed me home one day from the zoo, and well, Dad had to pay a lot of money to keep the zookeeper quiet. A lot of magic users had familiars, but, well, my baby is more like a super one.

This is a cluster fuck of epic proportions. College is supposed to be my time to finally be out from my father's thumb. The perfect, magical family with two and a half kids and a white picket fence. You know, the American dream.

I look around my father's perfectly maintained study. Custom desk, custom chair, and I'm sure the fucking air is customized for his highness. I scoff. American dream, yeah right. I'm sure the American dream doesn't involve magical families living within their sweet bubble of normality. And I'm pretty damn sure it doesn't involve one of those kids from some random magical family being adopted and thrust into our family, then suddenly moving in to maintain the perfect image for dear ol' Magic Chancellor Jacobs. Or a mountain lion, now that I think about it, yet X is a fairly new development, and no one, except anyone on the estate that is, knew about her.

Everyone thinks my dad is charming, and I suppose he used to be before he suddenly wasn't. My stepbrother moved in when I was ten and he was fifteen, apparently to show the American Council that my father cares about our magical youth. Suddenly, it's Zane this and Zane that. My personal favorite, 'oh Zane is excelling well with his magic, Hudson, you can learn a thing or two from Zane'.

Well, you fucking think? He's five years older than me.

He snarls. "You'll go where I tell you to go, things have changed. I donate way too much to that university for you to go to some random non-magic, human school in New York. I think not. You'll be going to school with our people. You have a duty to this family. You're a child of the council!" he sneered.

I roll my eyes. "Silly me, I thought I had the unfortunate honor of being your child. This is ridiculous, I've spent enough years under your tutelage. I'm the strongest user of any child of the council," I punctuate that with air quotes and heavy sarcasm.

I mean seriously, after that fucktwat Zane left, things were finally a little easier around here. The prodigal son had left, and I was free at last. And by easy, I mean I'm literally able to walk around without the creepy fuck staring at me and laughing uproariously, with his own personal council, or band of dicks as I liked to call them. They were always with him, whenever Dad would comment on my magic. Council kids stick together, except me. I can't stand the pretentious attitudes, the snark, and expectations that I'm supposed to be prim and proper underneath all of that. No. What you see is what you get. Sarcasm, top of her class in all magical classes and human relations. Another thing I took to piss my father off. He thinks humans are useless, I disagree. They have guns and we certainly aren't bulletproof, so we need to get off our damn pedestal.

"You're trying my patience, Hudson. You'll not only be going to the university, but you'll be expected to be at the top of your classes and extracurriculars that I have chosen as well." He hands me my new schedule.

DeLorean University of Magic. My heart stops. This is Zane's school, but he should've graduated by now. I release a heavy breath. I never asked what he did after university. I assumed he left and died in a ditch, you know, naturally. Well, that was my dream anyway, until he showed up for the holidays and shit for like five years. Dream deferred, but a girl could hope. At least, I haven't seen him in two years, not since I was eighteen. The last day I saw him, changed me in more ways than one. If I saw him again, I would probably nut punch him, or lick him. I haven't decided which.

I shook my head and took a closer look at the schedule and my eyes flew open. "Father, this is an accelerated schedule. You want me to jam pack four years of study into two years? When am I supposed to be able to enjoy college? And how in the world can I possibly take all these classes?" I continued to read through the schedule and rule book as he ignored my complaints and screamed. "Dad, okay, seriously? This is insane. A UNIFORM," I shrieked, "It's supposed to be university and I have to wear, what is this? A red pleated skirt, black blazer, a black button-down, and a freaking red cravat? Why couldn't they just tie? And oh, this is rich, black kitten heels, that's a major no. If I'm going to this forced Hell, I'm wearing my combat boots. How is anyone supposed to kick ass in heels, Father?"

He smiles, for a moment it looks like the father I remember in passing memories, then as quickly as it appeared, it disappears. Welp, there goes that possible sitcom moment. "Hudson, you're leaving tomorrow to prepare for your schedule. You're not there to have fun. You're there to succeed and work for the Council, in whatever capacity we need you. Period. If it'll shut you up, I'll allow the combat boots, but not the ratty ones you insist on wearing. I'll order several pairs and they'll be in your apartment when you arrive on campus."

He lifts his hand before I object. "Yes, you'll be living in an apartment instead of a dorm." He shudders. "No, I had this apartment built on the outskirts of the university for easy access but still hidden from prying eyes."

I growl, and X growls with me as we both stood up, ready to just fucking leave this stupid ass customized box. He rubs his nose, which pretty much means I'm getting on his nerves and am about to be dismissed anyway. "You won't be alone. Some of the other Council children will be there, but you're the only one on the accelerated path. I expect only the highest marks and I'll be checking in often with the school board and your instructors." He smirks. "Your extracurriculars will be focused on combat, both magical and physical. You've been excelling in those for years here, I expect nothing less. I even cleared it for your cat to be there with you."

"You know, if you keep repeating the same damn words over and over again, it's just going to cause your intellect to remain stagnant, Father." I grin and walk out of his office, slamming the door before he can respond. If I'm being forced the fuck out, I'm going to make his life hell.

Chaos and cats are coming DeLorean, buckle the fuck up.

CHAPTER TWO

As I finish packing up my sluttiest outfits and sleepwear, with the occasional comfort clothing, a shit ton of tampons, and the necessary toiletries, I take one final look at my room. If I can help it, my ass isn't visiting for the holidays at all. Not that my father cares. He'd be too busy, and Mother would be too far up his ass pretending to be a Council wife socialite, which means martinis at eight in the morning, so no one will notice I'm gone anyway.

Deciding not to bother to wait until tomorrow to leave, I take mine and X's stuff downstairs. I load up my pretty, sleek, black truck, one of the few things I didn't bother to argue with Father about. It's a gorgeous Cadillac Escalade with all the latest technology and upgrades. He saw safety and top of the line; I saw the car I should've given my virginity to instead. At my insistence, he even had the inside reupholstered in deep purple and the console has a black glitter finish. It's heaven. It can definitely fit a small army and I don't need that much space, but he's insistent. It's a bit much, but it's also kind of perfect, especially since X has her own space to lay back and relax. I even had my license plate customized behind his back to Hermione1. Humans may not really know the truth, but Harry Potter is pretty spot on. Although, I'm convinced the Council here is more on par with the Death Eaters aspect of it all.

The packet Father has given me already has my keys to the apartment, address, schedule, and apparently, the receipt of the delivery of all my uniforms. Gross. I set the location in the GPS and prepare myself for a twenty-hour drive from Colorado Springs to DeLorean. With a sigh, I turn back into my thoughts, I'm totally hemming the fuck out of that skirt. I will wear the uniforms, but to my new specifications of freedom. No more proper outfits, no more frumpy shit like I'm supposed to wear with Father. Nope, I left all of that back in my old room and packed my suitcases with my newly purchased hidden clothes and gorgeous matching lingerie sets I'd bought in hopes that I would be able to get to New York, but that's not happening. I think that's what bothered me the most, I was on my way to Washington State. Seattle to be exact. Yes, you read right. Twilight world. If I meet a sparkly vampire, my ass is running away with him, Council be damned. Guys didn't really talk to me, not unless they were begging for mercy and even though I want to have sex again, I don't think anything would compare to my first time. Granted, this isn't for lack of trying but my dad being who he is, no one ever wanted to date or come around me anyway. Add my skills and crap half the time, no boy would even talk to me outside of school projects. And my only physical contact with boys in general, besides Zane and his friends, was during my sparring and martial arts training every day for two long ass hours. I guess that in itself would have got me off, there were definitely some gorgeous boys in my class, but even after, they would've run in the opposite direction as if I had the plague.

Being a Council girl sucks ass sometimes. It wasn't like I was ugly, although I thought I was for like three minutes, but no, when I hit puberty my hips flared out and my thighs actually took shape instead of looking like noodles and my waist tucked in, leading to toned abs from the consistent workouts. I was shown how gorgeous I was for one amazing night and then it was taken away. I repressed the thoughts. Point is, I grew up and now, I've grown breasts! I shouldn't sound so excited, but they literally just came out of nowhere last year. I thought I was going to be a sad A cup forever, but now I'm a solid D cup. Yes, at twenty years old, my breasts finally came in. They are so nice to look at, I even talk to them sometimes, but the Betty's are heavy and make my back hurt like a bitch, so I pick them up with magic half the time. Anyways, when you pair all that with my long white, yes white, hair down to my ass and green eyes, I thought I was okay. Still sexless. Fuckery, I tell you. Pure fuckery, the Fates were prudish assholes who didn't want me to get some, but they didn't own Amazon, so I have a small arsenal of toys and Kama Sutra books. I had to get off somehow, right? In fact, I'm pretty much an expert at this point at getting myself off, and hopefully, when I do have sex again, I can impress them with my practiced skills. Practiced with a vibrator and porn, mind you, but what the fuck ever.

To be honest, I think about sex a lot more these days, but pretty much nonstop since the Christmas after I turned eighteen. It was the last time Zane had come home to visit, and holy shit, did he look amazing. None of the boys in training looked like that. It wasn't even fair.

"Hudson, come downstairs, dinner is almost ready, and Zane just got here. Come say hello to your brother," Father yelled from downstairs. Okay, so Zane was here, and? Was that supposed to make me hop, skip, and jump in excitement? I rolled my eyes as I took a look at myself in the ensuite bathroom mirror and sighed. I hated these stupid dresses that were bought for me, two more fucking years, and I swear I was going to leave and completely replace my entire wardrobe. I took in the gaudy red and black dress that looked like a long Christmas potato sack and the stupid kitten heels I was supposed to wear. Well, Dad could go fuck himself, if it was just a family dinner, I was going to put on my damn combat boots. I was going to look like a potato sack going to war, but it was better than those fucking funeral heels. I shuddered.

I finished combing my hair, foregoing makeup, and walked into my room where Zane was casually sitting on my bed like he owned it. I stomped over to him, the overall effect lost, I'm sure, in this outfit, but the meaning was the same.

"What the fuck are you doing in my room, asshole? You could've knocked."

"I did knock, but I'm sure you couldn't hear me wearing a sack, it must be affecting your hearing." He turned his head and looked at me quizzically.

I scowled, "Well yeah, it is hard to hear the sound of someone completely unwanted knocking on my door, then coming in my room like they belonged here..." He stayed silent with a smirk on his face. "For fuck's sake, Zane, stop staring at me you fucking weirdo and let's go get this pony show over with. Father has a Christmas dinner with the Council, *I need to be sick by then."*

He laughed at that and stood up and gestured for me to go first. In my fucking room. I scoffed, figures. I rolled my eyes. "This is my room, Zane. You go first. You know, ladies first and all." He glared and walked out of the room and I smiled with my small victory. I'll take them when I can. I didn't even look at how nice his butt looked in his slacks, I was so proud of me.

I sighed and put on a smile before walking down the stairs and heading into the dining room, which was decorated like a Hallmark movie threw up and then played in its vomit. It was ridiculous, but it's the only time of year my mother did more than drink and go to the socialite clubs. No, she just drank here and ordered the staff around to put shit places. I preferred her gone, when we were together, she would either stare at me or completely ignore me. I didn't know if I liked the attention or the lack thereof, but it was my norm. I'm not exactly sure why she never wanted to be my mom, but it was the same since I was little. I didn't really care too much, I trained too much to pay attention. What really hurt was when my father stopped caring and he brought Zane around. But then, shortly after, he had hired Kalen, my trainer who felt more like a father than Chancellor Jacobs did, and I ignored the pain. I was good at it too, until Zane came to visit, and the pomp and circumstance started up again.

We sat down and Zane and Dad joked around while Mother drank herself into a stupor and I sat silently playing with my food, lost in my thoughts and losing my appetite.

"Hudson, Hudson, Hudson..."

"Huh? I'm sorry what?"

"Zane was just asking how school was going and I was telling him you are at the top of your classes and training. You're blossoming under my tutelage. I'm glad you finally started to be worthy of the Jacobs name," Father rattled off. Zane had a soft smile on his face.

"I'm sure Zane is very interested in hearing how I'm not a complete and utter disappointment to you now that he has been gone, what? Five years now? Fascinating, Father. Please, continue. I'm sure you haven't insulted me enough yet, don't let me interrupt you."

He sighed and narrowed his eyes. "That is not what I was doing, Hudson. Can I not just talk about how great you're doing without the backtalk..." I waved him off and he turned bright red.

"That's not how that works. You can say I'm doing well and leave it at that. Even though I have been at the top of classes since I was old enough to go to school. You don't get to mix in an insult with a compliment and then have the audacity to think it's a good thing. Just say it like it is, Chancellor," I sneered. "I just wasn't the son you wanted." I stood up from the table, no longer interested in the food. The staff looked away, used to me and Father arguing, and my mother looked up at me with vague interest in her eyes, or maybe that was the vodka. Zane's eyes were full of some emotion, probably upset I was insulting Father. I rolled my eyes.

"Sit down, Hudson. Dinner isn't over, and you are not excused," Father yelled. I laughed. He is full of shit.

I pointed at Zane. "You see him? Him and you are the only two people you care about at this table." I then pointed at the vodka bottle. "That bottle is the only thing your wife cares about." I started to walk away but not before finishing, "Me? I'm the shiny toy you take out so you can remind people that if you have a kid, you may have a heart. No one here cares about me unless they can take me off the shelf and dust me off to show off my skills. In two years, I'll be gone, and you'll regret thinking money can buy love when all I wanted was the father I had when I was a little girl. So, FUCK you!" I ran up the stairs while everyone's jaw dropped. I didn't curse at my father; I may let a word slip but never towards him.

I stripped off the stupid sack and threw on another sack that was supposed to be a night gown and crawled into bed with the remote. I was so fed up tonight, this pony show was ridiculous and I'm over it. A few moments later and I heard the door slam and I'm sure they left to go to the stupid dinner. I'm glad I didn't have to fake being sick because I would have had to punch someone if I was forced to go. I leaned back and put on Lucifer, it was a show I had started to watch, and I was infatuated with his accent. I wanted to be Chloe Decker so bad, I mean I was more of a Mazikeen type of badass, but Lucifer and I totally would be a match made in Heaven, or Hell. Whatever.

My door opened and I looked at the door in irritation when Zane walked in, wearing sweats and a tank top. I scowled deeply at him. "Don't you have somewhere to be that isn't around me? And don't you knock?"

He smirked as he closed the door then flipped the lock and came to sit next to me. "I tried knocking last time and you didn't answer, so I figured it wouldn't make a difference. There is also a nice thing called a lock you could use." He pointed at the now locked door. "I figured I should show you how to use one, being the prodigal son and all." He smiled softly.

I scoffed. "Fuck you too, buddy. What if I had been naked?" Then he laughed. Laughed! As if me being naked was pure comedy. "What are you laughing at?"

"You have nothing I haven't seen and get over yourself. You weren't naked. I heard the television so I knew you were in bed. Relax." He laid on top of the covers and watched the show silently with me. I was musing over his comment, nothing he hasn't seen. Of course, he was off in university getting his rocks off while I was still here being a virgin. After a moment, I crawled on top of the covers to lay on my belly next to him, kicking my legs up and leaning my chin on my hands. He raised his eyebrow and looked back.

"You know, you are off doing big things, are there any hot guys outside this pony show?" He scowled at me. "What?! I'm just asking, I mean, take Lucifer for example. His accent is hot, he's a sex symbol, and he can get anyone he wants. I want someone like that. Do they sell those at the university bookstore?" I giggled and pushed him when he glowered at me.

"No, they don't. You don't need to look for boys. I'm not having this conversation with you."

I sighed, "Of course. Silly me thinking you came here to actually be a person and talk normal stuff with me."

He sighed and turned towards me leaning on his arm, his body facing me. "This is normal to you?" I mimicked his posture and turned toward him as well.

"Well yeah, and... can I be serious for a moment and you can be honest and not a dick?" I bit my lip, wondering where I was going with this, but I just had to know. He is the only guy besides his friends that actually spoke more than a word to me.

He nodded his head, curious. "Sure. I know you may not believe me, but you can tell me pretty much anything. We may not be super close but that's not because I don't want to be."

"Okay... whatever that means... too late to play brother now... anyways... do you think I'm lacking in something?" He looked shocked for a moment.

"I mean like seriously, dude. You're out there getting girls, doing God knows what with your life and I'm eighteen and I haven't been kissed yet. It's frustrating. At this point, I'm going to make out with a teddy bear." I flipped on to back in frustration, staring at the canopy over my bed.

We were silent for a minute and he laughed. No seriously, he is really laughing right now. Ugh, I shouldn't have asked him at all. "Ugh, forget it, I'm sorry I asked."

"You're not lacking in anything, Hudson. You are the whole package," he whispered, his voice tight. "The right guy hasn't come along yet. But when he does, you'll know."

"How does someone know? Every girl my age has had a few boyfriends, I just want to be kissed for goodness fucking sa..." my words trailed off as Zane shifted and was suddenly on top of me, his body and his lips pressed against mine, heat and confusion suddenly flooded my body before I moved my head.

"What, what are you doing?" I stammered out, cheeks red. Zane looked at me with something I've never seen in anyone's eyes. Desire.

"Showing you that you are wanted. You just didn't see the right guy in front of you..." he whispered against my lips.

"But..."

"Don't finish that. I'm not really your brother, Hudson, and you are eighteen years old, there is nothing wrong here." He groaned. "Stop wiggling, Hudson. You're driving me crazy and I've wanted this, wanted you, for a long time." I didn't realize my hips were moving back and forth. Apparently, they knew what they wanted. My brain just hadn't caught up, still in a fog. I didn't really want to think though, I wanted to kiss him again, it felt... right.

"Kiss me again... please." He groaned and took my lips with his, quickly taking control and I followed his lead, opening my mouth while he teased my tongue with his. We kissed until we were breathless, and he hardened against me.

He pulled away, his breathing uneven. "Okay, we should stop now." I nodded, as I threw my legs over the side of my bed and stood up.

"We should," I sighed, but fuck that. I have no idea when I was going to get a chance like this again and I was feeling things I've never felt before and I wanted to explore more. I didn't want to just stop. I lifted my gown over my head, and he sucked in a sharp breath.

"We should, but I don't want to."

"Hudson..."

"No, this is me taking control. I know what I want, and I know you want me to, you said as much. So, let's enjoy it and not think about it." I kneeled down on the bed next to him and brought my lips to his. He groaned and wrapped his hands around my hips, right after he quickly took off his tank top and pulled off his pants. Thank God the light from the TV was still on, because holy fuck, he was perfect in every way. He got on his knees too and pulled me in flush against his body, one hand tipping my head to grab my lips, the other grabbing my ample behind.

"Are you sure, Hudson?" he said raggedly.

"Zane, shut the fuck up and just fuck me. Show me what I've been missing." He growled against my lips and laid me down on the bed and started to kiss a path down my breasts, sucking on each of my nipples and teasing them while I moaned at all the new sensations I was feeling. He licked a trail down my toned abs before reaching my bare pussy and opened my legs.

Without pausing, he started to lick and suck, swirling his tongue over my clit and I bucked my hips completely lost to this.

"Oh my God, oh my God, oh damn."

He growled his approval against my clit. "You taste like fucking honey. Look at me, Hudson. I want you to watch me while I taste you for the first time. The only man to ever take you and savor you." I moaned at his words and looked down while he licked from bottom to top, dipping his tongue inside of me before reaching my clit and sucking it between his lips, and flicking it with his tongue.

"Fuck, Zane, fuck." Then my hands flew to his head as I came with a loud moan grinding myself on his face like a hussy. He groaned and kept going. I tried to push his hands away and he snatched my hands and pinned them to the side while he settled himself closer and ignored my pleas, another orgasm building. Fuck, it was too much. I closed my thighs around his head and the licking and sucking from that position just intensified the oncoming orgasm and I screamed his name as I came again, my body shaking. He finally stopped and he grabbed my head roughly and kissed me, I groaned as I tasted myself on his lips.

"Don't ever fucking tell me to stop eating that pussy again. Make no mistake, Hudson, it's mine, you're mine and they damn sure always will be." I don't even know what I responded, nothing was making sense, my body felt like I was floating. He leaned over me and kissed me softly. "Look at me, Hudson. I want you to watch me. That hasn't changed. I want you to watch while I take this virgin pussy for the first time. I want you to watch while I make you cum with my dick inside you for the first time. I want you to look into my eyes and never look away, do you understand?"

I nodded. He wrapped his hands around my neck and squeezed lightly, I moaned. "I want your words, Hudson. Your words."

"Yes, Zane," I moaned again. I looked down and saw how big he was, and my eyes widened. How the fuck was he going to fit?

"Look at me, Hudson. Don't worry, it may hurt a little at first, but you'll be fine. Don't look down. Just look at me." He ran the tip of his dick from my clit down to my pussy a few times making me moan from the anticipation. He positioned himself and started to work himself in slowly, my breath *hitched but I did as promised and looked in his eyes. He looked at me with such intensity, I didn't know what to feel. What did that look mean?*

I lost all thought as he filled me with one thrust, and I gasped. Holy fuck, that hurt. "Breathe, sweetheart," he said softly, and he leaned over and kissed me, reaching one hand between us to play with my clit. He didn't move inside of me, his strain visible but he continued to focus on me, kissing my lips, my neck, teasing my nipples. I felt another orgasm building and I didn't feel the pain anymore, just an overwhelming need to have him move inside of me.

"Please..." I whispered. He smiled at me and started to move, still playing with me and that building orgasm hit me, and I came and clenched around him.

"Fuck, Hudson. You're so fucking tight," he choked out and rolled his hips like he was dancing with me instead of pumping me like in those corny videos. I didn't expect this, he moved so sensually, it was as if he was playing my body like an instrument. His hips flexed and he moaned, his eyes never leaving mine.

"Fuck, Hudson, you feel so damn perfect. You're fucking perfect for me, baby. Every fucking inch of you is fucking perfect. You've always been mine; you just didn't know it yet."

I moaned his name. "Zane, please..." I don't know what I was asking for, but he cursed and started to move his hips faster. I gripped his back and drew my nails down, the eye contact never wavered. At the feel of my nails, his face turned almost feral and he leaned down and bit my neck. I felt my eyes roll back and choked back a scream as I came and clenched harder than before. He swore and came, pounding into me. A few minutes later, he pulled out of me and laid down next to me, pulling me towards him, kissing me gently.

"Wow," I whispered.

"How do you feel?" Zane chuckled.

"Amazing. That was incredible. It was perfect. Can we do it again?" I asked and he laughed and kissed me.

He caressed my face and looked at me. "You're perfect, Hudson, never doubt that. You are everything anyone could ever want. Everything I want."

I gasped as he brought me closer to him and kissed my neck and moaned, and I felt him getting hard again.

"Fuck, we didn't use a condom," he groaned.

"I've been on birth control since I was 14, we are fine." I had to regulate my irregular periods and severe cramps and was put on them shortly after starting my first few periods. Also, magic users didn't get STD's. It was definitely a perk for the sexual overachievers out there.

"Let's go clean up." He got out of the bed and picked me up and carried me into the bathroom, I laughed.

That night, he fucked me in the shower, on the bathroom counter from behind, making me watch while he pounded into me, then twice more on my bed. It was incredible and I was so happy, my heart and pussy full. When I woke up the next morning, he was gone, no note. Over the next couple of days, between crying myself to sleep and training, my hair started to turn white, like snow. The doctors couldn't explain it and Father said it was just premature hair changing. Except that was for grey hair and not white. X followed me home from the Zoo shortly after, during my pitiful attempts to cheer myself up.

Kalen looked at me with shock, his gaze filled with worry when he saw my hair and Xena. From that point forward he trained me harder than ever before, as if the hair and my lion were personally offensive to him. He wouldn't explain why, but I took it all in and trained with an animalistic ferocity until I felt like I was superhuman. Kalen even made X train and learn how to attack, pounce, and fight with me and my rhythms. Every day, I got stronger, smarter, faster and knocked Kalen on his ass more times than ever before. I was full of anger, resentment, and confusion, and I took it out on every training session and every training battle for school. No one wanted to spar with me anymore, magically or physically. And still, even though I grew up after that night, I didn't know if I loved him or hated him for giving me the best night of my life and then disappearing. I cried until I was empty but instead, I filled it with violence and power. If I ever saw him again, the first thing I was going to fucking do was nut punch him.

Lost in my head, after about thirteen hours I called it a day and drove into a hotel for the night. I threw a shielding spell over X to get through the lobby and when we finally got into the room, I stripped off my clothes and took a warm shower, groaning as the heat worked my sore tight muscles from sitting for so many freaking hours. X jumped into the shower after me, weird ass mountain lion, before jumping out and shaking herself everywhere. I shook my head, silly ass cat.

I sighed and settled in, groaning as my body relaxed, *getting out to fill up the gas tank and load up on coffee totally did not count as relief.* I had already thrown away the clothes I had on, the last of the frumpy shit I would ever wear for a while, set my alarm for just a few hours, and died, X curled next to me, on top of the sheets.

I GROWLED AS THE STUPID ALARM WENT OFF THEN LAUGHED WHEN X bit it in half, and I dragged my ass into the bathroom to brush my teeth and take a cold shower to wake myself the fuck up. What I needed was some fucking coffee. Cold showers suck, but fuck, it would be okay with instant coffee. I brushed my hair, not that it ever did anything spectacular after I blew it out. When it was wet and curly, it was a different matter. Thank God, I didn't have to deal with that this morning. I remembered that I didn't have to put on a shitty outfit, and I squealed as I ran to just one of the suitcases I brought up and put on a matching set of underwear that weren't white granny panties and a glorious pair of tight jeans that hugged my ass, hips, and thighs. Holy wow, this was amazing, I felt so powerful and I was still half naked! I quickly tugged on a white low cut halter crop top that tied around my back and then again at the bottom across my back. My sheer black bra was on display but with my long hair hanging, it wasn't visible. Hmm, on second thought, I took off the bra and just used magic instead of underwire to alleviate the extra strain. They were perky enough but no point in pretending that they still don't need extra help to save my back. My back was completely exposed, revealing my full back tattoo of a lion, mandala style, in black, then from my lower back to the crack of my ass, were the words 'never give in to weakness'. I got it after that Christmas. It also tied into the fact that being surrounded by elitists was exhausting and giving in to the whims of pretentious assholes for their benefit and powers was a weakness. Fighting against the consistent stifling atmosphere was just a few forms of rebellion really, until now. I threw on a pair of cute pumps instead of my normal combat boots to give myself another confidence boost, made my way out of the room, and checked out, and got ready for the last part of my trip.

"X, how does it look?" She looked at me and walked around and roared her approval.

"Thank you, sugar lumps," I rubbed her head and gave her a kiss while she preened at the attention.

With only seven hours to go, it was going to be a better drive. I grabbed food and coffee from a drive-thru and kept going, only stopping for gas and more snacks for me and X. I turned up the music and sang along to every rap song I could, until I pulled into the University town, where I rolled my windows down to enjoy the nice summer air. It was about three in the afternoon and everyone was walking around the town. It looked cute; lots of stores, cafes, a movie theater, a bowling alley, and what looked like the cutest retro skating rink. There were even a few bookstores, I squealed at that; *nothing like a good book to make shit better*. Luckily, being here early gave me a couple of days to explore before I settled in to have to work out. I drove another fifteen minutes or so and pulled up to a large gate tucked seemingly into the forest. I showed my identification to the very attractive guard, scratch that, downright mouthwatering sex symbol, and he directed me to the side of the drive with a roll of his eyes, muttering about rich magic kids. Well, there goes that attraction and my tongue.

"Uh, all that shit doesn't mean I'm deaf, asshole. I'm also not like these other dickheads who go here. I'll gladly drink a beer with you or kick your ass. Your choice, bitch." Then I drove off leaving him with his mouth hanging open as X rolled down the back window and growled. I laughed at her while rolling my eyes at the warm welcome, I rolled to the side of the road, following until making a sudden right onto another road that had a no trespassing sign. I felt the tingle of magic as I drove onto the driveway; ah, it was shielded! Well, that makes sense. I finally arrived after about a fifteen-minute drive and I shook my head. Of course, Daddy would have the apartment fifteen minutes away from the school and all forms of civilization. Asshole. But when I glanced up from my GPS, my jaw dropped. Yeah, what should have been an apartment was a huge house. God, he was such a pretentious fuck. I have to give it to him though, it was beautiful. I sighed. "Sucks I would have this fucking place to myself," I grumbled, but it is what it is. At least I had X. God knows how roommates would react to my lion familiar. When they probably had little shitty ones.

The house was all grey and black brick on the outside, a gorgeous patio in the front, with swings! A perfect reading spot. The red door was the perfect touch to the small three step staircase leading to the door. I spun around taking in the small fountain in the center of the driveway and the huge trees around the property, the house was nestled into the forest with what looked like a well-worn path near the side, probably for running. X bounded out of the car and ran for the trees, probably to hunt and use the bathroom too.

"Be careful, X. Come back soon. Don't kill anyone!" I snickered when she roared back. We can talk telepathically, not very well but I could get general impressions of what she wanted and her intentions. It was getting better; Kalen said a familiar took quickly to their matches but since she was such an oddity, it may take a bit more training. I didn't think much of it, I was sure one day it would click, she was my best friend. Well, I also hated people, so there was that.

I looked back at the house, damn it was perfect. I quickly opened the door and brought in all of my things, I needed to pee before I died. I found my room upstairs all the way in the back of the hallway, it's the only door the second key opened, so it had to be mine. I was confused about the other rooms being locked but the thoughts disappeared when I walked into the room, *holy fuck. HGTV took a shit in here.* Oh my goodness, it was huge and painted purple with a black ceiling that had those cute little stick-on stars. The bed was dead center and looked bigger than a standard king size bed with a canopy and a bedspread that matched the color of the walls. I fawned over the pretty cherrywood furniture and soft plush dark grey carpet, as my bladder yelled, and I ran to the bathroom to pee and took in the gorgeous grey tiles and walk-in shower. It was beyond perfect. After I washed my hands, I made my way back to get all my and X's things brought up and unpack it all. After that I looked around my room again and noticed a door to the side that was covered by a blackout curtain, explaining why I didn't notice it. Opening the door, I noticed it led to a larger covered area that had a huge pool with a waterfall backdrop and a huge jacuzzi on the side; a pool X was already swimming in; cheater.

Forgetting everything, I ran back into the room and went into my bathing suit drawer, and picked a white suit that matched my hair perfectly. It could technically be classified as a one piece but dipped all the way down past my navel before crossing up in a thick band right at my hips giving the illusion that the suit had a full back, but actually, the suit was completely backless, showing off my back tattoo and the start of the crack of my ass. The band simply wrapped to connect the barely there panty portion that didn't really cover my ass. Realistically, my ass was too big for that anyway, my rap video curves were a blessing to every outfit in existence. The top tied around my neck, pulling the material tight against my breasts, holding them in from falling out on the sides but having the full-blown cleavage in the front. "Fuck," I whispered as I looked in the mirror. Frumpy, chancellor's daughter was fucking gone and Hudson the porn star has arrived! *Cue the porn music.* I squealed in excitement, it was hot, and I felt like a rock star. Don't let anyone ever fucking tell you a nice outfit wasn't empowering, because it sure as fuck was. It wasn't a white pantsuit, but a white sexy bathing suit will do.

I grabbed my phone and ran down the stairs, hyped as fuck. I noticed a built-in outdoor speaker when I peeked through the door and I connected my phone to the Bluetooth and blasted my Pandora reggae station. Crap it was loud; thank God I was in the middle of nowhere because the party of one plus lion has begun! As "Action" by Terror Fabulous started to play, I dipped my toes in the water, admiring the barbecue area with an outdoor kitchen and large outdoor television set. It looked like it was all carved into grey and black stone. Ugh, this accelerated program sucks ass, I would have loved four years in this place. With a little sigh, I gave a little spin and threw my hands in the air swerving my hips to the song while walking over to the waterfall ridge. I shook my ass like I was in a rap video, laughing before jumping in like a fucking dolphin with legs. I swam back and forth across the pool, singing to whatever song came on next. After a while, I jumped out of the pool and grabbed my phone, changing the station and just kicking my feet in the water. Cardi B's "I Like It" started to play and I started bopping my head and leaned back, my suit is pretty much see through and my nipple piercings show clearly through the thin material. Another moment during my rebellion; hurt like a bitch too. I got up to put my phone back down, shaking my ass and rapping along to the song and I was so lost in my own world that if it hadn't been for X's roar of anger, I would not have realized the sliding door for the back of the house had opened, and right in front of me was my worst fucking sexual nightmare. Zane... and not only him, but his merry band of dicks too, Ryder, Hunter, and Grayson. FUCK. ME. Not literally. Well, maybe.

CHAPTER THREE

Fucking shit. My little slice of paradise, which let's be honest, was a facade, to begin with, is now blown to hell. He graduated. Should be long fucking gone, but no, here he is just, breathing. I really hate that he is breathing. I could get past the fact that he has been working out a lot more since I last saw him. Scratch that, the fact that he looks like he eats a gym for breakfast and goes on about his day. I can look past the fact that he had on a tight black t-shirt, that highlighted every ab and made his golden skin stand out and dark jeans. Fuck, it should be illegal to look that good. I had to check myself for drool as his five o'clock shadow, black hair, and green eyes just completed his entire bad boy, demi-God look. However, getting past all of that, I couldn't get past the fact that he was standing there just breathing my air, for God knows how long. Did he see me dance, rap, swim? He definitely caught me shaking my ass, it was a lot of ass to shake, I thought with a smirk. Eat your heart out, asshole. These past two years I had changed. I was curvier, more toned, and had bigger tits.

"X, calm down, I know the assholes." She sat down next to me with a humph and narrowed her eyes at them before laying down and closing her eyes.

I ignored the fuck out of them, snatched up my phone, and called my father, who surprisingly answered.

"Yes, yes, I'm here, I'm fine, the house looks good. Let's cut to the chase, Father. You couldn't mention the fact that Zane was still here... What do you mean he lives here? What do you mean they all live here?...They are my what? Dad, with all due respect... I hope you spontaneously combust in the most gruesome of ways." And I hung up my phone. I pinched the bridge of my nose and took a deep breath, resisting the urge to turn around and either punch Zane in the nuts or lick his face instead. The struggle of my hormones, who didn't understand betrayal.

"Still dramatic I see," Zane said with irritation, the fucking audacity by the way. I turned around and put my hands on my hips and took in the bored expression on his stupid, handsome face, but the heat in his eyes didn't lie. So, I did the only thing I could think of. I walked up to him and nut punched him.

"FUCK, HUDSON," he yelled while he bent over and grabbed his nuts. Well, I did promise myself years ago.

"Fuck, yes that is exactly what you did you piece of shit. Fucked me then left. You're lucky I don't fucking rip those balls right off and shove them down your fucking throat. In fact, I wish you had a pussy so I can fuck it and leave it too. Don't drop the soap, sister-fucker."

Ryder, Hunter, and Grayson were laughing so hard, they started wheezing while Zane hunched over, glaring at me. *Little bitch.*

The longer I looked at him, the more I realized, with a pang in my chest, that I still had lingering pain from those days. X pawed at my hand and I didn't realize she had gotten up.

You okay, Hooman?

I'm fine, Xena, he just makes me crazy.

Eat?

No, you can't eat him. I laughed at her when she gave me the sad version of a lion look and went back to sunbathing by the edge of the pool.

Sighing, fuck, I gave him more than my virginity that night and I think I just realized that. I wish I could explain, I truly wish I could without looking or sounding like a hypocrite. I spent so many years feeling resentful towards him, angry. By association, his friends could go fuck themselves as well. However, something inside of me took them all in and I settled, the anger receding. I tried to ignore the confusing and conflicting and down-right annoying swirling emotions and stood up straighter. It must have been the fact that I touched his nuts, yeah. Nuts confused people; I mean look at men. They are all fucking stupid.

Clearly immersed in my nut thoughts, I didn't realize that he and the merry band of cock rings had come closer, hands in front of their dicks. The merry band of dicks all stared at me, heads cocked and interest in their gazes. Well, I assumed it was. I wouldn't know, boys have been running from me for too long for me to know what interest was, and the last time well, that didn't end well. Regardless, it looked like the guys in the pizza porn videos look at the cougars. I reached over and grabbed my hair, wringing the water out of it while I looked at them, needing to keep my hands busy. I was still twitchy. I can admit, hell anyone with eyes could see, that Hunter, Ryder, and Grayson have definitely gone from boys to men. Hunter was lean but muscular with his arms covered in tattoos, his grey eyes standing out on his cleanly shaven face with messy brown hair. He radiated danger, like if he was just a breeze away from punching someone in the face, *swoon*. And God, did his chest have a chest?! I can't deal. And Ryder, fuck, looked like he lifted pick-up trucks for his meals instead of eating his protein like a good boy. Seriously, he flexed just standing still, and with black hair, hazel eyes, laugh lines, and a sharp jaw, he looked like a sexualized Marvel character. I want to lick him. I suddenly had to press my thighs together, stupid hormones.

Finally, I took in Grayson. He always did have a boyish, boy next door thing going on with his dark blond hair and cute blue eyes, but now he had more of a Lucifer Morningstar next door thing going on, wrapped in tattoos. I mean, come the fuck on. Did these guys come here and get smacked with a 'Make A Pussy Soak' stick? Now, they were no longer the annoying ass teens that laughed at me, they were now the older, about to make my life a living hell, grown ass men. Or make your life wonderful and full of orgasms. I ignored that thought though and shook my head.

I raised a single eyebrow and grabbed my hair to the side to settle over one shoulder, turned around and went to start the music again. I winked at them, blowing them a kiss before I walked to the pool and dove back in, laying back and closing my eyes to float. It was quiet for a few moments and it was nice until I opened one eye and I noticed how they all just stared, eyes kinda glazed over like when you see the last donut about to be eaten. Fuck man, the day you have to ask yourself, what's wetter you or the water, is the day...well it's today. Sigh, if I was a donut, I'd be an overfilled Boston cream, I chuckled to myself at my little dirty joke, and hummed to the music playing. Suddenly, the sun was gone, and I adjusted myself to stand in the water, to see fucking Zane blocking my light. *Shouldn't he be fucking getting an ice pack? Gotta hit him harder next time.* I groaned internally, I looked up at him, fucking 6 foot plus monster, and crossed my hands under my chest. "Can I offer you some assistance? Maybe offer to remove that spiked stick up your ass?"

Someone cleared their throat and I looked over. "I have no idea what you just said, sweetheart, but all I heard was stick and ass and I'm intrigued," said Ryder as he kneeled by the edge of the water, his jeans straining as he looked at me. I laughed and licked my lips, his eyes drawn to them immediately. What would the new sexually free Hudson do, should be the next official saying at DeLorean because it was about to get steamy, and I was going to piss Zane off.

I swam to the edge of the pool and put my hands on the edge of the pool in front of him, pushing myself up, my arms flexing, until I was eye level with him. "Really, Ryder? Let me ask you... with those two words in mind, can you live up to your name?" I blinked up at him innocently as his eyes widened and he choked. Zane growled and Grayson and Hunter laughed then coughed when Zane glared at them.

Ryder leaned over to whisper in my ear, "I can and will do way more than that, Hudson. You'll see." And he bit my ear lobe. A shiver worked its way up my spine and at his smirk, I smiled. I couldn't have him having the last word. So, I reached up and pretended to reach over to touch his face, when I grabbed his shirt and pulled him into the pool with me. I laughed, as he came up and sputtered.

"You little witch!" he yelled, Grayson and Hunter bent over laughing. Ryder pouted,

"You owe me, these were Italian leather combat boots."

"Wah, wah, wah, when you left, how long did it take you to become a pussy?" I yelled and he growled and swam towards me, I shrieked and jumped out of the pool right as he got to the edge. I stuck my tongue out at him. "Na, na, na, na, na," I sang. I was having way too much fun with people I thought I was still resentful towards.

I spun around when he jumped out of the pool and walked straight into Hunter and Grayson, and Ryder pressed against my back. I looked up at them and it took everything I had to not rub against their chest and purr like a kitten. "What was that about me not getting you?" Ryder whispered.

I huffed. "Well this is just an unfair advantage to use your *walking sex* friends to distract me from running away successfully..." I tapped my chin and smiled. "Actually, I think it means I win because you couldn't get me on your own."

Ryder grabbed my waist and leaned forward to whisper in my ear, "No, I still win, because I'm the first one to have his hands on you," he chuckled. I rolled my eyes.

"Actually, that was Zane, and look how fast he ran. Be careful, I may have the fucking crotch cooties." I heard Zane make a sound and I ignored him. "Anyways, whatever, sore loser..." I grumbled and pushed against the wall of muscles in front of me.

"Are you guys going to let me pass or are we having an orgy? I read about those; totally fun." They choked while Zane reached over and grabbed my hand, bringing me up against him. Seriously, all this manhandling is doing shit to me, secret vaginal things. The kind that are going to have me humping my damn pillow. X took that opportunity to throw her full strength at the three boys behind me and they all fell into the pool.

She swished her tail and walked off. *"My hooman."* I shook my head at her declaration and laughed.

"She isn't a big fan of manhandling, apparently," I giggled as they all trudged out the water but quickly stopped when they stripped off their shirts.

"Holy shit," I whispered, I swiped my hand across my mouth because I was most assuredly drooling. I mean, how couldn't I? Ryder, Hunter, and Grayson looked smugly at me while I stared until I felt my hand get tugged on again.

I looked up at Zane, who had the cutest tick in his jaw and refused to look past my eyes. "What are you wearing and why are you wearing it?" I laughed at him. Really laughed. It's been two years, and honestly, it could've been two hours and it wouldn't have made a lick of difference, we were not going to just be okay. I was still hurt, apparently, and I couldn't get a read on him. I wish I could just completely avoid him right now; my stupid heart was in pain. Although now, what Dad told me is certainly a complication. I sighed, I was going to have to deal with that come Monday, today and tomorrow were mine and I was going to enjoy it, with pranks, torture, and sexual tension. He could bitch all he wants but I know damn sure despite how we felt about each other right now, nut punch and all, deep down we still thought about that night.

Don't get me wrong, it doesn't suddenly make me that girl who forgets everything, but I was going to embrace my freedom, whichever way I wanted to. Ryder, Hunter, and Grayson were fucking gorgeous and I felt something weird around them. Have you seen Hotel Transylvania? Yeah, I felt the zings. Sigh, women can be sexually free, they just needed to embrace it, even if you zing the shit out of some extra dicks.

"It is a bathing suit, Zane. See, there are these things that you wear in the water that cover up private parts from being exposed to the world. Would you like me to demonstrate how I put it on? I could take it off and slide it back on and show you how if you're confused. It would be hard considering how wet I am but..." I laughed at his expression. "I imagine you're dressed every morning by a fucking house elf." I went to untie the top of the suit and he grabbed my hand and snarled. He and Father should have a snarling contest, I'm sure it would be quite entertaining to watch, with a face shield of course. I caught the sound of choking from one of the guys in the back, Ryder was thumping Hunter in the back while Grayson just looked at my hands being held by Zane. I turned my head to look at Grayson's face taking in the hyper focused, heated look, the way he licked his lips and shivered. He winks at me and I look away, *my vagina is my own worst fucking enemy.*

"What I mean," he bit out, "was why are you wearing this bathing and not something less revealing. For fuck's sake, Hudson, it is see-through." He waved his hands as if that was going to suddenly conjure Dolores Jane Umbridge's kitten covered snorkel gear.

"Oh, you mean like the shit I used to be forced to wear back at home? Yeah, I threw all of that shit away and have fully embraced being a sexier version of me. You should try it, but maybe not with this bathing suit." I turned my head and pretended to look him over. "Well, not all of us can get the good genes." I winked at him and reached over to give him a nice hug, soaking him. He pushed me off of him and I laughed and side-stepped him to get into the kitchen through the sliding doors behind him, suddenly hungry. Except, I was hungry for something else at this point too, *I'm going to put my toys to work tonight.*

I walked in expecting a kitchen, but it wasn't just a kitchen, it was a freaking playground with knives. It had every chef's dream; stainless steel appliances and the most charming light granite waterfall style island surrounded by stools on one side. The entire kitchen led into an open concept living room with two large light grey brick columns on either side of the area, the only indication that you were going into another section of the home. God, it was beautiful. I looked around in a daze until my stomach grumbled and I realized I was still hungry. Fine, stupid stomach, discovery later, food now. And with a house full of grown men, there should definitely be something to eat.

Noticing the music from outside played inside, I danced and sang along as I started taking stuff out of the fridge to make a sandwich and searched around the kitchen looking for the bread. My lips pursed and I started going through the cabinets and drawers and realized one drawer was full of condoms. I rolled my eyes, even as a spike of jealousy went through me. Ugh, I ignored that and reached up to one of the cabinets and found the bread, but, of course, with these 6 feet fuckers, that shit was high as fuck, I reached for it and I felt a warm body press up against mine and reach over me to pass me the bread. I turned my body to see Hunter now firmly pressed against me, and I swallowed thickly at the expression on his face as he looked down at me hungrily. His body radiated tension, he felt like he was a coiled snake ready to strike and sorry, but unlike Samuel L. Jackson, I was totally ready for some snakes to board this motherfucking pussy plane. I shifted my body as much as I could with the damn granite sheetrock parked in front of me and pressed closer against him. I drew my hand up his chest, reaching up to caress his jaw, then I moved across his shoulder, down his arm and snatched the bread out of his hands.

"Thanks, dickhead. Much appreciated. Chivalry and all that." I ignored their pointed stares and pushed him off, ignoring him as he adjusted himself and then I continued to make, then eat my sandwich. I chewed and looked at them while they stared at me.

"So, are you guys going to just sit there and stare? I haven't seen your asses in a few years," I said, pointing at Ryder, Hunter, and Grayson. "And I haven't seen or heard from Zane in two, hell I didn't even know he was still alive. All this big dick energy is stifling. I'm sure you'll be glad to have me and X around to balance it all out." Speaking of said lion, she pranced herself right into the room and sat down next to me.

Ryder laughed, "Yeah, we're looking forward to stifling something all right." Zane smacked him upside the head.

"That's not even the correct use of the word, idiot," Zane grumbled. Ryder just laughed harder. I smiled and rolled my eyes, finished off my sandwich and cleaned up, walking around them to put everything away.

"You lost the right to smack anyone who wants to flirt with me two years ago, asshole," I threw over my shoulder while I cleaned up.

They even watched me while I did that. I walked to the other side of the island where they were sitting and pushed myself up to sit on it. Not sanitary but whatever.

"What's with the lion, Hudson?" Grayson asked, stepping closer to try to rub her head, X narrowed her eyes and watched him while he scratched her ear.

Eat, now?

"No, X, no eat." I laughed as Gray pulled his hand back slowly.

"Like him, he is not scared, no one is. I like that."

"She said she likes you all because you're not scared of her."

"But still eat if they hurt you."

"But she will eat you if you hurt me." They laughed, but X growled. She wasn't joking. I smirked.

"X?" Ryder asked.

"Short for Xena; she's my warrior. Wait until you see her fight with me. It's like we're one person." I rubbed her head affectionately. I looked up to watch them staring at me again.

"Alright, what is with the damn staring? Seriously, you guys never seen a girl and her pussy before? I'm sure there are plenty of them, both girls and pussies, looking to hook up with the hot magic instructors on campus." I smirked and waved my hands around pointing at them.

"You think we're hot?" Hunter said with a smirk on his face, pressing his hand on my leg. Zane smacked him upside of his head too.

I laughed. "You would have to be blind, no scratch that, I'm sure even the blind can see how hot you guys are." I shrug, truth is truth.

Grayson jumped in, "One, not all of us hook up with girls on campus." He looked at Zane and Ryder when he said that. I felt something in my stomach catch fire, I ignored it. *No reason to get jealous, Hudson. He left you, remember?* "There may not be any rules against it since we're all of age, but I don't shit where I eat." I wrinkled my nose at the imagery. He laughed. "Besides," he walked up to me and pushed himself between my legs, still tall enough that I had to look up at him, "Why bother anymore, when you're here. Not like anyone can compare to you." His voice sounded husky, but his eyes looked sincere. I shifted uncomfortably, pushed him away and jumped off the counter, as he chuckled.

"Haha, hilarious." I rolled my eyes, admittedly confused. There was sexual tension and flirting, then there was admitting actual feelings beyond that. I didn't want that right now, not after seeing Zane. "Besides, you couldn't handle me. I'm sure I'm much more than what you're used to. Wouldn't want you having to worry about coming too fast," I quipped, my humor the best deflecting mechanism I had.

I wonder if there were more hot guys on campus. God, I wanted to try so much of the sexual shit I read about in all my books and saw in videos.

"Okay, you all had your fun. Hudson, I'm laying down some ground rules. You will not be having sex in this house," Zane snarled, as he stood up, he crossed his arms and went to lean on the counter.

Just to at least get the edge off... wait, what... my inner reverie interrupted as Zane got in my face, his mouth moving but I'm not sure what came out, X snarling right back at him her claws out. "Huh? What did I miss, X? I was busy thinking." I looked between her and Zane. "What are you talking about now?"

He looked at me, clearly pissed off. "I said, you will not be hooking up with anyone in this house, on this entire campus actually." He must have lost his ever-loving mind. Some hunk was going to get this pussy, even if I had to shove it down his throat.

"I see." I walked up to him. "Who is going to stop me? You? Are you going to monitor my every move? Are you going to sleep in my room, in my bed, or are you going to try to be gone when I wake up again?"

He huffed in frustration. "Hudson..." I waved my hand and cut him off.

"Listen, despite whatever shit Father told you, you're not actually my keeper, Zane."

"Don't I fucking know it..." he grumbled low. I chose to ignore it.

"Therefore, you will not interfere with who I fuck or don't fuck, suck or don't suck, who's cum I swallow or don't swallow..." The guys choked in the back and Zane's face turned an interesting shade of red.

I stepped close to him and looked up at his handsome face, the tall fucker, I saw his eyes widen with panic, *easy prey*. I ran my hand down his chest, holy fucking shit he was sexy. I shook my head and ran my hand lower, slowly, watching his eyes heat. "Listen up, Zane. You had your chance and you fucked me over. If it wasn't for the fact that you set my teeth on edge and these three merry bands of cock rings were associated with you, I would break down every door in this house and ride every fucking dick I wanted. In fact, I would waltz around just sucking dicks because I felt like it and it was a Tuesday," I fumed, but I reached my hand lower, our eyes never leaving each other.

"Merry band of what?"

"Is it Tuesday yet?"

"She is so getting fucked," the other guys said at the same time.

I smirked, internally but Zane and I kept up our staring match. "I'm not your keeper, fine, but that's beside the point. You won't be doing any of those things. You are on an accelerated pace, remember? You will have no time to worry about any of these punks on campus because you will be busy studying," he finished with a self-satisfied smirk.

I ignored that as my hand finally reached its destination and I grabbed his dick through his pants. He took a deep breath. "Oh, Zane, you think that matters? I'm an A student. Cute really, but you'll be amazed how much I can study while bent over a library desk. Besides, if the boys on campus don't interest me, I always have you four." I winked, stepped away, tossed my hair back and walked to the staircase and headed up to my room, Xena following closely. It was still a little early, but I suddenly needed a warm shower and my bed. After a nice long soak, and some self-play where I may or may not have moaned all four of their names, I threw on my PJ's, turned on Netflix and settled in to watch Lucifer. Mmm, that was one sexy devil.

CHAPTER FOUR

Zane

I LET OUT A BREATH AND TRIED TO REIN IN MY SWIRLING CONFUSING emotions.

"Fuck, she is beautiful, Zane, and feisty as hell too," Hunter says first, breaking the silence from watching her strut away from the kitchen and up the stairs. Her curves and ass are on display in that bathing suit, not to mention that tattoo and the perfect swell of her tits, definitely bigger from the last time I saw them. I blew out a breath, I still felt the heat of her hand on my dick. I refused to back down, but fuck, if I wasn't going to think about it every second of every day.

We always had this sibling rivalry thing going on since I was brought into the Jacobs' house at fifteen. I excelled at everything that was thrown at me and the Chancellor was always proud. That's all that really counted to me at the time. Not having a dad, I wanted to be the best son I could be. Then there was Hudson. She was so sweet and beautiful and kind, but she was consistently being pushed by her dad to be the best, and you can tell it was affecting her. She stopped being sweet abruptly and became wary and calculating, pushing herself harder and harder every day.

When I met Hunter, Grayson, and Ryder, it was after I moved into the Jacobs' house, and we became friends so naturally, always easy to be around each other. We would spend our time laughing and joking while we sparred and practiced our magic together. Hudson, you can tell, wasn't too happy with having us there. We would tease her and laugh at her sometimes, but overall, we looked after her, even if she didn't see it. Three years too soon, we had to go to University and Hudson, naturally, was alone again. I think she liked it that way though, we never really saw her hang out with anyone, even at the insistence of the Chancellor. She would say the girls were too prissy or too high-mannered to spar or train with her, and she didn't want to waste her time. After a while, the Chancellor gave up trying to care and just rode Hudson harder.

Hudson, despite being his daughter and being made to dress up in frumpy clothes and go to events with the Chancellor, wasn't like every other girl. She was alluring, she drew your eyes even if you didn't want to look in her direction. Beyond that, she wasn't like every other awkward teenage girl, she was gorgeous. Perfect in every single way, anyone with eyes could see that. To the boys, and I more than most, it was almost magnetic. During our cool downs, we would talk about how we felt this strange connection to her. At the time, it was easier for her to hate us for some frivolity like sibling rivalry, than get closer to her. Our age differences being the major problem really, so we did what we could. We protected her. So, before we left for DeLorean, she was thirteen and starting to develop, we put the word out that if any boy even looked in her direction, we would beat the shit out of them and hide the bodies. We even went as far as to let them know that if anyone so much as disrespected her, there would be consequences. Now, we wouldn't hit a girl, but a nicely placed glitter bomb in a bully's room or a few well cast spells would be hard to trace.

We shouldn't have worried much, but we did. We kept tabs on her, and I would even visit during the holidays. She was getting stronger, always top of her class and first in all her combat classes. She was lithe, fast, and for someone who is a rich kid by most standards, she got down and dirty and never gave up.

When the time was drawing closer for her to go to University, I had called the Chancellor and he rambled on about her wanting to go to New York for school. He was very...animated, to say the least; completely against the overall idea and I knew it would never happen because, despite his aloofness, he did love his daughter in his own way, and wanted her safe and in a bubble. No, she would go to DeLorean and finally be where we can be with her all the time. But I needed to make sure that every moment she was near me, she understood how much I, we, wanted her and how sorry I was. It was a fine line. She was so incredibly irritating, and her mouth and sass made me want to bend her over my knee, but she was perfect.

Almost too perfect, to the point of otherworldly means, if you believed in the myths anyway. During her senior year combat exams, the boys and I snuck in and hung around the back to watch her final testing before her graduation ceremony. We looked on as she entered the ring, head high, her air of confidence never wavering even though she was matched with a boy three times her size. Grayson was pissed, but I remembered us smiling as she smirked at her opponent. The moment the signal to fight sounded, Hudson had ran straight at him and jumped high and wrapped her legs around his neck and took him down to the floor and was beating the shit out of his face before the poor guy knew what was happening. He never stood a chance. I had laughed and we had left before she saw us.

I had stopped visiting for holidays when she was eighteen, she had two years left before University. I visited that last Christmas and tried to make her feel better after an argument with her father and instead, I ended up spending that night having the most intense sex I ever had. She was incredible, so damn sexy and for that entire night, she was mine. I took her virginity, fucked her senseless and left before she woke up and stayed away. I was a fucking idiot. I hated myself every day. And every moment I was alone in my room, I remembered how she felt around my dick and stroked myself, coming so hard, I saw stars. I couldn't even hook up with another girl since then. I knew it would never be the same, so what the fuck was the point. I knew at the time I had already given my heart to her; hell, it was impossible not to. But it was terrifying, there is commitment, then there was Hudson. I could lose myself in her and it wasn't until I saw her again that I realized that maybe I should have let myself get lost.

Every time the chancellor asked me if I was visiting, even though I ached to see her, to the point of distraction, I told him that I was an instructor at the academy having graduated with honors with the boys, as an excuse. It was the truth, I did graduate right at the time of retirement for several of the professors. And to be honest, the pomp and circumstance of being around the Council was stressful and grating on the best of days, but having to go to those events, watching her grow more beautiful by the minute was something I couldn't bear anymore. I don't know exactly when I fell in love with her. It was before tasting her for the first time, before even seeing her I think; it was the moment I heard her voice as she ran around the house playing when I arrived at their house. Ryder, Hunter, and Grayson? They were never with her like I was, but the attraction, the need to protect her, to be around her? Yeah, they all felt the same and it was distracting to the point of madness.

I sighed. "Yeah, she is. She is absolutely fucking more amazing than I remember." Fuck, this is going to be harder than I thought, and I knew it was going to be almost impossible. Even now, I just want to go upstairs and bury myself inside of her, even if her damn lion tried to kill me. I groaned and sat down on the kitchen stool, but not before grabbing a beer from the fridge and taking a long drink.

Ryder chuckled and slapped my back. "You're the fucking idiot who fucked the most amazing girl in the world and ran." He shook his head and I growled at him. He laughed. "Come Monday, you'll have to taper that down, but yeah, I know exactly how you feel; hell, we all do." He shook his head and grabbed the decanter of whisky and a glass instead.

I put my head in my hands in my head then looked at Grayson.

"Nothing to add, bro?" Always the quiet and observant one, it was a little shocking to see him take the initiative and walk up to Hudson when she was on the counter, even if it was to throw me and Ryder under the bus. In fact, he was usually so aloof, it was the occasional game to fuck with him, but his ass was fast despite his size and it ended up in a brawl in the house most times. He looked at us but was lost in his thoughts. I sighed and looked away; I know how easy it is to get lost in anything Hudson related.

Seeing her today was like a punch in the gut. When we saw her car parked, we assumed she would be in her room, when we walked to the kitchen, heard the music and saw her through the glass, swimming in the pool, we were drawn like moths to a flame. I don't even know how long we stood there, but it was impossible to move. Fuck, gone were the Delores Umbridge clothes her dad would make her wear and here was a grown woman. I mean shit, she had more than grown up, she filled the fuck out from the last time I saw and felt her. Her white bathing suit looked painted on, her ridiculously curvy thighs and plump ass on display and the material was pretty much see through. The way that suit hugged her waist, and teetered on a thong suit, I was convinced it was made specifically for her and put on with magic. Her hair had gotten longer and brushed her ass as she danced around and sang to the music playing. Even with the color change, it was amazing. She looked like some type of Goddess. When she spun around, and we saw the nipple piercings on her fucking amazing breasts, I felt all of us suck in a breath. She had abs most men would kill for and breasts women pay for. But it was when her green eyes met mine, when she finally noticed us when we had stepped outside, that I lost all sense. I missed her. I wanted her. I needed her.

"You know what I'm worried about? Tomorrow," added Gray finally. Hunter cursed and Ryder groaned.

"Tomorrow?" I looked at him in confusion, then it hit me. Our annual, before the year mixer, was tomorrow night, which realistically was a party not a mixer, but the school board didn't need to know that, and no one would dare say anything against us. I growled. Fuck, a room full of college guys, horny girls, and instructors that were our age. It was one of two times the younger instructors and students mixed together, at the start of the year and then again at the end of the year, and always here. We were literally tossing Hudson into a pack of wolves.

Gray smiled slowly. "You know she will be the most beautiful thing here. Can you imagine her walking around in anything like she wore today? We're fucked."

"So why are you smiling?" Hunter snarled, always the volatile one. He had a point though, the smiling put me on edge.

"I'm always ready to teach a lesson or two. Hudson is off limits, and this is the perfect time to make it known." He shrugged.

"Well, tomorrow just got a little bit more intriguing." Ryder looked at his watch. "I got to go pick up the liquor for tomorrow. Hunter, you're driving." Ryder laughed as he finished his whiskey and stood up. Hunter groaned and followed Ryder out the door, bitching about always being designated driver to a bunch of pussies. I laughed. I loved my assholes.

"Tomorrow is going to suck, isn't it?" I asked Grayson.

He smiled viciously. "Fuck I hope so, I'm a little blood thirsty." I laughed and we got up to go to our rooms to take a shower before coming back down the stairs to grab a few beers. We sat down on the couch until Ryder and Hunter came back with a few pizzas.

❧

Hunter reached over and snagged the controller for the Xbox and declared war on Grayson but after a few minutes started cursing.

"Gray, you can't fucking play this game if you're not going to fucking revive me when I need you to. You are a shitty Call of Duty partner," growled Hunter.

"I wouldn't need to revive your dumb ass if you stop fucking dying," Grayson laughed. Hunter threw the controller at him and Gray dodged it while jumping over the back of the couch to avoid Hunter's fist. Ryder and I shook our heads and kept eating, ignoring them. They can't play games for shit without it ending up in a fight. They were the worst.

"Hudson! Protect me, Hunter is trying to kill me because he is a pussy," Grayson yelled, and my head snapped up as I saw Hudson leaning against the stair banister, smiling at the two idiots. She had her hair in a messy bun and was in a pair of short shorts and a tight tank top with no bra. I almost whimpered.

Grayson ran behind her, all six feet five inches of him, hiding behind a five-foot-five woman. I rolled my eyes, Ryder was laughing. Hunter stopped his attack and stood in front of Hudson.

"Are you going to protect him, Hudson? This is where we draw a line. You're going to have to pick a favorite," Hunter grated out and Grayson stuck his tongue out at him. Hudson laughed.

"The fact that you know I can protect you is cute, but I don't know if I should even bother, seeing as not one of you came to tell me there was pizza. I'm not sure if I want to help anyone right now." She stuck her middle finger out.

Grayson pretended to pout, and she laughed and turned to give him a hug, having to get on her tippy toes to get her arms around his neck. Hunter was momentarily distracted as her ass popped out of her shorts from the bottom. Grayson smiled smugly at Hunter, who flipped him off.

"Okay, you big baby, I'll protect you from big bad Hunter." She turned around, reached up, and bopped Hunter on the nose. "Bad boy, go sit down." Hunter looked shocked, and I busted out laughing. He walked back to the couch, grumbling about unfair advantages and she rolled her eyes.

"Again, maybe if you would have told me there was pizza, I would have chosen you. Besides," she shrugged, and she walked to the pizza boxes and grabbed a box of pepperoni, "Grayson is my gentle giant. I must protect him at all costs. Hunter, you look like you eat humans for breakfast. It's kind of scary for my gentle giant." She hid a smile behind her pizza, which she was disrespecting by taking two slices and putting them together like a sandwich. We stared at her.

"What?! I only eat carbs once a week, and Friday is my freaking day. Leave me alone. You think a body like this is made from cucumber sandwiches?" She scoffed and took a big bite and moaned. I shook my head and Hunter stomped back to his seat on the couch and Grayson sat down next to Hunter on the floor.

"Two things here. First off, I'm not scared of Hunter, I'll put his angry ass on the floor. Also, I like the idea of being your anything. So am I your favorite then?" Grayson asked. Hunter cut his eyes at them while he played his game solo, watching her for her response. She laughed.

"Uh, nope, you are not going to trap me into saying favorites. I'm here for the pizza and big dick energy. Also, because I'm ready to kick someone's ass on Call of Duty."

"You could never kick my ass in COD, angel," Hunter scoffed. "Also please tell Grayson that if I have to get up from here, I will beat his ass."

She scoffed and stood up to snatch a remote. "Switch it to two players, you asshole, and we will see who wins."

"You're on." Hunter's eyes glimmered in challenge.

"Big dick..." Ryder started.

"Don't finish that statement unless you plan to show me. Which reminds me, do you guys have batteries?" Hudson asked with a smirk. We all groaned, and she cackled.

"That's fucked up, Hud, totally fucked up," grumbled Hunter.

"Maybe." She picked up more pizza and shoved it into her mouth. Where the fuck is it going?

"But I'll torture you all in every way I can since Zane has tried to ban me from all dicks. Even though he did a good job at playing keep away from his dick for the past two years," she grumbled the last part as she shoveled pizza into her mouth. She was like a fucking machine, eating and shooting at the damn television at the same time.

Grayson scoffed and bent over to whisper something in her ear that made her blush bright red. She cleared her throat. "Good point. Are you volunteering?"

"I think we all would, Hudson. I'm sure of it." His voice was dark, and I was jealous that he made her blush.

I cleared my throat. "Where's Xena?" I asked. She shrugged and whooped at her body count on the game before tossing the controller back on the table.

"You have an advantage; I want a rematch," Hunter said indignantly.

She stretched her arms above her head and my mouth started to water. "Nope, but if you can go more than one round in other things, I'll consider it." She winked and Hunter's eyes glazed over. I held back my anger and smirked.

She looked at me. "Anyways, she said something about food and safety and ran out the back door right before I came down here. When she is ready to come back, she will knock on the door until someone lets her in, or magically appears in my room. I don't know, she comes up with the weirdest shit every day. Speaking of, do either of you have a book on familiars? Dad kept her hidden, unless she went out at night to hunt in the woods, so I would be interested in learning more."

"Actually, yeah, I do. Let me run up and grab it," Ryder said as he got up and went upstairs and came back down just as fast, tossing the book her way. She smiled at him and mumbled her thanks around her pizza.

"It's amazing that you have a familiar that's a fucking lion. I don't think I've ever seen one up close, let alone as a familiar. Most magic users have birds or some shit. The guys and I don't even have ours yet. I'll admit, I'm jealous as fuck," Hunter grunted out while shooting at the TV.

"Thank you, she is pretty special. Just walked out of the Zoo and followed me home and told me I was hers. Dad had to pay a lot of money to shut them up." We laughed.

"I have an idea!" Ryder stood up and went to the kitchen and came back with shot glasses and a bottle of Apple Crown. Hunter and I groaned, and Grayson just shook his head, laughing. Hudson looked at him, confused.

"We're going to play a drinking game called three truths and a lie. We have to guess the lie and if we're wrong, we drink! You get to ask the person you want to guess if they get it wrong, they have to do a dare," Ryder finished explaining.

"I'm down, can we skinny dip after?" Hudson teased and we all turned to look at her, she laughed but blushed. I loved that color on her. "Okay," she clapped, "I'll go first."

She took a second to think, and Ryder poured the shots.

"Okay! Number one, I watch videos to learn how to dance. Two, I watch videos to learn how to cook. Three, I watch videos to learn how to suck dick properly. Four, I have four piercings. Zane, you answer," she finished and my dick immediately got hard at the thought of her watching those videos for anything. We never got to that part, and now, I was anxious to try. This was easy though; she only had her ears and nipples pierced so that was true, she clearly knew how to dance very well from what I saw earlier. We had a cook in the house, but that doesn't mean she didn't try to learn.

"Okay," I leaned back on the couch staring down at her. "Number one, two, and four are truths, three is a lie."

She licked her lips. "Wrong." She smiled and I frowned and took my shot. She paused and pretended to think. "For your dare, hmmm, can I cash in on it later?"

"Nope, uh, uh, nope, it has to happen right here, Hudson. Stop changing the rules," Ryder said.

"There weren't any rules given actually, Ryder... so I'm implementing a clause. Instead of daring Zane, I'm going to go ahead and dare all of you instead." She threw her head back and laughed.

"I don't like that either," said Ryder.

"I'm intrigued," mumbled Grayson.

"I can outdo you anytime, angel," said Hunter.

I shook my head. I knew that the one dare she wanted to give me was one she wasn't ready for, so I let it go and just watched.

"Okay, I dare you all, to skinny dip with me, right now." She jumped up and ran to the pool, stripping off her clothes as she ran. We all looked at each other and Hunter shoved the shit out of Ryder, who fell to the floor but then grabbed Hunter's ankle and then Hunter fell, and the pizza spilled to the floor. *Fucking children.* Grayson had side stepped them and was already in the kitchen and I jumped over Ryder and Hunter, who were now beating the shit out of each other, yelling about seeing titties. When I got outside, Hudson was already in the pool and Gray had already jumped in to splash her while she laughed. I looked at her, stripped, and jumped in just as Hunter and Ryder had gotten outside. Ryder pushed Hunter into the pool and jumped in after him to hold him under. I laughed and swam away from that shit while they settled down.

"Alright, alright, the liquor is out, so let's get back to the game, Hunter, it's your turn to guess," She clapped her hands and stayed under the water. Hunter pushed Ryder off and came closer and leaned on the side of the pool and looked at her, still breathing hard from roughhousing with Ryder.

"Um, one is true as we saw you dancing, I had a feeling two is true as well, but if Zane got it wrong," he shrugged, "then that is false so I suppose four is true, and three is true?" he finished with a hitch in his voice. She laughed and shook her head and splashed him. And he huffed, wiping the water from his face.

"Okay, so what's my dare? You already got me naked, so I don't know if there is much more you can do now." He looked at her and turned his head. She smiled, I've seen that smile before, two years ago.

"Your dare is easy, kiss me and touch me." She looked at me briefly when she said it but focused her attention on Hunter. *Fuck.*

Hunter

"Kiss me and touch me..." When she said those words, I wasted no time with that dare at all. I swam to her and pushed her up against the side of the pool. I felt the other guys watching and I'll be honest, I loved having a fucking audience. It's what I loved most about what I do. Granted being a professor was vastly different than being a voyeur, but whatever.

I hovered in the water against her, her breasts brushing against my chest, her nipples hardening and her breath hitching. Fuck, I've been dying to kiss her for years and I was going to make this count. I grabbed her chin and pressed my lips against hers. I teased my tongue across her lips, and she opened for me, so fucking sweetly. I teased her tongue with mine and I felt her tongue piercings running down her tongue and I groaned when I felt them. Fuck this, I grabbed her ass and wrapped her legs around my waist, pressing my dick against her, deepening the kiss. Her hands ran up my chest and wrapped around my neck and she moaned into my mouth. She ran her hands into my hair and pulled, making my eyes roll to the back of my head. If she likes it rough, we were going to be fucking perfect in bed. I ran my hands up and down her body, caressing her rock hard abs and dipping lower to her pussy. Fuck, even with her legs wrapped around me and being in the pool, I could feel how wet she was, I dipped my finger into her and curled my finger teasing her G-spot. Fuck, she was so tight and when she clenched around my finger and moaned, I almost lost it right there.

She started to move gently with my hand, and I slid another finger into her, and she froze and threw her head back. "Fuck," she whispered, and I leaned over and grabbed her lips again with mine, not wanting to waste a second of those lips and sweet tongue on mine. I had her ass firmly in one hand while I worked her over with the other, her moans turning into short pants, her tongue rubbing firmly against mine. Fuck, I could die happy with her kisses. Remind me to kiss Ryder for this fucking game. I had been ignoring her clit on purpose, but the moment I moved my thumb and applied pressure, I felt her clit piercing and lost it. I growled, bit her lip, and stroked her the way I needed my dick to and tugged and flicked her clit. She clenched and moaned my name into my mouth as she came, her nails running down my back. This was just the way it should be; my name on her lips. No other woman should ever moan my name, this was it for me. It was always Hudson.

I finally let go of her kisses and she opened her eyes, and they were glazed over. "Well, shit," she whispered. "I'm going to need more games like this. Can we make this a mandated house meeting thing?" She went to move her legs off of me and I growled, and I turned her around and pressed her back against my front, I wasn't ready to let her go. If ever.

The guys were staring, their eyes heavy, and she cleared her throat, and I kissed her neck, and she bit her lip.

"Erm, Ryder, can I give the right answer now?" She breathed heavily.

"Go for it, sweetheart," his voice low.

"Well... Hunter, I swear I'm going to move away..." I chuckled and stopped my hands from wandering, her body responding again. "So yes, I watched videos to learn how to dance, I also learned videos to cook because it is interesting to me, three I definitely watch videos to learn how to give proper fallatio, I want to make sure I'm great at it, but four is wrong." I smirked at fallatio and my dick jumped.

Grayson frowned, and my dick jumped at the thought of her tongue rings on my dick. I groaned and hid my head in her neck. She laughed softly, rubbing her hands across my arms, I don't even think she realized she was doing it.

Grayson looked at her. "You have your ears pierced and we saw the nipples through the bathing suit earlier." He looked at her, hell they all were looking at her like their eyes were some type of metal detectors. She smiled slowly, that look sending shivers up my spine, knowing exactly what was pierced; every second with her was driving me crazy.

"Nope," she popped the p, I needed her to pop another p, preferably on a handstand like the rap song goes. "I have my ears, that's two, my nipples that's another two, you three guys haven't seen or felt," she laughed and winked at me and my dick got harder. She gasped and thrust against me. "my mouth," she finished with a gasp. Then she stuck her tongue out, then back in, and I smiled when the guys froze. "I have three tongue rings down my tongue, and I also have my clit pierced." She shrugged and tugged away from me and started swimming around the pool, all eyes tracking her. "About two years ago, I was... rebelling..." her eyes flicked to Zane; we knew what she meant though. She was hurt, I almost beat the shit out of him when he told us what happened. Grayson had to take me off and I went into my room and didn't come out for the rest of the day. Just thinking about it made me clench my fists.

"Anyway, that day I got my tattoo, the bottom of it reads 'Never give in to weakness'. The artist started talking about how much piercings hurt, pain is weakness, so I laughed, and I got everything pierced at once right after he finished and used a healing spell to prevent having to wait for them to heal on their own."

She swam around the waterfall letting the water fall on her, her body glowing under the lights.

"Enough about me! Your turn! And it better be juicy," she yelled.

"Fuck, I don't think any one of us has anything that juicy, so I guess we can just do a truth for a truth? Guys? Is that cool?" Ryder swam around to be next to Hudson, and Gray and Zane shrugged.

"I'll go first then," Grayson started. "I have a Jacob's ladder." We started laughing when Hudson's mouth dropped open.

"I wonder if my tongue rings would get caught on that. I have to do some research," she whispered low. We groaned; she was going to kill us.

"Ah fuck, did I say that out loud?" She looked around sheepishly.

"Yes, you did. And we can find out, soon," Grayson promised in a low voice.

Zane cleared his throat and I laughed, he looked at me and I resisted the urge to roll my eyes at his expression. Dumb ass, I couldn't think with so much Hudson in the air, *if that even made sense,* I mused. Regardless, the fact that he fucked her and left her was insane, even now, the need to pick her up and touch her was relentless. So how the fuck did he do it. *There was no way this was remotely normal*; I shook my head, took a deep breath and went next.

"Um, hmmm, fuck, I didn't think this through. I don't remember much of my life before moving to Colorado, it was as if I woke up and I was there. My family said I had repressed memories from my childhood, but it always bothered me, and I feel like there is more to my life, but I never found out anything and I let it go," I shrugged. I had mentioned that to the guys before. I knew the consensus. Childhood amnesia was normal but honestly, it was different for me. I felt like my slate was wiped clean. I just can't remember. Magic can alter, it can break minds even, but to be able to wipe clean? As intricate as the mind was, to even function after something like that was impossible. That took a level of power that was unheard of, so it had to be repressed memories, but I just wasn't convinced.

Hudson made a sound in the back of her throat, and swam up to me, hugging me tightly. I wrapped my arms around her and hid my face in her neck and just breathed her in. This topic always bothered me; I'm surprised I mentioned it, but I just didn't think of anything juicy. She tugged my head back gripping my hair and pressed her lips against my neck. "Hey, hulk," she said, and I laughed. "Let us all make some new memories for the ones you are missing. We can even start with me kicking your ass in Call of Duty." I pressed a kiss to her temple and settled her firmly against me.

I'm usually very worked up, always ready to fight and expecting danger at every corner, it was how I was wired, so letting go and feeling relaxed felt amazing. Ryder, Gray, and Z all stared at me and I shrugged. There was relaxing with our friends then there was... Hudson. I'm not sure why this girl affected me so much, so quickly. But I didn't care, I didn't need an explanation or a long plot to figure it out. This girl was just it, and I didn't need to jump through hoops to figure that out. I would say she was a witch but uh, yeah.

"I like to read romance books," Ryder said sheepishly. "Actually, I follow your Goodreads profile and I, uh, kind of... readallthebooksyoureadsowecanhavesomethingtotalkaboutwhenyoucametoschoolhere," he finished quickly, his face red and he dunked his head under the water, and I laughed.

Hudson looked at him when he came back up and took a deep breath. "That is actually one of the most amazing things anyone has ever done for me. You and I are definitely having a book club date. My room, popcorn, our Kindles, and chocolate. It's going down."

"Are clothes optional?" Ryder teased; I rolled my eyes.

Hudson laughed. "I don't think strip reading is a game and I don't think we can book club if we're naked."

"We can if we act out the parts. I'm a good actor," Ryder insisted.

"Well, you know, a lot of those books were reverse harem, we can always act those parts out."

Ryder's smile froze and he swallowed. "Fuck. Guys, we need to book club the fuck out of each other right now." Zane, Grayson, and I looked at him like he lost his damn mind. Hudson just smiled. I put it in the back of my head to look it up later.

"No idea, but I'll look it up and text it to you guys later," I remarked.

"Hey, no fair, I want to be in the group chat too!" Hudson pouted.

"It's a guys group chat, you would be bored," Grayson teased.

She stuck out her tongue at him. How I didn't notice her tongue piercings was beyond me. Fuck, she was so sexy.

She smiled evilly and I narrowed my eyes. "Hunter will add me to the group chat, won't you Hunter?"

"Huh? Why would I do that?" I smirked. She shifted and ran her hand back to grab my dick and stroke it. I choked and bit back a moan while she worked me over under the water.

"Because you really want me in the group chat so we can send each other pictures and texts all day," she said huskily, turning herself on as much as she was turning me on. I groaned, fucking torture.

"Hmm, pictures and texts? All day? You're going to have to prove that, if I add you, we will want to see at least one picture of you a day. And several messages," I grunted out as her hands gripped more firmly and she quickened her pace. She squealed and smiled up at me. Never stopping her pace, and I started to thrust into her hand. She was fucking driving me crazy.

I moaned and grumbled about pussy power and they laughed at me. Funny sure, but it was my dick getting the fucking best hand job ever. Jokes on them, I thought as I closed my eyes and leaned over to kiss her neck.

"Well, fuck, that escalated quickly," Ryder said gruffly. Yeah, yeah, the fuck it did. *Fuck, she was going to make me cum like this.*

"Don't be jealous, bro. I have the sob story, you get a date, Gray is going to detangle tongue rings from his dick. So, all in all, the only loser here is Zane," I said smugly. He threw his middle finger up at me. I laughed but choked as she touched the tip of my dick and discovered the piercing there. Her eyes shot up to mine, heat in her eyes. I grabbed her hand and leaned over to whisper in her ear. "Let's stop this for now before you make me explode and we have to clean out the pool and I'll come up to your room later."

She winked at me. "Deal." *Oh, it was fucking on.*

Zane cleared his throat. "Well, my truth may not get me any of that, but it will definitely set me free."

Ryder rolled his eyes. "Shut the fuck up, Z. Are you going to start playing a violin?"

He laughed. "Nope. My truth is I've been in love with Hudson from the moment I saw her 10 years ago."

Hudson let out a low squeak and froze in my arms, fucking shit. She was going to run. *Don't worry angel, no matter where you go, I promise I'll be there from now on. Nothing would keep me away, even if I have to break every fucking jaw and door down to get there.*

Hudson

What the fuck just happened? I had just wanted some fucking pizza. What do I get? Skinny dipping. An amazing orgasm, which was okay, a pierced dick, a book date, a promise to make memories, and a declaration of love. Love. From the guy who took my virginity and literally fell off the face of the earth until earlier. He had some fucking nerve.

To top it all off, my vagina was still on fucking fire. I'm totally done for the night. Yup. It's my time to go to bed.

"Um, well." Everyone was just staring at me like the news was only news to me. The way they were acting with me today, the pull I've been feeling has been intense, I knew they felt it too. But love, Zane? Really. Mother fucker. Okay, I needed to breathe. Go to my room, hide. Yup. Hiding. Hiding sounds fucking amazing actually. I slid away from Hunter, really fucking hoping he came to my room later, and swam to the edge of the pool. Everyone was staring at me, like I was going to combust.

"Hudson, wait," Zane started.

"No, oh no. Not waiting. Two years, Zane. You took my virginity and left me two years ago. I didn't know what I did wrong, I didn't know if anything was wrong with me. I felt... broken..." God I hated to admit this, but he needed to know. "I cried; you know. For days," I whispered. "Days. Then my hair started to change to white and I thought it was stress, thought I was going batshit, granted it wasn't anything like that, but I lost my damn mind, Zane. You didn't call, you didn't text me..." My voice sounded pitiful even to myself. "You left me, Zane. You don't get to tell me you love me, because if you did, you wouldn't have left." I straightened my spine, embraced my fucking badass-ness, and strutted my sexy naked ass out of the pool and put my hands on my hips to face him. "I won't be weak again, Zane. So, take a good long look. I do not cry for anyone anymore." I marched myself up the outside stairs to my room and slammed the door and locked it. Stupid fuck.

I took a quick shower and laid in my bed, in the dark, and punched my pillow. He loved me? That annoying little shit. How dare he love me? In the words of the great Will Farrell, this is horse shit.

I flipped on to my back and stared at the starry sky stickers, trying to help myself breathe calmly, turned on some music and a few minutes later, I heard a knock on my door. I didn't bother to look up as my door opened and closed.

"No hablo inglés" I grumbled.

Hunter chuckled and I turned my head towards the sound.

"You're such a dork," his said softly.

"You just used the word dork, so that automatically makes you one first." I sighed. He laid down next to me and looked at the stars with me, reaching over to hold my hand.

"You know, I have to say this, and I won't mention it again. He didn't say what he said to make you run away." He sighed.

"That's not it though. It's not about running; it's about self-preservation. There is a difference. What he did was wrong, Hunter. I gave him a part of me and yes, it was amazing and everything it should have been. It was perfect honestly. But after..." I blew out a breath.

"If it makes you feel better, I beat the shit out of him when he came back and told us what he did."

I laughed. "Yeah, that makes me feel a little better, thanks." I bit my lip. "But I'm a new version of me. I'm stronger and I'm actively embracing who I am. The other shit doesn't matter. I have always been a bitch, smart, and damn right unbeatable." I smiled and laughed when he groaned. "Shut up, it's true, but this time, I want to embrace everything I want. My sexuality and the power that is inherently Hudson. It's exciting." I leaned up and caressed his face.

He looked at me intently and leaned closer. “If you keep touching me, Hudson, I’m going to kiss you again and I don’t think I’ll be able to stop.”

I don’t know who spoke at that moment, but whoever that horny bitch was needed an applause when she said, “Maybe I don’t want you to.” His control snapped and he pressed his mouth against mine, his tongue teasing until I opened my lips. His tongue immediately caressed mine, teasing my tongue rings. His mouth moved against mine, completely taking over my every thought as I moaned and pulled him closer. His hands tugged gently on my hair, making me clench my thighs in anticipation.

“Fuck, Hudson.”

“Did I fucking ask you to stop kissing me?” I replied as I grabbed his neck, fusing our lips back together. He positioned himself over me, and I opened and put my feet on the mattress. He moaned against my lips as his dick pressed against my pussy but not going in. He leaned back on his knees and started to touch me and massage me everywhere. When he pinched and teased my nipples, I moaned my approval, and scratched lightly down his arms. He hummed and he followed his hands with his lips, kissing, licking, and biting my neck roughly before licking a path to my nipples and sucking one into his mouth and swirling his tongue around the peak. He bit down hard then flicked his tongue around to ease the pain.

“Fuck,” I groaned. He switched his attention to my other breast while his hands brushed against the inside of my thighs and I bucked against him when he replaced his hands with his mouth, pressing kisses and bites against my thick thighs while he opened them and stared at my waxed pussy.

“Fuck, Hudson,” he growled. “I’m going to make this all mine tonight,” he whispered as he pressed a kiss on my swollen clit and sucked it into his mouth. I bucked off the bed and he wrapped his arms around my thighs and brought me closer to him. I put my hands on his head as he fucking licked, sucked, and tongue fucked me. Nothing could’ve possibly prepared me for this. He groaned about how good I tasted while he worked me over from top to bottom, and I grinded my hips against his face. He slowly alternated between fast and slow tempos, never letting me catch my breath, flicking and sucking and kissing my clit. Then he grabbed hold of me, pressing me down while taking my clit through his lips, flicking it with the tip of his tongue and I came apart for him.

"Fuck, Hunter, yes. Oh my God. Yes, fuck, please." I don't even know what I was begging for, but he knew what my body wanted better than I did at that point.

He flipped me over. "Get on your knees, Hudson, and open your legs. I want to see that pretty pussy from the back," he said darkly as he reached over, grabbing me by my neck, choking me, and pressing kisses down my spine. I groaned as he teased my pussy with his piercing, never actually going in.

I tried to rub myself against him and he choked me harder until tears streamed out of my eyes, then he let go slightly and he smacked my ass three times, making me scream. I was so wet, it was dripping down my legs. He ran his finger up and down my soaked pussy and moaned with approval.

"You're not in control here, angel. I gave you something already, this is now for me. I want you dripping just like this the entire time. Say you understand, Hudson."

"Yes..." He smacked my ass and reached over to pinch my nipples, hard. I moaned, shaking from need.

"No, you're going to say 'Yes, sir'."

"Yes, sir," I moaned, and he reached down and pinched and flicked my clit, taking me to the edge then stopping. I groaned and he opened my legs wider and smacked my pussy. I screamed in pain and pleasure.

"Little girl, you're playing with fire. I let you come. That was a favor. These are all favors from your Sir. That is the way this works," he growled before he bent down and sucked my clit in his mouth, pulling my piercing with his teeth, making me leak and groan in the pleasure and pain combination. He groaned as he licked and sucked my clit and lips, then shoved his tongue inside of me, tasting me. "Fuck, baby girl. I'm not sure if you taste better on your back, or this way, with this fucking sweet fat ass in my face." He smacked my ass, massaging the sting away. Yeah, he was an ass man, which was good because I had plenty of it. He grabbed my ass firmly and separated my cheeks, running his tongue from my clit all the way to my ass, where he ran his tongue around my tight rim, making me moan in surprise. He was relentless, between my pussy and my ass, he had me shaking. He switched all his attention to my ass, kissing and licking around the rim, grunting his approval as I lightly pushed back to accept the onslaught of the unexpected pleasure. Fuck, Hunter was incredible.

Suddenly, he leaned up and pushed my face into the mattress, holding me down by my neck and slammed into my tight pussy. I screamed, not having had sex since Zane. I was soaked and sensitive but still tight as fuck. He groaned and grabbed my tiny waist and had a good firm grip while he slid back out and rubbed his dick against me. I moaned.

"Yes, Hudson, I'm going to make that ass mine, just not today. But when I do, you're going to beg me for more," he said low and he slammed back into my pussy. She was hungry for him, and I started to clench around him, moaning into the mattress.

"Fuck yes, you're so tight, your pussy is fucking perfect," he growled, and he pounded into me, reaching under my hips to play with my clit. I clenched around him and felt my orgasm building before he slammed into me a few more times, then stopped moving. I was going to cry if he kept this up. It was so damn good, but fuck, I craved him, I didn't want him to ever stop.

"Were you going to come without permission, Hudson?"

I whimpered and he reached down to wrap my long hair around his fist. "Answer. My. Question. Hudson." He punctuated each word with a thrust of his huge dick, and I was fucking drooling with how amazing he felt inside of me, his piercing hitting my cervix, making every thrust a fucking Christmas gift.

"Yes, sir. I'm sorry, sir," I moaned and then cried out as he tightened his grip on my hair.

"No sorry, baby," he stroked slow, pulling out and rubbing his dick on my ass before sinking inside of my pussy and doing it again. I moaned.

"I wanted an excuse to punish you and you just gave it to me." He smacked my ass again, then slid a thick finger in my ass and I bucked against him, groaning at the strange feeling. It felt good, especially with his dick inside me at the same time.

"Your ass is tight, baby. Maybe I don't have to wait long. You like this, don't you, Hudson?"

I moaned and he started to fuck me again with his dick and his finger and I pushed myself back, wanting more. He chuckled and worked another finger into me, and my eyes rolled back, and I started asking for more.

"Uh, you didn't say sir. Now, I'm going to have to stop. Too bad, that ass could've been full tonight." He took his fingers out and I whimpered at the loss and then he started smacking my ass over and over again, hard, until I begged him for mercy, he laughed.

"Mercy, Hudson? Every time I smack this fat ol' ass, your pussy tries to milk my dick. And fuck, I don't know when you became my wet dream, and I don't know where these curves came from, but I swear to you, I'm going to fucking worship each one until you fucking melt at the idea of my dick inside of you. I waited too long for you and I'll be damned if I miss any moment. I want you to look at me, no matter where you are, and remember how I feel when I fuck this pussy raw. So, you're not getting mercy, baby, we're just getting started and I can go." He started to smack my ass and work his hips slowly into me, pushing his huge dick all the way inside and dragging it back out again, his piercing sliding against me. "All. Night. Long." He finished his point by pulling me up all the way, my breasts in the air, my head on his chest, and pounded into me, this new position driving him deeper inside and I screamed his name, completely at his mercy. He pulled out of me and laid down on the bed and picked me up, his arms flexing as he settled me on to his dick.

"You're going to ride me and I'm going to see those pretty tits bounce and feel that fat ass on my thighs as you slide up and down. I want you to go all the way to the tip of my dick and back down, Hudson. Don't half ass this," he demanded and then he thrust inside me and my eyes rolled back. I moved myself up and down like he wanted, his dick hitting me so damn deep each and every time.

I started to shake, needing to come. "Please, sir, can I come?"

He smiled evilly. "No, Hudson. You don't get to come on my dick yet. You haven't earned it, but for being a good girl and asking, I'm going to spank you, and every time, you're going to thank me. Do you understand?"

"Yes, sir." I wanted to fucking curse but when he reached over and spanked my ass, I thanked him each time. I moaned and I clenched around his pretty dick. He groaned when I clenched and he smacked me four more times, and I screamed thank you and each time, he groaned as I got tighter and tighter.

"Fuck, Hudson, this pussy is going to drive me crazy. I wonder what else is going to drive me crazy." He reached up and grabbed my breasts, caressing them and tugging on my nipple rings.

"Ride me, Hudson, don't fucking stop and don't fucking cum," he demanded.

I rode him hard, loving the feel of him inside of me. He groaned, cursing and tossing his head back. He thought he had it bad? I was losing my fucking mind and when my eyes started to roll back, he grabbed my hips and made me stop and then smacked my breasts. I yelped and he drew his hands down my abs, mesmerized, and reached down and played with my clit, which was fucking soaked from the juices leaking out of me. Every touch brought me closer to the edge.

"Yes, Hunter, yes, please," my words started to just blend into a bunch of nonsense at this point. He smiled and he held my waist with a bruising grip as he pumped inside of me, holding me still while he worked me over.

"You can cum now, Hudson." And holy shit did I. I let go and he didn't stop fucking me. His dick never got soft and I had to wonder what the fuck he was on. I came twice more, and I felt like I was dying.

"Oh no, sweetheart, if you think we're done, you're wrong. You're going to cum in my mouth again, then I'm going to cum in yours, then I'm going to cum in that pretty pussy a couple more times tonight." *How the fuck was I going to manage that?* I had no idea.

He snatched me up and picked me up until I was sitting on his face. I moaned as he sucked on my clit and I had to hold on to the headboard as he tongue fucked me and then tightened my thighs around his head just like I liked it and gently licked up and down my over sensitive clit until I was moaning his name over and over and screaming yes sir with every flick he gave me. Then he nibbled and sucked on my clit, grabbed my ass and started to make me ride his face. The pleasure was fucking unbelievable and with a groan he bit my clit and I screamed.

"Fuck yes, daddy, I'm going to come." He stopped everything he was doing and shifted my pussy off his face and looked at me. I whimpered on edge; my eyes unfocused. I looked down at him and gasped at the intensity of the look in his eyes.

"Say it again," he demanded. One hand reached up to grab my long hair. "Say it again, Hudson."

"Daddy," I said softly. His smiled turned feral and he put my pussy back on his face and started to tongue fuck me. He smacked my ass and I moaned. I was right there and with one last lick from him sucking my clit into his mouth, I came so hard, I thought I was losing my damn mind.

"Yes, daddy, yes fuck yes."

I was shaking while he lapped me up and caught every drop and I thought he was going to move me, so I shifted and he looked at me and growled, "One more time for daddy, princess, then I'm coming down your fucking throat." And with that, he grabbed my ass and started all over again. I gripped the headboard with everything I had as he tongue fucked me, urging my ass to ride his face as he tongued my asshole between shoving his tongue inside of me. I bucked against him as he slid a finger inside of my ass while he started licking and sucking my clit until I was about to fall over. When my body began to lean, he reached up and smacked my breast with his free hand, hard enough to leave his handprint, and he tugged on my nipple rings. Then he reached up and wrapped one hand around my neck. "Don't fucking move," he growled under my pussy and started to lick and suck even harder, using his other hand to urge my hips to move on his tongue.

Well fuck, is it possible to die from attraction? I moaned his name, bucking into his mouth. He reached up, looked into my eyes then smacked me, hard. Putting his clean fingers in my mouth, Hunter smirked and grumbled out, "Suck on daddy's fingers, now." I was a fucking goner for him, I sucked his fingers as if I was sucking his dick and he groaned, eating me out. I started to shake and clench my thighs as I flooded his face. I screamed, grinding my pussy on his face no longer needing him to do it for me, until I was completely spent. He cleaned me up with his tongue and moved me off of him.

"You're fucking honey, Hudson. I'm going to taste that pussy whenever I want it, understand? If I call you, you come and you'll cum on daddy's tongue, then on my dick. And whenever..." He grabbed my hair and pushed me to my knees, lining his dick up with my mouth, sliding in between my lips, I sucked him in deep and swirled my tongue around the tip of his dick. "Fuck, yes, angel. Whenever I want this mouth, you're going to give it to me each and every fucking time." He grabbed my hair tighter and slowly pushed his huge dick down my throat. I gagged a little but then I adjusted as he slowly worked himself in over and over again, his eyes rolling to the back of his head.

"Those fucking tongue rings are going to drive me crazy, I'm going to fucking spill down your fucking throat and you're going to swallow every fucking drop when it's time." He pistoned his dick in and out of my mouth with one hand while reaching over to play with my breast with the other.

"Hmm. Yes, Hudson, fuck. Suck me harder, baby." I suctioned my cheeks and teased him with my tongue, and I took him all the way into my throat and hummed. "Fuck yes, baby. Yes, you know how long I can last, baby, so don't make me punish you. Suck this dick, baby."

He wrapped both his hands in my hair, making me moan. This rough shit was just what the fuck I needed. He was a fucking god. He grabbed my neck and held me to his base, his dick in the back of my throat and I moaned at the sensation of being filled this way. He slipped out and slammed back in while I sucked and licked and teased him like he did to me. His hands controlled my movements. I felt my pussy dripping.

"Fuck, baby, yes. I can't fucking wait until I'm in your fucking throat, ass, or pussy, and the other guys are taking you in other places. We're going to fill you up with cum, Hudson." I moaned at the thought, sucking a lot more enthusiastically, making him buck into my throat. "Oh shit, baby, you like that, right? The idea of Grayson in your ass, Ryder in your pussy, and me coming down your throat? We will take turns too, baby, until you can't walk and can't talk. Until you need days off from the number of times you're going to cum."

"Mm," I moaned, and he slid all the way out and looked at me.

"I want to hear you say it. I'm about to cum and I want to hear you say it. Lick my fucking balls and say it."

I leaned over to take his balls in my mouth gently and lick them. "I want you to fuck my ass daddy, Grayson in my pussy, and I want to suck Ryder empty while Zane watches. Then I want Zane in my pussy while I drain you dry with my throat. I want it more than anything. Sir."

He moaned and I licked his balls a few times, dipping lower to lick his taint and swirl my tongue on the edge of his ass before he choked my name and slapped me hard and shoved his gorgeous dick down my throat.

"You're a fucking dirty little slut, Hudson. You're my dirty little slut. I'm going to teach you so much, baby. Ahh, yes suck me, baby, yes. Take me deep." He gripped my hair with both hands and pumped into my throat while I licked sucked and hummed and he shoved his dick as far as it could go and he bucked as he came into my throat, stream after stream of cum coated the back of my throat.

"Yes, mmm, yes, baby girl, fuck," he moaned.

He let go of my head, his dick still hard and he leaned over and kissed me.

"You. Are. Fucking. Perfect. Hudson."

He hugged me close and laid down next to me, drawing his hands up and down my sides.

"Just don't leave me when I'm sleeping, Hunter. I don't think I can deal with it again," I whispered.

"I'm not going anywhere, ever," he promised. Then he slid inside me from the back, hand around my neck, choking me until I couldn't breathe, and I moaned in pleasure. Then he fulfilled his other promises and we really did go at it all night long. Thank God we had magic because I wouldn't be able to walk.

CHAPTER FIVE

It felt good to wake up knowing I didn't have to pretend to be someone I wasn't. I stretched my arms over my head and smiled and I looked at Hunter and had flashbacks of last night. I thought Zane was amazing, but Hunter could give him a run for his money. I may be stuck with the emotional abandoning fucker and have to take the majority of my time being in classes and studying but I wasn't home and that was awesome. I got up and pressed a kiss to Hunter's face and he groaned about sunshine and I laughed and got up to go to the bathroom. I washed my face, brushed my teeth, and jumped in the shower to rinse off the hot night and wash the sex out of my hair. It was supposed to be a quick shower until Hunter walked in, picked me up, and slid inside of me, making me cum twice before he did. I rinsed off before he got hard again, he really could keep going. What the fuck was in the water in DeLorean? I laughed when he grumbled, and he walked out to his room to get dressed when I told him I was going to work out. I smiled at the thought of actually putting on cute workout clothes instead of baggy pants and shirts.

Say what you want, but when you can finally dress the way you want after years of being stuck it gives you a whole level of confidence. I threw my hair into a high, tight ponytail and put on a She-Fit sports bra and work out shorts that looked more like booty shorts, but I felt cute, so whatever. I threw on my trainers, and before I headed downstairs, I took a peek at the uniforms for classes in a couple days. As I suspected, the skirts were long as fuck. I put one on over my shorts and took a scissor and cut off about 4 inches from the hideous things, then I re-hemmed the bottom using thread and magic, then happily threw the extra fabric away in the bathroom and skipped my happy ass downstairs, phone and earphones in hand.

In my glee, I forgot that men lived here as well, ahh what's a little sunshine without sexual tension! All conversation and laughter stopped, and they looked at me and stared with their mouths open. I rolled my eyes and walked in, looking for stuff to make a protein shake with. I figured with their gym clothes on, they had to have plenty here.

"The staring bit is getting kind of old, guys. I assure you I look the same as I did yesterday."

"Yeah, except now it's day time. No more shadows," Hunter grumbled. I laughed. I turned to look at him while I made my shake.

"Yeah, I suppose that is true, just wait until you see my thong bikini," I joked, with a deadpan face.

"Like hell you're wearing a thong bikini," Zane said with a low voice.

"You know, at the rate I'm rolling my eyes, I have a feeling they are going to get stuck in the back of my head. Kind of like when I lost my virginity, come to think of it, and last night, of course." I winked at Hunter and he licked his lips, my clit jumped and I smirked. I put my shake in a glass and chugged half of it down.

Grayson chuckled darkly, goodness gracious. Can a voice have muscles? Because this is what a muscular voice would sound like laughing. His vocal cords must bench press 350. He sauntered towards me, I never really realized what that meant until now. *Well shit, saunter away you sexy book men, saunter the fuck away.* He put his arms on either side of me, caging me in. "You keep on teasing, you're just going to make things a lot harder for yourself when school starts." I breathed him in. God, he even smelled like muscles. Steeling myself, making my voice nonchalant, I pressed up against my cage and rocked against him, side to side. Until he had to bite back a groan and he bit his full lower lip and stepped back.

"Hmmm, the only thing hard here is you, Gray. Now, if you'll excuse me, I'd really like to swallow," I paused and looked at his hard-on with a smile and quirk of my head, his nose flared, "my protein drink." I stepped to the side and sat on a stool to finish my shake while the boys cleared their throats, with a smile on their faces. Except for Grayson, who looked starved. Poor guy. I read too much to lose. Want to learn the art of teasing? Read some A.J. Macey, your vagina will combust, but it's so worth it.

I finished up my shake and went to rinse out my glass when I heard the words party and prepare.

"Party? What party?"

Zane barely spared a glance at me and said, "We're throwing a party tonight before school starts."

"Of course, you're invited," Ryder threw in. Well, I would fucking hope so. I live here it would be hard to not be invited to my own damn house. When I said as such, Zane laughed at me. Was he always that beautiful when he smiled? I couldn't remember honestly, but I admit I liked him when he smiled, despite myself I felt myself wanting to lean up and lick his lips. I could imagine how they would feel against me again, so soft and per...

"What are you thinking about?" Zane asked, suddenly in front of me. I really need to stop zoning out around these guys.

"Jeez, personal space, bro and none of your damn business. I'm just mentally preparing myself to go do a warm-up run before hitting the gym. I'm sure you guys have to have one in this big ass house." I changed the subject and tried to walk around him.

But he gripped my wrist and leaned down, "I'm not your brother and you're wrong... everything that goes on in that head is my business.

Remember that." A shiver worked it way up my spine and I felt myself clench my thighs. He caught the small movement, because, of course, he fucking would, and smirked.

He straightened up. "Yes, we have a gym. We were going to go out for a run and do the same. Before getting things ready for the party. Everyone should be here around 9, so we have a few hours." I nodded, ignoring the smirks from the other guys and pretending what just happened didn't just happen. You don't fuck me, leave me, tell me you love me, and expect unicorns to fly out my ass in gratitude. Nope, you get to atone for your sins, motherfucker. And atone he would!!

I cleared my throat. "Right. Well I'm going to go. I saw the path when I first pulled up yesterday, I'm going to go Katniss Everdeen in that bitch, but I suppose you can follow along." I grabbed my phone, arm strap, and earphones, turned on the ball of my foot and got the hell outta dodge before whatever tension in that room sparked even more. I sighed, one day here and this connection just got stronger every passing moment. First second I had, I was going to do some fucking research about this shit. There had to be a magical explanation, like a fucking spell, *it happened in Harry Potter, granted the potion ended up being poison but you get the drift.* Thinking about that, I quickly typed out a text to my dad, telling him to order me a MacBook with the highest memory, with all the programs and all the extras. Once I sent that, I also told him to order me an iPad Pro with all the extras too. I needed one for ease and one for extensive research. My old computer lasted me about six years and with school, it was time for an upgrade. He kept insisting to upgrade every year, but I told him it would be stupid to waste money for things I already had. Well now, I'm calling it in. He responded with a thumbs up, I rolled my eyes. Parents using emojis will never not make me feel weird.

I left the door open while I marched out, went down the short steps, and walked to the path. I strapped on my arm band for my phone and slid my Bluetooth headphones in, turning on my music, as I observed the trail. It was certainly well worn, I thought to myself as I started to stretch. The surrounding forest was looking bright with the sun filtering through the trees. It looked so picturesque that I was looking forward to exploring the forest beyond the path one day. I spread my legs apart and leaned over to my right, grabbing my calf and stretching, before switching to my left and doing the same. I shake myself out and pulled my arms over my head, while getting on my tip toes. You ever catch a fucking cramp when running? Yeah, not fun.

I turned around, wondering where the guys were and almost ran into Ryder and Hunter, who were standing just a little too damn close. Hunter smacked my ass. "Remember what I said last night, angel," he growled, and I rolled my eyes, smiled and started to jog. Xena jumped out of the woods and started to run with me. I had wondered where she was all night but with blood on her face, she must have been hunting. I smiled down at her, it felt good to just do something so simple as running. Just me, my lion, the road, my music, and deep breathing. I started to pick up my pace as my music started to become upbeat. Ignoring the guys running behind me, I once again picked up my pace, Xena following suit, and let my mind wander. With the guys having a party, I wondered what it will be like. I can't imagine them doing much other than staring everyone down trying to incinerate anyone who came near me. I had a feeling, with the way they were acting, it wouldn't be far-fetched to assume just that. I hope I at least made one friend tonight; it would make Monday a lot less lonely for me. I just couldn't let myself fall into the same pattern. This time, I'm going to attempt to try. Even if I only make one good friend, that's all you ever really need. I read somewhere that friendship was essential to the soul. Well, I was trying to grow a soul, might as well make a friend too.

Reaching the end of the path, I moved to turn and start the run back. There is nothing worse than stopping and starting up again. Of course, the guys are hot on my tail, so I had to do some quick footwork to avoid the giants behind me; you would think I stole their fucking magic beans or something. Their eyes widened as I side stepped with a spin to face the other direction and kept running all the way back home. Home, God that feels weird to say knowing I was sharing it with this lot, I had to come back home to my teachers, and lovers? So complicated. Father didn't specify what they taught and honestly, I didn't even want to ask, I could always check my schedule, but I don't think I want to know just yet.

I got inside the house a few seconds before the guys did. I bypassed the cases of liquor that I missed on my way out and went to the giant see-through refrigerator for a bottle of water, as Xena bounded outside the back door and threw herself into the pool. I shook my head and laughed.

I unstrapped my arm band and took my earphones off and I observed the guys as they walked in and grabbed their own bottles. Their sweat covered t-shirts clung to their abs and fuck, if it didn't make my mouth water. I bit my lip as I took my time taking in every detail. In my defense, I was never around boys much back in Colorado, not enough to really get a good look like this. Last night, we were in a dark pool, then me and Hunter, oh I felt every inch of him, but still, in a dark room. So, this was a treat. Scratch that, this was a 40 course meal. I don't even think they had those, *ask me if I cared.* I, unfortunately, tore my eyes away, once again catching the last bit of the conversation during my mental undressing sex party.

"...Yeah, a few of them confirmed. You know the house is going to be full. We just have to ward the staircase, so no one goes up stairs," Hunter finished, as he looked pointedly at me.

"What are you looking at me for? Why would I go upstairs when all the hot guys will be down here?" Uh oh. Hunter stalked towards me, I backed up slowly, my hands up and turned around to go to the sink and wash the sweat off my face. More flies and shit with honey or whatever. My honey can be backing down.

They sucked in a collective gasp when I turned around, and I turned back once I dried my face with a paper towel. "What? Do I have something on my back?"

"Your shorts are up your ass, Hudson. God, who the hell told you they were athletic wear?" Zane bit out.

"Oh." I jiggled my butt and pulled them down and out of my ass, they groaned. "They are athletic shorts, well for other girls, I guess. But as you can clearly see, I don't have the ass that would be classified as typical." I shrugged. "My waist is too small to go a size up too. Anyways, I love my body, so leave me the hell alone. I'll wear what I want." I fixed my ponytail and went to grab another water so I could head to the gym. I seemed to be filled with restless energy the more I was around them and I needed to get it out.

"Well, I'm going to kick something. Is the gym downstairs?" When they nodded, I made my way in that direction. "Oh, by the way, since this is technically my house party too, I wanna control the music. God knows what you all listen to." I found the door and started down the stairs. When I got there, I gaped. Now this was a home gym. A sparring area, a weapons area, punching bags with wraps and gloves on the side! I was so giddy, I started to clap as I ran to the punching bags. There were two side-by-side and I was totally ready to beat their asses. Just look at those fucking bags, looking at me, just hanging there, begging to get their asses handed to them.

"You can choose the music if we can choose what you wear," said Ryder. I looked at him, raised one eyebrow, and looked away, not bothering to respond as I started to wrap my hands, forgoing the gloves, to feel the contact. I was okay with the lingering looks, their reactions to me, even the harmless flirting and amazing sex. However, let the court take note today, your honor, that they have me all the way fucked up if they think for one second that they will dictate what I wear. I didn't leave one oppressive house to enter another. It was not going to happen, and I would gladly show them just how advanced I became in my studies if they tried.

I started to punch one bag in a one, two punch combination to get a feel for the bags. Feeling good, I blocked everything out and started to move my feet and switch between both bags. After years of being ignored, it felt good to be wanted, even if it was on a basic level. It was a bit empowering if I was perfectly honest, and I knew that self-confidence and self-worth came from the inside, and I had those things. However, it didn't hurt to get a power-up every now and then. *Sigh*, I felt myself getting worked up and I roundhouse kicked the bag. Keeping my leg extended, while balancing on the ball of my other foot, I kicked the bag in three quick successions before pivoting back to face the bag.

. . .

Ryder

It didn't escape my notice that she never answered my request. I don't know why I even thought that she would be okay with it. To be honest, I thought she would have turned around to give me a smartass response. When she walked away and started to expertly maneuver around the punching bags with perfect forms and well-timed hits, I figured I had my answer. I laughed, she was completely focused on her task as the boys and I walked behind her to the sparring portion of the gym.

This was usually our time to practice our maneuvers and come up with ideas for the students when we were in classes. Hunter taught self-defense and hand-to-hand combat and he was fucking good at it too. His students would always come out bruised and battered, but they always learned fast and excelled. Zane was the instructor for weaponry, and he bore the scars to prove it. He was committed to his students and oftentimes he would be down here practicing using different weapons at once, trying to hone his speed and efficiency. When we came down here together, like now, he would start sharpening his precious weapons and would occasionally pause to take turns in the sparring ring. Grayson was usually quiet and very calculating in general, so you would never guess that he taught magical theory and practice. His low tone would have his students on the edge of the seats, trying to hear what he was saying so they wouldn't mess up when they had to put their knowledge to the test in the front of the class. I was the magical weapons instructor, meaning I had to teach students how to use their magic with their weapons at the same time. I enjoyed teaching. I didn't think I would, but I admit most of the students were fucking clueless. They would come from Zane's class and Grayson's class to mine, and still have no idea how to isolate the skills and simply use them in tandem.

I had a feeling this year would be different with Hudson here. She was enrolled in the advanced version of the classes, taking classes with the students who were set to graduate at the end of the year. I looked over to where she was unwrapping her hands and taking a sip of her water, her perfect chest rising and falling with each breath she took, her muscular thighs flexing with every step she took closer to the sparring ring.

"I got next in the ring, after I whoop someone's ass in weaponry. Who is my first victim?" she said confidently.

Interesting indeed.

Hudson

The guys smiled and chuckled while Zane laughed. Like an actual belly laugh. Oh, he truly had no fucking idea.

"You're laughing, so I assume I'm teaching you a lesson first?" I smiled at him, as I approached the weapons wall.

"You seem quite confident, so I guess you really didn't check your schedule. I'm the weapons instructor on campus." He shook his head and walked up to me. I tipped my head up to look at his stupid, loving me, ass face, keeping my smile firmly in place.

"I assume you have a point in telling me that. Although, for the life of me, I can't quite figure out what that point is. So," I point at the weapons, "choice of weapons?"

Grayson laughed and sat down on the floor, the other two followed suit. "I gotta see this shit." Zane gave a cocky smirk and reached down for two short swords.

I rolled my eyes. "Guess you chose the short swords so your dick wouldn't feel left out in size. Poor little guy," I deadpanned as I picked up a similar short sword and a hand scythe, my favorite weapon. I always felt like a miniature grim reaper when I used the wickedly curved death tool.

As the boys laughed, Zane gave a self-assured smile. "Sweetheart, now, now, we mustn't tell lies." I laughed and covered it with a scowl. Harry Potter references will get me every time.

"Yeah, okay whatever, so let's make this fun. I win, you AND your merry band of cock rings stop cock blocking so I can actually get some tonight. It would be a shame to waste the outfit I'm going to be wearing tonight," I said, looking pointedly at Ryder. The men growled. I really wasn't thinking beyond them but fuck it, all is fair in love and vagina. Besides, they were acting like Neanderthals.

"No deal. You're not getting some of anything," he growled.

"Oh, Mr. Toot It and Boot It, I thought you were so confident?" I raised an eyebrow. "If so, then there is really no risk."

"Not true, there is a high risk from me," Hunter growled.

"And me," Grayson threw in.

"Fuck it, definitely me." Ryder laughed.

He ignored them. "True. So when I win, you have to talk to me about what I said last night, and hear my side of it, and listen to what I say, *and* be in the same room as me," he finished. I pouted; fuck, he found my loopholes.

"Deal, I look forward to someone peeling my dress off for someone tonight, love em' and leave em." I winked at him. He advanced with no warning and swung with one of his swords toward my neck and arched the other to stab towards my stomach, expecting me to do a backbend to avoid the first sword; savage... smart too. I bent low and pivoted to the side, avoiding both hits, before standing and taking a step back. I smiled evilly and said, "okay, since you want it that way, fine. First blood. Oh and," with barely a thought, I infused my weapons with magic and set them alight, "magic counts too." I threw myself in his direction, doing a full body turn and with my back facing his, I used my hand scythe to play with him and tear his shirt off his back before I laughed and stepped back before he could pivot and attack. I loved this, I've always loved these parts of my lessons. It was when I was able to get my frustrations out and I was damn good at it.

If I came home with a scratch, Father would book extra lessons at 5 am, before school. I would be so tired that I had to learn to never be injured. I didn't mind the extra lessons, I loved Kalen, and they got me out of the house, but I didn't like feeling like a zombie throughout the rest of the day.

I focused on Zane, who had to remove the remains of his shirt. He observed me a bit more closely, realizing that he needed to slow down and consider his next move. I took that time to look for a weakness and an opening, but pretty much just took in the perfection that was his body. It should be illegal to be that perfect. I mean, truly, he was carved from warm stone. I had a tough time convincing myself that this attraction was wrong, but realistically, other than him being an asshole, the only thing that pissed me off was that night. *It could be worse. We could actually be related and be somewhere in the Midwest, fucking each other and our own cousins and shit.*

I saw him decide to move a split second before he moved and I sent an extra boost of magic down my scythe as he spun and made contact with my sword, I parried before quickly swinging it back around, breathing through the motions and I repeatedly blocked, hit, and spun. Expertly, he backed his swings with his upper body strength and his hips. Most people thought that power was only from their arms, however, in order to truly land a strong hit, you needed to activate your hips slightly in order to really pack a hit. Zane was good, I'll give him that, but Kalen would use brutal hits too, so I learned to really focus on my full body workouts to get stronger. I could take the hits longer than most people but eventually everyone tired, Kalen and I just never actually got to a point where I was tired, and we trained for hours. He never tired either, I thought suddenly. Regardless, to avoid my arms being battered down, I used a trick I learned back at home and quickly turned out my scythe and wrapped it around his blade and quickly jerked my arm to the side and he lost his grip on the sword and it went flying toward the men. I heard one of them curse and Zane's eyes flew open in shock. Then his eyes narrowed. Well, fuck. Guess he was determined to win now, so let's see how this plays out. This would be an appropriate time for a cackle. Where the fuck are the Sanderson sisters when you needed them?

I needed to get the other sword out of his hand, but I knew he wouldn't fall for the trick twice. He spun the sword between his hands trying to confuse me and I smiled as he advanced, spinning the blade behind his back to his front but I parried as he attacked. This time, I swept low and brought my leg around to knock him on his ass, but he expected that and, with a smirk, he jumped, but with a similar smirk, I quickly stood up, dropped my scythe and uppercut him on his way back down. He stumbled back and I kicked the other sword out of his other hand. I threw my sword to the side and crooked my finger as we stepped further into the center of the sparring circle. He looked a little bewildered and put his hands up. He punched forward, slightly grazing my ear and then followed up and got a good punch to my stomach, I grunted and laughed. I spun on the balls of my feet and danced away. That hurt like a fucking bitch, but I wouldn't let him see that. At home, if I showed weakness after a hit, I had extra drills, so I showed none. To Zane and everyone else in that room, my ribs and side didn't hurt at all. I took a deep breath and took a risk.

I ran toward him, my intention was to wrap my legs around his neck with a running leap, but I had a weird feeling that he was expecting that, don't ask me how. Instead, I ran and slid between his legs instead, before jumping up back-to-back, reaching up, and wrapping my arms around his neck from the back. I used that momentum to kick up and then slide my leg back, using the leverage of my body to flip him onto the floor. Except on his way down, he grabbed me and spun me, effectively pinning me underneath him. This was typically a bad position to be in, and with a man Zane's size and me five feet and five inches, it most definitely was. My legs were pinned, and he reached over to pin my arms down by my wrist.

I would be pulling my magic at this point with anyone else but the look in his eyes had me stuck. We both were breathing hard, our chest rising and falling, sweat slicking down his abs and likewise between my breasts. He looked at me intensely, and I licked my lips, suddenly thirsty as fuck and needing a shit ton of water. He followed my tongue and then without pause, leaned down and crushed his lips to mine. He teased his tongue across my lips, begging for entrance and against my better judgement, I opened my lips and his tongue clashed with mine, for the first time in years. He groaned and pulled back. He took a shuddering breath and whispered, "I win." I smiled.

"Not quite," I whispered back. I pushed my magic to use air energy, just enough to dislodge his hold then I drove my elbows into his neck, and I kicked my leg out and had him pinned on the floor with my magic. "We can go ahead and call this a tie. I will listen to you, even though you broke my heart and I," I punctuated my next words by grinding my ass onto his hard dick and he groaned, and his eyes became hooded and he gripped my waist to stop me. I smiled, "I get to get fucked tonight." I jumped off him before he could respond and walked out the gym. A chorus of, like hell's and the fuck she will, sounded behind me. I laughed.

Zane

Holy shit, I haven't been bested in a long ass time. I don't know who the fuck was training her back in Colorado, but they were bad ass. The way she showed no pain, even though I punched her in the ribs and side pretty damn hard, then she fucking laughed, was seriously the sexiest shit ever. I was already half-mast throughout the entire session. I could ignore her amazing body, her ass that was just like two floating beach balls rubbing together on her perfectly matched thighs, her perfect breasts and the way her body curved like an hourglass. I could even ignore the way sweat ran down her abs and sheened over the rest of her body, but fuck, when she ripped the sword out of my hand with that sleight of hand? It was like someone punched me in the fucking heart. It was all I could do to keep going at full strength and when I lost my other sword and she tossed hers and crooked her finger to follow her to switch to sparring hand to hand, I lost my mind. I felt like I was drowning in sensations: possessiveness, lust, love, obsession and pride. She wasn't just amazing, she was everything. When I gave in and kissed her, I could see myself drowning in her passion. Watching her walk away and not grabbing her to bury myself inside of her, wrapping my hands around her ponytail and fucking her until she screamed my name, was the hardest thing I have ever done. I groaned; I'm so fucked.

"Dude, you are so fucked," Grayson chuckled. "She handed you your ass and your manhood in twenty minutes. How does it feel?"

"You laugh, but I'm the one who just had her grind on my dick with her perfect ass and kissed her." Grayson stopped laughing then and put his calm face in place.

"Yeah, but I'm the one who will have to teach her how to suck my Jacob's ladder," he teased. I went to punch him, and he danced away, laughing. Dick.

"Yeah, but I'm the one who actually got his dick sucked last night. Those videos did pay off," Hunter laughed.

I threw a fireball at his ass and he cursed while he ripped off his shirt. Point.

"Well, it was a tie, so how are we running interference tonight?" Ryder asked, shaking his head.

"We could always have someone else watch out for her. I mean, technically it wouldn't be us cockblocking, which is Hudson code for making us jealous, it seems. Her eyes light up and she has that little smile on her face. I really think she is just fucking with us. Besides, I made a deal with her last night," Hunter mused.

"I'll ignore that. But yes, I don't think interference in that regard is needed. More like someone to make sure no one gets handsy or approaches her. So we don't smack everyone tonight." I sighed. "But who? We clearly can't ask any of the guys we know, they will fall in love with her faster than they can catch their next breath." We thought for a few minutes. "What girls do we know? There has to be someone we can have keep an eye on her."

"Wasn't there another girl who was doing the accelerated program and starting this year too? We just got an email this morning, I have to check my roster," Grayson mumbled and made his way upstairs with us following close behind. We walked into his room, decorated in cool green tones and dark furniture and a huge bed in the center of the room, and I walked across the room and leaned against the opposite wall, while he pulled up his roster on his computer. "Her name is Remi, and looked like she had a pretty good transcript, so she and Hudson should get along pretty well."

"Hudson has always been antisocial. Well technically, that was our fault, still, she may not be too receptive to a friend." I rubbed my head in consternation. Fuck. Stupid ass bet.

"I wouldn't count on that. She looks like she threw away her old life and is trying to start off on fresh footing. I think if we introduce them casually, they'll be fine. The real problem is who the fuck this girl is, what she looks like, and how do we invite her to a party that mostly has upperclassmen and instructors. The only new kid we know until Monday is Hudson." Ryder started pacing back and forth trying to get his point across. Fuck, she had us in here, plotting protection plans to keep her away from a bunch of guys without looking like dicks ourselves. In all honesty, she valued confidence, strength, and skill. Most of the people wouldn't be up to her level anyway, and we would be quick to let them know that I thought with a smile.

"Nah, that's easy. Look, it says here," Hunter grabbed Gray's computer, "she's dorming over in Blythe. Reed is the RA there this year, isn't he?" Hunter pulled his phone out and his hands flew over the keys before we could respond. Reed was a senior we met. Technically, if the boys and I hadn't done the accelerated path, we would have graduated last year. So, we were pretty close, and hung out often. After a few moments, Hunter smiled. "Yeah, he is, and it looks like he spent the day helping people moving in and has already met her. Says she's a knockout, and he was thinking of asking her out, but will invite her over to the party tonight. Says he will go ask her now to give her time to get ready." Reed had apparently sent him a picture from her social media account, and he whistled. "He isn't wrong, she is pretty." And passed his phone around.

I scoffed; I didn't care about anyone other than Hudson. No one would ever compare. He rolled his eyes at me. "Dude, we all know there is only one end game, doesn't mean I'm blind."

I took the phone, the naturally tanned girl in the photo with bright eyes was indeed pretty. She had a nice shape too, although, nowhere near Hudson. Hudson was a fucking scientific anomaly with those curves. The girl had long hair, although it was dyed bright blue. So, she was a bit of a rebel too. I had a feeling her and Hudson would have gravitated toward each other anyway. I figured this was just us speeding up the process. Hunter's phone beeped and a message flashed saying that she agreed as long as there was alcohol. I laughed. Oh yeah, they would get along just fine.

CHAPTER SEVEN

Hudson

I SKIPPED STRAIGHT TO MY ROOM TO SHOWER AND CHILL AND YUP, watch Lucifer. I checked my phone and saw Father had sent me delivery tracking information for arrival tomorrow and another thumbs up. I replied with a quick thanks and opened the group chat Hunter had added me too. I ignored the pings from earlier, a bunch of useless information about party preparation and I smiled remembering my promise. Before jumping in the shower, I stripped off my clothes and stood in front of a full-length mirror and snapped a few pictures before sending them all in the group chat. They all started to reply at the same time.

Hunter- Yeah, I'm about to make good on my promise. 😮

Ryder- Fucking shit! I dropped my phone and cracked my screen.
Grayson- Fuck your screen, bro. Look through the cracks.
Ryder- Fuck you.
Grayson- Only if you look like the pictures.
Zane- I hate you all.

Two minutes later, Hunter walked in the room and flipped the lock on the door and threw me on the bed and ate me out like a starved man. He wrapped my legs around his head and wouldn't stop until I came over and over. My ass still stung from the smacks from when he made me sit on his face and suck his dick at the same time. He had me completely under his spell, he was that good. And when he came down my throat, I moaned and swallowed every drop. Of course, his dick stayed hard and he bent me over, fucking me, choking me, and grabbing my hair until I screamed his name over and over. Just when I was catching my breath, he laid me on my back and picked up one leg and fucked me slowly, with sure, even strokes. All while caressing my face and my breasts, playing with my clit, and making me cum over and over as he pressed kisses to my neck, face, lips and breasts. He whispered how beautiful I was, how amazing I felt, and how he never wanted to stop being inside of me. I loved rough Hunter but the soft, making love Hunter blew me away. I moaned because of how amazing he felt until he filled me up with his cum. Best two hours ever, that guy can fucking go. Holy fuck. After he left, I took a quick shower, still having time before the party, and laid down on the bed with just a tank top and no panties to watch some Lucifer. *You know, in case Hunter came back* I smiled. Zane knocked on the door a few minutes after my shower and sat down on the edge of my bed. He was dressed in some low hung sweats with no shirt on, looking like a wet dream.

"Can we talk now?"

"I guess," I grumbled. What I should have said was yeah after you fucking cover up those man nipples, they are making me horny. If breast-feeding women have to cover up, man nipples gotta go too.

"Hudson, I'm sorry." He sighed and started to pace up and down the room. "My intention wasn't to break your heart. I promise I went in your room that night to just hang out and make you feel better and then one thing led to another."

"I see, so I was a mistake?"

"No, yes. FUCK, not in that way, Hudson. It was the best night of my life. You were eighteen, a virgin. I was twenty-three, I had had my fair share of women, Hudson."

"Oh, this apology is going great, please, continue." I rolled my eyes.

"I slept with a few women after you, Hudson, to get you out of my head, to pretend that what I felt for so long wasn't real. That night you rocked my world, I mean fuck, we literally fucked all night and my dick never got soft around you. It doesn't work that way with you. I was scared as hell, I knew I loved you at the time, I may have denied it, but I did. Everything you said that night, every moan, every whisper I remember like it just happened." I looked away, I refused to cry for anyone.

He walked up to me and kneeled at my feet, pulling my chin up and toward him, so I could look into his eyes. I was painfully aware that I had no panties on.

"Hudson, I admit I was an asshole, I was a punk. I left that morning and ran because I didn't understand how something could feel so real, everything was so explosive, so incredible, and I freaked out. Yes, two years was a long time. But I'm here now, I promise I'm not going anywhere anymore. I'm not running. I can't fight what we have. None of us can. I love you, Hudson. I really do, every moment I have, I'll prove it to you. Just, please, don't shut me out. I made a stupid mistake."

"You are stupid," I whispered, his head dropped but he kept eye contact like he did those two years ago. "You broke my heart, you broke me. I promised myself I would never ever break for anyone ever again, Zane. I will not break that promise to myself. But I'm not stupid either, never was. I got it; it was intense. For me, it was downright magical. I hoped for more but realistically, while I was still home and with you all the way over here, it would have been impossible. We were magic together, no pun intended, and..." I sighed and rubbed my head, suddenly having a headache. "I cannot fucking believe I'm saying this shit, but I'll tell you the same thing I told Hunter last night. Do not disappear when I wake up. Be here, Zane. Because I can't handle it if you weren't." I reached down and held his face. "But we have to go a little slower. I hope that's okay with you. I'm scared too, except now it's for a different reason."

He leaned up and pressed a kiss to my cheek. "I understand, baby, but I'll be here every moment. I promise. I'm never leaving you again. I love you, Hudson." He grabbed my legs and pulled me closer. "I love you." He opened my legs and pressed kisses to my clit. "I love you," he repeated while he ran his tongue up and down my pussy. "I love you," he groaned against my clit as he swirled his tongue around it and sucked it between his lips. He dipped his finger inside my pussy and curled it stroking me, drawing out a moan. "I love you," he whispered against my slit before he wrapped my thighs around his face and started to lick and suck without letting up. I moaned and grabbed his head. Shit, this was supposed to go slow but fuck if I'm turning this down from the fucker who left me high and dry. So, I'm enjoying one hell of an apology, and he grabbed my ass, inserting one finger in my ass and one in my pussy while working me with his lips and tongue. I screamed his name as he made me cum, shaking, and in true Zane and Hunter fashion, kept going, while I bucked my hips into his face. His tongue fucked me, alternating between his tongue and finger, his other finger still fucking my ass and groaned against my clit, sucking it between his lips and stroking it firmly yet gently with his tongue until I came again, his name on my lips.

"Yes, Zane. Fuck, you know just what I like, hmm, yes," I screamed as he lapped me up. I laid back breathless, jelly.

He got up off the floor, gave me a wink. I gave him a small, dazed smile, and he walked out of the room. I felt the air leave my lungs and I threw myself back on the bed. *Well. That was a good start.*

Three hours later

. . .

I TOOK A LOOK IN THE MIRROR AND SMILED SLOWLY. FUCK YES, THIS was going to piss them off so much. My inner bitch cackled. When I had gone shopping, I made sure all my clothes were perfectly suited to fit my body like a warm hug. I put on one of those sexy but cute thongs that left no line on my hips and had pulled on a light purple, tube top style body-con dress. It was like putting on a second skin. Every curve on display, my ass looked perfect and the top of the dress was tight enough that I didn't need to use magic to slightly help lift my breasts. They were pushed up and on display. The dress fell to right below my ass, it hugged me perfectly but if I bent over, my Brazilian wax would be on full display. I heard people start arriving about half an hour ago. I certainly wasn't going to be down there like a newbie, getting to a party early.

I had taken my time, I had already showered, washed and blown out my hair, and put on black eyeliner and black lipstick over my pouty lips. I'm not big on makeup, it takes too long to put on but tonight, I felt like a rebel and this was a giant fuck you to Father and old Hudson. I pulled out and put on my new gorgeous Goya Ruban Alta Louboutins that I couldn't resist during my secret shopping trips. They wrapped around my ankle, had a peekaboo style and were slightly see through. Honestly, if I could've lost my virginity to a shoe, this would have been it. I practiced, in secret, walking in them since they were higher than I was used to wearing from the times I had to go to functions with Father. But honestly, these were so comfortable, it was like an extension of me. I was all giddy. I took a final look, did a little spin, snapped a few pics and sent it to the group chat and walked out of my room a little swing in my hips.

Gray, Ryder, Hunter, and Zane were in the living room laughing with a few of their friends and I gave a little smile seeing them relaxed. They have been so strung up since I arrived. I knew it was the sexual tension between us all, I wasn't expecting it at all, let alone to have it be so intense. I didn't know they would be here, but hell, even my feelings toward Zane were leaning further from anger and more toward forgiveness. When Zane kissed me, every cell in my body caught on fire, but when I rubbed my core against him, I almost lost it. If I had to bet, I'm sure it would be just as explosive if Gray and Ryder kissed me, too. Two down, two to go. I laughed to myself. Funny, I read about this situation in so many books that my first thought after reading a reverse harem novel was, fuck yes sign me the fuck up. Now, I didn't want a broken vagina, but I figure with some kegels and ice packs I would be fine, right? Plus, I had magic, those bitches didn't have magic.

I peeked and saw the guys look at their phones and quickly start typing.

Grayson- Really? You're going to make me catch a fucking case. I'm too pretty for jail.

Ryder- You need to change, that barely covers your ass.

Hunter- Am I the only one picturing her in heels while I fuck the shit out of her?

Grayson- Not at all.

Zane- Fuck, you look amazing. Now that we saw and we're the only ones that matter, go change, into a potato sack.

I laughed.

Hudson- I'll make you all a deal, let me live, and how about I model these for you later, no clothes, just my heels and a thong?

Grayson, Ryder, Hunter, Zane- Fucking deal.

I smiled to myself and snapped myself out of our messages and started to walk up the stairs. One of the boys' friends tapped another and they all stopped to stare at me. I ignored the looks and smiled brightly, especially when I saw the heated looks from my boys. I kind of like how that sounded. I strutted up to them but before I could get very far, a guy grabbed my elbow gently. I turned his way with my eyebrow raised.

"Most people speak before touching," I said, pointing at his hand with a small smile on my face.

"Yeah, you're right. I'm sorry. I just had to actually come talk to you before everyone else had the chance to. I have a feeling after that entrance it is going to be hard to actually get a word in edgewise in a few moments." He laughed and rubbed his neck, looking nervous and embarrassed. I sort of felt bad, he was cute, only a couple inches taller than me with dark hair and hazel eyes. Despite how nervous he looked, he had a very easy smile, "Okay, that's fair." I laughed. "What's your name?"

"I'm Joshua. I'm a senior here." He reached out his hands to shake mine and I took it, very sweet indeed.

"Well, hello, Joshua. I'm Hudson, it is a pleasure to meet you." At that moment, two guys bumped into me, laughing.

"Wow, you are hot. Fuck this loser, let's talk." As I was about to open my mouth, Xena decided to make her appearance, bounding through the door, knocking them down on their asses, roaring in their faces, swiping at their heads, keeping her nails sheathed.

"Holy shit," Joshua whispered. I laughed.

"Joshua, this is Xena, she's my familiar. She doesn't really take kindly to people being disrespectful. Neither do I, for that matter. Tsk tsk, should I ask her to get off? I mean, that's 200 pounds of muscle." I pretended to think while the guys on the floor continued to shriek. Distantly, I realized that the room was pretty quiet, and the heated angry stares from the guys burned into me. I looked up and smiled at Grayson and nodded at him. Let him deal with it.

"X, we're good, get off of them." She roared loudly one last time before prancing off to my side, pausing and taking a long whiff at a now nervous, Joshua.

"He's good. Other boys are bad. Grayson must eat them if I can't." I laughed out loud. Grayson had already grabbed them by the scruff of their collar and was walking out the door.

"Hey, Gray, X said if she can't eat them, you can." His angry scowl turned into a wide smile while he 'escorted them out the door'.

I turned my attention back to Joshua. "She said you're okay. Since you have her approval, how about I save you a dance later?" He smiled and nodded.

"Deal. I'll talk to you later. I need another drink after that, or six." He laughed and sauntered away. I smiled and turned to face the guys and their friends.

I walked up to them and snatched Zane's beer from his hand and took a deep drink, he wasn't officially my instructor yet, so fuck propriety. Not to mention, I'll be twenty-one in just a few weeks, October was close. After a few quiet moments, where the strangers stared between me and Xena, jaws open, I rolled my eyes and introduced myself.

"Hello, I'm Hudson Jacobs, nice to meet you, and this is Xena," I said pointing at the gorgeous girl next to me. She nuzzled me affectionately before focusing her gaze on the men in front of me.

"Jacobs?" said one of the men, who looked about the same age as the guys, looking at Zane curiously. Instead of introducing himself, fucking rude.

"I believe the proper response is' hello, my name is, insert here', but since your curiosity won out over proper manners, yes, Zane was adopted into my family when he was a teenager. Would you also like to know the color of his bed sheets before you tell me your name?" I said evenly with a raised eyebrow. Grayson, who had walked back in at that point, choked on his beer and Ryder laughed outright.

Hunter shook his head and smirked instead of laughing. "Hudson, angel, that idiot with his foot in his mouth is Logan. He will be your instructor in complex magical history and theories. Come Monday, you'll call him Professor Logan. To his right is Reed, he is a senior here. To Reed's right is Blair, he will be your instructor in human studies, and because of your schedule, you'll also have Professor King, who is next to you and he will be your potions professor. Gentlemen, this is Hudson, she will be living here and is on the accelerated path." Xena, lifted her paw and smacked Hunter. He laughed. "Yes, and this is Xena, Hudson's familiar."

They all had a fit physique and attractive faces. King had that sexy man bun thing going on with black hair and blue eyes, laughter and mirth in his eyes, laced with interest. Logan was the opposite, he had blonde hair and dark eyes, his eyes filled with a strange manic glee, like a mad scientist. It would have been funny, if I wasn't sure or not if it was for show or his actual personality. Overall, weird. Blair, well, he was more attractive with silky looking hair and hazel eyes, a sensual mouth and eyes filled with lust, no mistaking it. Pure lust, it was disconcerting, then he smiled at me and the look faded into one of welcome. Well, that was something to tuck away for later. *Multiple personalities, check.* Reed was your regular boy next door, nothing truly memorable about him, other than a kind smile and kind eyes.

I smiled at all of them. "It is a pleasure to meet you all, I'm looking forward to Monday. You'll get to know me more very soon, although I hope it's not in one of those awkward, tell me one thing about yourself introductions." I pretended to shudder, and they laughed.

"Familiar, huh. I have never seen a familiar quite that large before. There is a theory that the bigger the familiar, the stronger the magic user. That is quite the display of power there, Ms. Hudson," Logan, I believe, said.

"Yes, well. I don't like to be cocky," Zane cleared his throat. I rolled my eyes. "Okay I do, but yeah, I guess you can say that. I take pride in my studies is what I sure Zane was trying to insinuate. You know how big brothers are." I smirked. He scowled at me. Xena stared at Logan for a long time, unblinkingly.

Something is wrong with this one, strange. I will watch. I frowned, I caught that too, but knowing she shared my opinion was good. Then she suddenly snarled at Blair. *This one is bad, I kill.*

I grabbed her by the neck. "Xena, baby girl, why don't you go hunt? I'm sure I'll be good here with the guys." She looked at me sullenly and slinked away out the door, throwing one last look at me before she nodded.

Ryder, Hunter, Gray, and Zane raised their eyebrows, and I shook my head subtly. "She's a little protective, new place and all." I smiled. They all nodded and started talking to each other while I spaced out. Xena's reactions were always spot on, so that was rather interesting, I can shelve that information away for later though. I really did want to have fun.

The room was quickly filling up with people, looking around I saw quite a few cute boys and pretty girls here. It was nice to be around people who were in your general age group and it made things easier for me to attempt to blend in and have fun. I turned back to the men who were going down memory lane, and I noticed that King, Blair and Logan seemed to be diverting their attention and pretty much just staring at me. *Have to admire their ability to multitask.* I resisted the urge to roll my eyes and just stared back. *If you can't beat em' join em'.* Grayson noticed where my gaze was, and his entire body tightened.

Biting back a laugh I purred out, "Hey, Grayson, remember that bet we made earlier?" Ryder, Hunter, and Zane's eyes snapped to me while their friends looked on curiously.

"Yes, I remember that bet you made with Zane. Why do you ask?" He casually sipped his beer, looking at me. I narrowed my eyes at him and stepped a little bit closer, my breast on his chest with my new heel height. Awesome.

"Grayson, I plan to collect on that bet. Do not interfere, before I put your ass down on the mat instead of Zane this time. Clear?" Then I leaned up and whispered in his ear, "Besides, I'm with you guys, so chill, no one else matters. Xena would eat them anyway." I winked at him, and I turned my ass around and walked to the kitchen, my hips swaying. Not that they can help it, I had a natural swing. I ignored the beer and went straight to the whiskey. I took a sip from the cup I poured and sighed. My mission was to make a friend tonight and definitely get some. So, I took a look around the kitchen and my eyes focused on a girl about my height, dressed in a similar tight dress but hers was black and she had bright blue hair and a bottle of whiskey in her hand instead of a cup. I laughed at her no care attitude.

Her eyes turned to me as she took me in, a smile slowly forming on her lips. She was gorgeous, athletic but still curvy, and she had a general air of not giving a fuck as if the bottle in her hand wasn't an indication of that already.

She walked up to me. "Hi, I'm Remi, you must be the girl in the purple dress, with a lion people are talking about." And she laughed sweetly, no false tones in her laugh.

I blushed. "Yeah, that would be me, a bad ass lion tamer."

She reached up and put her hand on my face, brushing my hair back. "No blushing yet, gorgeous. What's your name?" she asked. Was she flirting? Did I want her to? I wanted a friend, but don't close friends typically play around with each other that way? I shrugged internally, this is why I avoid people, this was too complicated.

"I'm Hudson and thank you for the compliment. You look bored."

She laughed that sweet laugh again. "I am, my RA invited me apparently to meet someone who is also on an accelerated path like me, and the music sucks." I laughed and I rolled my eyes internally at the first part, of course the guys would try to get me to meet people. Keep me away from other guys. *Idiots.*

"That would be me, so I guess we will be in all the same classes then. I'm glad we met, I typically don't really like people and I usually prefer to be a loner." Her eyes widened at that.

"I wouldn't have expected that at all, you seem so easy going and relaxed." She shrugged, "But since I'm the same way, I guess that means I have you all to myself," she says with a smile, and her hands touch the curve of my hips as she steps closer. Yup, definitely flirting. And honestly? I wasn't remotely bothered by it. In fact, I liked it. I never had a chance to explore my sexuality and what I liked, but fuck it, that's what college is about, right? I chugged my glass, took the bottle from her and drank. She laughed.

"I have a familiar as well, although he doesn't really ever venture into crowds. He tends to lean more toward volatile, I guess it's my bubbly personality." She smiled.

"Really? That is awesome. I'm not sure about the protocol for asking about other familiars, just being able to research about them now, but can I ask what form yours takes?" I asked curiously, sitting on the counter in the kitchen, opposite to where she was leaning.

"There really is no proper way to ask, people generally don't as not having one may or may not be an indication of power, or the size of the familiar having the same result." She shrugged. "I don't really mind, I don't attempt to hide him, he just isn't a people person but Cerubus can take two forms. He can be a very large snake or shift into a phoenix. Depends on his mood, what he wants to hunt or how sneaky he wants to be. Either way, picture Nagini from Harry Potter and there you have Cerberus."

"That is freaking amazing. I'm not sure if Xena can shift. As it is, she's freaking huge but I guess I also haven't asked her if she wants to or if she can change."

"Familiars were said to shift to human form in order to protect their person or take the shape of what was needed. Either way, it is a blessing not a lot of magic users have. There is a legend though that the stronger the magic the more likely you are to have a familiar, but the closer to magic, the stronger the familiar." I nodded.

"When you say *closer to the magic*, what do you mean?" There were strong magic users who were more intune with their magic but I wouldn't necessarily consider them closer to it. She smiled at me.

"Just some folklore," she glossed over my question before continuing, " I can give you some books and such to help guide you since you haven't learned much about them yet. It will be fun for you to learn as much as you can."

"Thank you! I'll look forward to that. In the meantime, you did mention lame music. Do you still want to dance?"

"Fuck yes, this shit makes me feel like I'm drowning." She laughed.

"Well, let's change the music. Fuck that bullshit, and we can dance," I pointed to the throng of people moving awkwardly to whatever the fuck was playing. I mean, fuck, didn't the boys ever hear about R&B and HipHop?

"How will you manage that?" she asked.

"Easy, I live here." I laughed at her expression. "No, I'm serious, Zane was adopted into my family when he was older, and my father wanted us to live together on campus. So, here I am."

"Wow, well, then lead on. Let's change this shit." She whooped and we made our way to the living room where the guys were now settled on the couches that were pushed further back to make space. I leaned over Ryder and grabbed his stupid phone out of his hand despite his protests. He tried to reach around me, and I sat on his lap and leaned over with the phone in front of me keeping him away and I logged into my Spotify playlist. His fingers dug into my waist to stop me from moving.

He leaned down to my ear. "You need to stop wiggling on me, or I won't be able to get up from this couch anytime soon," he growl. I laughed and waved him off.

Finally getting to my playlist, I popped my head up, suddenly remembering my manners. "Gentlemen, this is Remi, she is also in the accelerated rated path. She is my new friend; she also has whiskey, and we're going to dance to good music now, not this funeral shit. Also, I know you guys wanted me to meet her. You're still cockblocking you know," I sing-songed, the whiskey making me forget present company. "But I'll forgive you because she is hot as fuck." I winked at them and they attempted to hide their laugh, failing miserably. I got up and jumped a bit to fix my dress, slightly flashing Ryder, oops, and they all groaned. Well, actually, Grayson growled. I started my playlist and "Sleeping in My Bed Remix," by Dru Hill started blasting on the sound system booming throughout the entire house.

This was a real fucking party, no more YouTube twerking for me folks! I'm a big girl now and I didn't even need pull ups! I grabbed Remi's hand and walked closer to the now dancing people, the guys watching. We started to dance to the beat, singing and rapping along, taking turns with the whiskey bottle. Each drink making us a little bit bolder. Joshua found me, and we danced to a couple of songs, while Remi danced with another girl. We laughed and at one point, Joshua and I exchanged numbers. He winked at me, thanking me for the dance before going back to his friends, even though I felt his eyes continue to follow me.

My playlist switched to the reggae portion of my playlist after a few more songs, the whiskey bottle long gone. The beats switched, prompting dancing that was more melodic and smoother, yet coupled with sensual movements of your hips. I learned well from sensei YouTube, I refused to be someone without rhythm. So, when Remi pressed her body up against me, her back to my front, we rolled our hips together without missing a beat. She reached up and wrapped her arms around my neck, tugging me closer, and heat spread throughout my body. I'm honestly not sure where this was going, but I'm not going to fight it. I gave as good as I got, so when the song changed to something more fast paced and she turned me around and grabbed my hips, I moved against her, slightly bent over, moving my ass and hips to the rhythm.

She ran her hands around my hips and reached up to grab my hair and tug me back and she pressed a kiss to my neck. Her other hand roamed across my abs as she hummed in my ear, her hand grazing the underside of my breasts, which were thankfully contained by the tightness of the dress, but still gave a show to whoever was looking, which was pretty much everyone at this point. "Drive Me Crazy," by Kevin Lyttle, started to play, how appropriate. I turned to face her and I'm not sure exactly where the boldness came from, but I tipped her head to mine and captured her lips with mine. Still swaying to the music, she caressed her tongue with mine, moaning into my mouth. She grabbed my ass as we deepened the kiss before pulling apart and breathing heavily looking at each other. Half the room was full of writhing bodies and lip locked couples. The only people aware of what was going on was me, Remi, and about 8 grown ass men on the couch. Four of which looked like they were turned on, the other four looked like they were ready to punch everyone who was looking at me.

I leaned into whisper into Remi's ear, "more whiskey?"

"Mm, among other things, yes." And she pressed a soft kiss to my lips.

I grabbed her hand and we walked into the kitchen without a second glance at the boys and went to get some whiskey. Half of the party had moved into the pool, so we sat by the pool sharing the bottle between us, as we laughed at people's antics and kissed.

Grayson

That did not go as expected. When Hudson had walked down the stairs every single guy focused on her. To the point that she immediately made a friend and two very well thrashed enemies, everyone else who attempted to talk to her was confidently sidetracked by one of us and after a few well-placed threats, they knew better. The other instructors next to me though, were as lost as everyone else was. I groaned. I assumed that after she found Remi and started talking, she would make a friend and hang out for the rest of the evening. But no, in true Hudson fashion, she surprised us. She changed the music, started dancing and we were fucking goners.

Seeing her dance, sing and rap, was funny. We laughed at that and continued to talk and ignore the party, this being more for the students than for us. But after a few quick glances, we noticed her fun moment had turned into sensuality and then gyrating. When they started to press their bodies together and grind on each other, it took everything in me to not grab her and take her upstairs. Shit, I have no fucking doubt Ryder, Zane, and Hunter wanted to as well, considering they all became laser focused as her and Remi's dancing had turned into a make out session on the dance floor, with Remi grabbing Hudson's ass, our ass. The same ass that belonged to me. Hudson whispered in her ear and pulled Remi in the direction of the kitchen. We looked at each other, definitely not as planned. Looked like Hudson was going to collect on her debt after all, just not in the way she first intended. Well, fuck.

Hudson

Remi and I ended up getting roped into a truth or dare game by the pool with Joshua and some of his friends, and ended up jumping into the pool with our clothes on. But not before taking off my shoes, I'm not that fucking drunk. We were laughing and joking around with people by the pool and I finally felt like a real young person. I knew Monday was going to bring its own challenges, but right now I was a normal college student, and I was having an amazing time.

"Okay, okay! Truth or dare, Joshua!" Remi yelled across the pool.

"Dare!" He laughed, drinking from his beer.

"You have to go streaking!" I fell over in giggles, as he stood up confidently and stripped before taking off at a sprint.

It was drawing closer to two am, and my guys stepped outside, probably looking for me, as people were slowly leaving. When they spotted me, they frowned and walked over.

"Hey, boys! We lost a game of truth or dare. I would ask if you wanna play, but you're probably all chicken shit. Joshua is currently streaking around the house." I laughed. Ryder smiled and Hunter laughed. Gray lifted an eyebrow, but Zane just stared.

Hunter grabbed his phone and started taking pictures of me, laughing about drunken nights.

"You realize, when you come out of there, that dress will be completely see-through, right?" Zane pointed out.

"I'm counting on it," said Hunter as he kept taking pictures. Zane growled and smacked him upside his head.

"Probably, but I'll go straight to my room." I shrugged.

"Everyone is going to see you," he bit out.

"Hmmm, really? Okay. Well then, I'll go up quickly. Remi and I were going to go up to the room and eat pizza and watch Netflix anyways. When they deliver can you bring it upstairs please?"

They nodded. Hunter asked, "Are you okay, baby? Sober?" He is so sweet, my walking muscle snake. He busted out laughing. Oops, totally said that out loud.

I climbed out of the pool with Remi and realized that yes, this was all indeed see through. I cringed, not ideal but fuck it, I'll own it. I bent over carefully to pick up my shoes and walked over to the outside staircase that led to my room. Before I got there, I leaned over and hugged Hunter on impulse. "Thank you for asking. Yeah, I'm sober, but pizza will definitely help with the headache we will have in the morning, for sure. I ordered enough for all six of us, if you want to join us. You'll just have to get rid of everyone." I blew them all a kiss and grabbed Remi's hand and went up the stairs in front of her to undo the ward on the door. The entire time she was running her hand under my dress and suddenly, I couldn't wait to get inside the room, and I hope the pizza took a little longer than planned.

"I'm sure the pizza will take a while, want to take turns showering?" I barely finished the words when she locked the door behind me and pressed me against it, kissing up my neck and working her hands under my dress. I let out a low moan as her hands grazed my thong, and she bit my neck gently. Fuck, I felt myself getting wetter as she licked up my neck and sucked on my ear lobe, whispering, "Definitely showering together. Lead the way, Hudson."

The way she said my name sent shivers down my spine. Taking a deep breath and gaining control of my legs again, I walked to the bathroom. Turning on the shower to the rainfall feature, I turned and started to take my dress off, when Remi moved my hands to the side, already having stripped in that short time. She was beautiful, her hair dripping from the pool laying across her full breasts. I followed the curve of her hips with my eyes noting the soft flare and supple thighs. Her lips were full and every flicker in her eyes screamed lust. She licked her lips as she peeled the dress off of me, licking her way through the valley of my breast with each tug. As she peeled lower, her tongue followed, stopping right above the apex of my thighs.

She gripped the thong and pulled the rest of the dress off, pressing a kiss to my waxed mound. I drew in a deep breath as she got up and wrapped her hands around my waist, grabbing my ass and pulling me in for a kiss that I felt all the way to my toes. As her tongue caressed mine, she guided me into the floor-to-ceiling shower. We pulled apart enough to lather ourselves in soap and rinse and condition our hair, eyes never leaving each other. Although she did take a minute to lather her hands and rub them in between my folds lightly, caressing my clit, drawing a deep moan from me that she swallowed by pressing her lips against mine. She chuckled as she pulled away and I pouted.

We stepped out of the shower and dried off and I took a few minutes to add a cream to my hair for my hair to curl nicely instead of in a hot mess. We took time to brush our teeth, seeing as I had an extra brush under the sink before walking into the room. I went to grab one of my nighties and she grabbed it from my hands, tossing it on the bed. Her eyes on me she walked me back until my thighs hit the bed and I had no choice but to lay down.

Hiking myself further onto the center of the bed, she crawled sensuality, following my every move. Fuck. If this was her version of foreplay, it was certainty working, as I was trembling and trying to catch my breath. She came up close and grabbed my breasts in her hands, taking one nipple into her mouth and tweaking the other between her fingers. I threw my head back and moaned. She alternated between each breast while she climbed on top of me and nudged my thick thighs apart with her knees. My heavy breast forgotten, her hands now caressing my sides while she licked her way down my stomach and dipped into my belly button. At this point, I was biting my lip, enjoying every single touch, my first touch from a girl and fuck, it was incredible. I felt sexy, desired, worshipped, and needy in a way I never expected. Sex with Hunter and Zane was amazing, but there is clearly a sensuality difference with a female that I didn't expect. It was like every touch was charged with heat.

She passed my navel and pressed kisses and licks to my mound as she settled herself between my thighs, kissing each one before she looked at me and licked from the bottom to the top of my pussy, flicking my clit before sucking it into her mouth. I bucked in surprise. I didn't think anything would ever feel this good.

"Fuck," I moaned loudly.

Remi

Fuck, Hudson was fucking gorgeous. I wasn't expecting that. It made it harder to do what I needed to do but fuck, I lost myself as I ran my fingers down the curves of her body. She looked and felt like something out of a fantasy. I groaned as I settled deeply within her thighs and savored her taste. When she moaned and bucked into my mouth, I growled and wrapped my arms around her thighs and pinned her down as I sucked and flicked her clit. I felt her getting wetter and wetter soaking my chin, faster than I could lap her up. I stiffened my tongue and thrust it inside her to capture more of her juices and her hands wrapped around my head with a husky moan. I slowed my pace and savored as I licked my way back up to her clit, running my tongue up and down the inside of her lips, keeping her on edge arching to get my tongue where she wanted it. I smirked, then gave her what she wanted as I kept her on edge not letting her cum. I pulled away and climbed up to kiss her deeply, letting her taste herself on my tongue while I kept my hands stroking her and not letting her come back down.

"Do you want to cum, Hudson?" I pressed my breasts up against hers, feeling her perfect body against mine and I bit back a groan. "You're going to have to beg me to let you cum. Then you'll be a good girl and cum on my face." She groaned, shaking her head, bucking her hips into my hands. I fluttered my hands over her, cupping her sex while she groaned in frustration.

"Let go, Hudson, give me control," I said as I kissed down her neck and chest and took her nipple into my mouth. She groaned and arched her back, her curves looking all the more delectable, direct contrast to her hardened abs. Jesus, I don't think I have ever seen or tasted anything as perfect as her. I knew I had a job to do, but from the moment I saw her, I knew she was more than that. She was mine. Her white hair was a complication, but it proved to me that what I felt wasn't temporary lust. Until I had to deal with the future, I was going to drown myself in her juices.

"Remi, please, make me cum," she said breathlessly. I smiled and slowly licked my way down, dipping through the warm carved abs before her desperate moans prompted me to continue my trail downwards. Kissing her clit and then sucking it into my mouth, my pace relentless, quickening then slowing, over and over. Her moans grew louder, and she grabbed my head and clenched her thighs around my head, squirming, and sensually rolling her hips into my mouth. I loved that she knew what she wanted. Every roll of her hips, desperate for what I can give her. Being a female, I understood that eating pussy was like a slow dance, you savored, rolled and swirled your tongue to the rhythm of the body you were experiencing except in the end, the song never ended.

"Remi," she screamed, coming so hard, her body was shaking. I lapped her up, making sure I caught every drop of her sweetness. I moaned against her, not being able to stop as I ran my tongue slowly up and down her slit, caressing, kissing, and savoring her. I wasn't quite finished with her yet, in more ways than one, but to be honest, I don't think I ever will be. She just tasted and felt so fucking good, it was amazing.

She tried to pull back from the onslaught of my tongue, moaning and breathlessly asking me to stop. I smiled, "No." I renewed my passion, which never really left, I don't think it would with a girl like Hudson. She was an addiction, a sweet temptation that can break you and fuck, if I didn't want to be broken repeatedly. She thrashed and arched her back, and I reached my hands up her body and rolled her nipples between my fingers while caressing her breasts gently. Being sensitive from her previous orgasm, she moaned, and my name was whispered from her lips as she wrapped her legs around my head. I let my tongue ring graze her clit and sucked her back into my lips, groaning. I don't think I could ever stop at this point. I shifted her and had her sit on my face. Goodness, from this angle, I could look straight up her abs to her perfect breasts and her neck as she threw her head back and rode my face at the urging of my hands on her hips. She reached for the headboard as I delved my tongue inside of her, tasting her before dragging my tongue up her slit slowly and lovingly.

There was never a rush to eating pussy, you had to savor it to make them beg for it, and I was no exception. I made her beg, I made her plead, I made a girl who never gave up control clench her thighs and cry for her release. And I gave it to her. I let her cum but then she thought she could get up off my face. I nipped her clit, making her yelp and moan and grabbed her ass and thighs tighter as I licked and sucked and swirled around her swollen clit. Licking up and around ever so slowly, I made love to her pussy with my mouth, but this time, she took more control. That's my girl. She reached down and tugged my head, riding my face in earnest. I moaned at the taste of her and the pain/pleasure from her tugging me closer into her pussy. I nipped her clit again as she grabbed my head with both hands bucking as she came again and again, covering me in her cream. I placed one last kiss on her swollen pussy and laid her down.

When I came here tonight, I figured I would come and leave early. When a gorgeous woman with curves for days walked down the stairs, I was stuck. I couldn't leave without talking to her. When she came into the kitchen and locked eyes with me, I was definitely lost, I couldn't help myself from flirting with her. When she told me her name, my stomach twisted and churned but I pushed it down, enjoying the moment for what it was. When we danced, I couldn't help myself from touching her, kissing her, falling into her. She was magnetic. It was surreal.

We laid there for a few moments just caressing each other and kissing softly, her eyes were glazed over, and her lips were swollen from our kisses, her skin flushed and if I thought she couldn't get any more perfect, I was wrong. So very wrong.

Hudson

With a final kiss, Remi went to the bathroom to wash up. I blushed when I realized just how much I came, my cream on her neck. I laid there for a few seconds, just basking in my first ever girl on girl sexual experience. God, that was just incredible, I thought as I got up and put on my less provocative nightie from one of my secret shopping trips. I looked down and frowned, this was definitely not appropriate pizza party wear. I turned the TV on to Netflix and when Remi stepped out of the bathroom, I gave her a pair of sleep shorts and tank. At that moment, there was a knock on my door.

"Come in," I said loudly.

"This isn't over gorgeous," Remi whispered, and she went to settle herself on the floor as the guys walked in in their pajamas. Zane had the pizzas, while Hunter had soda, Gray the glasses, but Ryder had a bottle of liquor and shot glasses. They set everything down and suddenly focused on us. Their eyes flit back and forth between Remi and I and the bed. It would have been funny if it didn't immediately want to give in to my overeager vagina's wishes. *Dumb horny bitch. I'm sorry, I love you,* I internally whispered to her.

I cleared my throat. "So you guys just gonna stare or are we going to eat? I'm starving." I sat down on the floor and grabbed a box of pizza, grabbed two slices, made a sandwich, took a bite, and moaned in happiness. The guys shook their heads and sat down on the floor in a loose circle, taking a bite of pizza. I looked at them appraisingly, this quickly building friendship and connection was exciting but distracting. This is totally a normal college experience, right? Sigh, if only it felt that simple.

"Hmm, I'm full," Remi said and pressed a kiss to my neck, and I blushed, and their eyes heated.

I laughed and pointed at the guys, "Don't start, we had a deal. I technically haven't collected yet."

I winked at Hunter then choked on my pizza and laughed when he growled and mouthed the words, "I'm collecting."

"A deal?" Remi asked.

"Yup, I challenged and beat Zane's ass in weaponry, then sparring." I ignored his growl. "And it was so they wouldn't cock block. Fuckers."

"I don't feel bad about that bet, you should have seen the looks you were getting," grumbled Ryder. "It's like they smelled the virginal blood in the proverbial water. Gray punched a couple of sophomores who were talking about you, by the way, after you went upstairs. Technically, school hasn't started yet, so it was a free for all."

"First of all, I'm not a virgin. Second, I would have liked to see Gray punch anyone. Kinda hot," I said and threw him a wink, thinking about how his abs strained under his tee shirt. I looked over at Remi, who was laughing at us.

"You see the shit I gotta live with? Pure fuckery I tell you." I reached for the soda and a glass and scowled at them; fuck, they were so ridiculously gorgeous. "I'm going to make your lives a living hell when you bring a girl home. I'm going to put mayonnaise in her hair and then I'll probably drown them in the hot tub when they try to be sexy." I took a sip of my soda, wondering if they knew just how serious I was as they all laughed at me.

Remi shook her head and laughed. "I'm loving the dynamics here and one, the cockblocking stunt, I can't be mad at. I mean, I saw you for all of five seconds before I even wanted to punch anyone in the face for looking at you." I scowled at her, the traitor, and she put her hands up. "No, I'm serious. Five seconds, I counted, and they have to live with you and watch over you. Shit, you're lucky they haven't tried to tie you down yet." The boys looked at me with a smug look on their faces. As if they could take me anyway. If I'm going to be tied down, it's going to be for sex. "Second, drowning a bitch? They won't bring anyone home. Like I said, I see the way they look at you, am I safe to say that Hudson is pretty much the end game here?" She directed that question towards the guys. They agreed, and I blushed. She nodded and reached over to take a bite of my pizza sandwich, bitch. "Anyways, fuck, that's brutal, but I'm thinking poison is easier. You won't get your hands dirty, but keeping your men away from other women? That's hot and hot. I will help." I laughed at that; she was so similar to me, it was frightening.

Zane rolled his eyes before taking a few bites of his pizza and staring at me. Actually, they were all staring at me while they ate, well Remi mostly stared at them staring at me, with a smirk on her face. We finished the pizza in silence, but it was a comfortable one. We put the boxes to the side, and I had to ask, "Okay, what is with the shot glasses and liquor? It's like 3 am."

Ryder smiled. "Well, we figured we can all play a little game." I looked at them warily.

"What kind of game? The games we played yesterday? Not happening. I am not skinny-dipping. But if it involves kicking your asses again, I'm down."

Remi raised her eyebrow at that.

"Well, technically, I dared them to skinny dip, but still not happening," I explained and she laughed.

"Well, it's simple really," Ryder said with a smile. "This is called, never have I ever." I shook my head, I knew the game. Basically, someone has to say something they haven't done and if a person has done it, they have to take a drink. Strategy wise? Stupid, I haven't done a lot of shit, so this game wasn't ideal.

"Really? You know damn well there is a lot of shit I haven't done, so let's skip the liquor part of it all." Ryder pouted at that, I laughed. "Shush, we still have a book date, sweetie, but..." I thought and rubbed my chin. "I'll tell you all one thing that you all really want to know, so ask away."

Before anyone can say anything, else Grayson spoke up, "Deal, I will go first. Who taught you how to fight the way you do and why? Those techniques go beyond normal training."

I considered him for a second. "Father always had a rule. If I came home with a scratch or a bruise, or anything that indicated I was losing to anyone, he would make me undergo extra training. I would have to wake up early, before school and work with my instructor, Kalen Dochloite." Remi took a sharp intake of breath, but when I looked her way her face was blank, so I continued. "I would train before and after school with him. In fact, Father had me taken out of training in school during that hour to train with him instead. He was brutal, but kind and fair. He didn't accept weakness. I did drill after drill, ran for hours until I was able to outpace him, until I was able to best him in hand to hand, until I was able to beat him in weaponry.

"In fact, I was thirteen when I started training with him, right after Zane left. That first day," I smiled at the memory, "he wouldn't let me leave until I could summon magic and infuse my weapons. I was so pissed that I told him to stick his sword in his ass." I laughed, "He laughed at me, and told me to shut my smart mouth and focus. I did and after a few tries, it was like it was always inside of me, it became second nature. He became more of a father figure. There was nothing I couldn't do in his eyes, and believe me, he made sure I could do it all. When I was eighteen, the training became more brutal, more intense. He would say if I have a tattoo about weakness, then I needed to hone the skills to back it up." Kalen was just amazing. "In fact, I felt like we were holding back, but for some reason, he saw my white hair and told me I was getting old early and I needed to train harder. We laughed, but for the past two years, we trained every moment I was free; it was so brutal but it was exhilarating, and I never tired and we would go for hours. It was during that time that I put him on his ass a few times and he was so proud of me. My dad didn't look at me like that anymore; his approval was like a drug to me. I love him." I smiled softly. I would kill for that man, and fuck anyone who got in my way.

"Wow, that's impressive. The name rings a bell, but I can't place it. It's like at the tip of my tongue. That's so strange, maybe I read of him somewhere," Grayson said pensively.

"Probably. You've been teaching for a while, it's probably in there somewhere and you drank it out of your memory," Remi teased then laughed when Gray gave her the middle finger. "Sorry, bud, I like what you like." And she winked at him and he shook his head and busted out laughing.

"Fair, everyone here likes the same thing." And he winked at me. I rolled my eyes. These guys were going to kill me.

"In more ways than one apparently." Hunter pointed at the middle of my legs, I blushed, and he laughed. "Okay my turn, I'll make this really good, I have been thinking about it a lot actually." He clapped his hands. It looked ridiculous, he was just so damn muscular and dominant, to see him be silly was endearing.

"When are you going to put Zane out of his misery, so he can stop being a grouchy asshole, and just kiss him, and make up?" Zane choked on his soda.

"Haha, asshole, we already spoke today, so mind your business." I stuck my tongue at him. The guys smiled in approval and it made me feel warm that there was no hint of jealousy.

I mean hell, Remi and I just hooked up and it was like a consistent flip between friend and lover in my head. Has it only been a few hours? I feel as if I knew her my entire life. It's the oddest sensation. I shook it off and focused on the boys instead.

"Aww, we missed the make up? Not fair, I wanted to watch," Ryder jokes. A small smile formed on Zane's face as he leaned close and his lips grazed mine.

"Yeah, you missed it, but it's okay. She isn't going to make this easy and that's okay with me. I love the challenge." He grabbed my face and looked into my eyes as he said, "as long as Hudson knows that she will always be my entire heart, I'm okay with that." I nodded and gave him a small kiss and his face lit up and it sent warmth to my heart.

Remi looked at us and smiled. "Well, I'm going to go ahead actually and go. I have to get some stuff ready for tomorrow. Did you see those fucking skirts? Fuck no. I'm cutting them all. I'm not fucking walking around with a kilt." I laughed.

"I already cut mine; I'm not dealing with that shit either. Fuck that." We got up, picked up the boxes and cups, and headed down the stairs. I gave her a hug at the door, and it turned into a lot more as she tried to push me up against the door to kiss me, but I pushed her back instead, pulling her hair and biting her neck then kissing her soundly until we both looked dazed. I gave her my number and closed the door. I smiled as I turned around and the guys were leaning against the stairs looking like a sexual HGTV episode. I rolled my eyes. I looked around the mess and cringed, and I walked to the kitchen to grab a bottle of water.

"Bedtime, boys! We must prepare for the new year like good boys and girls!" I announced as I tried to head upstairs but Ryder grabbed my hand before I was able to. I laughed and blinked up at him as he brought me close to him.

"Uh, I didn't ask my question." He leaned back and hugged me, wrapping his arms around my waist. "We have established that you're pretty much it for us we have said it a few times. You haven't mentioned it though. Does it bother you?" I looked in his eyes and saw real worry there. Nope, not my jokester, he wasn't allowed to look sad. I reached up on my tip toes and pulled him down and kissed him, rubbing myself against him. He bent me slightly back, taking control of the kiss and taking my breath away at the same time. When we pulled apart, I looked up at him.

"This may not be conventional, and I will say it's strange how fast this even got to this point, but it feels right and I'm going to go with that. My gut is normally not wrong, so I'll stick to that. You all feel like you're a part of me. To be honest, I can't even see past a couple days ago. I'm good, I promise I would tell you otherwise." I smiled as I looked at them.

"Good, because I can't see past you. Even if it is a sausage fest," he grumbled, and I smacked his chest.

I looked at Zane. "What is your question? You never asked either."

He pulled me toward him and whispered in my ear, "Can I take you on a date tomorrow? Book shopping and some coffee?" He said book shopping. He wants to take me book shopping. I can't say yes, because now I have to go plan my wedding. If a man wants to take you book shopping, you marry him, period.

I smiled, well actually, I beamed like a fucking perverted horny firefly. "Fuck yes, it's a date. You keep it up and I may have to marry you. Books are my weakness." He laughed and hugged me tightly, giving my forehead a kiss. I loved how he was truly trying. It just made things a lot better for me to heal.

"Actually, we'll all have to go into town tomorrow, so while you guys have your date, we'll go shopping," Grayson mentioned, and the guys nodded.

"Oh yay! Then after me and Zane have our date, maybe we can all meet for lunch around one?"

"Works for us, sweetheart. We have a little surprise that I think will make tomorrow a lot better too," Hunter said, and the guys smiled. I was jittery and excited, and I needed to go to bed so I could wake up!

"Okay bedtime, bedtime, everyone, go, go, go we have a big day!" I started to go upstairs, and Hunter grabbed my hand, I almost growled in frustration. I needed to get ready to go fucking book shopping and I will fucking shank him.

He rolled his eyes at my face. "You and the books. We need some ground rules. One of them is whenever you leave us, you need to give us a kiss, no discussion." Okay, I can do that. Then sleep. Then books. I jumped up on him and he caught me with a laugh and kissed me sweetly before setting me down. Then Ryder grabbed my ass, horny fucker, and brought me in and kissed me until I blushed. He winked at me and passed me over to Grayson, my sweet giant who must have had some type of pent-up passion. He wasted no time to turn me around and press me against the stairs and kiss his way up my neck before tangling his tongue with mine teasing my tongue rings, his hands sliding up and down my sides teasing the rim of my shorts before letting go. I was in a little daze and Zane took up his spot and gave me a sweet kiss, filled with promise and hope. Ugh, these guys were just perfect. I skipped my happy ass upstairs and went to bed, but not before I took a picture of me laying down naked to the group chat.

Grayson- Not cool.

Ryder- We need to book club and chill, soon.

Hunter- How do I type in a growl in a chat? You're lucky we have to get up in a few hours.

Zane- I want a picture of...

I laughed and sent a picture of what he wanted.

Zane- Fuck.

Grayson- Evil.

Ryder- This is some bullshit, I'm going to bed.

Hunter- I swear I'm going to poke a hole through my sheets.

I went to bed with a smile on my face.

CHAPTER NINE

Remi

"Were you able to meet her yesterday, Remi?" Alvor asked. We met off campus at a little cafe in town at his behest that we meet every few days for regular updates about Hudson Jacobs. I had no idea why he insisted on meeting at this ridiculous time, on a Sunday none-the-less, after being requested to go to a damn party. I would have gone with or without Reed's invitation, but it provided a better cover, I admit. Having those guys head over heels for her will make this year a hell of a lot easier for us, the perfect distraction. Slight problem was, I found myself craving her too.

"Alvor, was this meeting at 8 am really necessary? I could've just called you, I'm exhausted."

He looked at me reproachfully. "Remi, you know very well I hate those silly devices, face to face..."

"Meetings are a lost art, I know, Alvor, I know," I interrupt, rubbing my head, sipping my coffee.

"Well?" he prompted.

"She certainly looks just like him, uncanny really. She is also gorgeous. It's a wonder her powers haven't manifested earlier. She seems to pull the attention of everyone around her," I thought. "During a conversation with her brother and his friends yesterday, she admitted to receiving training from Kalen Dochloite. He hasn't been seen in several years, Alvor. That is not a coincidence. She also bested Zane in combat." I shook my head proudly, a smile making its way on my face.

"I know that look, Remi." He reached over to grab my hand, his handsome face and white hair, dyed black, a sharp contrast to his hazel eyes. "You have a duty; we have a duty. We need to keep an eye on her. She has the potential to be dangerous. If she is attracting the eyes of others already, we may have a bigger issue than young magicians. I have the school warded strongly, with the help of the prince."

I gasped. "The prince? But he never comes this far. Are those precautions necessary, Alvor? I spent time with her, she's vulgar yes, but kind and lonely."

"Maybe not, although I doubt it, but what she represents, her destiny is paramount. The prophecy is what it is, Remi. I will do what I can, but you know as well as I do, this is our duty now. Especially, since you won't do yours." He looked at me reproachfully. "The boys, do they suspect anything at all?"

"No. But we have a slight problem."

He sighed. "What would that be?"

"Her hair is pure white already, and she not only has a familiar, but a lion. She's almost complete with her change." He looked startled.

"That is certainly a serious complication. Try your best to keep an eye on her, and I'll take the steps to test her powers during school hours. If she's powerful, we can save our home after all." He gives me a serious look, stands up and walks out, looking smart in his suit. At eight in the fucking morning.

I grumble into my coffee and settle in to enjoy the little peace I can. "Well, goodbye to you too, Uncle."

HUDSON

"FUCK, OH WOW," I MOANED SLEEPILY, SLOWLY WAKING UP. I OPENED my eyes to light streaming through my room and Grayson's face in between my legs. Now, this was a fucking alarm clock.

"Good morning, sweetheart," he said, looking up at me before dragging his tongue up from my ass to my clit. I gripped the sheets and moaned as he swirled his tongue around my swollen clit and sucked it into his mouth.

"Fuck, Gray." He chuckled as gripped my thighs and spread me further apart, pressing kisses on my lips between flicking my piercing. I groaned and gripped his head, grinding my pussy into his face. I heard a ping go off on my phone and I reached over with one hand to grab it, firmly keeping my other hand on Gray's head. I would die if he stopped. Moaning, I looked at my messages.

Ryder- Wake up, fuckers.

Hunter- Fuck you 🖕

Zane- I've been up, you're the late one.

Hudson- *sends picture of Gray in between legs* Currently being woken up right now. 😈

I moaned as Gray picked up the tempo and clenched my thighs about his head and shuddered as I came all over his face. He slowly lapped me up.

"Fuck, baby. You taste so good. We're going to finish this later."

I stretched my hands over my head and pulled away, I have a fucking book date.

I leaned over and gave him a kiss. "Mm, thank you for the alarm, Gray. I'll definitely have to pay you back later."

He laughed and shot me a wink. "Anytime, baby. Anytime." He gave me a final kiss before stepping out of the room. Shit, a man who gives and doesn't ask for anything back? Yup, keeping that gentle giant. I hummed as I skipped my happy ass to the shower, getting ready in record time. I squeezed into some leather pants, threw on my combat boots, and a tight black tube top that showed my midriff. I was so excited that after making sure my hair was perfectly coiled and hanging down my back, I even threw on some bright red lipstick and black eyeliner. I gave myself a once over and smiled. I'll skip the picture this time, they can see this badass vision in person. I grabbed a leather jacket on my way out of my bedroom and walked down the stairs and into the kitchen. I saw Xena outside sunning on the pool and sent her a mental message that we were going out and to hold down the fort. She lifted a paw in response, and I smiled.

Then, I frowned when I didn't see the boys, but I grabbed a bottle of water and followed the sounds of voices coming from a door towards the front of the house I never gave mind to. Pushing the door open, I smiled and rolled my eyes as I took note of four ridiculously handsome men laughing at Tik-Tok videos while leaning against the wall of a very spacious garage. While they were distracted, I took in the fitted jeans and casual tee shirts and combat boots, they either all got dressed together or shared the same closet, but they were still each uniquely them. Hunter still looked like he was expecting a war to break out at any moment, Ryder laughed with his entire face lighting up, Grayson chuckled instead of outright laughing, always quiet until he had something to say and Zane? Well, Zane was intense, his eyes having the ability to pierce your soul, but his smile having the ability to melt me completely. Damn, they were perfect, and I wanted to lick them.

Looking around the garage, I noticed a few cars and four gorgeous motorcycles. I couldn't help myself, I walked into the garage and my feet led me to the sex bikes. Four of the newest model Ducati Panigale V2's.

"Fuck, these were only supposed to be in red and white, how the fuck did you get them customized and fully loaded when they haven't even hit the market?" I asked.

Warm arms wrapped around me, hands splayed on my belly, before I was pressed against a hard body. Yum.

"Mm, whoever this current sex God is, won't distract me from the question about the sex bikes. These are top of the line; I've been stalking the Ducati website for months for an announcement."

"I'm glad you think I'm a sex God, princess. You look absolutely beautiful," Zane rumbled with his deep voice, pressing a soft kiss to my neck. I sighed, God, being this close to him felt so damn good.

"Mm, thank you." I turned around and reached up to give him a quick kiss. Well, that was the plan anyway. He trailed his fingers down my back, making me shiver, staring into my eyes with so much emotion before he pulled me in and pressed his soft lips against mine, caressing the dip of my waist. He teased my mouth with his tongue, and I opened for him, our tongues exploring, and I moaned softly before pulling away. I smiled at him and stepped out of his reach.

"Hey, the kiss comes after the date and the books, Zane. Stop taking advantage of my weakness and someone tell me about the sex bikes." Zane laughed and the guys shook their heads at me.

"It amazes me how you grew up with money, yet you never really realized its benefits, angel," Hunter said. I shrugged. I grew up with it, but it didn't mean I ever thought much of it unless I really needed something, like the laptop and iPad, for example. I didn't like asking my father for anything.

"We have a few connections, gorgeous, so we made it happen. Which reminds us." Ryder smiled mischievously while Grayson smirked and walked towards the back of the garage and snatched a cover off the exact same model, painted purple and black with glitter. I screamed and jumped and ran over to the bike. I walked around the bike admiring the color, it matched the inside of my car perfectly. It was fucking perfect. Oh my God, I was going to be such a glittery badass on this.

"Gah, I'm sorry, who do I thank for this amazing sex machine of steel and porn?"

They laughed and Ryder, Hunter, and Zane joined me and Gray next to my bike.

"We all chipped in for this one, baby girl. You would leave your computer open around the house when we were younger. You were always researching bikes, so when we found out you were coming, we all got the bikes and customized them, but this one we made sure matched your truck," Ryder finished explaining.

I turned my head, confused. "How did you know the color of my truck? Father got that for me not too long ago." They all looked at Zane, who stood with his arms crossed, and he reached up and rubbed his neck.

"Um, now, remember we're moving forward, Hudson," he said nervously, and I raised my eyebrow. "I was still calling the Chancellor every few days and during one of those calls, he was ranting about customizing the inside of your truck with black, purple, and glitter." I frowned.

I felt a serious spike of anger and pain, he could call my father but couldn't call the girl who he fucked and left? I closed my eyes and pinched the bridge of my nose, taking a deep breath, reminding myself that we were going to move forward, and it was in the past. But fuck, if the past didn't hurt, then who the fuck would we be today? Rafiki may have been smart to kids back when Lion King came out, but just because it was in the past didn't make the pain any less meaningful or, in this case, potent.

"I'm not going to even go there right now, my parade will not be rained on. I'm still liable to nut punch you. Again. I'm going to climb on my sex bike, and we are going to go have a date, and if there are any pieces of you left, the boys can help you get back home."

He winced, and Grayson shook his head and clapped him on the back. Hunter punched him in the arm and glared at him, stopping to give me a kiss before getting on his bike. Ryder just looked at him and shook his head. You know he is serious when my goofy one isn't smiling.

We sped off into the town, and I thoroughly enjoyed the ride with my new sex toy. It was such an incredible piece of equipment. I took a deep breath and absorbed the energy around me. I can bitch about going to Delorean but this area was absolutely gorgeous. It was just green forests all around and I felt so alive and exhilarated in a way that you just can't if you're surrounded by concrete. In a way, I guess I was happy my plans to go to New York were stopped. I didn't even have a real reason to go other than to piss off my father. Realistically, I can study human relations anywhere.

These trees, nature? Was just pure magic, literally as magic comes from the energy and elements around us. Magic, at least, was honest. We had the innate ability to use it, manipulate it and build a world dedicated to the protection of magic users. We weren't too different from humans, but to them, we magic users were witches, wizards, Death Eaters. While yes, like I said before, we resemble a lot of movie depictions, who I am secretly convinced were made by witches, we mostly kept to ourselves. Occasionally, you had the dick head who used blood magic, sacrificed, and did stupid shit to defile nature and go against our basic nature, if they weren't hunted down and brought before the council, they always escalated in violence. I joke a lot but the reason I read so many books and watch so many movies and shows about paranormal beings is because it is important to see how humans see us. Especially because knowing how much they know, or rather think they know, can be important to our relations with them. It was all fascinating to me. Also helped that a lot of those authors have some kick ass sex scenes with like demons and shit.

I pulled into a spot near the bookstore I saw on my way driving in, leaving space for Zane to pull in next to me, while the boys drove further into town to do whatever grown magic boys do. I hopped off my sex kitten and waited for Zane to hurry up. I like the sauntering stuff now that I can witness it firsthand, but books wait for no one.

"Come on, Zane! They even have coffee inside! It will be integral to your survival if you plan to keep up with me there!" He laughed and we went inside to breathe the air of literary magic.

Four hours and six coffees later, Zane was sitting in the middle of the aisle arguing with me.

"Hudson, baby, you can't carry all these books with you on the bike. It's impossible," he said for the fifth time. The disrespect I had to deal with was astounding.

"Excuse me, what good is being magical if I can't buy one hundred books right now and find a way to carry them with me," I whispered angrily.

“You just said it, one hundred books, Hudson, and no, you can’t just shrink them. You’ll draw too much attention to yourself,” he whispered back, throwing his hands in the air. The nerve. How many nut punches can he take? I grabbed my phone and started texting the group angrily.

Hudson- Guys, 😔 Zane will not let me get all the books I want. He’s ruining the best date ever.😩

Zane- (picture of the books in the aisle) This is why.

Grayson- Holy shit, Hudson

Ryder- You can’t say no to books, Zane.

Ryder- Wait, is that the pile or a book aisle?

Zane- It’s the fucking pile bro!

Ryder- Holy shit.

Zane- Yeah. no shit. Tell her no. She’s not listening to me.

Grayson- I’m the gentle giant, she likes me more. I’m not telling her no.

Ryder- Hunter said to tell you, ‘your Daddy said no?’ Does he have your dad’s number?🙄

Hudson- LOL, tell him that only works when I’m in trouble, I can’t be in trouble for book shopping, that's like against some academic rule, isn’t it? Aren’t you all teachers? The fuck?😂

Grayson- 🤦‍♂️🤦‍♂️ Literature porn is not academic.

Hudson- You take that the fuck back. 😬It’s human relations. I learn about paranormal creatures from a human's perspective.

Ryder- That actually makes sense, if you’re studying the relations of dicks and chicks. Also, Hunter said to tell you, to shut your mouth when you're talking to him.

Hudson- LMAO, 😂🤣stepbrothers, nice. Seriously, guys, can you come back and create a diversion so I can Hermione these books into my bag after we buy them? Also, wtf is Hunter doing? Why can’t he text?

Grayson- Why not have them delivered? Also, not telling you, he made us promise.

Ryder- Because you can’t let someone else touch your books. It’s a rule.

Hudson- I think I love you, Ryder.

Zane- I tell her I love her, and I get a voodoo doll made, this is some bullshit.

Ryder- Don't give her any ideas, there is a magic section in that store. BTW, I love you too sugar, we're going to make sexy book babies during our kindle and chill.

Hudson- Deal, Best book husband ever.

Hunter- Okay, I'm finally done here. We will meet you and you guys can create a diversion.

Zane- You are such a pussy for her, what happened to the tough guy?

Hunter- He is busy making a voodoo doll of you to stick in his ass so you can smell like shit.

Grayson- LOL fucking twisted.

Hudson- LMFAO OMG, the lady in the front is going to think I'm having a fit.

A few minutes later, I heard the bikes purr as they parked in front of the store. I was making Zane carry my books to the front while he bitched and moaned, and I laughed. He gets serious points for dealing with this for so long.

The bell to the store door rang and when the cashier lifted her head to greet them, her eyes popped open and her jaw dropped. "Holy fuck," she whispered. I smiled behind the books and gave the guys a thumbs up behind my back.

"Yeah, they are my brothers..." I leaned over to check her name tag, "Rosie. And I know for a fact they like to share. If you think you can handle it?"

Ryder chuckled and went to lean on the counter and winked at her. I think she came right there, her cheeks turning pink. "Oh, Rosie looks like she can definitely handle us," Ryder drawled.

She giggled and packed up the books and handed a huge bag to each of the guys, while Ryder flirted with her and gave her a slip of paper with a number, and walked out the store with Hunter, who was whistling Red Light Special, and Gray while Zane paid for the books.

I wrapped my arms around him and with a teasing note in my voice, said, "Oh, baby, don't be such a grouch. If it makes you feel better, I can tell Rosie that we share too." His arms tightened around me and his eyes flashed in warning.

I leaned across the counter, my breasts on display. "Rosie, tell me, baby. Have you ever come with a girl between your legs?" I whispered in her ear, she blushed and stuttered to respond.

"I'm so sorry for her behavior. Thank you, Rosie," he apologized, and I turned back to wink.

"Wait," a small voice said. We turned back and Rosie slid a paper into my hand. "Text me anytime." Then she stepped closer and whispered in my ear, "I have never been with a girl before but there is something about you. Definitely text me." She leaned forward and pressed a kiss against my lips before walking back behind the counter. I hightailed my ass out of the store.

Zane busted out laughing, barely catching his breath. I scowled at him.

"Shut the fuck up, Zane." Then I turned to the boys. "Did you shrink the books to fit in my bag?"

They nodded. "What happened?" Gray asked.

"Hudson... Hudson..." Zane couldn't stop laughing, that dick. "Hudson flirted with the girl inside and told her we share, and the girl came back and kissed Hudson. You should have seen her face."

"Fuck you, guys. Let's go have lunch." I swung my legs over my bike and sped off while they guys laughed and followed. Fuckers. I had only been with Remi. I was fucking with Zane, but I definitely did not have any inclinations towards the same sex except for Remi it seemed. Well, at least for now, who the fuck knows anymore. I, apparently, like four guys, a girl, and want to have a baby with a motorcycle. I mean, what else is going to be thrown my way?

I SPENT THE REST OF SUNDAY GETTING READY FOR SCHOOL. WE ENDED up having pizza before we headed back home. The computer and iPad had been delivered, and I set them to the side to update and download all the software while I put my books away on a bookshelf I stole from Zane's room when he was downstairs. I also stole his speakers and blasted music from my phone singing and dancing along to my randomized Mary J Blige playlist; the good stuff. I snapped a picture and gave him my thanks and he responded with several middle fingers. I sniggered, honestly, he should be fucking honored that his shelves were being graced with authors like B.C Morgan, E.M Moore and Nikita, my favorite new dark romance author. This bitch gave me so many ideas. If Zane fucked up again, I'm just gonna stab him and tell him that Nikita told me to do it. Fuck it.

I took out my uniform, gag, for tomorrow and my combat boots. I'll be damned if I was wearing heeled penny loafers at any point in time. There were people, like me, who wore heels to look cute for a party, then there were fucking idiots, that would be the not me person, being caught in a fight with penny loafers. I looked at my skirts and frowned, God I hoped I didn't cut them too much. I groaned; I didn't want to start school looking like Britney Spears. I was more of a Genie in a Bottle chick. Don't judge me, Justin was just not a good decision. Although, hitting people one more time was a good idea. Yes, I knew it was the other way around, but you won't catch me singing that version.

Fuck, I was brain rambling, ugh. I sighed; well, I guess I'll see how short the skirts are tomorrow after they ride up my ass all day. I threw myself on my desk chair, looking over my schedule, and I gave another grimace. Partially this was the reason I didn't really want to leave my brain right now, I'm literally in school for over 12 hours. The least I can do is hide out in my room for a bit to breathe before I had to deal with this shit tomorrow.

Jacob, Hudson: Schedule

7am-8am - Breakfast - Common Dining Room (fuck them)

8:15am-9:30am - Magical Theory and Practice - Room 234 - Professor Grayson (going to fuck him)

9:45am-10:45am - Complex Magical History - Room 236 - Professor Logan (looks like a mad scientist)

11am-12pm - Human Studies and Relations Room 239 - Professor Blair (CREEP)

12:15pm-1pm - Lunch - Common Dining Room and Outdoors

1:15pm-2:15pm - Magical Weaponry - Professor Ryder (yum)

2:20pm-3:20pm - Alchemy - Professor King (totally nice guy)

3:30pm-5pm - Self-Defense and Hand-to-Hand - Professor Hunter (professor DADDY)

5:15pm-6:30pm - Weaponry - Professor Zane (asshole who stole my heart, ate it, and gave it back)

6:45pm-7:30pm - Dinner - Common Dining Room

8:15-9:30 pm - Study Hall (Tuesday & Thursday) (nap) Magical Tactical (Monday, Wednesday, Friday) (kick ass)

I pretty much was lost in my thoughts, making little corrections doodling, as I looked over my schedule and sighed. To be honest, my non study hall nights could've been spent in swimming or running, but I ran every day and I already know how to swim. So, what was the point? At least magical tactical is a combination of all the shit I'm good at; self-defense, weaponry and magical practice. I also thought alchemy was going to be boring as fuck; do I look like I aspire to be Professor Snape?

I heard a knock on my door and said, "come in", lost in my thoughts.

"Hey, I found some extra books on familiars for you. I know Ryder was getting some together, so I grabbed a couple that may also help you as well," Grayson said, walking into my room. I smiled at him.

"Thank you. It's insane how much I don't know about something so close to me. So, I appreciate these." I started to thumb through them, excited to sit down and really pick up as much as I can.

"I don't think I have ever seen anyone as excited as you are about books. Today was especially impressive," he teased as he leaned against the wall next to my desk.

"Well, it's safe to say you have never met anyone quite like me before." I stuck my tongue out at him. He laughed.

"Yes, well, that part is true. There is no one like you at all. It makes you even more special to me; to us." He leaned over and caressed my face, making my heartbeat like crazy. Xena gave a lion meow and walked up to him, rubbing her head against his leg. He laughed and rubbed her face.

"You're special too, X."

"Attention whore," I laughed as she swatted at me.

"I admit, Gray, I don't think I have ever heard you speak so much in the entire time I've known you." I smiled at him and turned back to the books on my desk, looking through them. "You have a voice that's just made to be heard, and I love it. I kind of want to keep it all to myself in a box." I laughed as he mockingly held his throat.

"And keep this magic from other women? I can't do that to my fan club."

I narrowed my eyes but laughed when Xena jumped on him and knocked him down, sitting on his chest calm as ever.

"X, I was joking. Get off," he grunted, while I laughed.

"Yeah, that's what I thought. Good job X, claim what is mine." I got up and walked over to my dresser. It may be late, but I was a little restless and maybe a good run with Xena will help with the jitters.

"Xena, want to go for a run with me?"

Yes, I keep safe. I smiled and blew her a kiss.

I went into the bathroom to change into my gym clothes and put my hair up. When I stepped back into the room, Gray and X were fake wrestling on the floor. I rolled my eyes. I grabbed my phone and tucked it into the side of my shorts. I started to head out of the room and Xena and Grayson got up to follow me.

"Do you want us to go with you?" Grayson asked.

"No, it's okay. I can meet you at the gym after though."

"Okay." He reached out to grab me and kissed the side of my head. "Have fun." He winked and walked towards the gym.

I made a quick protein shake before going out and while I drank it, I looked around, startled to realize that the house was spotless. The boys must have had someone come and clean while we were gone. I didn't even realize; I had books to store and shit to steal. I smiled at the thought of them, the urge to see them all unfurling in my belly. I finished up my shake and stretched before walking out of the house and starting off at a jog with Xena by my side.

We ran the path a few times before calling it and going back into the house. Xena ran into the pool and I laughed as I closed the front door and headed to the gym.

I walked downstairs and paused when I saw the guys training and sparring, looking perfect. Ryder and Zane were sparing with magic infused weapons, sparks of magic being let off into the air while they fought. Grayson and Hunter were sparring and using magic at the same time, using some impressive strength and power, but still there were some things I know if Kalen were here, he would smack them upside the head until they corrected.

I smiled and switched their music and stuck out my tongue at their shouts while

"Perfect" by Simple Plan started blasting through the radio. How appropriate. I jumped on the treadmill and started to jog, not tired from my run at all. I usually only trained with music at full blast if I felt comfortable in my surroundings. So, the fact that I have been able to let myself free here spoke volumes. I felt safe here and I wasn't going to overthink it, so I blocked everything out and just ran. I felt my feet hit the belt, moving and urging me to go faster as song after song blasted through the room. I hit a full out run without feeling even a little winded. My eyes flicked at the clock and I've been running for 45 minutes straight at a flat out run. I should at least be breaking a sweat by now or dying. Clearly, this wasn't working, so I slowed down and turned off the machine, taking a drink of my water before turning around to do something else. Well, I tried to turn around but suddenly, there was a wall of muscle in my way. I rolled my eyes. Seriously like fucking dick magnets.

"Yes?" I asked as I pushed my way through the wall of warmth. Pausing briefly, a low growl leaving my throat when I touched them, yum. They cocked their heads and looked at me strangely. I tried to keep moving and Hunter reached for my arm and brought me close enough that I could smell the sweat from his body. Yuck, I don't care what these books say, sweat isn't sexy, but fuck me if being this close didn't make my heart race. I tipped my head and leaned up for a kiss, a low moan escaping from my throat as he reached around and grabbed my ass and brought me closer. When we broke apart, it was as if our bodies fought against it.

"I like when you growl for me, baby," he teased.

"You also like when I call you daddy." I took a step back and danced away laughing as he went to grab me.

I would try to process this feral reaction that was increasing every moment I was around them, but seriously, did it even matter? I mean it was cliché, but this is what all the women from my books must feel like. I always laughed, thinking it was all a lie; 'oh look, I suddenly met a walking cock, and I can't think'. I used to scoff. Well, jokes on you, Hudson, you slutty whore you, after a bunch of dicks at once. Father would be so proud. But you know what? When he asked, I'm going to blame the Harkwrights', and while he tried to figure out who they were, I was going to hang up the phone. Nothing like a good ol' book reference to get you out of an argument.

I walked to the weapons wall to warm up, the guys, who were following, stepping back. I grabbed two long swords, testing the weight in my hands, and found the weight comfortable, like an extension of my arms. I turned the blades in my hands, testing them both together before turning around. "I had fun today, boys. Thank you for coming out with us. Hunter, you never told me what you were buying at the store." I sliced the swords through the air, picking up speed and pushing my body to fall into an easy rhythm of blocking and parrying against fake opponents.

"You'll see," he grinned while he shared a smile with Ryder and a scary smile with Grayson. Okay then. Weirdos. I rolled my eyes, and I flipped the swords into the air, did a flip, and caught them behind my back, before stabbing an imaginary home wrecker in the gut. I was not leaving this gym until I felt like I was going to pass out, then I was going to eat dinner and set my alarm for my regular 5 am run. It is time to get back into a routine. Maybe that is why I'm restless, not my hormones. The guys stayed for a while but eased out when I went from weapons to sparring to the punching bags and then back to the treadmill. After a while, Hunter came down and literally picked me up and took me upstairs to eat. I glared at him but mumbled, "thank you" while I ate my food.

"I'm not sure what time you guys leave, but I do five am runs if you want to join me," I spoke around swallowing my food.

Ryder looked at me appreciatively, "Thank fuck, these guys never want to get up that early and run with me. I'll join you. Students and teachers are expected to eat in the common area for breakfast by the way, so at least you'll have time to get ready."

"Yeah, I think the fuck not. How about I play nice the first day and then everyone else can eat a dick? I don't play nice with others and I have a strong feeling after the first day everyone is going to hate me." I smile. "I'm actually counting on it. I'm suddenly bloodthirsty for whoever is hot for the teacher." I winked at them and they laughed at me. I wasn't joking though. *I will cut a bitch.*

CHAPTER TEN

I walked in after my run with Ryder and quickly jumped into the shower to shave my legs. Fucking skirts. I even washed my hair and blew it out. I smiled as I thought of the little delay Ryder and I had during our run. We were on the way back when he suddenly grabbed me and kissed me. Xena even made herself scarce. He was huge and muscular, but he was so fucking sweet and tender with his lips. Except then it was like we were starving for one another and he pushed me up against a tree and tugged my shorts down and slid inside me.

I didn't register the pain from my back as he brutally pounded into me while making me come apart when he bit my neck and growled,

"Fuck, Hudson, how can you make me feel so fucking weak around you? I can feel myself falling harder for you every fucking second I'm with you," he said, filling me as he came. It took a while to come down and he slowly kissed me before we made our way back to the house. *Yeah, running at 5 am is going to be my new favorite thing.*

❧

Ryder

Fuck, that girl was going to drive me crazy. These past couple of days have been impossible. I've been stroking myself in the shower like a teenage boy just knowing she was down the hall. Being around her, joking, laughing, playing around; it just felt natural. I feel this ridiculous pull towards her, like I have to be near her and touch her. Hell, we all did. This wasn't just us liking her and wanting to be with her like before, when we were younger. No, this was stronger, a physical and emotional attraction so deep, our souls clashed, like it was inevitable.

I sighed as I finished getting ready and headed downstairs. This morning, we were just supposed to run, but I took one look at her face and had to kiss her. Except, it turned into more. I have never cum that hard before. Shit, just thinking about her tight pussy had my dick getting hard again. Fuck, my dick didn't even get soft after. I got in the shower and stroked myself, her name on my lips.

I went into the garage and swung my leg over my bike, the guys and I usually rode together but it was nice out and the weather would change soon. I glanced at Hudson's pimped out truck. Seriously, that shit should have been on that show that used to be so popular; it had all the bells and whistles.

Her dad always seemed to be overcompensating, despite always pretending she didn't exist when they were in person. She has every right to be mad at him. We would see how her heart broke every time she was told she wasn't good enough, like Zane was. We would laugh it off, but she always grew more distant and angrier as the years went by. I sometimes truly think she thought we were laughing at her. The truth was, laughing with her dad would distract him and he would start talking about trivial things. We hated to see her face look so sad; even then, we wanted to protect her. I sighed as I rubbed my face and shot her and the guys a quick text, and I headed out.

The guys and I parked in the lot in front of the dining room, attracting the eyes of several students and female faculty, and I laughed. We noticed, we flirted, we even let ourselves indulge sometimes, but we knew Hudson was always it. It was almost magnetic, like we were meant for her, but whenever we discussed it, we can never truly put it into words other than the caveman version "mine".

We stuck around for a bit talking to Logan and Blair, who were outside before we bothered to head inside. We heard the rumble of a bike behind us as Hudson pulled in next to us and we all just stared. "Oh, fuck," whispered Grayson. Oh, fuck was right.

Hudson

I tossed on some gloss and took a look in the mirror. I looked edgy with my combat boots and black blazer and my ridiculously short red plaid skirt. I cut too much, not compensating for my butt. Sigh.

"Xena, how does it look? Bad ass?"

Look like I need to kill people for you. I like it. I laughed.

"I'm not sure if you're always hungry or just murderous, but I like it. Also, your speech is getting better." I smiled at her and she gave me a toothy grin, jumping off my bed.

I looked at the mirror one last time. Oh well, I would own it, but I did put on some booty shorts underneath before grabbing my backpack and my phone. I smiled when I saw the message from Ryder. I wanted a bike for so long, so knowing the boys got me one was amazing. I looked forward to riding it again. I skipped to the garage and I took in the beautiful glittery magical Ducati and realized my poor baby never got a name. I shall call her *Nimbus 2003*. I turned her on, and she purred underneath me as I took the fifteen-minute drive to campus, after using the remote on my keys to lock the garage. Xena, refusing to stay back, ran alongside the bike on the empty road. I wondered if other students took their familiars or if they even had any. I was also curious if Remi would bring Cerberus.

I was thoroughly enjoying my bike and I pouted when I approached the parking lot. I parked the bike next to the boys and warded it to keep it from dirt and fuckers. I turned around and saw Ryder, Hunter, Zane, Gray, Blair, and Logan standing next to their bikes as well. I walked up to them, Xena by my side, before heading inside. "Yay, look at us. We're a little academic Bike Gang. We should come up with a Quidditch-related gang name. Anyways, good morning, Professors, today is going to be fun. Chin up, I'll make every single class I'm in very interesting and sometimes violent. Scouts honor!"

I waved and walked away looking down at my phone as a text came in from Remi to meet her in front of the dining room. Fuck yes, walking in alone sucks. You've seen those teenage angst movies; it is the same thing no matter what school you're in. Especially when you're mandated to attend and if I were a betting woman, and I'm not because I would always win, there is probably a group of stuck up bitches in here and some cocky boys thinking they are God's gift to women. Joke would be on them; that award goes to my men.

Xena and I were drawing quite a bit of attention but a lion and a new girl kinda went without saying that it was inevitable.

I see Remi and give her a hug, nibbling her ear discreetly. She shuddered and I smiled. Yup, just Remi then. Being near her warmed me up like the fucking sun. We walked into the dining hall, and up to the huge buffet while looking around.

The room was huge with gray stone walls that looked carved. There were dark cherry wood tables with matching chairs, and when you looked up the room was lit with beautiful antique chandeliers. There was a black table near the front that looked like it would be the staff table. In short, it was gorgeous and well done.

I noticed Joshua and his friends at another table, I waved and smiled before diverting my attention back to the food. I grab a tray and fill it up with fruit, avocado, eggs, toast, and almond milk. As I'm ending the line, I spot a center table that people seemed to be staying away from. Interesting. Remi nudges me and I smiled at her, noting that she didn't have loafers or heels on either and laughed. "You weren't going to do it either, huh?" I said as I pointed at her shoes.

"Fuck no, you can't kick ass in stupid loafers."

I laughed. "I said the same thing, ready to go play nice?" She groaned.

"You noticed the same table I did, didn't you? Should have known." She shook her head. "Fuck, it might as well start the day with something exciting. We have Magical Theory and Practice with the seniors, that's going to be fun." She rolled her eyes.

We walked to the table and sat down. "It will be, Grayson is the teacher." I smiled and winked. Xena settled in next to me, watching the room and licking her paw dramatically as people walked by, giving her a wide berth.

"Xena, you're being silly," I whispered.

No, people smell strange here, I must watch. I rolled my eyes and let her do her thing and turned back to Remi.

"What's up with you five anyway?" Remi asked casually, no hint of jealousy. I think I was more relieved than I should have been.

"No idea honestly, I'm drawn to them in a way that I can't explain, like a cat in heat if I'm around them for too long. It's intense. Sex is great too." I shook my head and took a bite of my food and my hair moved in front of my face. Her eyes focused on my hair.

"When did you dye your hair?" she asked slowly, suddenly looking at me very strangely.

"I didn't," I shrugged. "I woke up one day and it had started changing, I thought it was stress. Doctors didn't stress, so we eventually just let it go. I even did some research, figuring there must be something out there about tough bitches getting white hair prematurely." I joked.

She rolled her eyes. "If there was anyone who did that research, it would be fucking you." She laughed.

"Ha-ha, shut it. Did you bring Cerberus with you? I thought it would be cool if you brought him too."

"I would have, but he said he would show up when he was good and ready and not a moment before. He tends to just pop in and out at will, like interdimensional traveling."

"That is fucking awesome." I gaped and looked at Xena. "Is that how you randomly appear in my room if I don't open the door?"

Yes, but it makes me tired. I must practice.

"She said it makes her tired and she has to practice more, but that's freaking awesome. Imagine the battle benefits. If I had known, I would have been making her practice a lot more."

"She will get the hang of it. Maybe if Cerberus isn't grumpy, he can help her."

Xena looked at her and growled.

"Okay, or maybe you don't need help," Remi laughed.

We chuckled at Xena's reaction and continued to eat breakfast when suddenly the room got just a tad quieter. Remi and I looked at each other when two guys sat down in the chairs next to us and smiled.

"Hello, ladies. I'm Jensi and this is Luca." Luca smiled at us. "We just wanted to come say hello."

"That's nice," I drawled out. I blinked at them.

"Did you need something?" Remi asked and I hid a smile while I took a bite of my breakfast. Jensi and Luca looked confused but smiled anyway.

"Nope, we hung out at the mixer this weekend and saw you and we wanted to come by and say what's up. Also, you sat at the table typically reserved for the snobs. Figured you would want a heads up. They can be brutal," answered Jensi, with a roll of his eyes. I smirked, well that's nice. I guess.

"Ah okay, you looked a little familiar, but we were totally done that night," I laughed. "It is nice to meet you sober."

"Yeah, that night was definitely a night to remember, even if I only remember half," Jensi grimaced.

"Yeah, because you spent Sunday throwing up half your memories, dude," Luca teased.

We joked and laughed about the truth or dare games that got us drunk until Luca sucked in a deep breath. "Incoming, queen bitch and her posse of cunts," he sing-songed and smiled.

"Don't worry, boys, I have a feeling they won't last long," laughed Remi. Jensi and Luca looked at each other and grimaced. I smiled at them, they needed to relax. I was a loner, not a pussy.

A high-pitched shrill voice sounded behind me. "Who are you freshman bitches and why are you at the seniors table? This is ours."

Xena growled, but I sent her a mental message to let me handle it. I turned around, barely sparing the redhead a glance but noting quickly her sharp nose, pretty blue eyes, false eyelashes and a face full of makeup. Her shirt was one size too small, to bring attention to her chest, and her skirt was short, but not in a sexy Hudson way, but in a more desperate kind of way. She looked like a socialite hanger-on. She probably thought the world owed her something too. Well, I grew up in that world and I hated it there, and I damn sure didn't appreciate it trying to take human form and breathing down my neck.

"Hmm," I drummed my fingers on the table. "I suggest you walk away and sit somewhere else then. Because not only is your annoying ass voice interrupting my breakfast, but also, I don't give a fuck about what ever social hierarchy you think you got going here," I said calmly.

Remi smiled behind her glass of juice and I felt eyes draw in our direction. I groaned internally. When I said I wanted to meet people, I didn't mean this way.

"What's this, Trish? Who are these..." he sneered "degenerates? Freshman? Must be, looks like Jensi and Luca decided to go fishing for fresh meat." A blond Malfoy looking guy walked around and put his arm around the red head's shoulder, a group of guys following suit. Do people travel in packs here?

"Real original there, Derrick." Jensi pinched the bridge of his nose, "Go the fuck away."

Derrick laughed. "You know it does not work that way here," he drawled and sat down at the table with his friends.

"Okay," I finished eating and cleaned my mouth with a napkin. "So, tell me. How does it work here?"

"We don't have time to educate you," Trish huffed, clearly annoyed at being ignored. "Besides," she slammed her tray next to mine. Bold. "Derrick, don't worry about them, they were just leaving," Trish said.

"Actually, no, Malfoy, we weren't leaving. We're going to sit here, relax, and the rest of your sycophants can go sit in the dungeons or wherever assholes like you congregate for sacrifices."

"I think they generally hang at the cemetery, you know, at the grave of Voldemort's dad," Remi spoke up happily.

"Ah yes, bones of my father unwillingly taken and all that. Fucking Death Eaters." I nodded calmly.

"Fuck this." Trish reached around to grab my tray. Horrible mistake, really. I mean, we clearly warned her; we even tried to be nice, I think. I quickly turned, grabbed her arm, pulled it behind her, and smashed her head into the table. It got quiet then.

"What? Not going to defend your friend?" I looked at her group, then at her boyfriend. "Derrick? What about you? Not going to stand up for her now?"

"I don't know. I mean, I should. But there is something about a gorgeous girl pinning another girl beneath her that does it for me." He winked and took a bite of his food. Pig. Trish growled and bucked underneath me, but I laughed.

"Yeah, not that easy. You'll actually need some skill," I joked. Remi, Jensi, and Luca shake their heads with a smile.

Suddenly, Professor Blair walked up to the table as Trish screeched that I was going to pay or some stupid shit like that. Shut the fuck up, slyther-whore.

"Hudson, want to explain why you are holding a student down on the dining room table?" Blaire asked calmly.

I blinked and looked at him with my head turned to the side. "Because killing her would be frowned upon?"

Remi busted out laughing, Luca choked on his juice, and Jensi had to hit his back. Blair shook his head, a frown on his face but laughter in his eyes.

"Hudson, please, let her go. You're making a scene," he said as he looked around, prompting me to look and see the guys also staring at my direction, texting furiously. I'm sure I would have a shit ton of messages in a few moments.

I pouted. "Fine, I shall let her live, but she should know that Voldemort died in the end." I released her and grabbed my things to go. Class was going to start soon. Derrick and his friends' eyes laser focus on me now that I'm standing up. Xena stood up and swiped Trish's tray off the table and roared furiously. I laughed at her reaction and rolled my eyes.

We started walking out of the dining room with Remi linking with my elbow, and Luca and Jensi bringing up the rear. I guess I have my own posse now. See? I'm a big kid now! Professor Blaire saw us out, and stood closely as he watched us leave "Yes, well, be that as it may, Ms. Jacobs," his eyes twinkling, "they did kill Sirius Black," he said with a straight face. I burst out laughing, drawing the eyes of the students near us.

"Professor, you're not giving me much incentive to stay away." I wagged my finger jokingly.

He shrugged. "High society was never my forte, neither were the pretenders. Some of them need to be knocked down a peg, and I think you'll be the one to do it. Just try to not draw too much attention to yourself. Although, I have a strong feeling it was too late for that the moment you graced these halls." Xena growled, deep in her throat.

Bad man smells evil.

At that, Blair walked off, and I stared after him. Luca whistled and Jensi looked at Blair with a frown.

"He was definitely flirting with you there, Hudson," said Luca with a low whisper.

"Yeah, I'm not sure I like it, really," added Jensi. "Not like that. I mean, he kind of gives me the creeps. Always did. Spends more time tutoring the female students than any of the other professors here."

I frowned, was he flirting with me? Remi was also frowning.

"Hmm, yeah, I think he was. Well, I guess there is only one thing left to do." Remi smiled.

"What would that be?" I asked. She leaned in close to me and bit my ear. "Show them you're mine. I'm willing to share with Hunter, Ryder, Grayson, and Zane, but everyone else will learn to back off," she said with a smirk and gave me a peck on my lips, and I laughed as we started walking in the direction of the classrooms.

"Jensi, Luca, what's your schedule like?" Remi asked, hers in her hand. Jensi passed her his and she passed him hers.

"This is a senior schedule," Luca said, looking over to the paper in Jensi's hand.

"Yup, we're in the accelerated course," Remi explained. They continued to chat as I pulled my phone from my jacket, tuning them out.

HUNTER- Who are those boys?

GRAYSON- I punched two people already, I would rather not punch more.

HUNTER- How do you not feel your phone vibrating?

I rolled my eyes at the earlier messages and ignored them. Charming. They are willing to play four dick hockey, but get jealous if I try to make guy friends. Yeah, I won't dignify that shit with a response.

ZANE- It's only been forty-five minutes. How could you have possibly needed to be escorted out the dining room already?

HUNTER- Jensi Grey and Luca Adams, seniors, 4.0 students, competitive swimmers. Grew up together, mom and dad all work with the council. They are pretty well off and Luca drives an all-black Maserati and Jensi drives a deep green Aston Martin. Luca was potty trained at two and Jensi at three. They both have sisters and brothers that graduated from the school, and they live over in the west side dorms.

GRAYSON-

RYDER- You know, I was joking when I said you should find out when they were potty trained.

HUNTER- I don't see Hudson until lunch and until class, I had to let her know about her two walking corpses.

GRAYSON- I see her in a few minutes, looks like they are all in my class.

RYDER- Smh, fucking weird, Hunt, just fucking strange. They are in my class too.

ZANE- Mine too

HUDSON- You guys are ridiculous . Zane, that bitch started it, she had to die. Well, she got her head slammed into the table, but same difference. Hunter, you're such a creep, they are nice and respectful, so leave them alone. They haven't even flirted like the other guys who were at the table. Ryder, to be fair, no one knows if you're joking or ever being serious.

HUNTER- Who the fuck was flirting?

GRAYSON- We are talking after class.

ZANE- Who? Answer the question.

RYDER- Ah, fuck. Sorry babe, they are crazy.

HUDSON- Bye, see you later. Xoxo. Love you.

I laughed as I put my phone back in my pocket and I couldn't help the smile on my lips, despite the whispers of the new girl hitting a senior filling the hallways. It's good to have a few friends and it felt good to have the guys just a text away. I don't think I have ever had a moment where I wasn't ridiculously lonely.

CHAPTER ELEVEN

Walking into class was like walking into a different time zone. No, seriously. The room was dark with huge stained-glass windows, an arched ceiling, with just enough light to see clearly, and the desks looked worn. Not at all like HGTV artistic worn furniture either. More like if I sit here, I either may get a splinter or impregnated by wood. I didn't like either option. The desks were set up in a semicircle formation, I'm assuming for the practice portion of the class, so, naturally, Remi and I settled in dead center, making sure I had the perfect view of the class, not Grayson or anything. In all honesty I was a great student, so I had no qualms about being in an advanced program. I don't expect to really break a sweat. Jensi and Luca settled down on either side of us and we fell into an easy conversation.

The other students were starting to file in and of course, the cluster fuck of the seniors, AKA the merry band of cunts, from breakfast walk in. Trish sneered when she saw me, and I gave a little wave and blew her a kiss.

"She can blow me, not a kiss though; she's hot as hell," a random boy whisper shouted to his friends and they snickered.

"Shut your fucking mouth dickhead and show a lady some fucking respect before I shut your mouth for you," snarled Luca.

"We were just joking, Luca, calm down. You and Jensi can piss on her all you want..." He didn't finish his statement before Jensi was up and out of his chair, punching the kid in the mouth. I laughed, shaking my head. Yeah, it was good to have friends. I'm not sure what inspired this amount of loyalty so quickly, but I wasn't going to make them feel bad about wanting to. I did, however, ask them to calm down, assuring them that I'm more than capable of defending myself.

Noticing Trish still staring at me, I flipped her the middle finger and she turned red, flipped her bottled red hair and stomped to one of the seats, dragging Malfoy's doppelganger and her flock behind her. I rolled my eyes and caught Remi's smirk as she opened up her book and notebook. I followed suit, ignoring the fact that the senior boys were making lewd comments and the girls were throwing the evil eye. I sighed. I'm twenty, why was this still an issue? Xena walked around the room, walking close to everyone's desk, making them cringe, until she walked to the front of the room and sat down, staring everyone down.

Grayson stood in the middle with his arms crossed, now flanked by Xena, eyeing Jensi and Luca with a grudging respect in his eyes and I smiled behind my hand. My gentle giant may have been a little jealous, but I think he feels a little better seeing how quickly the boys defended me rather than being just as crude. He was dressed in grey slacks and a dark black button down, sleeves rolled up to show off his tattoos, paired with an expensive pair of Italian loafers. Basically, he looked like pure sex and an unexpected wave heat and possessiveness hit me so hard, I had to clench my desk until my knuckles turned white. I took a few deep breaths giving Remi a reassuring smile as she threw me a concerned look. I had no answer for her, it freaked me out a little too. I shrugged it off and focused as much as I could.

Grayson gave off an air of power as he looked at the students and gave them what was supposed to be a welcoming smile, before his smooth voice filled the room without him having to raise his voice. "Welcome to Magical Theory and Practice. Some of you are here for the first time," he nodded to me and Remi, "and some of you I've had as my students for years. We will not be slowing down, and we will be jumping right into where we left off." I shuddered as he finished, his voice affecting me on a cellular level. What the fuck was going on? Trish, of course, noticed my small movement and smiled.

"Professor Grayson." her voice grated my nerves. "It looks like one of our new students may be a little nervous, maybe we should provide her with extra time before she is in this class?" Trish came off as sweet as a candy covered in ants and I rolled my eyes. Bitch.

Grayson looked at her with an eyebrow raised. "Really? That is unfortunate, like I said full speed again," he responded darkly, his voice and gaze pinning her to her seat. He moved to the center of the room and started his lesson. "So, as we all know, magic can take many forms when you are practicing; think of our usage of elements, for example. Logically, it stands to reason that you can control that form, like using those elements to create fire and then using it to attack. When considering 'form', you have to decide if you want a flame shaped into a ball, a blade, or even a throwing star; whatever you need to maximize your attack." He held his up and controlled fire in the palm of his hand, willing it to change shape as he spoke. Impressive.

"Keep in mind, you need a proper form to navigate that attack. Why?"

I raised my hand. "Otherwise, you lose control."

"Yes, you can lose control. So, what are some versions of proper form? Can anyone demonstrate?"

Derrick stood up and walked into the center of the room, bending his knees, one leg slightly back for balance, his arms above waist level. Grayson nodded. "Stay there, Mr. Derrick. Yes, that is one of the proper forms for controlling your magic, what else?"

I raised my hand again. "Mental form. You need to be able to clear your mind. Of course, it cannot be seen, but it is rather easy to tell if you have proper form as your attacks would be weak and you'll be harmed." Grayson, nodded.

"Hudson, front and center. Let's see if you have proper mental form by attacking Derrick."

I smiled and stood up and walked to the center of the room. Well, this just got interesting.

I took form and faced Derrick, forming my fire into a large ball, letting it hover and get larger and larger as my concentration increased. Derrick, eyes wide, formed his fire into a blade. I smiled.

"Okay, let's see whose mental form is stronger. You are both shielded. Essentially, to tell if your form is strong, throwing your fire shouldn't throw you off balance. Begin."

I threw my ball, and it engulfed his entire shield, burning brightly. Without the shield, he probably would have been incinerated. My stance was the same, my focus sharp. Good thing too, because when Derrick threw his attack, he fell back, and it aimed for my heart and I was not shielded. I quickly countered and pulled from earth to obliterate the fire, versus it hurting, or rather killing me, like it was intended to do.

"What the fuck?" I hear it echoed by Remi and Grayson.

Grayson frowned. "I shielded you. How the hell did that not take?"

"No idea, but it's going to take a lot more than that to hurt me. I realized last minute I wasn't shielded." I frowned, thinking.

"It's okay, we can figure this out later. I'll go sit back down." I smiled, my thoughts whirling. If I was a weaker person, I would have been injured or dead. School just started; who the hell would want me dead? I pushed the thoughts out of my head and focused on Gray.

"Okay so, moving forward," Grayson continued, a crease in his eyebrow.

"So, knowing we can control the forms our magic takes, you should be able to manipulate the magic to push through objects to fortify them in battle. Some push magic into objects to cause harm or cause good fortune. Rather, they cover them in magic, to be more specific."

A student raised his hand. "Professor, I am confused. Is that the same thing as infusing our weapons like we do with Professor Ryder, for combat?"

"Not necessarily, although the concept is the same. This would be more geared to making a sword stronger with a spell or pushing a bit of your magic into the sword, beyond that of coating it during battle. In effect, it is not visible." The student nodded.

Grayson's voice flowed through the room as he passionately described how we should be able to use magic to create and, in turn, destroy.

"So, what is magic? Trish?"

Putting her on the spot made me smile, but she tossed her hair and responded airily, "Well, Professor, it is a manipulation of what is around you."

"Close," he continued but I interrupted as I raised my hand. He raised his eyebrow with a smirk.

"Hudson." He nodded his head with a wave of his hand indicating for me to proceed.

"Magic is not only the manipulation of what is around you. Rather, it is a deep connection to the various elements and energies in the air."

"Correct." He smiled. "What are some of the limitations to magic?"

"Limitations are that you can only use what is in your immediate area," Trish responded.

"Not necessarily," I interrupted. "The various forms of manipulations do not necessarily have to be with elements in your immediate vicinity."

Grayson lifted his eyebrow. "Interesting. So, you're inferring that you can pull from energies that are, let's say, miles away? How do you manage to do that?" he asked. He looked genuinely interested.

"You can't. She's full of shit, there is no way you can pull from what isn't around you. That would take more power that anyone has," one of the students said. But before Grayson could respond, Luca threw a paper ball at him, I smiled and continued. I knew this information like the back of my hand from the insane amount of advanced studying I had to do, but also from what Kalen would go over during our various training sessions. He wouldn't let me just do the basic forms of magic; he taught me beyond that. What I assumed was advanced, was in all actuality less than basic. It was child's play. He taught me the strengths we can really have but warned me the dangers of a quick burn out, without consistent practice.

When we first began, I would tire quickly but got better. I slept like the dead after those training sessions. I was relieved that after my 18th birthday, the exhaustion never manifested again, I was able to always keep going. But of course, he trained me harder and harder and we still had not reached a bottom. During one of our cool down talks, he told me that magic had its limitations, however most of those limitations were due to lack of knowledge and/or willingness to do what was unknown. Those limitations just stopped applying to me, and, when I thought about it, truth was, I enjoyed the knowledge I was just one pantsuit away from ruling the world. Not really, but a girl could dream.

I raised my eyebrow and waved my hand towards him. "Despite the idiot over there, the power you have is internally driven." I nodded my head and clapped sarcastically. "Just like the standards for stages of growth as a person, your abilities grow the same way. The more you practice, the longer your endurance. Like training for battle or for sports, even. That being said, magic is energy and manipulation, right? You can infuse objects? Have you ever considered using the elements around you to infuse YOURSELF with power? Like magical coffee, it won't last forever, but it can give you a boost to continue to use your magic." I paused and looked around the room and caught Gray's eyes, flickering with interest.

"Now, the elements are everywhere. So, by definition, if magic is about a deep connection with oneself and the elements around you. Once you ground yourself, you should be able to pull from distances. Furthermore, it is about mental clarity. I'm sure you were all taught the merits of mediation?" Everyone nodded, Remi looked at me curiously. "Meditation isn't about sitting down and focusing only; that ability to touch the deepest parts of your soul can be achieved even when practicing. You need to breathe deeply and ground yourself to the very elements you wish to use. Magic is a gift to be used. If the elements rebel, it is because your ability to ground yourself is weak, and then you lose control of your magic, which is dangerous to you and others around you. Oftentimes, that is why some people rather use blood magic. They lack control but seek a way to ground themselves, even if it is unnatural. If you're connected to the energies, then they will infuse you further and add to your abilities."

Grayson nodded, eyes twinkling. "Ms. Hudson is correct, granted that was later in the semester. However yes, the better you ground yourself the more you can achieve with your magic. So where do we start? How do we use these theories we just learned and put them into practice? Does anyone want to give it a try? Ms. Hudson, these were your theories today, so you can come forward. However, I do need another volunteer."

I got up from the chair of splinter death again and walked into the center of the classroom to the collected whispers of lust, envy, and anger from Trish and her cronies. I keep a smirk on my face and ignore everyone. The only two people in this classroom I care about are Remi and Gray, and I guess a little of Jensi and Luca, though they were newer. Ha. Everyone else can eat a dick with ketchup. When no one raised their hand, Grayson picked a random student from the room named Brent. He was built like a swimmer, had striking blue eyes, messy blonde hair like he did it on purpose to look sexy, and a sharp jaw. In effect, to any other girl, he would be breathtaking. He walked up with a cocksure smile and sauntered to the middle of the floor. I rolled my eyes internally. Oh boy, pretty boy syndrome.

"Hudson, Brent is one of the strongest students here. I do think he would be a good match to bring out your theories. Now, I want you to both center yourself and pull a small amount of magic and try to, as Hudson said, pull from elements farther from you, and attack and counterattack. During this practice, you also MUST shield. If you don't protect yourself, that's on your shoulders; take responsibility." Grayson nodded and indicated for us to begin.

I didn't need to truly ground myself; I already was. It has become so ingrained in me that I'm constantly ready to protect myself. I focused on Brent and felt his magic building. Right as he brought his hands up, sliding his right foot back and slightly bending his knees, he threw a blue and green swirling ball of energy in my direction. As directed, I shielded in a different way. I smirked, as I brought up my hands and blocked the attack with a wall of flowing water and ice that came from my hands and I used the element to absorb his power back to myself. Water is in the air, therefore an easy element to wield, to absorb energy without taxing yourself. A few gasps went up around the room. If any one of them would have flipped through their books for this semester, they would have seen that you can absorb someone's energy in combat.

Grayson laughed. "I see someone read ahead. Go ahead, Ms. Hudson, counterattack."

I pulled my energy in a different matter. I used everything around me and beyond me and without a thought, sent orange, yellow, green, and blue swirling magic towards Brent, and he flew across the room and crashed into the wall, hard. The only thing that saved him was the fact that he shielded his body before battle. However, he was going to be sore. Oops.

Everyone ran towards him, making sure he was alright when a dark figure I didn't notice by the door started clapping. "Well done, Ms. Hudson, that was quite impressive. Mr. Brent," this man nodded as Brent got up a little red in the face and sat down, glowering at me, "I'm glad you shielded yourself adequately and are okay."

I was still confused and about to open my mouth to ask who he was, when Grayson spoke, "Mr. Alvor, what a pleasant surprise. Class, this is our new dean of students." Everyone murmured their hellos and he smiled warmly before settling his gaze on me once again. It was strange; I felt like I knew him, but I have never seen him a day in my life.

I took in this tall, muscular man with black hair that didn't seem right on him, and hazel eyes. He was dressed in an all black suit that was tailored to his perfect body. He was quite the looker, and by the eyes of the girls in the room, they thought the same. Trish even removed the sneer from her face. She can actually look like a normal person. Shocker.

"Ms. Hudson, that was quite a display of magical practice. I did hear quite a bit of the class and my interest was piqued by your conversation as I was passing by. May I ask what combination of elements and manipulation you used in order to accomplish that?" he asked sincerely, yet there was something in his eyes; not necessarily curiosity, but a hint of wariness, caution and excitement, maybe? It didn't set me on edge exactly, but it made me less inclined to want to do anything in front of him. And a bit confused.

I replied with a sure voice, he may confuse me, but magic did not. "Well, sir, all the elements." I shrugged. "They could always cancel themselves out, but not if you can concentrate on keeping the forms separated just enough. Magic users often disregard that everything is made up of atoms. Atoms are nuclear energy, and theoretically, we should be able to manipulate those aspects of energy. If we can understand the science beyond nuclear weapons, we can use that to create a similar, yet nowhere near as destructive, unless intended, form of defensive magic. Like a rebound from the energy around him, that didn't necessarily touch him. Had he not been shielded, his injuries would have been from what he crashed into and he would have been knocked out, not killed. Theoretically, of course," I smiled at him. "Then again, he may have exploded, but I didn't think Professor would appreciate the mess." I smirked, as the class laughed. He quirked his head at me, tapping his long finger on his chin in consideration of what I just said.

"Quite extraordinary, I must admit." He then looked at Brent. "Mr. Brent, I hope you're okay, although you look no worse for wear. Wonderful." He clapped his hands and turned to Grayson. "Professor, I apologize for the intrusion, I'll go now. Marvelous class. I'm very impressed." He bowed slightly, as did Grayson as he walked out of the classroom.

Grayson cleared his throat. I was still standing in the middle of the classroom, not knowing what I should be doing. So, I lifted my head, and walked confidently to my chair, the murmurs now full of awe as well as lust. I don't really care either way.

"Professor Grayson, Hudson is clearly dangerous. You heard her; she could've made Brent explode! Should she really be allowed to practice in class anymore? This isn't a battlefield," Trish said shrilly, finally gaining her voice back. God, her voice was fucking annoying as fuck. Besides, it was a theoretical and practical application class. Buckle up, bitch, it's only going to get harder for her dumb ass to be anywhere near me.

Grayson sighed. "Ms. Trish, I highly suggest you can the attitude and try to learn something instead of being so combative. Save that for Professors Zane, Ryder's, and Hunter's classes. I do not have the patience for it." He turned away and started asking questions. I tuned him out as Remi ran her hand up and down my exposed thigh while everyone was listening. I turned to her and she gave me a wink. I smiled; something about having

Remi near gave me peace in a way I have never felt, other than with the guys, as if nothing could get me. I tap my pencil on my notebook absent-mindedly. Come to think of it, even with Kalen, I knew he would protect me with his life, but it wasn't that type of solace these five gave me. It was a deep sensation of being settled, I just wish I knew why.

CHAPTER TWELVE

When the bell rang, I packed up my things and let everyone leave, letting Remi know I'll be a few. Xena trotted off after the students, observing everyone. I had a few moments before my next class and I hadn't really spoken to Gray today yet, other than through text.

"Hey, handsome, good class today." I walked up to him with a smile and lightly caressed his arm. "I missed you this morning." I gave a fake pout. He laughed and warded the door so no one could come in.

"Yeah, you missed me so much you went and made a couple more friends I see." He raised his eyebrow and I laughed.

"Mmm hmm, jealous? Is that why you warded the door? Want to punish me, professor?" I said quietly.

His eyes flashed and he stepped closer, pushing me back to the desk, a shiver went up my spine. Mine, Mine, MINE, a whisper floated through my head, getting more and more insistent. I ignored it and looked up at him. So damn perfect. He put his hands under my skirt and gripped my ass, grinding against me. I bit back a moan. He laughed and leaned closer to my ear, "I love how quickly you respond to us, sweetheart. I admit this uniform has never turned me on until now. Now, I just want to see it off you." His eyes darkened and a smirk lifted his lips. "And yes, the professor is going to punish you," he said gruffly, one hand on my ass, one hand trailing up my thigh, and my breathing faltered.

"Hmm, what's the punishment?" I asked, looking up at him. He raised an eyebrow, and trailed his fingers past my shorts and panties, groaning when he realized how wet I was. How could I not be? I mean fuck, those tattoos, those eyes. God, he had this Lucifer next door look down pat. He radiated pure sex.

He looked at the clock. "You have 13 minutes before your next class. You're going to cum all over me," he whispered against my mouth, kissing me, sliding off my shorts, opening my legs, sitting me on the desk, and quickly unzipping his slacks. His dick fell out and my jaw dropped. I knew he had a Jacob's ladder, but my focus was on how big he was. He laughed when he saw my face. "Don't worry, Hudson, I'll be your gentle giant... this time." I shuddered at what would happen next time.

He opened me wide and ran a finger down my pussy lips and licked his finger clean and hummed. "Yes, you taste so sweet, baby. I'm going to fucking live between these thighs, but right now, you are so wet, sweetheart, and so ready for me. So, don't scream." He winked.

"Wha...." He went inside with one stroke, my new perch and his height perfect for him. I bit my lip so hard, I drew blood. Fuck, I was fucking stretched so tight. He pulled me to the edge of the desk and slid out and slammed back in again, making his desk shake.

"Fuck, Hudson, this pussy is so fucking tight. What the fuck?" he groaned, pushing me to lay down, my ass hanging off the table and my legs wrapped around his waist. His piercings were such a new sensation. Every stroke was making me pant with need.

Suddenly, my entire body got hot and I needed more, I didn't give a fuck about how big he was.

"Yes, Gray, yes, fuck me harder," I groaned. Hope the ward held out sound too.

"No problem, baby." He picked me up and bent me over his desk and grabbed my waist and thrust inside me again. I screamed as he pulled my hair with one hand, fucking me until I saw stars.

"Mmm, I love seeing this ass bounce on my dick, baby," he moaned, letting go of my hair and smacking my ass. "Eight minutes, sweetheart. You're going to come for me." He reached around and grabbed me by my neck, choking me while he flexed his hips driving into me. This height difference was a fucking delight. He grabbed one of my legs and set it on the table, driving into me and I came hard, clenching around him so tight, he cursed, and he had to really work to keep moving inside me.

"Fuck, Hudson, you drive me fucking crazy, baby. You're so fucking perfect. We have six minutes; you're going to come again for me, baby, then I'm going to fill up this pretty pussy," he growled, taking my leg off the table he pulled me off the side and turned around, so he was against the desk instead. "Bend over and touch your fucking toes, Hudson. You're not getting any fucking mercy from this dick." He smacked my ass and spread my legs further, I bent forward grabbing my ankles, Grayson kept me from falling over while he pounded into me, this angle hitting every spot making me moan and clench uncontrollably. He worked a finger into my ass, and I came, my entire body shaking, and he cursed and came inside of me a few thrusts after. I stood up shakily, flipping my hair back and picking up my panties and shorts while he tucked himself away. He grabbed me and kissed me while fixing my skirt and helping me tuck in my shirt quickly. So fucking sweet, even after being a savage.

"You can go to class now, Ms. Jacobs, but you're not allowed to clean yourself up. You're going to drip with my cum all fucking morning." He bit my lip and smacked my ass as he ushered me out of the class. Okay, maybe not so fucking sweet.

Luckily, that insistent voice in my head receded. I walked into Professors Logan's classroom, Remi, Luca, and Jensi waiting for me near the front. The room had the same overall look as Grayson's class, except all the chairs faced forward in rows. I'm starting to see a theme; they were all watching way too many magic themed movies. I felt my phone vibrate in my pocket and looked discreetly.

GRAYSON- Jensi and Luca are good, they almost beat the shit out of some kid mouthing off about Hudson.

HUNTER- Who was mouthing off? I'll kill them.

RYDER- Noted. First class and these fucking kids couldn't infuse a cup with water from a fucking sink. I need a drink already.

ZANE- I agree with Hunter, and I'm teaching a freshman class to help out a new instructor, and they can't fight worth a damn. I don't know what they are teaching in these secondary schools, but I second the drink comment.

HUDSON- You are all distracting. By the way, send dick pics, thanks.

I switched my phone to silent as Professor Logan greeted the entire class, gaze lingering a little on me and Remi. "Hello again, students, let's just jump right into it. This term we will be delving a little deeper into our magical history. Now, we all have learned the basic governmental bodies, how they came together, and how they control the magical population by making sure everyone adheres to certain protocols around humans. Also, on why we focus so strongly on a curriculum that includes heavy defensive and offensive magic; for example, career choices and protection of our people and our counsel from outside forces. But does anyone wonder beyond the simple history of actual magic and instead the source of magic?" His voice wrapped around the classroom like a lullaby and an energy drink at the same time, and we were woven into his words. Someone had responded with what we were taught that the earth and elements were the source of magic and only a few were able to manipulate it. It was all pretty basic information, and I was just enjoying the relaxing atmosphere of the classroom, basking in my afterglow, until I looked at Remi, who was hyper focused and tense. I frowned and tuned back to what was going on.

"...entities, who are pure magic mating with humans," Logan completed his statement. Wait, what? Remi scoffed, and various students raised their hands.

"Professor, do you mean like Gods?" a short girl with glasses asked from the back of the room.

Logan smiled. "No, no, a lot purer, Megan, born from the earth itself, pure energy, and magic from the elements themselves."

Remi didn't bother to raise her hand. "Professor, if that were true, wouldn't that be the same thing as being born from the Goddess Gaia? Therefore, the derivative of magic would indeed be from the Gods bestowed upon certain families and therefore passed through their lines until it was diluted enough to just be magic and not Godlike powers. It doesn't seem logical for anyone to be born from energy," she said with disdain and menace in her voice. What was up with her? This was interesting; the possibilities of the routes of our magic. It's one thing Kalen never really went into detail about during our long conversations.

Professor Logan stared at her for a minute before responding, "That would make sense, yes, but this is why this class is complex history! We need to look at this from all angles and delve into the most outlandish of theories. As often, this is where those who study history find more than mystery, they find the truth," he finished, his eyes gleaming.

I must have tuned out most of what was going on earlier because before I knew it, he was dismissing the class but not before assigning a ten-page single spaced essay on the possibilities of various origins of magic and why they could be important, due Friday. I could've been imagining it, but he stared directly at Remi when assigning the assignment, her jaw ticking as she refused to break eye contact. He then turned and gave the class a warm smile and said his goodbyes.

We stepped out of the classroom and headed into the bathroom in between this room and our next room. I grabbed her by the arm and had her face me. She looked furious. I just couldn't figure out why. "Hey, Remi, Mimi, what was that about?"

She looked at me, her eyes blazing, something flickered in her eyes and they briefly... changed colors? She closed her eyes and took a deep breath before she opened her eyes again and they were back to normal. It must have been a trick of the light, the bathroom did look like a replica of the girl's bathroom on the third floor in Hogwarts. I have expected Moaning Myrtle to pop up. *Seriously, too many freaking movies.*

"Nothing, really, except I hate when people try to teach and present myths and old bedtime stories as truth. The way he got excited about it, as if it was true, just upset me that's all. He was overly excited about teaching fairy tales for a history teacher." She tried to smile but it fell flat. "I'm okay, and I'll do the damn paper and reference Walt Disney and Tinkerbell as my sources, that will piss him off and I'll feel a little vindicated." I laughed, and I used the bathroom. I laughed again when Remi came out putting chafing cream in her bag like I had just done. Anyone who says having a butt this plump and thighs like this, and not needing chafing cream, were filthy liars.

I washed my hands and turned to Remi. "Hey," I said, "the class itself is interesting. It's cool to see how he weaves myths and tries to tie it to history. It may not be ideal, and it may not be rooted in truth, but it helps us think and really come up with our own theories. Yeah, he may have seemed a bit over the top, but just enjoy the class at face value and don't put too much stock into it. It's not worth it. Just take it all out during training," I finish with a laugh and she gives me a real smile, finally, as we head out of the bathroom and start to walk to our next class.

She bumps my shoulder when we're outside. "So Mimi? Is that my new name? I like it." She pressed a kiss to my lips, briefly caressing my tongue before biting my lip with a smile. God, being the same height had its benefits.

"Ugh, the fucking hot girls always end up together. I wanted a crack at the new girl. That ass is fucking amazing. God, she must be so hot in bed."

"I don't know, I did some asking around. I heard she lives off campus with her stepbrother and the other professors. They probably pass her around."

I froze and had a quiet fury in my veins and turned around to see some of the boys that we saw at breakfast.

There was a difference between lewd, whispered wishes that women were pretty much trained to ignore, and then there were guys like this. Comments that could implicate the guys in anything untoward, degrading shit that was impossible to ignore, and anything hateful towards same-sex couples, that shit does *not* fly with me. Of course, the moment the comment was made, Zane was walking by. He turned, pissed as fuck. Knowing him, his would fucking kill a student. Can't have that, so I stepped up to the group of guys.

Unfortunately for them, Xena chose that moment to materialize out of nowhere and stalk towards them too. The fear in their eyes sent an unfamiliar thrill of excitement down my spine.

"Who said that?" I said quietly.

The rest of the hall seemed to get quiet as they looked on, walking to class. A cocky, redheaded 20-something-year-old, with no hair on his chest, but at least a decent physique, stepped forward. He would have been cute, if he wasn't a pig.

"Relax, Hudson, is it? Think of it as a compliment. I'm quite the catch," he laughed.

I scoffed. "I'll take that with a grain of salt. You seem to know my name already. Wonderful, saves me the trouble, but like I asked, who the fuck are you?"

"I'm Justin, you may recognize me from this morning. We're at the top here. You'll do well to remember that." He sneered, then tried to grab my hand and I leaned back, a snarl on my face. He laughed. "Anyways, what's up, baby? Did you want to stop being a dyke and be with a real man?" He laughed and his friends followed. They expected a reaction. That's okay. They will get one. Just not one they expected.

"Dyke, real clever." From the corner of my eye, I noticed a massive snake making its way towards the group. In a second, it had wrapped around his legs and knocked him down, fangs drawn, hissing menacingly. Xena started circling the group. I smiled as his face turned red and fear leaked into his eyes. It was intoxicating.

I stepped forward and leaned against the red brick wall in the hallways. "So, I take it you're a senior then. Cool. You realize that means you'll be in my combat classes? Let's make a little wager." I looked at Zane and he nodded his head, a tenuous control over his emotions. He knew I could defend myself. I needed him to take a deep breath and just hang back and let me handle it.

"We fight. You win, you can have me, anyway you want me." My tone laced with heat. "I win, and you become my bitch."

Justin looked up at me and scoffed. "Yeah, as if this frigid bitch could ever beat me in anything other than a dick sucking competition." Zane growled at bitch. I laughed.

"Good to know you like sucking dick, I'm sure you all take turns in the locker room. That's cool, I'm sure your girlfriends now know where they all got the chlamydia from." I pointed at them, "Sharing is not caring boys," and I fake shook my head.

"Listen, bitch," Justin's friend started as he stepped closer to me. I punched him straight in the jaw and he fell back onto the floor. His friends let him fall, not expecting him to get hit. I stood on top of him and crouched low.

"The other insults were a freebie, but you're not going to disrespect me. In fact, I don't even know your name yet, but you can be a part of the game as well." I looked around and saw Hunter, Ryder, and Grayson, and even the Dean near, but he didn't intervene. Strange. "We're going to go at it alright, baby," I sneered. "Just not the way you wish you could," I said it loud enough for my voice to carry. "In fact, I'm going to make it my mission today to take on your bitch asses and beat your asses in every class that involves any form of combat. I would ask permission but, truly, I don't give a fuck. You're vile and disrespectful and need to be taught to keep your mouths shut." I turned and stood up from my crouch and quirked my eyebrow; surprisingly, the professors and even the dean nodded.

"Cerberus, come," Remi said low, the snake hissed and was suddenly gone. Xena threw her weight at the rest of the guys and they shrieked and jumped back.

I laughed and turned around, faced the crowd, crossed my arms and smiled. They walked away quickly. I sighed and rubbed my temples. "Fuck, first day of school and I'm in a low budget fucking sitcom," I muttered. I waved at the guys who looked ready to burst, and quickly walked to class with Remi, Jensi, and Luca, who were both ready to exact their own revenge. Today was turning out to be a blast.

Before walking into class, I reached out to Xena, who was still following and looking very agitated, *"Xena, go hunt. I will meet you at home at the end of the day."*

"I want to eat people." She looked at me with wide eyes and I chuckled. Bloodthirsty, just like her momma.

"No, silly girl, I'll handle that. I will fill you in on the rest of the day later." She growled and ran off into the wooded area. I smiled and shook my head.

Blair

I leaned against the hallway wall watching the entire interaction with Hudson and the other senior boys, and it made my fucking dick hard watching all that sass. All I wanted to do was part those thick thighs and sink into her fucking juicy pussy. It's all I have been thinking about since I saw her walk into the party in that skintight dress that left nothing to imagination. She was sexy as fuck and I found myself drawn to her in the strangest of ways. I yearned for her. Every time I looked at her, I wanted her, brutally. I adjusted myself and made my way to my next class where I can stare at Hudson and fantasize for the entire hour.

I walked into the class and stayed behind the desk to hide my hard dick from the incoming students. Hudson and Remi sat front and center. Hudson was in that short ass skirt, if she opened her legs, I'm sure I would see that pussy. When she jumped off her bike earlier, I got a glimpse of creamy golden inner thighs and had to bite back a groan. That pussy was going to be mine; it was promised to me already. Regardless, it would have been, even if I had to take it. She will want it though. I saw the way she was with Ryder, Hunter, Grayson, and Zane. She was fucking them; I know she was. So, she would be willing. I'll have her screaming my name, and scratching my back. She will want it. The female students here always do want it in the end. Even if she fought, that was okay. Sometimes, they fight it at first, but in the end, they give up, be it by force when I break their spirit or when I break their pussies. Recently though, I find they prefer it when they bleed. Or was that me? It didn't matter anyway. *Mine.*

Remi

I sat down in my seat and took my supplies out, quietly. Despite my ire, which was evident by the way Cerebus popped in, I let Hudson handle the situation. She needed to figure out how to handle shit like this without anyone stepping in. So instead, I looked around cautiously, sensing something unnatural in proximity. Then, I noticed the strange way Blair was staring at Hudson and it made me cringe. I looked over at Jensi and Luca, who were sitting next to us and I saw the curious looks on their faces as Blair's stare intensified. It certainly wasn't my imagination then, I picked up on the danger coming from him this morning. He was someone I needed to watch for, and I'll be sure to mention it to Alvor. We may need a different Human Studies teacher before this semester has even started.

Fuck, this was becoming more complicated by the fucking minute. Logan, with his fucking theories, unstable students thinking with their dicks, and now, a potential stalker teacher.

We surmised that her presence would have the ability to pull out the best or the worst in people, and I had no doubt in my mind that this was going to be difficult, but it is one thing protecting someone as a duty, and then there was protecting someone you find yourself feeling more for. Everything becomes personal and more difficult to handle. Passionate people act and react passionately. You can't look at everything emotionally. I mean sure, in certain situations, it can make you stronger. It is often the ability to be compassionate that can make leaders great. However, emotions can cloud your thoughts, and those same leaders put themselves, and their people, in danger. It was a vicious cycle in the real world. I groaned internally; my heart, crazies, hornies, and stalkers, oh my. Yeah, shit just got real. I wondered how else this can become fucking worse.

Hudson

Human relations class passes by quickly, easily one of my favorite subjects, especially once I got over Blair staring at me. There was something off about that guy. Regardless, I loved the idea of integrating with humans peacefully and doing good in the world with our powers. The magic boards usually wanted to stay within their cities and never expand, but I always thought that was ridiculous. If you stayed within your own world and traditions, could you ever truly grow as a person, both intellectually and emotionally? If only people really understood that we could make so many positive changes in this world. It was a dream, but it was my dream. By the end of the class, we were assigned a five-page paper on the importance of human relations in a particular country of choice. I was excited about it and the endless possibilities. Remi laughed at my excitement but looked genuinely interested in my point of view and we decided to do the papers together during study hall tomorrow.

Lunch passed in a blur, the food delicious, but knowing I would be doing more strenuous activities before dinner had me filling myself with proteins and greens. I even grabbed an extra protein shake, freshly made, to go. We didn't see the assholes from earlier. They probably were preparing for the ass beatings of the day. Remi and I finished lunch and went to change for the second half of the day, where we were able to switch into tactical wear. For girls, that consisted of fitted stretch cargo pants with various weapon holders and a tight black crew neck tee and cargo boots. A lot of good that shirt did for me. My breasts were so big, the crew neck still showed my cleavage. I snapped a picture and sent it to the boys.

. . .

HUDSON- (Picture)

ZANE- No.

HUDSON- I wasn't asking for permission, asshole, this is what it looks like. 🙄

HUNTER- No one should be able to put on tactical gear and look like a wet dream. That shit looks more like a scuba suit. You sure you got the right size?

ZANE- No, she bought a toddler version. That shit is way too tight. Put on a sports bra or something.

GRAYSON- I prefer the skirt, your ass looked delicious making the skirt bounce, but this outfit outlines every curve. Those curves are ours. Your breasts look like they are about to pop out though.

HUDSON- I'm putting on a tighter bra so that they don't bounce and knock me the fuck out. But you're all sexist. Everything you guys wear looks all stretched out across your sexy ass muscles. You're all just pissed because my muscles come with tits.

RYDER- We aren't sexist, we're Hudson-ist. We don't care about anyone else. Besides, sweetie, we're mad because we can't see your tits right now, tease. It's a true tragedy.

HUDSON- That's fair (Sends picture of said tits)

I did put on a SheFit to keep the girls contained. The boys changing had looser fitting gear, but the effect was the same; we looked dangerous and bad ass. Muscles on display. The overall look filled me with excitement and full-blown blood thirst.

ZANE- Fuck! 😩

HUNTER- Fuck me! 😩

GRAYSON- Not okay. 🤯

RYDER- I'm only giving the people what they really want. 🤣😂

HUDSON- Okay all adjusted; I'm going to be late for class. My next professor is a real dick.

RYDER- No, but he does have a big one. 😉🍆

. . .

I LAUGHED AND LOOKED OVER AT REMI, WHO WAS DONE GETTING ready.

"Well, you look fucking hot." I smiled and walked over to her.

"Duh, it comes with the badassery. I mean, what bitch can pull off blue hair and tactical gear?" She rolled her eyes and giggled. An actual giggle. Adorable.

Yeah, Remi looked sexy with her fitted clothes and her soft curves on display, she was incredibly beautiful. She must have seen the look on my face because she gave me a soft smile. I have a serious crush on this girl, in my case, five times over. I've heard of people meeting "the one" and being so sure, but what the fuck does it mean when you meet five ones and they were all so different? I couldn't resist the voice in my head to be near them. I frowned; not an obsession, no, it was almost intrinsic. Almost as if I knew them on a base level, like DNA? Sigh, that is what it felt like. Even if Kalen would kick me for being impulsive, I wanted to embrace it.

CHAPTER THIRTEEN

I smirked, as I walked into class and saw that Justin and his cronies were already there, leaning against the wall in the room, devoid of any seating. I went to stand next to Jensi, Luca, and Remi. Ryder stood in the center of the room in all black, looking like he ate a McTruck sandwich. Jesus, he was so damn muscular and beautiful it made me ache. 'Mine, Mine, Mine, Mine.' I rubbed my head, discreetly. The voice was back, and I felt the urge to go up to him and just wrap my legs around him. I threw him a heated look and he gave me a soft smile before he cleared his throat and focused on the class.

"Two things," he started with his gravelly voice, devoid of his usual humor. "We're picking up where we left off last semester. Most of you still can't infuse magic into your weapons and after all these years, it's fucking pathetic. I'm not going to sugar coat it or make you feel good about it. I'm here to teach you and hope that you get it this time around. You need help? Fine. Let me know, or I can assign you a tutor. You need to fool around? Then you'll get the fuck out of my class. Second thing," he smiled then, "I hear there is an issue of disrespect and a challenge has been issued. I won't step in. I won't protect. I will observe. As will Dean Alvor." He nodded his head to the shadows where the dean stepped out. Fucking creepy how he keeps doing that, as if he can blend into it.

"Hudson and Justin, grab your weapons from the wall and then front and center." I walked to the wall without glancing at Justin and grabbed two short swords, while Justin scoffed and chose a long sword. If he hasn't learned that just because it's big doesn't mean you know how to use it, after four years, that's on him. I went back to the center, grounded myself and nodded at Ryder.

"Let this be a lesson for all of you. Never bite off more than you can chew." Ryder smiled and shook his head.

Justin smiled and replied, "Don't worry, dyke, I'll go easy on you. You heard the professor, you bit off more than you can chew."

"Oh, Justin, you misunderstood me. I was referring to you," Ryder said with a dark laugh and stepped back. "BEGIN," his voice thundered, turning me on.

My swords immediately coated with magic without a second thought and the class gasped, Justin still hadn't infused his weapon. *Pitiful. Oh well.* I stepped forward slowly with a smile on my face. His sword finally lit, but I had already started my swing and knocked his sword to the side and landed a kick to his chest and pushed him back. He advanced and swung the sword towards my neck, and I bent all the way back in a low bridge. Using my forearms, I flipped low and back up without losing my weapons, then pivoted while I crouched. I landed a roundhouse kick to his face, lifting my weapons and knocking his sword to the side. He stumbled to the side with a snarl, and he stepped back and circled me. I felt him pouring magic into his weapon, trying to build his next attack.

Never give your enemy a glimpse into your next attack. I didn't need to pour magic into my weapons. As I tried to explain in class this morning, we are magic. He pointed the sword at me and let loose a particularly strong spell that smelled of decay. I narrowed my eyes, hoping that it wasn't what I thought it was. If it was, he turned a challenge of disrespect into an unnecessary death match. I threw my weapons up in a cross formation and applied a counter spell to what I suspected was a particularly nasty killing spell that ate at your flesh, and it rebounded and absorbed into my weapons, infusing my weapons instead. The class was quiet. A fury rose inside of me, I growled low in my throat. Ryder looked particularly pissed and Remi held Luca and Jensi in place, looking ready to beat their ass and Justin's ass. The dean's focus seared into me and he stared at me with interest, but I blocked them all out.

Seeing his spell backfire, he stepped back quickly, eyes flicking to the dean, and regrouped, walking around me. I ignored my past advice and while I followed him with my eyes, I filled my weapons. When he saw me coming, I advanced in two long strides and knocked his sword to the side as he tried to press his attack. We met in the middle and for a few seconds, all you heard was him grunting, our swords clashing. He stepped back, breathing hard, having used way too much magic to attack, and especially to use that last spell. Have to wonder how the fuck he learned that shit. It was my understanding that it was frowned upon to use death magic at DeLorean.

My intention went from beating his ass to really teaching him a lesson. You don't pull shit like that on anyone in a learning environment. Hell, even if you weren't in one, that type is rarely ever used. I stood still, not lacking in energy or strength, and he attempted to pretend he was on his "A" game, I simply winked at him as he swung his sword in a circle formation in front of him, trying to be cocky. I laughed, and he looked pissed. He swung, I tossed my swords in the air, turned on the ball of my feet low and knocked him on his ass, and caught my short swords, midair, in a quick spin. I walked over to him on the floor, while he still held on to his sword, attempting to use a spell. I crossed my swords over his, letting the steel clash and let loose a basic counter, and his sword went out. I kicked the sword from his hand and stood over him. My lit swords at his neck. I was feeling a blood thirst that was begging to be released and it took everything I had to reel it back.

"Yield, Justin," I said with a snarl, barely restraining myself. "Murdering skeeze. You can't just be one or the other, you gotta be both?"

"Fuck you, you got lucky we will see how lucky you are during the next class, or on your way home, or when you're alone in the hallway. Cunt." He spat at me. I froze. Did he just... was that a... this fucker threatened me. A thick voice unfurled in my mind; *you will not be threatened. You're the power they are, but a watered-down version of your majesty. No threat shall go unpunished. Kill.* I took my swords and brought them up over my head and drove them down as fast and hard as I could into his heart. At the very last minute, the Dean shielded him, but not before I was able to get a half of an inch of the blades into his chest. The blades were infused with a paralyzing magic, and I was going to use it to make his death slow and painful. Justin laid on the floor, shock on his face, not being able to move, but his fear was leaking through his pores, boosting my high.

I pivoted and snarled at the Dean, and he held his hands up. "Easy, Hudson, come back to yourself. Everything is going to be fine. He lost, and I prevented him from being killed. You would have regretted it otherwise. You know it being your first day and all, murder isn't good on your transcript," he tried to joke, the concern, more so glee, clear in his eyes.

Ryder came up behind me and touched my back and I calmed instantly. The Dean looked at him for a second and then nodded approvingly, then clapped. "Well then, that was an exciting show of power and abilities. I highly recommend that you all learn that your words have consequences. This year is a little different. There will be no petty calls to parents and swinging money around. This year, every issue will be dealt with in combat." The class gasped and began to protest, and he held another hand up, "And no worries, your parents have been informed, so calling them will have no effect either. Welcome, officially, to DeLorean University. I suggest you truly start to care about the things you say, because I promise you, the next person will. Spread the word."

The Dean left after waking up Justin and healing him. "Can't have you weak, can we?" he said happily, as if he was talking about unicorns and rainbows. *What the fuck?* "You still have some classes with Ms. Hudson today, so I suggest you prepare mentally to see the rest of your comrades fall." He walked out of the classroom with a flare, and Remi just shook her head next to me. Jensi and Luca stood to the side, watching me from the corner of their eyes while they practiced with Remi. The rest of the class continued quietly while the students tried to infuse their weapons. I stood to the side against the wall, processing my sudden blood lust and how I almost lost it. No, not almost. I lost it. The fucking voice told me to kill, and damnit if the Dean wasn't there, Justin would be dead. Granted, not a huge loss, but shit. And what is worse? I wanted to kill him. It excited me; his fear driving a strange need inside of me.

Alvor

I walked quickly to my office, deep in thought, rubbing my dyed hair, still in shock to see it black instead of white. It was strange for sure. I sighed, so many changes in such a short time.

It took all I could to shield the students from Hudson's glow during her fight. She was truly magnificent and powerful, and would serve her destiny well, if she can be directed in the correct way. She hasn't come into her full powers and I just hoped that the wards would hold off those that would be attracted to her power, like starving vampires. Remi tried to look casual, but I knew this was hard for her. To be honest, I didn't expect to see the look of yearning on Remi's face and the fierce protectiveness. If my suspicions were correct, it was more than that.

Unfortunately, that was only heading to heartache and complicated decisions. I reached my office and closed the door behind me, sat down and sighed. Resting my hands on my desk, I lost myself in my thoughts.

I was drawn to someone once, it was unnatural. My heart ached for someone else now. I had goals, our home was steeped in tradition, in the need for power. It's why Hudson was important. Sigh, her and Remi, they were drawn to each other. Maybe I could use it to my advantage. Gaia knows my last attempt failed.

I knew the men would be drawn to Hudson, always being in close contact with Hudson, her energies and power, but Remi? Not only was it unexpected, but it is also unprecedented. I didn't know how to protect Remi. In all my years, I was swimming in uncertainty, and uncertainty led to blind decisions. No, I needed more information. Fuck, I never understood the word until now. So, double fuck!

Hudson

We only had a five-minute time frame to get from Ryder's class to Potion Making. He had been throwing me glances for the rest of the class, but I was lost in thought. Absentmindedly, I was infusing and defusing my weapons while I mulled over my thoughts. It isn't that I felt badly because that little fucking poor excuse for a man deserved it. It was more of the burning rage I felt to kill him. No... that wasn't right... it was more like to destroy him. I wanted to make sure he never lived again, at that moment.

Fair combat was one thing, but he tried to kill me because he was a saggy nut sack, so I defended myself. Period. I sighed as the class let out. Following everyone one out, I was pulled out of my thoughts when Ryder, standing by the door, blocked my exit and wrapped his arms around me. Remi and the boys nodded and left a few seconds before to, I assume, grab seats for our next class. Ryder, I tilted my head in thought, he was another thing spinning through my mind. The instant soothing sensation I felt when Ryder touched me, as if he grounded me, brought me back into myself, was incredible. It was as if he snuffed out the darkness inside of me at that moment. Why?

"Are you okay?" he asked and peered down on me. His hulking presence was overwhelming when I was only five feet five inches. I laid my head on his chest and breathed him in. Being with him this morning calmed me physically, in a way, but God, I wanted so much more. It was driving me crazy just being around them. At the same time, being around them calmed me emotionally. See? Confusing.

"Yeah, now that I beat the little shit, I feel better, and um," I hesitated, "thank you. I'm not sure exactly what you did but when you touched me, I felt better... so whatever you did... thanks," I stammered out. The cool Hudson being vulnerable was kind of lame, I admit.

He kissed the top of my head and tightened his hug, drowning me in muscles before smiling down at me, lighting up the gloomy thoughts. "Well, anytime you want me to touch you and make you feel better, just let me know. I'm right down the hall, you know." I rolled my eyes, if he wasn't trying to get me drunk, or run and fucked, he was always joking; he was so silly. I loved that about him. The ability to take tense situations and make them disappear, if even temporarily. Mine. Mine. Mine. Oh, shut up hussy. MINE.

"Ha-ha, yeah, well, I'll consider that. I'll see you later." I reached up on my tippy toes and grabbed him for a kiss, tall ass fucker. He grabbed me tighter and groaned, and I felt him get hard. I winked at him and crossed the hall to Alchemy.

RYDER- Kiss and run? I don't think that was in any of the books we read.😂

HUDSON- We can just write our own book.

RYDER- Dibs on the sex scenes.

I rolled my eyes, *of course.*

HUDSON- You can write the M/M scenes.👬

RYDER- Still totally down for that, M/M turn all the girls on. And who knows dicks better than dicks?

HUDSON- We are getting married, set the date. 😍

RYDER- Vegas. Noon, tomorrow. Xoxo😘

CHAPTER FOURTEEN

I admit, I was totally prepared for the same type of dark room and worn tables for Potions, but when I walked in, I burst out laughing. Professor King looked up from the podium at the center of the room in the front, and smiled at me, laughter in his eyes. The room was set up with desks on either side, dark wood, worn, but not as much as other desks I've seen today. At least I wouldn't have a splinter baby by the time I left class. The room itself was very dark, and in the back of the podium was a staircase that looked like it led to an office. Professor King had his dark hair down instead of in a sexy man bun and had a black cloak on. I kid you the fuck not, he designed this room to look like Professor Snapes classroom in the Harry Potter films.

"Well, I'm glad someone picked up on reference for the new change in my room and attire," he chuckled.

"You change it every year?" I inquired walking up to the front of the classroom and sitting next to Remi. Jensi and Luca were next to us in the nearby row of seats.

"Yes, last year I had it set up like the city of HalloweenTown, no one got it then either." He rolled his eyes dramatically and I laughed. "No, Hudson, you're the first to get any reference to my magic movie addiction. Now, everyone, turn to page 394." He tapped a wand on the podium. He smiled and I literally had to hold my belly as I cried real tears from laughing so hard. He laughed and once we were both back to normal, the entire class was just staring at us.

Of course, some little bitch angry asshole had to speak up, her nose in the air. "We don't concern ourselves with human movies that depict magic. They are beneath us."

King rolled his eyes and gave her a soft smile. "That is unfortunate, Ms. Janie, as you would have learned in your first year of Human Studies and Relations, knowing how people without magic perceive us as well as how they believe they can identify us as different, is very important to not only your survival and safety, but for those in the community as well." He clicked his tongue in disapproval. "You must learn to think outside of your self-imposed bubble, otherwise you'll be as much of an empty shell as the others in our society who refuse to see reason. The word progression exists for a reason," he finished smoothly, maintaining a sweet smile on his face. I blinked. I genuinely think that being kind is just ingrained in his personality, you cannot fake that kind of look in your eyes.

She looked at him with indignation. "Are you insulting the Councils?" The class started to whisper at her words.

He kept a serene expression on his face. "Not at all. What I'm saying is, eyes forward and let's begin our Potions Mastery Class. Any questions pertaining to the values of Human Relations can be taken up with Professor Blair."

He ignored any further comments and started his lesson on the use of certain elixirs that can improve strength when failing during battle. I instantly loved him. Now this is a person I can see myself being friends with; a genuine kindness that superseded any malice.

"Now, class, what would be the benefits to using elixirs in a battle versus using them in real life?"

Remi raised her hand. "In battle, some elixirs will hone your strength and magnify your abilities. This is also true in non-battle situations. However, when in battle, the elixir blends with and feeds off of your adrenaline, but when in regular situations, it draws upon your regular energy, therefore the temporary boost will end up giving you something akin to a hangover."

King nodded and smiled. "Exactly, Ms. Remi. What else? Someone else this time." Jensi raised his hand, King nodded. "Mr. Jensi, go ahead."

"Sir, it makes you addicted to the elixirs."

King nodded. "What else?" He pointed to Luca. "Mr. Luca."

"Once addicted, the energy made to use the elixirs, and then taking said elixirs, will cancel out then eat at your body. Your body will start to deteriorate, and sometimes your mind too, depending on the severity of the addiction," Luca finished.

"Good, now is there a cure for this? Class?" I raised my hand.

"Not a known one... or rather... not a viable one, sir..." He raised his eyebrow and I continued.

"One of the problems with consistent use of elixirs is just like Luca and Jensi mentioned, addiction and deterioration. Magic is energy, so when energy cannot be contained in its form, it will be let loose back into the environment around them... when people started to die hundreds of years ago, they sought a way to cure themselves before essentially exploding... ancient texts studied by magical philosophers hinted at a race of beings that were pure magic and therefore, could save the body of the addicted."

His eyebrows rose even higher and Remi stiffened beside me. I had once snuck into my fathers' Council's libraries and read some of the older texts in my fathers room. When I asked him, he said they were written by a philosopher who was a bit addled. However, the next time I went to look at the book, it was gone. I know these 'origins' clearly made Remi uncomfortable, but the best growth is not brought along with comfortability. Admittedly, I didn't think it was truly possible for a being, in general, to save someone whose addiction had grown so great, their minds and bodies started to truly deteriorate.

"Now, I don't necessarily believe that, so the solution hinted at isn't possible. However, I do have some theories beyond that," I finished.

King hesitated before speaking, "Yes, well those ancient philosophers did indeed touch on that. Truth is, there is no proof, nor has there been any proof of such beings existing. Magic comes from what is around us; our elements and energies..."

I interrupted, "Yes, absolutely my point. The problem with the addictions is that as the mind and body fails, the energy is more potent. The body, which is technically the host of our energies, tries to fill these cracks the only way nature knows how, by trying to heal itself. It starts to draw more energy, like a solar light used by humans. Those addicted, in effect, become almost nuclear..." I tapped my fingers against my desk and leaned forward. "So, while we cannot cure the body or the mind from deteriorating, much like, again, humans who suffer from Alzheimer's or severe cancer, theoretically, another magic user can help those suffering pass in peace by absorbing that excess magic into themselves instead, to avoid anyone getting harmed by the explosive release of energy." Trish sneered at that.

"No one could possibly do that, could they, professor? They would be subject to the same death. No one person can hold that much power in their bodies and survive, so you'll have two releases of energies and a bigger problem." She rolled her eyes.

I nodded, "You know, she would make a good point, however," Trish turned bright red and curled her fists, *so extra*, "before I was interrupted, Professor King, there might not be one person who can but rather a large group of people who can absorb it instead. In Professor Grayson's class, we discussed imbibing tools with magic. We also theorized pulling magic from distances beyond our normal range. If you wrap all that up then ideally, small boosts of power can be given from other magic users in times of need. Technically speaking, souls are beyond our range so this would be the same thing, rather, absorbing instead. Just reversing the process with enough focus. Because of the deteriorating mind of the user, it won't be as if we are forcing magic from a user unnaturally, therefore causing one to fall into darker magic, rather the mind will give freely because it has no choice to. In theory, it isn't difficult."

King nodded, eyes bright, burning to ask me the question on everyone's mind, how did I know that? Well, I practiced with Kalen. They didn't need to know that though.

"Yes, well that is one possibility that would require research, trial and error, but everyone is right, in both facts and possibilities. As possibilities are simply the beginning for something new. I wanted to start you off with this information, class, because senior year tends to be very taxing; you'll be pushed, tugged, and tested. You'll be exhausted, and you'll want to come to class, maybe learn how to gain energy, or make an elixir without my consent or assistance and possibly cause yourself more harm than good. Or, and I hate to think this of my students, make any type of elixir that will cause harm to a fellow classmate. I will warn you; I will always come up with an antidote. There is a reason I'm in this position. I have a certain affinity for it. However, you will not be welcome back to this University, nor any other University, as you'll be brought up on charges for attempted harm to another magic user by the councils. So, do not test me; in this, I will show no leniency." He ended with a fierceness that fit his character for the day. Yup, definitely loved him. He will be my squishy. I will make sure he knows that.

By the time we wrapped up our discussion, it was time to head out to our next class. Before I was able to leave, King called me and asked me to stay. I smiled at Remi and the boys, who went ahead, and I sauntered over to my squishy.

"Yes, Mr. Squishy?"

"Squishy?"

"Yes, I like you and I usually hate people. So, you shall be mine and you shall be my squishy."

He groaned and smacked himself in the head. "A Finding Nemo reference? Really? Jesus, Hudson, you really know how to destroy a man's ego," he joked.

"Hey, hey, not every man gets to be my squishy. You should feel very honored." I jokingly punched his arm.

"Yeah, whatever," he muttered, and I laughed. "Anyways, I held you back for a few seconds to let you know to be very careful who you mention possible folklore and ancient whisperings to." I frowned, realization dawning from the start of our discussion.

"You're the second person today to get upset about this topic, so while

Remi explained she hated people teaching myths as fact, what is your excuse?"

He sighed and leaned on his dark desk. "Hudson, a lot of people believe those stories; fanatics if you will. They have led witch hunts, so to speak, to find people of these myths. They can be dangerous and unstable. I'm not saying this to freak you out, but what I am saying is, word gets around quickly. Don't fuel the fire."

"You might want to tell Logan that. He has us writing a ten-page paper about the validity and importance of old knowledge and possible roots of magic." He frowned, then sighed, then groaned.

"Yeah, I'm not very surprised. But yes, I'll talk to him about it. Anyways, come on, I'll walk you to your self-defense class. I hear there is going to be an epic showdown at high noon, and this cowboy doesn't want to miss it." I rolled my eyes as he threw his cloak over the podium and put his hair back up in the sexy man bun; *cute little squishy cowboy.*

CHAPTER FIFTEEN

We walked into the gym where we would be having our next two classes. I made eye contact with Zane and smiled slowly, his gaze becoming soft briefly; my heart skipped a beat. Ryder, Grayson, King, Logan, and Blair, along with Dean Alvor, sat to the side on the highest level of the bleachers. Did no one have a class to teach at this time? Goodness, I walked over and drank my protein shake while I waited for everyone to get settled in. Three hours of combat, I'm going to need it. I sighed as I finished, placing my bag down, and nodded to the guys who followed me and walked over to Remi, who, of course, was in the front.

"You know," Jensi said, throwing an arm around me. "You're gaining quite the reputation, little sister. I've had to nudge a few..."

"He means a lot..." added Luca, shoving Jensi and putting his arm around me, instead laughing as Jensi punched him in the shoulder.

"Yes, well, a lot of little fuckers in the hallway for talking about the new girl." I laughed as he stood and puffed out his chest and pretended to be Superman. Remi chuckled.

"Don't laugh, Remi. We saw you trip a few of the posse earlier with magic," laughed Jensi.

I raised an eyebrow at Remi, and she smirked. "Why, I have no idea what you're talking about. I'm a good girl." I laughed.

"Little sister?" I asked Jensi. I liked it. The only brother I had, well, we fucked. So, it would be nice to have one or two, in this case, that felt real.

He smiled. "Yeah, it fits you, I think." He leaned over and kissed my cheek, and I smiled widely. "But make sure you let them," he gestures at Zane and Hunter, who looked an interesting shade of red, "know that." I laughed and shook my head.

"No, but seriously, it's only day one and you have a few people gunning for you already. Give us your numbers. We want to make sure we can text each other if shit is about to go down and we need someone to hold a camera," Luca laughed.

"You guys are so extra, but yeah, let's do numbers at dinner. Sex, I mean class, is about to start," I licked my lips, looking Zane and Hunter up and down, and they groaned. "Groan all you want but those two," I pointed at Zane and Hunter and gave them a wink when they noticed me, "are a walking aphrodisiac."

"More like aphro-dick-siac," Remi muttered, and I busted out laughing, Jensi and Luca tittering next to me. Oh yeah, I found my fucking tribe. Then the demanding started. *Motherfucking, swoon. Damnit, his voice is pure sex.*

"Line up, now!" Zane barked at his students, Hunter following suit with a portion of his class, which was technically on the other side of the room. In effect, we now had both classes facing each other, and Hunter and Zane walked into the center of the section of the room we were in. Zane nodded at Hunter and then Hunter's voice echoed around the room. "We are going to do things a little differently today. Yes, it is your first day, but we are still picking up where we left off. Except, we are going to be somewhat combining classes. While there will be students practicing their weaponry and others hand to hand combat, others will be combining the two." I gave a slow smile. Holy shit, they were going to replicate what Zane and I did the other day.

Zane continued, "We recently learned the merits," he looked at me, "of fighting with both forms seamlessly. This isn't a fight with weapons to transition to fighting hand to hand. No, this is if you lose your weapons during a fight, you don't freeze up. You use everything you have to keep fighting despite losing your weapon. In class, the moment you lose your weapon, you call the fight. In real life, you die." Some shifted nervously, others looked excited to learn something new, others, like the "head" seniors, looked pissed. Ten dollars from me to me if they complain first.

"Professors, some of us," Justin's friend from earlier, who also needed an ass-kicking, looked at me, "have been doing this for years. It should be easy to do that in the heat of battle. I don't see why combining the classes has merit."

Zane and Hunter aren't your typical teachers. They weren't the jokester like Ryder, or patient until pushed like Gray. No, they were explosive first; Zane with his urge to protect, and Hunter with his urge to fight first talk later. Zane was now instantly pissed, and Hunter was pissed just because he was Hunter.

Zane barked, "You have a lot to learn if you think that by being here longer you know more. In fact, let's make an example of you, Mr. Alexander, come forward. Ms. Remi, you also come forward." Remi immediately stepped up to the mat, her hands behind her back, blue hair tied in a ponytail, looking in front of her but not before she threw me a wink and I blew her a kiss.

Alexander scoffed. "The dyke, protected by the bitch who got lucky. Yeah, I'm sure I'll learn a lot," he said loudly and laughed, a few people joined but most saw the showdown with Justin and I and looked away.

I immediately stiffened, anger flowing through me at his disrespect at my girl. Hunter and Ryder's eyes bored into me as I visibly restrained myself from a smart-ass comment. Jensi and Luca shoved their shoulders into me with a sure smile making the universal neck slash symbol for "he's dead". I chuckled.

Zane spoke low, "We already have two challenges today. Your words, Alexander, will have been up to Hudson, but since you're already on the floor, I guess that's being handled now. I believe Dean Alvor made his wishes very clear. I agreed then but now," he laughed, "now, I'm truly going to enjoy this lesson more than a teacher should." He stepped back with Hunter.

"You have your choice of weapons; no magic allowed," said Hunter quietly, barely restraining his anger.

Remi and Alexander went to the weapons wall and Remi turned back and asked, "Professors, how many weapons allowed?"

Zane smiled. "As many as you can fit on your person." Remi nodded. She put short knives, daggers, and a short sword across her back that came with a holster, which she adjusted to her, and she palmed a staff as her held weapon of choice. Alexander mocked her for needing so many weapons and Remi simply smiled and walked back to the center of the mat. Alexander had chosen a very sharp needle sword and a broadsword. It took tremendous strength to fight one handed with a sword like that. I wonder if he knew how or if he truly thought he could best her quickly without getting tired first. I have yet to see Remi fight, but I had a strong feeling that she was fast, quick and deadly.

"Oh, and unless there is danger of actual death, I will not intervene. Which means injuries will not be cause for a cease fire," Zane chuckled, "Begin!" Okay, fuck, I had a feeling that Remi would be fast, but she pulled out dagger after dagger and aimed them at the side of Alexander's legs, cutting him superficially but enough to bleed. The shock stunned him before he started to move. He went to swipe the sword down while swiping the needle sword towards her middle, giving her limited options. If she ducked, the sword would hit her down the middle, and if she moved away from the long sword the needle sword was still coming towards her. She could jump back, but he would press his attack unless she moved fast enough. But she could...

Remi smirked and quickly tucked and rolled going under his widened stance. *Sucked to be tall now mother fuckers*, I laughed to myself. She got up from her roll, spun on the ball of her foot and kicked him in his lower back, bringing down the staff on his head before he had the chance to react. Stunned, his grip on his weapons was weak as he tried to regain his balance, but he still had a hold until Remi used the staff and brought it down in quick succession, knocking both weapons out of his hands. He took a breath and turned around with a snarl.

I took note of the training that continued in the other classes. Behind them, the other class fought with their weapons seamlessly, looking well matched and sweating. They were impressive; Zane did teach them well. However, they had several small tells that would get them killed. I would have to let Zane know. The self-defense classes were beating the hell out of each other. I smiled. I loved the bloody nature of hand to hand. I loved to feel the fight, blood and bone on my fists.

It looked like Alexander kicked out and snapped the staff Remi was holding, essentially giving her two weapons now. She spun both and blocked his fists with the sticks. He was taunting her, and her face remained serene the entire time. For some reason, it felt like she was holding back, which was sexy as hell. Then Alexander had to run his mouth with more taunts, but now, those taunts were directed at me.

"It must feel good to lay between her thighs at night, lapping her pussy up, especially in a few days after Derrick and his crew fuck her. I hear they are running a train on her soon. I hope you're bi, because you're going to be a cum guzzler soon too." He laughed, panting in exertion. His words processed but it was just the wrong thing to say to Remi, to any of my guys really, including Jensi and Luca, who looked ready to join in.

Remi's eyes blazed, and she flipped back and threw her broken pieces to the side. She approached him with fury in her eyes and crouched, launched, and punched upwards in an arc, uppercutting him. He tilted back and she sidestepped, tossed an elbow into his ribs and while he was hunched slightly over, she jumped and punched down, smashing his nose. Blood spurted and instead of letting up, she kicked his legs out and he fell... hard. Groaning, with some hidden strength, he kicked his legs, knocking Remi down, but she used that momentum to turn, tuck, and roll then kick him in the face. Once, twice, three times, until he wasn't moving. She then got to her knees and punched him in the face in a one-two combo. He had already been down, but she was better than me; at least she didn't try to stab in through the heart. However, she stood up, stood back, looked at the class and licked the blood off her hands, her eyes flicking to everyone in the room and smiled, her teeth and lips covered in Alexander's blood. The class shuddered.

While the medics took Alexander to the infirmity, Zane spoke with a fierce pride in his tone, nodding at Remi. "Again, your words will issue the challenge, and your skills will speak for you. Don't talk if you can't back it up. It is the first day back and so far, two - soon to be three - students have had their asses handed to them by two new students. Now, that can mean you didn't train all summer or that they are simply better than you," Zane shrugged.

"Or it can mean that you're shitty teachers," said Trish. I groaned loudly.

"I swear," I pinched my nose before I continued, "You don't learn, you have been running your damn mouth all day. Try listening. You see those students over there?" I pointed at the students' training. "Sweating, kicking ass, all evenly matched. Clearly, they have been instructed well. Those teachers you want to call out so badly are unsurpassed in skill by most people. I'm sure if you fought them, they would kick your asses. Your fucking problem is that you haven't been challenged yet; Mommy and Daddy running to save you. You're too safe in your own bubble. If you aren't challenged, you don't learn. Thank goodness I'm here to save the day. I'm a fucking Powerpuff Girl." I shook my head.

"Professors, if I may, two things. I would like to fight both Justin and Trish at the same time. I would also like to fight Remi, who is clearly my equal if not better, to show them a few things." I smiled.

Trish rolled her eyes. "Now we're promoting domestic violence, great."

I smiled and my voice became low and husky. "It's not domestic violence if you like things rough, honey. You should try it. Maybe you wouldn't be such a bitch if you got fucked as well as I do."

She gasped and I turned around and ignored her once again. I looked at Zane and Hunter, their eyes filled with dark promise, oops.

Hunter cleared his throat. "Remi, if you're okay with that, we will have some time."

Remi murmured under her breath, "For which part." I laughed and winked at her. "Yes, we can do that tonight. I would like to add the magical aspect as well, to give a really good example."

I nodded. "Good point, in that case, Justin and Trish? Ready? Cool." I sauntered over to collect my weapons, my favorite choice of a scythe and short sword with a few daggers for good measure. I ignored them and their choices. It didn't matter anyway. I walked to the mat and twirled my sword short between my fingers and closed my eyes. Sometimes, your other senses told you more than your eyes did. I felt the attack, they swung at the same time, I would have done the same, which is why I knew they would be swinging from either side.

With a yell, I used my scythe and turned it in my right hand and pulled as I snatched a sword from someone's hands, and used my short sword to parry the other sword, while pivoting and kicking backwards, knocking down whoever was behind me on their ass. I opened my eyes to see Justin about to stab me in the neck with his other weapon and I bent back slightly and brought the scythe up to stop that blade, hard, and then roundhouse kicked his other sword out of my way, and it crashed to the floor next to me. Trish had gotten back up at this point.

I mentally regrouped; each of them had one weapon, and I had both. At this point, the best plan for them would be to take out my legs or at least one of my weapons. They would probably take out my legs, thinking it would be the quickest way for them to overpower me, and then take my weapons. I thought about all of this in less than a second- muscle memory. Knowing my legs were going to be taken out, I did the only thing I could do, I took a hit for a win. I jumped up and turned, putting me in the path of Justin's blade, but wrapping my legs around his hips jerking my body to the side, before jumping off, catching him off guard and while I rolled to the side, Trish knocked him down and sliced his back open, he let out a loud yell. Trish screamed at the blood, and I laughed low. When fighting multiple people, pit them against each other.

The slice I got was superficial, but as his blade was coming down, he did slice my shirt down the middle and scraped my stomach when I jerked up and to the side. My shirt is open now, some cleavage showing. Thank God for good sports bras though, whoop whoop. To avoid my shirt getting in the way, I stripped my shirt off quickly, much to the dismay of my men and Remi, who glowered, and much to the excitement of the other boys watching. Trish stepped over Justin with malice on her face and she pressed her attack with one weapon, throwing some impressive combinations and spins. Zane taught her well.

Except then she became predictable, I feel like Kalen was speaking in my head, "always watch for your enemy's patterns and also don't ever have a pattern." So, I never did, and I always watched closely. She was going to step forward with the right leg and arc the sword to come at me from the top, so I used both weapons, stopped the arc and jerked up slightly, bending her wrist enough for her to let go of her weapon. She growled, pissed, and took up a fighting stance instead. Justin never did get back up. Oh well.

I laughed and tossed my weapons to the side, her eyes widening in surprise. "No, bitch, I'd rather feel your face break under my hands than beneath a sword." I laughed and stepped forward, quickly fake punching her face to distract and instead kicked high, smashing her stomach and making her double over, while I punched her face from the side and made her neck snap to the left and then to the right as I followed up with another hit. She kicked out and instead of me landing on my back, I flipped up, arching over and landing in a crouch. I smiled and let her come to me and I circled her, playing around. I started to sing, just to piss her off.

"I'm a Barbie girl, in a Barbie world. Life in plastic, it's fantastic. You can brush my hair," I sang.

"Shut the fuck up, bitch," she snarled.

"You don't like that song? How's this one? Hush, little asshole, don't say a word. Hudson's gonna buy you a mockingbird and if that mockingbird don't sing, no refunds, bitch." I snickered.

She threw a kick and I sidestepped. "What? So, what if it didn't rhyme? It was solid work. People don't appreciate good artistry anymore." I sighed and I finished her off, kicking her in the face, and as she fell quickly, side stepped and punched her in the opposite direction, completely knocking her out. Justin was taken to the infirmary, so I shrugged and stood in the center of the mat while I reached up to fix my ponytail. I smiled and faked a bow. Remi shook her head, but what I noticed was the smirk on the

Dean's face. I still don't trust the fucker. The students looked at me and Remi in awe and grudging respect. This is the way it should be in the movies. First day, lay down the law and win a few battles, then bitches back down and we ride off into the sunset. Unfortunately, pettiness was just the start of my problems.

CHAPTER SIXTEEN

King

I had to laugh as she gave a fake bow. I rolled my eyes at her and she smiled back. Damn, she was magnificent. Remi was as well, in a terrifying, eat your soul kind of way. When she licked the blood off her hand, I knew she wasn't someone that you should ever take lightly. Hudson though? I knew she was tough; she took hits when only necessary, with eyes like a hawk, picking up on patterns and movements seconds before they were made.

We watched as Hudson and Remi squared off using magic, hand-to-hand, and weapons to teach a lesson about the benefits of the cohesiveness of magic. To be fair, they had a point. You can't run off in battle and clap your hands and say, "oh wait, it's magic time, let me ground myself." We stressed this, but it fell on deaf ears.

"You know, when you guys spoke about her, I certainly wasn't expecting to have her be so incredible. When Chancellor Jacobs let us know she was coming, I was expecting skills, but this magnitude of efficiency is disconcerting at the worst times, but damn formidable at the best of times."

Gray chuckled beside me, "You're telling me, we have to live with that terror every day. This weekend was just a taste. She's going to be bloody impossible to deal with after today," he groaned jokingly.

We watched as Hudson and Remi both threw magic so powerful, Zane hastily tossed up a shield around them to protect the rest of the students. The girls laughed as they flew back but used the elements to outmaneuver each other with clashing weapons. It was like watching a fucking movie right before my eyes.

"A taste, huh?" Blair whispered beside me in a low tone. I turned my head and raised my eyebrow.

"What I mean is, if that is just a taste, you guys are in for quite a banquet of fucking destruction." He chuckled darkly.

"Not the words I would use." Ryder frowned. "But the general idea is there, she's going to be insufferable."

"You know, her talent could only get better from here on out. Let's see how she does after a couple of weeks in her classes. Surely from skill alone, she can surpass quite a few students. I want to make sure all of the academics are on par as well," Deal Alvor chimed in from next to me. "Maybe an apprenticeship with me would be in order, but I don't want to pile too much on her plate at once."

He said this distractedly as Hudson pressed an advantage and threw a combination of magic that knocked Remi on her back before crossing her swords across Remi's neck. Remi laughed and they knuckled. Giving each other a hug and joking while they walked back to their new friends, Jensi and Luca. They were good boys.

I nodded my head at what Alvor had said, she was bright, I'll give her that, and quick on her feet; academically as well as with her magic and combat alone. In fact... "It certainly would be useful to see her help train some of these students after she does her own combat warm ups. She is very advanced." Ryder and the Dean nodded and Grayson steepled his fingers under his chin.

We started to get up to file out of the combat zone before the students headed to dinner.

"She definitely surpassed my expectations in practice today," Gray sighed and straightened. "I agree with the Dean. Let us see how she does in the next couple of weeks. I have a feeling she will continue to surprise us."

That she will; I'm sure of it. What I'm not sure of is if I liked being friend zoned. I shook my head as I thought about being her squishy. I had a warm feeling in my chest. Being her anything made me a little giddy, even if it wasn't in a romantic way. Still, I have a feeling that being friends with her would be better than to not be. In more ways than one. No one that skilled is ever free from the challenges that will come from those who want to prove themselves, or worse, those who would rather destroy the good in her. Being her squishy would mean I can keep her close and watch out for her too. Oh, the tangled webs life weaves, and my life is tugging me toward her direction.

Logan

Watching Remi lick the blood off her hand, I knew what it was. Briefly, her eyes had touched mine, but that was enough. It was a warning. A warning I wasn't going to heed. I knew she knew more or was more. There was something off about her. I was excited at the prospect; I knew I was right. No one understood me. They warned of telling old stories, calling them myths. They said that those stories were falsehoods, that they couldn't possibly be true. So why couldn't I tell them? No. Only those who seek to hide the truth forbid you from talking about it. I knew... I knew... I knew...

I loved when me and my twin sister went out to play in the forest behind our house. There was a pretty stream with the prettiest of flowers.

"Laillaaaa, wait for me!" I giggled and ran behind my sister. We were only seven, but my mom and dad always said that if we stayed only by the stream and no further that we could go out to play. They could see us from the window. Our home was warded against intruders, so we were safe.

"Logan! Hurry, I want to play with the flowers and pick some before supper!" Laila giggled while she squealed. Her beautiful, long blonde hair trailing behind her, her white dress getting tangled around her legs as she ran and laughed. She is my best friend.

"Okay, okay, Laila, I'm coming. Supper is hours away, Lai." We reached the stream and put our toes in the water. We spent hours out, until we fell asleep right next to the flowers. Until my mom shook me awake.

"Where's Laila, Logan? It's time for supper."

"She is right here..." I trailed off, not seeing her next to me where we fell asleep holding hands. "Well, she was here. Maybe she went back home?" I bit my lip, knowing Lai wouldn't leave me. We are best friends; two halves of a whole. I saw the doubt and panic creep into my mother's eyes. She smiled tightly and picked up my small frame, rushing back towards the house, looking around her whipping her head back and forth.

"Laiiiiii, you left me sleeping!" I yelled into the house as we got to the front door. Except she wasn't here. Dad chuckled, but then seeing my mom's face, immediately questioned what was going on.

"Laila wasn't outside with Logan. Lo said they fell asleep. When I looked out there, they were still there. Where could she have gone so quickly?" Ma said.

That night we didn't sleep. My dad sent up a search party and that's how we spent every day for three weeks. My mom started to pray to whatever God would listen, my dad spent his every waking moment throwing himself into his work. And I... I stood by the window staring at the stream every single night and day until mom would put me in bed. Lai couldn't be gone; she would never leave me. She would come back. One night before bed, I was staring out the window when I saw a flash of a white dress. I ran out of the house with my mom on my heels. "Mom, I saw her dress. I saw it. She's here."

She broke down in tears. "Don't cry, Mom, she's here I just saw her dress! Let's go get her!"

"Lo, listen to me. I never want you to go out there and search for Lai," she choked out, "you need to stay inside where you're safe... I. Can't. I can't have them take you too."

"Mom, who? Who took Lai?" I started to get angry, stomping my feet. "She's my sister, I want her back!"

She never answered me. It took weeks of eavesdropping before I heard her pray to people called the "Fae", begging them to bring her back Laila.

It took another few weeks before I learned that my mom had been looking into gaining more magic, except she bartered wrong and lost a child in the deal. I didn't know what that meant. Bartered wrong. Did she make a deal and with who? My father called her foolish and said grief was making her mad. She fell deeper within herself, becoming so quiet, I never really saw or heard her anymore. In a matter of months, she passed away, a shell of her former beautiful self; I had lost my mother and sister.

The day of her funeral, my father held me close and I saw something glimmer in the trees from the corner of my eye, but when I looked, it was gone. In a matter of days, we had packed up and moved, leaving that home and those memories behind, but if we left, how would Lai eventually find us? So, I left a note in the woods before I left, telling her where we were going and that I loved her and forgave her for leaving me and not taking me with her on her adventure.

A year later, during dinner, I brought up what I overheard from my mom during her discussion with Father, and he immediately shushed me. "We will not discuss that part of our lives anymore. We will remember them with good times, Logan, never with the days of panic or the ramblings of a mad woman, stuck in her grief." His sad eyes pierced me, and he sighed. "Logan, your mother lost her mind in the end. We must never discuss such things because the last thing we need is people looking further into false myths."

I looked at him genuinely confused, wringing my hands in front of the dinner table. "What false myths, dad?"

"The kind where people try to look into magic as more than what it is. Practice makes us stronger, son. Power comes from practice. Power cannot just manifest. That kind of thinking makes us weak, for if we're always seeking more power, we are never content with the fierce pride that comes from genuine practice. Remember that, son. It will always be your most important lesson."

I went to bed that night with thoughts of what my father said floating through my head as I tossed and turned. He was wrong. I was obsessed after that moment, feeling like something was missing. I went back to that little stream at our old childhood home every year. I took opportunities when my father started working with the council to read everything I could about magic in their libraries. Oftentimes, when I was sixteen, I found myself there after dark, taking my father's keys and going into a section that was always blocked off and warded. It took me weeks to figure out the ward, but it was worth it. There were references, never full descriptions of the origin of magic of pure magic. Theoretically, that meant pure power. So, my mom wasn't crazy. For years, I couldn't not figure out who she could have bargained to. Who were the Fae and why did she barter? I questioned myself every moment.

But unlike what my dad said, while I obsessed, I trained, and I excelled. When I went to DeLorean on an accelerated path, it was the same year that Hunter, Ryder, Zane, Grayson, King, and Blair also went. We became teachers shortly after, and teachers due to retire soon came at a good time. Everything clicked when I was given the opportunity to teach magical history. Pure magic, prayer, Fae. You can practice all you want but there will always be those out there stronger. Did they practice more? Or were some simply more gifted? Who made people more gifted? Rather what? I brought up my musings to the men and they would tell me that I shouldn't spread 'such lies'. Then I met Remi this year, she felt... more... her warning... almost made me snap. They don't want to share that power. They want to promise it and then kidnap the kids of those who ask for it. They want to kill mothers slowly from depression.

We walked out to go have dinner and I caught her gaze and smiled. I knew she knew something. She was possibly inconsequential, but maybe she was a part of something grander. Something that must come toppling down. Pure magic belongs to me... no... no... I mean us, I... no... we shouldn't have to barter for it. I felt my fists clenching and I had to catch myself and take a deep breath. I settled in at the teachers table in the dining room and laughed along to whatever the guys were talking about. No, we shouldn't have to barter. Some were more worthy to be there; they took my mom, they have my sister... clearly, I deserve to be a part of them too. It was my right. They owed me... I mean us.

CHAPTER SEVENTEEN

Zane

Fucking shit, looking at her had my dick hard as fuck. Trying to maintain my face was the easy part. My eyes though? Couldn't help themselves, following the beads of sweat as they crawled over her defined abs. I was jealous as fuck, wanting to be doing the same with my tongue and fingers, before ripping her training pants off and drifting lower. I needed to taste her, feel her, worship every fucking curve. She didn't know it, but I was going to make sure she screamed under me, my dick worshipping her just as my mouth and tongue will again. Fuck, I had to discreetly adjust myself, but Hunter noticed and laughed at me.

"Don't give me that fucking look. You know damn well she had the same effect on your dumb ass too," I grumbled.

"Yeah, yeah she does, but I fuck her and don't leave after." He looked at her as she got ready to head to dinner, hanging back slightly. Before I responded to his smart ass comment, he continued, "Fuck, she better have an extra fucking shirt. She's not walking around like that. These fucking assholes won't stop staring." I had been too busy lusting and wanting to punch Hunter to realize that Hudson was indeed still in her sports bra, her breasts straining underneath. Her confidence rocking it. Amazing. My temper with it? Not so amazing.

"Not happening." I walked over to Hudson and Remi, Hunter stalking behind me. "Good work, princess. Now that you have successfully made every man's dick hard in here, how about you put on a shirt?" Hunter rumbled in agreement. She gave me a little smirk and took a step away from the bleachers and closer to me, having to strain her neck to look me in the eye.

"I don't know. I was thinking of making this my new uniform. Very comfortable, free range of motion... I like it."

Remi turned to look at her and then back at me with a smile in her eyes. "You know, telling her what to do will probably have the opposite effect." Hudson nodded, sagely.

"She's right, but I mean, I can be persuaded by other means." She blinked up at me, so goddamn beautiful that I almost missed her insinuation. Right as I was going to respond, a senior student, Maddie, who I may or may not have slept with a few years ago before I became a professor, and a few dozen times after, walked up to us.

"Zane," she giggled and put her hand on my arm, and I raised my eyebrow at her. "I mean, Professor Zane," she giggled again while putting emphasis on the professor and I had to stop myself from rolling my eyes.

"Yes, Madison?" My tone bland and disinterested. Her eyes faltered but she quickly looked at Hudson and back to me, her hand sliding up and down my arm.

I heard a low growl and a whispered but ferocious, "mine", but when I looked at Hudson her eyes were cool and her face was blank.

"I was thinking maybe we can do some extra training. You know, so I can make sure I'm in perfect shape." Ugh, she came on too strongly then, and apparently, now as well. The gym was empty now except for her friends in the back, Hunter, Remi, Hudson, and me. I took her hand off of me and looked at her with a hard stare. She stepped back a little. She was pretty, with long red hair, green eyes, freckles, tall, thin with slight curves, but she wasn't Hudson. Shit, no one was.

Before I was able to reply, Hudson jumped in and her voice sounded downright feral. I smiled internally. "Yes, that would be a great idea..." her voice trailed off and she looked at me, indicating that she needed to know her name.

"Madison," I told her gruffly.

"Yes, well, Manuel, that sounds like a good idea. Your form could use some work. So, I'll go ahead and volunteer to help you with extra training." She smiled, but it looked more like a wolf ready to pounce on their meal than friendly. Jensi and Luca, who appeared out of nowhere, laughed and whispered bets. I had to hide a smile at their antics.

"It's Madison," she snapped at Hudson, and Hudson nodded in understanding with a small smile. "I'm good, thanks. I'd rather train with an actual professor, not a new student."

"Yes, yes, Melinda, I can see the appeal in that. Zane is actually busy that day though, with another student he will be training." She was no longer smiling, her eyes flaring and... wait, were they swirling in different colors? I blinked and her eyes looked normal again, trick of the light, I guess.

"Madison," she snarled, "I didn't say which day and I was talking to Zane, not you, new girl."

"You owe me five, bro. Told you she was going to say something stupid in less than two minutes," Jensi laughed.

"I was thirty seconds off, asshole," Luca said, passing him the money. I shook my head.

Remi shook her head and couldn't hold back her laughter anymore. "I swear, I'll never understand huma.... the people in this school." She tugged Hudson's hand and pulled her away, whispering something in her ear. Hudson smiled brightly and winked at Madison.

"Hey, Madison, if it's any consolation, I'll take my deal off the table. But it will be a cold day in hell before I let Zane bend you over his." She saluted and walked backward slowly before turning and walking out the gym, still in her damn sports bra. Jensi and Luca follow behind, guarding their backs. I liked those fucking kids.

"That bitch is crazy..."

"Watch your mouth, Madison," Hunter and I snapped at the same time.

"She is right, on both accounts. We aren't happening and I'll be training more with younger students who need some extra help, Madison."

"But you liked it, loved it actually, when I was bent over." She stepped closer, her voice low, both of her hands now on my crossed arms. Hunter laughed and clapped me on the shoulder and headed out the gym after Hudson and Remi, fucker.

"I'm taken, Madison. Not happening, I'll see you in class." I side stepped her shocked expression and walked out of the combat zone. Fucking shit, I'm taken. I knew that, but saying out loud to someone else, it just felt right.

I walked down the corridor in my thoughts and when I reached the dining room, my eyes sought out Hudson immediately, noticing her with Remi, Jensi, Luca, and a small senior girl named Megan. That took me for a loop, Hudson isn't really a social butterfly and the moment she did try, she ended up with a girlfriend. I rolled my eyes. So, while it was strange to see her with more people, it was nice too. I fought the urge to walk over to her and wrap my arms around her. There were no rules, technically, of teachers and students being together, as we were all of age when we started, even more so since we were all in our early twenties, but it wasn't done, not publicly. I'm considering changing that. I settled in at the shared faculty table next to my brothers, their eyes also fixed across the room as Hudson threw her head back and laughed. She lit up the entire room when she smiled and all I could think was I wanted to wipe that smile off her face and replace it with a moan. I rubbed my face; fuck, I was so lost in her and it has only been a few days. Taking out my phone, I start texting the group text.

Hudson

. . .

"Babe," Remi whispered in my ear as she tugged me away from possibly catching a murder case. "She's desperate, any idiot could see how they all look at you. Now, smile and walk away. I'll reward you later..." She trailed off and licked my ear. I smiled, winked at Missy or whatever, but not before a few parting words before leaving the combat area. I was able to take a deep breath as I walked out into the corridor and Remi grabbed my hand, pulled me close and kissed me senseless. The slight copper taste in her mouth reminded me of when she licked her bloody hand after her fight, and that just made it hotter. Fuck, she was just walking sensuality. It took a second to blink the lust out of my eyes and she laughed at me. Laughed, the bitch.

I gently pushed her away. "tease," I grumbled, throbbing with excitement and need.

"Am not," she laughed again. "Fuck. I need some food and liquor. We need to consider that shit for tomorrow. It would make people a lot more tolerable if I didn't actually remember them." I laughed; I was inclined to agree. It was only the first day and we still had to go to the tactical course.

I groaned, "Yeah that sounds perfect, remind me to add that into our classroom discussions. The fucking benefits of drinking in class so I don't punch people in the face... Do you think the Dean would appreciate that course diversion?"

Jensi and Luca tossed their arms around us and joined in, agreeing to try to come up with the best possibilities.

"Absolutely not." I turned around to see Hunter walking in our direction. He gave me a tight hug and knuckled Remi and the boys. What the fuck? Is the dab between him and Remi like a bro code hi? A, 'we're all after the same girl' consensus dab? Is it called a bro code if it's a lesbian and a guy? We need a term coined, if not.

I shook my head and looked into his grey eyes. "You suck. The least you can do is let us get drunk the rest of the term, after the day we had." We were almost at the dining room, so we stopped for a few.

"Most people do that at the end of the day, not during classes." He pointed out, raised an eyebrow and ran his hand through his messy brown hair. He was such a ham, I sighed. He grinned at me.

"Most people aren't named Remi and Hudson," I gave a little laugh, "but I'll consider your opinion. Maybe." I winked as he shook his head and walked around us into the dining room. Party pooper. We walked in and grabbed a tray full of protein-filled food, needing fuel for the last part of the day. We settled down at the table we stole this morning and as we were about to tuck into our food, a small girl I remember from earlier was suddenly standing next to me.

"Hi," she said nervously and bit her lip. "I'm Megan. I was hoping I could sit with you four." I looked at her shuffling her feet, looking shy and super sweet. Her demeanor was very endearing, I looked at Remi and the boys, who all smiled at her and I shrugged.

"Sure, sit down." I smiled. It was nice to have a few people actually want to get to know us. We ate for a few minutes, when I felt familiar eyes on me, and I knew it had to be the guys. And my phone buzzed. They were always so intense when they were together, like they fed off each other's energies.

Which reminded me. "Alright fuck faces, numbers now." We started rattling off each other's numbers and saving them. The buzzing was getting more intensive, I rolled my eyes.

"Are they always so protective and intense?" asked Megan, her question took me by surprise, and I tossed my head back and laughed. *Oh, honey, you have no idea.* I shook my head and Remi just smirked.

ZANE- You keep tossing your head like that you're going to give us other ideas. 🤪

RYDER- Like yoga?

HUNTER- Yeah, if yoga comes with handcuffs and paddles.

GRAYSON- I swear, eating was never this damn difficult before. 😪

HUDSON- Oh, I don't know, Gray, you seemed pretty good at it. 👅 😉

GRAYSON- 😌 No comment.

RYDER- Technically, that is a comment.

GRAYSON- Fuck you. 🖕

ZANE- By the way, I think we all agree that Jensi and Luca are some pretty good guys. You can keep them.

HUDSON- Major eye roll there, 🙄 they aren't dogs.

HUNTER- So about this flexibility and sex toys...🙄

HUDSON- I studied Kama sutra, we should totally try some stuff out. I read about anal beads and those remote panties. I want a pair.

RYDER- Sweetie, you lost everyone at anal. I take that back, you lost everyone at Kama sutra- anal just sealed the deal.

I smiled, looking up from my phone. "Yeah, you can say that they have been like that the entire time I have known them."

She chewed thoughtfully. "Yeah, I can see that. It's like they are drawn to you though. Like magnetic. I noticed it at the party, but the energy flare is typically when they are all together."

At that, Remi's eyes sharpened, and she looked at Megan shrewdly.

"What do you mean energy flare?" Remi asked, her tone suddenly very interested. Megan looked at her and put her head down slightly, but her gaze met Remi's. Impressive.

"Like, at the party, the moment she was with them, all their attention was on her and they went into protective mode... it's hard to explain but when they are in class alone... the connection?" She stumbled through her words trying to explain and I was genuinely interested, as was Remi. "They can pass as close friends, but when they are all in the same room with her, it's like a deep well of power; like when you're meditating to find your source of magic. Except they are her source of power? If that makes any sense. I know I sound crazy. It's just an observation. I feel bad for whoever tries to take you five on."

Right then, a group of girls walked by and started to flirt with Jensi and Luca, I smiled. They were super attractive guys. I was waiting for the moment they would start to show that side of themselves. Jensi pulled a blonde girl into his lap and whispered in her ear and she perked her head up and looked at Luca, who gave her a devilish smile and returned to his food and our conversation. I winked at him and he laughed, shrugging. "Can't deny the heat, you know. You're not the only one with admirers, little sister." I rolled my eyes at that. We were the same age. I was surrounded by protective people.

My head went back to the conversation, "Wait, five?" I asked. "I can take care of myself," I stated plainly.

"Oh no. I meant Ryder, Hunter, Grayson, Zane, AND Remi. I didn't factor you in, you clearly can protect yourself. But with all of them at your side? I think it would be like a supernova." She smiled. I looked at her and turned my head, she was interesting to say the least. She picked up on energies. That was strange and a rare talent, as in most people prefer to practice their magic but ignore that magic was energy, and picking up on that was just as important. Kalen literally and figuratively beat that into me. If I can pick up on energy and energy spikes, then I can tell how powerful someone is or how powerful their attacks will be.

Jensi stopped whispering in the giggling girls' ear and leaned over to say, "we would like to be the nova handlers. Lord knows we're going to have to beat ass next period during swim." Luca glowered.

"Yup, you heard Alex. Derrick and his crew are spreading rumors that they want to run a train on you. They take swim too, so Luca and a few guys are going to run one on each of their fucking jaws," Luca growled, looking menacing.

"Well, be careful. They come from pretty well-known families," Megan whispered.

Luca and Jensi laughed. "So do we, Megs." With that parting comment, they sauntered off with a wave and the girls but not before pressing a kiss to my cheek. I smiled at how quickly I was okay with the show of affection.

I looked back at Megan, she was... interesting. Like she started picking up on energies because she was a loner and used that time to pick up on energies to pass the time. I said as much, and she smiled at me sadly.

"Yeah, I haven't had that many friends here," she shrugged, but I knew it hurt her. "So, I just, I don't know, kept practicing until it felt second nature. It's useful. I'm so invisible that people underestimate me, so I can be formidable in a battle because I pick up on little things."

"You're not invisible, at least... not anymore. You can sit with and hang with us. Hudson and I pretty much hate people in general. We're loners and we were drawn to each other because of it. Jensi and Luca just saw us piss ass drunk and we all kind of bonded. We can all be alone, together." She laughed and smiled. Her blue hair tied back and her green eyes sparkling, she was fierce but had open acceptance on her face. I loved that; she was just so… Remi.

"I would like that, thank you," Megan said brightly, her shoulders back and her head straight, a boost of confidence making her look a lot less lost. She was pretty, with her round glasses settled over her hazel eyes, long brown hair and sweet smile. She was the classic girl next door. Dinner was just about over, and we got up to start putting our trays back.

"Do you have any extracurriculars, Megan?" I asked as we paused to the side of the dining room before heading to the second combat zone area that held the tactical course.

"Yeah," she rolled her eyes, "my mom kept insisting so I chose the one thing she wasn't expecting, the tactical course. She wanted me to run or swim because it was something she can pass off as more ladylike to her high tea ladies." She rolled her eyes and smiled. "So, I figured. I'd rather test myself as the invisible girl and try my hand at the course instead."

We laughed and then grabbed her hand. "We have it too, let's go."

Chapter Eighteen

Well, this was impressive, I thought to myself as I walked into the other combat zone and took in the tactical course. It was massive. From beginning to end there was a combination of walls, ropes, water pits, mud slides, and barbed wires that you had to crawl under, and each section was completely random, nothing ever being consistent. So, while one section had barbed wires and then a water pit, the next would have ropes and barbed wire. Definitely a way to make sure we didn't get complacent with the course. What I did notice though, was that there were various flat surfaces, I presumed for the combat portions of the course. The entire room was dark enough to make the course seem more daunting, add the fog machines making visibility low, the floor in the entire arena damp dirt, it was a death trap. I couldn't fucking wait.

I started bouncing on my feet as I walked to the front of the room. Remi laughed at me and Megan, still looking wide eyed at the set-up, followed behind. There were only about 10 of us here, which was a nice pace from a full class.

"Alright students," Dean Alvors' voice rang out as he stood in the front with Hunter, Ryder, Zane, and Grayson standing behind him looking all kinds of menacing and sexy. I made sure they saw me as I licked my lips slowly, their eyes turning heated. I laughed and focused back on the dean. "Okay, so the course, as you can see, is random. Whoever gets to the end of each section first will wait and combat whichever instructor is there at the time. We will be walking about, rotating our positions. Do not let the instructor choice confuse you; just because they are there at that time doesn't necessarily mean you'll be fighting with that instructor's taught course magic. It will be varied. You may end up getting two of the same forms of combat back-to-back. The entire point is to keep you on your toes."

Easy enough. Sounds like a good time. Focus on what's in front of you and keep moving. I looked at the course, considering my course of action, and taking in possibilities and weighing them in my mind. I figured out there had to be way more random surprises coming up. Turns out, I was right when the Dean smiled at us savagely and the men started to grin.

"Of course, this is timed. Fifteen minutes to get across and at the end of the course, there will be an instructor, or two, or three, or myself, waiting to combat everyone here. Your goal is to last as long as possible with any of us, using full strength." Jaws dropped around the group at Dean Alvor's statement. It was so fucking on.

They had us line up with me somewhere in the middle. Strategy. I wanted to see what everyone else did and their times. I liked to pick up on the small issues I had to prepare for, although I had a feeling everyone would have their own set of challenges. This first section had a wall to climb over first, but with no foot holds or rope, then a flame pit at the bottom of the other end. At this point, the room darkened slightly and the other sections weren't visible until the student got there. Fucking genius. I feel like Kalen would have built some shit like this himself and laugh as everyone fell behind.

The first student ran up to the wall and tried to climb it, realizing he couldn't. Technically, he could go around it, but on each side was a sudden drop and he couldn't. Frustrated, he paced the wall as if it were going to open up the Room of Requirement or something. He finally manipulated the earth and made small steps for him to climb, but as he climbed them, the ground started to shake and he had to jump to the edge of the wall, hanging precariously before swinging himself over. Underneath the other side of the wall was a fire pit and he had to get across it without falling into the flames. He tried to use the wind, but that fanned the flames even more. This poor kid just looked completely out of his element. When he finally reached the end of the first section, he had to combat Zane with a weapon of his choice, and he barely lasted a minute before he was flat on his back.

As he cleared, the next student went on with their own set of challenges, each of them getting their asses handed to them by the course, the guys, or both. So far, no one had made time. I was the sixth person up and I was ready to go. When the Dean called my name, I was already walking to the first part of the course. Knowing that I needed to get up the wall, I wasted no time and used air to propel myself to the top of the wall before they had the chance to really stop me from getting there, though right before I landed on the wall, I felt pressure and I did land precariously on the edge of the wall. I laughed. Oh, this was going to be a blast.

Remi

I saw Hudson land on the edge of the wall and laugh. She had been practically vibrating with energy from the moment the other students began the tactical course. She had run and propelled herself before anyone could really see what was happening, so the instructors last minute attempt did nothing to deter her, although, realistically, I'm not sure they could. I looked around to gauge their locations while they were all rotating. Alvor was closest to the end, I'm sure he planned it that way so he could test her strength in battle himself. I rolled my eyes. The other students who didn't finish by the twenty-minute mark, were given a five-minute grace period, then told to step to the side to observe the rest of the students.

"She really is kind of incredible, albeit, maybe slightly insane," giggled Megan from behind me and I had to laugh.

"Oh yeah, that is an accurate description of her that's for sure," I replied in a low whisper, my voice tinged with affection. We turned our attention back to Hudson; she truly was something else. Her 21st birthday being so close, I worried quite a bit about how much power she was able to exhibit. I bit my lip; I was supposed to see Alvor after classes today to debrief, but I think he will get his own answers if he continues to watch as closely as he has been. I rubbed my temples; this was only the first day of classes and I had a strong feeling that something was about to happen. Shit can only ever get more intense, never less.

Hudson moved the earth to stop the fire, jumped down into a crouch without flinching, and walked across the first section to find herself face to face with Ryder. Without pausing or looking, she picked up the sword for the students, then infused it with magic and started to fight Ryder with an intensity and speed in her skill, which I'm positive increased from this morning. It is as if the more she used it, the stronger she became. I looked on with interest as she sidestepped and disarmed Ryder, smacking his sword to the side. My eyebrows shot up as her sword glowed... purple... right before she blasted Ryder with magic. Well, fuck. Ryder was on his back and she was over that second wall before he had a chance to get up. Then, it was my turn to step up. Well, I couldn't let her outdo me, so instead of flying through the wall, I used magic to blow it up instead. Who said only Hudson can have fun? I smiled and went through.

Hudson

. . .

After I laid Ryder flat on his ass with a combination of magic I never used before but seemed instinctual, if that made any sense, I vaulted over the next wall in time to hear an explosion of the first wall. I smiled; Remi would be a fucking show off. I quickly bypassed the next two sections, crawling under barbed wires, climbing ropes, and vaulting over a chasm in the ground, before kicking Zane's ass in weaponry and Hunter in hand-to-hand combat, barely. I was eleven minutes in and wanted to finish the last section in four.

I focused my attention on what seemed to be a water pit earlier but looked more like a swirling vortex. It made me pause. I peered at it carefully, sensing its energy and trying to put out, what I like to call, magical feelers. It was water-based, but with a jelly consistency? I rolled my eyes, water quicksand. Must be an interesting thing to be stuck in. Never matter. I sent out a wave of magic to freeze the vortex, but it wouldn't freeze. Interesting. Whoever did this was a dick. Oh well, I shrugged. If I could not freeze it, then I would do the next best thing. Without thinking, I shielded myself and jumped straight into the vortex. The vortex was magic, therefore, it was energy. Energy can be absorbed and then redistributed. So, when I hit the center, I held my breath and quickly threw my hands out, allowing myself to be drawn in. I hit the bottom of the pool and absorbed the energy of the magic around me. The colors around me were swirling and beautiful, almost hypotonic. It took a lot more effort to hold my breath than I thought it would. Whoever built this vortex did so to trap the student and make the student lose time. I closed my eyes against the magical mind fuck, force of magic and water, pressing against my lungs and instead, I breathed in the magic through my pores. This magic felt different, unique, pure?

Mine. My mind opened and it was like my soul was absorbing the magic as tightly as possible, taking its fill.

What's yours? The magic?

Mine.

Fuck, I was talking to myself. I ignored my thoughts and focused on feeling the power fill me, until the vortex stopped, and I was able to swim to the top of the pool, no longer being held down by the force of the power around me. I was weightless, powerful and unstoppable. I felt, rather than saw, the power flowing through me. The rush was incredible. I could do anything-be anything-and no one would get in my way. No one could even try.

Mine. All power is mine.

Yes. It is mine.

I burst out of the pool to find myself face to face with Dean Alvor, smiling at me until he saw my eyes. He blinked and took a step back with a frown on his face. I took in the group behind him but dismissed them quickly. He moved first so he was my prey. I turned my head to the side, feeling like a predator stalking the pretty rabbit before tearing it in two.

Don't run, pretty rabbit. I heard them gasp and I smiled.

I crouched down to the floor; the rabbit needed to be taught its place.

ALVOR

THAT MORNING, AFTER HEARING FROM REMI THAT HUDSON HAD been trained by Kalen, I quickly contacted Chancellor Jacobs and demanded his contact information, brooking no argument. I called him minutes after stepping out of the cafe that Sunday morning, needing answers.

"Kalen, I see you're still as difficult as ever to pin down," I spoke slowly over the phone. I hated these damn devices.

"Yes, and yet, Alvor, you were still able to reach me. I assume you have already met Hudson?" He chuckled. "How is my little minx? She is full of spirit, that one; the best student I have ever had and the strongest," he said with a loving note in his gruff voice.

I was taken aback by his tone; Kalen was known to be the ruthless warrior not the ruthless loving dad in training. He left our home years ago, never breathing a word as to why and he was never found. Not that anyone who ever tried to find him came back. After a while, we realized it was futile. Kalen didn't gain his reputation from whispers alone, no, he truly was the best warrior and your worst possible enemy.

I cleared my throat. "I have not had the pleasure directly, no, but Remi has. She seems quite taken with her actually. Remi isn't usually taken with anyone; my niece is a loner."

He laughed darkly, "She's a loner because she is as ruthless and as cruel as her family namesake." His tone became dark, menacing, before he continued, "make no mistake, Alvor, if Hudson is harmed in any way, you wouldn't live to see the other side. I'll rip out your entire soul from your being and laugh while I'm tearing you to pieces."

"Kalen, that is not why we're here," I sighed. He was so damn intense. "We're here to protect her and bring her home, where she belongs. She is the last. She has a role to play, which I'm sure you know since you have been training her all these years."

He grunted. I smiled. "Tell me, Kalen, how did you know where she was and how did you, the greatest warrior of our time, become the trainer of a young child?"

"I have my ways. Just because I was gone, doesn't mean I wasn't keeping my ear to the ground. We all knew of the prophecy, but I knew my role. I felt it. It doesn't matter how we got to this point. She is here. What is interesting to me, Dean Alvor, is how you were able to locate her."

"I was sent; it doesn't matter how. The facts are she must be taken back safely and before her powers manifest." His knowledge of my position wasn't worrisome. Kalen was nothing if not thorough and lethal.

"Hmm," he seemed unperturbed. "Her powers have already manifested. I'm sure you noticed her hair. There is only one thing preventing the early onset of her powers. Speaking of, you realize the wards around your school are not as airtight as you believe. I suggest you remedy that soon; I'll be visiting my little minx before long. I suggest you prepare."

"What? You cannot..."

"Do not presume to tell me what I can and cannot do. I'll be there... in fact... sooner than you think. Goodbye... mate."

Goodbye, mate. His final words still made my stomach quake in anger, betrayal, disgust, and anticipation. He didn't even say goodbye the first time he left. I pushed those thoughts away, because I should have realized that with his training and Hudson's innate abilities that she would be more problematic. However, it wasn't until she jumped straight into the vortex that I realized just how problematic. The moment she touched that water, I had a strange feeling come over me. A foreboding, if you will. I felt a tap on my shoulder and when I looked back, my eyes widened. A shiver went up my spine as I took in the six foot five, muscular man with eyes so dark blue they looked almost purple, golden tanned skin, and long dyed dark blonde hair.

"Kal..."

"There is no time for questions, Alvor, dismiss the other students immediately," Kalen demanded, voice and hard eyes brooking no argument. His presence was always mind numbing. From the moment we met, he has always captivated me, even after these many years, he still did. I shook my head to loosen the cobwebs, I knew my duties.

I immediately threw a shield around us and called out to the class, "students, that is all the time we have today. Take your things and have a good night. We will see you tomorrow." The students, already exhausted, thankfully, hastened out of the room at the dismissal, not noticing the time.

Kalen, the moment the last student was out, had sent a burst of magic to the doors and warded them closed. Ryder, Grayson, Zane, Hunter, and Remi walked past the shield and stared at the vortex that had just stopped spinning, watching as Hudson climbed out. I walked closer and I tried to smile but it quickly slipped, and I stepped back just as quickly. She was glowing, her skin alight in purple, red, and black hues, her eyes bright, her long hair dripping water, and her chest heaving. She would look beautiful, alluring, and dangerous, it wasn't for the fact that her eyes promised destruction.

She quirked her head and crouched down to the floor, like an animal waiting to spring on its prey. *Don't run pretty rabbit*, echoed in my head and when I heard everyone gasp, I knew they must have heard it too. Her smile looked feral and this did not bode well. I knew she was powerful; I would have to be oblivious not to, however, having not reached her 21st year, even with her spilling her virginal blood, the amount of power, focus, and strength to absorb the magic from the vortex should have been impossible. In fact, only the strongest could possibly have *that* much within themselves and not burst from the strain alone. Although consumed by the force and free will of pure magic, she showed no signs of destruction of her person. However, the more pressing concern was that those consumed with magic are almost impossible to deter once they set their goal on someone or something, and that someone was me. And I had to wonder if it was her magic that knew who I was. *Fuck.*

Chapter Nineteen

Kalen

I had no idea what the hell I walked into, but I'm glad I had chosen that time to hide in the shadows and observe. I had cloaked my presence from the room, having gotten there shortly after Hudson had begun her time on the course. She moved and fought with a speed and focus that far outshined any of the other students. It was clear her talents were wasted in a place such as this, she needed to thrive and be with her people. However, until she reached her 21st birthday, it just wasn't a good idea. She was excelling when she was with me, that much was clear. I taught her things way beyond her years that she took to with an innate ability. She was unmatched by her peers, if you can even call them that. She wasn't their peer, she wasn't their anything. Genetically, they may be similar. However, Hudson was much more. When I saw the calculated look on her face when she peered into the vortex of magic and water, meant to make the other students use other means to avoid it, I felt and saw her split decision to jump into it instead. I cursed.

It was at that moment I realized that her potential far surpassed my initial observations. She took everything I taught her and wielded her knowledge as one would wield a sword; it was a weapon. I was proud of her, yet I knew at that moment as strong and as old as Alvor was, Hudson was coming into herself a lot faster than anyone could have expected. She would destroy him. Although, that part may not be a bad thing; considering the purest part of her, her magic, considered him prey. That was an interesting tidbit for later.

I quickly stepped up and stood in front of Alvor, Hudson's eyes followed him until her attention snapped to me instead.

"Hudson," my voice strong and my hands up in front of me showing her I was no threat. "Hudson, listen to me. You're too smart to let yourself be controlled by magic. You control power, not the other way around."

She stood up from her crouched position, and raised her hands, stepping forward slightly, bending her knees. The movements were the only indication of her thought process as she exhibited no energy spike before she let loose a storm of magic that arced towards me. In those few seconds, I had braced myself and opened myself to absorb rather than deflect the attack, hoping to get a feel for the magic she had absorbed. It hit me and I grunted and took in a sharp intake of breath as I was inundated with a feeling of pure magic; a combination of all elements and energies. It was as if I was back home. *Fuck.* I felt the magic from the top of my head to the tips of my toes and released it.

"You took my rabbit," her voice deep, almost unrecognizable, with the excess power coursing through her system. Her words took me by surprise, and I laughed, she was the only one to have ever made me laugh since I left my home. Even then, my smiles were few and far between. Somewhere between the past seven years of training, I fell in love with this sassy little girl with the fire in her eyes, who blossomed into a woman right before my eyes. I could not have imagined a better daughter of my heart; she gave everything she had and learned the same way. Her father was a spiteful man, who loved her in his own way despite the circumstances that brought me to her. I wanted to protect her, but I knew that if I taught her well and guided her path, she would grow into the best version of herself she could ever be. I was right, and despite her being thrust into a situation where her magic was quickly growing, I knew she would rise to the challenge just like she always had. I would make sure of it.

"Your rabbit is not the problem here. Hudson, take a deep breath and snap out of this shit. Release the magic through your pores, feel it leave through the soles of your feet, the crown of your head, and release it back into the environment around you. That magic is not yours to keep. Release it." She frowned and her eyes began to glow redder, she was pissed. I suppressed a chuckle. I was familiar with the stare, albeit her eyes weren't typically red when she gave it.

"No, I don't want to. All of it is mine." She started to pace back and forth, her eyes never truly leaving mine. "Nah, you can't have it," she started to sing. I rolled my eyes. She had more control than I thought if she was still able to be a smart ass, even if she was pissed. One of the guys, Ryder I think, started to laugh behind me and her attention snapped to him, her eyes softening slightly the glow receding just a small amount.

"Mine," she whispered softly.

I frowned and looked behind me, taking in the four men, realization dawning, and I shook my head. Figures. Something else to explain later. Fun.

"You four, come here," I demanded rather than asked. If anyone could help her let go of the magic, it was them.

Without hesitation, they stepped forward; Remi as well, to my surprise and anger, approaching Hudson without fear. That was either very stupid or very brave. I was interested to see which.

After she snapped out of this, it was going to be fun to explain. But first, I needed to get her to gain control of herself.

. . .

Hudson

The power coursing through me was intoxicating. A small part of myself registered Kalen in front of me instead of my rabbit, I mean the Dean. I heard everything he said and responded in kind. I was still here, but the magic also took my will and shaped it to baser needs and responses. I felt like I was in a werewolf book. I did not enjoy not being in full control of myself, and seeing Kalen reminded me of that. He was right. He had consistently repeated that magic should not control you, rather the other way around, during our training. I sighed internally, but it was so much fun this way too. Decisions, decisions.

"Nah, you can't have it," I sang. I felt a little more me when Kalen rolled his eyes. I loved being a thorn in his side. Then I heard Ryder laugh and the magic took control again. It has been hard enough controlling the urges during the day, but hearing any one of them when I had barely a reign on my powers, snapped me right back into those damn werewolf tendencies.

"Mine," I whispered. A part of me noticed Kalen calling them forward, but I'm not sure if I wanted that. I wanted them, sure, on a baser level. I craved them on an emotional one as well, but at this point, what I needed was to be grounded, not to give in to the urge to get closer to them. Somehow having a magical orgy didn't seem like the best course of action. So, I stepped back.

"Baby, we just want to help," Zane's dark tone sent a shiver down my spine.

"Yum, I want help too." I moved my hand down my chest and to my abs. Ryder and Grayson barked a laugh and Hunter shook his head.

"I'd be happy to oblige. You know I like an audience, angel," whispered Hunter.

Zane groaned. "Not that kind of help, we can go back to that later though. I promise." I stomped my feet in frustration. *I'm a fucking glowing goddess of magic and I'm still being turned down. I'm going to turn him over my knee and spank him.*

Remi cursed and looked back. "Kalen, Alvor. I'm sure you understand the dynamics here."

Kalen chuckled. "Oh I understand, the only way to ground her without her having a magical sentinel-don't worry, I'll explain that later to you, gentlemen-is if you all bond with her magically..." Kalen trailed off and Remi rubbed her head and grumbled about a sausage fest and Dean Alvor laughed.

"Babe, we're going to help you ground your magic, you don't have to necessarily release it, but this way you won't have the urge to hurt anyone and the magic will stop trying to gain control," Zane said smoothly.

I grumbled, "mine, mine, mine." I took a deep breath and closed my eyes, willing myself to come back to the front as much as possible. I grated out, "You fuckers always take all the fun, I. Have... control... what... next... now," I grounded out.

"We're each going to touch a part of you, and it will help funnel the magic through us, so it isn't too much for you at once," Remi said and nodded at the boys, who all stepped closer. When I stayed still, they all approached me and placed a hand on me, one by one. Remi, Grayson, Ryder, Hunter, and finally Zane. When Zane touched me, completing whatever type of fucked up sexually charged circuit this was, I felt, rather than saw, myself glow brighter. They all took a sharp intake of breath that knocked them to their knees, their arms started to glow red, and the guys grunted, and Remi let out a small cry in pain. I felt the magic become more intense, and I felt like I was burning from the inside out, until I felt the urge to just let it all go. I took a deep breath, tired of the burning, and I heard myself yell out as I let go of all the magic inside of me. The release shot us all backwards in different directions. I braced myself to hit the ground, but, of course, I ended up falling back into the fucking water pit.

I dragged myself out of the damn pool for the second time of the damn night. Well, at least it helped the burning. I stood up and walked forward towards Kalen and Alvor, the other five grumbling and getting to their feet. Well, at least I didn't hit the ground. Sucks for them.

"Is this national drown the fuck out of Hudson day? This is some bullshit you know," I pointed at the Dean, who looked away sheepishly. "Don't think I haven't noticed you in all my classes today, watching me like some creep on the six o'clock news; you and Blair can have a creep-off. Was this another test? See how fast Hudson can drown?" Kalen laughed outright, shaking his head. I rolled my eyes and smiled at him. I even threw in a hug for good measure, since I knew hugging freaked him out. He stopped laughing and grumbled something about personal space between trainers and students.

"You laugh, you get hugged..." I paused, "Wait, why are you here?"

He rubbed his neck and blew out a breath. "To check up on you, of course. I knew you could never get the training you needed here," he said lamely.

"Yeah, sure. Because that sounds believable." I waved my arm and paused.

"What the fuck..." I whispered? I looked up and down my arms and belly, which were now covered in swirling black ink. I looked at Kalen and Alvor, who seemed to notice the marks at the same time.

"What is this?" Zane said suddenly behind me. I turned back to respond when I realized he had similar, no... he had the exact same markings as I did. Hunter, Grayson, Ryder, and Remi stepped closer, transfixed by the marking on their own skin. We all had the same marks, same patterns. I reached over and lifted their shirts, ignoring the thrill of passion that coursed through me at the contact and noticed that, just like mine, the markings were also on their abs.

"What the hell is going on here?" I whispered.

"I think we can answer that..." Dean Alvor said, and Kalen looked at him, eyes wide.

Kalen nodded to their silent conversation and sighed, "Let's go somewhere more private. We will meet you at your house shortly." Then he just fucking strode out of the room.

I looked towards Remi, who was chewing on her lip, looking a little lost. Well, join the club.

"Well, let's go see what the fuck this means now. Today is proving to be too long of a damn day. There better be some chocolate in that house."

I walked across the combat area, grabbed my things, and headed straight to my bike, not bothering to look back. I'm sure they were all following. I tossed my leg over my bike and sped off. I was going to get some fucking answers, after a shower.

Chapter Twenty

I drove for about five minutes, before my stomach started feeling very unsettled and a heavy, pressing sense of danger in my chest. Then my headlights caught something in front of me. I slowed my bike, not understanding what I was seeing. It had wings, dark, inky skin, and swirling, fire-tinged eyes.

"What the fuck." I barely got the words out before the stupid shit flew at me with a knife in its hand. I swerved my bike and jumped off, cringing internally as my precious Ducati fell in the dirt, rolling to my feet and trying to see in the dark.

I was able to dodge the attack, but the fucker was clearly still out there. I heard laughter echo around me, and I spun trying to gauge where it was coming from. Fuck this. I pulled energy, cursing not having a weapon, and threw a fireball in the direction of the trees, I heard a shriek. *Was that me?* Fuck, at least the fucker on fire helped me see a little better. And what do I see? I see that I was fucked, I was fucking surrounded. *Where the hell were the guys? They drive like a fucking grandpa on a tricycle, on a beach, in a speedo. Don't ask.*

XENA! I yelled mentally.

"Little queen, little queen, we have been watching you, feeling you. Your magic," one of the winged fuckers stepped closer and breathed deep, "is intoxicating. We want it. All of it. For that you must die."

"First of all, you dickwad, you must have the wrong person. I'm not a queen. Second, fuck you." I gathered my energy and casted a spell to immobilize, except it didn't affect just that one. It stopped them all. Holy shit. Well, that was fucking awesome. I heard the rumblings of bikes, before I saw Xena run and start tearing through whoever was stuck. Taking her lead, I walked up to one of the frozen beasts, its eyes still moving and filled with fury, taking its weapon and cleaving its head off. I cast a lighting spell, illuminating the entire area a bit more clearly and holy fuck. This wasn't a small attack, there must have been dozens of these fuckers everywhere.

I barely registered the guys coming to my side as they took in the sight surrounding us.

"What the fuck is going on?" yelled Zane, taking charge while they all dismounted and ran to my side. I vaguely registered Remi pulling up in her car and running out as well.

"Dude, I don't know. I was driving home when one of them popped out in the middle of the road, then this dead motherfucker, called me a queen and said my power was intoxicating and that I had to die blah blah blah. It was all rather dramatic." I waved my hands around, still taking in the scene.

"Queen? What are they talking about?" murmured Grayson.

"Well, I'll always call you my Queen, sweetie, but I don't think this is what these guys meant," Ryder tried to joke but his eyes were wide as he took in the many frozen bodies around us.

"I have never seen creatures like these," I said, Xena continued to kill and maim whatever she could.

"Hudson, we need to get you out of here now. There are quite a few things that need to be explained to you," Remi whispered. She spoke as if she knew. One of the creatures started to move and I spun around with the boys at the sound.

"Oh, little queen, there is so much for you to know and you know nothing," it cackled. "Just know, you will die," it hissed. I was fucking tired; it had been a long ass day and I. Was. Fucking. Done.

"Fuck this, you will die." I pulled my magic, closed my eyes, and sent off a wave of different, yet familiar, magic that lit up the night sky as it burned every single one of the winged evil fuckers up and incinerated them. I held my concentration through the shocked murmurs of the boys, until I 'felt' the threat was gone. My chest felt lighter and I took a deep breath and opened my eyes.

Remi tugged my hand and the guys looked as confused as I felt. I followed her to my bike, before I righted in, cringing at the dirt before getting back on. I was hyper aware yet strangely numb as we drove back to the house, Xena running by my side the entire time.

What in the ever fuck was going on, and why do I feel like this was only the beginning of a very fucked Hudson's life plot twist?

I pulled into the garage and parked the bike. I heard the other bikes and Remi's car approaching and I walked straight inside and headed straight for the pool area, not wanting to stand inside, covered in blood, sweat and whatever the fuck else was on my body. After a day like today, I needed a shower and comfort clothes, or maybe a dip in the damn jacuzzi, but I guess that was going to have to wait until Kalen could explain what these marks were and apparently, whatever that attack was, if what Remi said is accurate. Of course, Kalen and the Dean were already there, and I nodded my head in their direction as I threw myself down on the lounge chair, Xena at my side.

The men and Remi approached from behind and followed suit with picking a lounger. I wanted to make sure they were there before I started talking.

I looked directly at Kalen. "So care to explain why I feel like someone is holding out on me and why I was just attacked by some dark winged assholes who called me queen and tried to kill me?" He looked startled. Well, he fucking should. My bike was hurt damnit. At least I was fine.

"You were what!?"

"Yes, catch up, Kalen, because I'm really trying to figure out how the hell you, the attack, those creatures, these marks and my... friends are connected in all of this."

"They were dark Fae, Kalen. They got past the school wards and tried to kill Hudson," Remi spoke up. Kalen rubbed his head angrily and looked at the dean.

"Okay," the Dean started, "so I'm sure you're all curious as to what happened earlier," Alvor began. I rolled my eyes. What was this, a fucking wedding? We are all gathered here today, type of shit?

"Understatement, Dean. What is going on," Hunter started, my forever angry one, already aching for an argument.

"Hudson, as I'm sure you have all noticed, is different. Her abilities with magic, and the way her mind works, makes her extremely advanced. More so than anyone her age or even beyond her age," the Dean paused.

"For goodness sake, Alvor, the time to sugarcoat it all is over. She was almost killed," Kalen snapped, and made eye contact with all the guys and glanced over Remi, his mouth tightening, before settling over me.

"Hudson, your name is not really Hudson Jacobs, it is Riona Fheall. You are not human. You are Fae."

THE SILENCE WAS THICK.

"Okay." My voice was steady, and Kalen smiled. "So today, I started school, played Buffy the stuck-up kid slayer, drowned myself in magic, got attacked, and now I'm a fairy. Anyone else thinks this is all going just a little too fast? So, hey, before Tinkerbell comes and introduces herself, let's take this in parts. Part one, get to why we..." I pointed at the boys and Remi, "have matching tattoos. The murder shit can come after."

Kalen growled, "This isn't Disney."

"Clearly," Ryder scoffed. "There is no blood allowed in those movies," he muttered. Kalen glared at him.

Kalen continued, "So you're not Tinkerbell and not a fairy, even though Tinkerbell is fashioned after the Fae version of a pixie, but we can get into details later. I said you are Fae, and the correct term is Faerie. I have been training you and protecting you for years, it is my designated duty to make sure you know all there is about Fae, however the informational part was supposed to be when you turned 21 and had time to come into your powers, but your powers started to unravel at a quicker pace, shortly after you must have lost your virginity."

"How..." I started but he waved me off.

"Your hair would only turn at the spilling of your virgin blood. It's part of Fae magic. For most children in our home, it happens at puberty, when powers begin to manifest."

"Great, awesome. So, you're an undercover Faerie. Two things. Where is your home and where the hell are your wings? Those fuckers back there had wings you never flew around for me, soooo..." I trailed off.

"I'll get to that," he sighed. "Now, I would say it was a coincidence that I chose today to come by, but..."

"You don't believe in coincidences," I finished for him with a small smile and he smiled with me.

"Okay, so whatever. I'm a Faerie. I'll roll with that. Care to breach the other stuff?"

"One thing at a time," snapped Zane. "What are these marks?"

Kalen chuckled. "Well, it would be Hudson to leave home and within days, find her fated Fae mates. Although, I admit, Remi was a shock, being as old as she is," he continued even though I froze and Dean made a sound of protest. I had a feeling that the information drop was deliberate. "The marks indicate that you're all connected on a level that goes way beyond marriage, beyond soulmates; it is a connection that is only broken by death. The more mates, the harder you are, as a whole, to kill."

"Mates?" Zane whispered, his eyes on me, then turning to look at the other guys. Remi refused to look up.

"I'm sure you have noticed that you four have been drawn to her since you met her. Protective even. Every day that bond got stronger, and even when you left, you couldn't stop thinking about her? The mates typically know, innately, who they will bond to. Hudson, being younger, didn't feel the same until she was with you all at the same time, so just recently. Or when she was alone with Zane a couple of years ago, they wouldn't have been able to stop the pull, with her being of age." He sighed and rubbed his head. "Her meeting Remi completed your group, I can surmise, making Hudson's connection to you all stronger, even if it wasn't sealed at the time. Again, most Fae have one or two mates. Hudson having five is not only rare, it is unheard of. Typically, these bonds are sealed when the mates have sex for the first time and her virginity is gone. However, it seems you have all been intimate with Hudson." It wasn't a question and I blushed furiously and coughed. Grayson came over to sit next to me and put me on his lap. Kalen smiled approvingly. "No need to feel embarrassed, Hudson. It is a true honor to find your mate and you seem to not only have found them but to have built a relationship with each of them as well. Now usually, sex, virginity, and a bonding ceremony with a small transfer of power is all that's needed to bond, however, the magic from today not only sealed the bond, but it also seems to have brought out Hudson's full Fae side."

"What? How?" I was startled but Kalen smirked and shook his head.

"Hudson, I have been training you for several years. Not only were you near the surface of your magic, but you also found your mates and wielded an amount of power that even a full-grown Fae would be unable to maintain. While having the men there helped you from losing control, that loss of control would have been more of a rampage. A magical tantrum, if you will. I don't think it would have destroyed you."

"Think?" I asked before the guys jumped in, and I glared at them. *My time to ask shit, dammit.*

"If it was going to happen, it would have happened quickly." He waved his hand, dismissing the idea. "Regardless, you'll all have to navigate the bond and the connections it will start to unravel between you all. It will come with a fierce overprotective feeling, the ability to feel each other's emotions and to always be able to track each other, just to name a few."

"Overprotection? They've been like that since forever. And I'm sure they are the reason I have never had a date. No one would come near me... fuckers," I muttered. The boys laughed.

"Guilty, we threatened everyone before we left. You were always ours, even if we didn't really know it at the time," Grayson whispered.

"Guilty also, you're the daughter of my heart. I loved you way too much to let any little punk mess with you," chuckled Kalen.

"Oh, you guys suck!" I said, frustrated. I smirked at the boys though. "Could be worse, though. At least I lost my virginity to the right person," I said softly, and Zane looked at me with adoration, making me blush.

I cleared my throat. "Okay, so that is all quite a bit to digest and I still have a shit ton of questions. So, we're mated. We haven't had a chance to look at the marks in full, so if we have more questions, I guess we can ask after a decent shower."

"Now the murder part, why were those things trying to kill me and why are they called Dark Fae? What is the difference between them, and I guess you or me?"

"Hudson," Kalen, sighed. "In short, we have two factions, if you will, of the Fae. The Dark Fae who we call the Unseelie and the Light Fae who are called the Seelie. You're of the light variety. Within the Fae, there are many, many, variations of our people. For those fascinated by Disney," he rolled his eyes and Ryder chuckled, "think of goblins, dwarves, and pixies but there are thousands more. Marks are not understood by anyone outside of Fae, however, and there are those out there who have suspicions of our people. Over time, we have been pushing into society that Faerie's are myths and tales and what not." He waved his hands in the air. "Hudson, you are extremely important to our people, to our home, even if it was brought about in a less than desired way. To make it short you, Hudson, are the embodiment of a myth, in more ways than one, because you are a result of a prophecy. Myths protect, they obscure truths in order to ensure the survival of our home, our people, and our secrets. That is now your role. Who you are may have been hidden, but it was to bring about good and positive things. Within our home, which is protected, and beyond, there are enemies of Fae. So, from the outside, in short, we have been protected by myths and as such your very existence has been concealed by those same myths. It is what has ensured your survival, but we are always at war." He leaned back and took a long breath.

"Am I going to hear this Prophecy or am supposed to take it at face value?"

"It's long and we will get to it. The short version is, there is a balance, light and dark. It is a tenuous balance, but one that has been held by eons; nature balances all. We are the natural creatures, from Gaia herself, and therefore, we are pure magic because we came from the source of all life. Over time, magic has been diluted due to mating with humans, but our race has remained pure because despite those dalliances, we always come back home. The Dark Fae have perverted our lands, destroying the balance by taking a throne that was not theirs, and while you are technically the queen of the Seelie, you have been prophesied to help bring the balance back to all. We have been preparing for years and have amassed a small army for you. We will stop the killing of Seelie's and help those who need our assistance."

"Right... awesome cliff notes prophecy. So, I'm using my people to fight my people so I can win my people. Well, that makes perfect sense. Guess it's time for bed then." I rolled my eyes, putting my head in my hands rubbing my temples.

"I know it's a lot, there is no way to explain it all at once, but we will discuss everything in more detail, over the next few days. As it is, I'm thinking I'll need to stay and try to educate you as much as possible and have the grounds warded properly to avoid further issues." He leaned forward on his knees, looking pensive. "Eventually, I'm going to have to leave and touch base with our camp, but until then, we might as well learn as much as we can. Get you guys up to speed." He got up and stretched. "Why don't you guys go freshen up and I'll get some coffee started? I think with all the questions you have it will be a long night, and to be honest, I want to go on a perimeter search. Xena, you'll come with me," he finished, nodding to Xena and she stood up with her chest puffed out. I chuckled and nodded. Yeah, it was going to be a long night.

"Well, I'm going to head out now. Kalen? I trust you have this in hand. I'll make sure the other students are safe," said Alvor standing up, I narrowed my eyes at him as he walked away. That should have been his first instinct as Dean of the school. It didn't escape my notice that he didn't seem very outraged or concerned about our run in with the Dark Fae. I didn't trust him, and I just couldn't put my finger on why.

Part II The Blade You Wield

"Breathing slow and breathing deep
Arise thy spark!
Arise and conquer!
Fire deep within the soul
Defend the boundaries of thy master!
I find my voice; I find my power
I hum my spell
I sing my tune
The star of nature is my shield
I am firmly rooted in this realm.
Emblazoned sigil in my mind
My throaty drone empowers thee
To cast false angels to the wind

As I WILL, So MOTE IT BE!
The spell is broken
My guests depart
I fall down exhausted
I sleep without a dream."

STORM FAERYWOLF

Chapter Twenty-One

While Kalen and Xena did a perimeter check, we all took turns taking showers. I stripped off my clothes and tossed them in the hamper in my bathroom, and I walked into the shower and stood underneath the stream of the shower, as hot as I could make it. People joke that women need their water hot to remind them of hell, where they came from. More like we need our water hot to remind ourselves of where we will be going if we murder the stupid assholes who hit on us all damn day.

I lathered and washed my hair, taking in the new marks on my hands, arms, belly and apparently my breasts as well, all the way up to my collar bone. The swirls were gorgeous, intricate, weaving and knotting all the way down to my pelvic bone before they wrapped around my lower back. As I rinsed my hair and then conditioned, I let the conditioner sit while I soaped up my body dragging the loofah across my skin. My skin felt over sensitive and I let out a low moan. I sucked in a sharp breath as I bent over to wash my legs and saw that the swirls hadn't stopped; they continued all the way down from the juncture of my thighs to my thighs and legs. These swirls were just as intricate, but as they progressed to my toes they were more of a deep purple. They were gorgeous- it was as if I was painted on by someone with the most incredibly steady hand and vision. They wove, turned and twisted, very similarly to vines on a tree or the way branches grew.

I sighed, taking my time in the shower as I worked the brush over my tangles. I was going to go downstairs eventually; they would have to just wait. At that thought I saw Remi step into the shower with me. Benefit of a rain shower? So much space and never having to fight over the shower head. We stayed silent as I continued to work through my hair, and she started to shower. I took in her matching swirls except hers stopped right at the hip, while mine kept going. I wonder why. I said as much, as she looked away and muttered that she had no idea. I frowned; she must be as confused as I am, so I brushed it off.

Stepping out of the shower, I dried off quickly and threw on some underwear and a pair of yoga pants and a tank top. Remi helped herself to my clothes and we walked out of my room and down the stairs. It looked like the guys were all settled into the living room with cups of coffee in their hands, no shirts on, in grey sweatpants, with their new magical ink on display. Who ever invented grey sweatpants are fucking amazing angels and we need to bow down to their greatness because holy shit, I had to check if I was drooling?

"Jeez, they really need to consider banning grey pants, seriously," I said as I settled down on the couch next to Ryder and Grayson.

Ryder laughed and leaned in to kiss my cheek, I know we're apparently at war, so could he not look like fucking sex? "Aww gorgeous, I'm glad you think we're sexy," he wrapped his arms around me. This felt magnetic; too natural, like we were always meant to be in each-other's arms. I guess the mate stuff all made sense now. How fast everything progressed, and how good it all felt.

I stuck out my tongue at him, "I didn't say all that now," I grumbled. Grayson laughed, and leaned over to press a kiss to my lips, teasing my tongue way too softly and pulling away way too soon.

"Fucking teases," I cleared to my throat, "So Kalen, I'm curious, Remi's marks go from her arms to her pelvic bone, it looks like the guys are the same." I looked at them for confirmation and they nodded.

He nodded and sighed, rubbing his face leaning back against the wall across us, ever the perfect guard. "Yeah, when I saw them come down, I realized, and I guess it makes sense. You are exceptionally strong Hudson, that much is clear. The Fae live in a matriarchal society, so the bonds that form and the marks that follow are based off the strength and lineage of the female, usually the mate marks are on the bicep or forearm; nothing as intricate and as full body as yours. I haven't seen anything like it in a hundred years, after our last matriarch passed, and yet she only had one mate."

I blew out a breath, "I feel like every-time you answer a question I have several more, but first, is there a secret Faerie reason why my marks go past my pelvic bone and wrap around my entire back and legs? Is it like a Queen thing?" Kalen blinked and looked at me standing very still.

"That has not been seen in our history," his eye quickly flicked to Remis', which was another fucking question I had, I put it in my long list of to be asked. "That would be an indication of a strength and connection to your powers beyond my current knowledge and understanding. Can you show me?" I shrugged and tugged off my shirt and pulled down my yoga pants.

I TURNED AROUND AND SHOWED HIM THE MARKS ON MY LOWER BACK, butt, back of my legs as well as the front. Brushing my long hair over my shoulder I showed them my arms, chest and collar bone. Honestly, every inch of me was covered. Even my toes. The only part left alone was my tattoo, and even then, it weaved within it. I tugged my clothes back on. Kalen's face looked shocked, I avoided looking at the guys because I had a feeling their looks were a little different.

Kalen cleared his throat, "yeah, I have never seen that. You fully coming into your power is going to bring its own complications, but you can certainly not go back to school like this Hudson. It will raise too many suspicions and paint a target on your back, even more so. Apparently, there is already a professor on campus obsessed with the origin of magic. As it is, I don't think any of you should be going back to campus actively."

"Well, fuck me." I whispered. I just couldn't stop my entire life for some fucking myths or prophesy. I opened my mouth to protest but he must have seen me gearing up because cut me off with a firm angry voice, "Your work can be sent to you and you can complete assignments here if you wish, but that time of your life is now over Hudson. Your education will take another route. As for staying here, the same thing goes for your mates- their marks cannot be seen, but they are extensive. I'm sorry. No matter how strong you are, you also cannot be left alone during the day, not because you can't defend yourself- I pity whoever tries to attack you- but simply because all it takes is one wolf in sheep's clothing." His voice darkened. "And I have a feeling that we have quite a few amongst us. I will not have you in danger. I hope Alvor will have measures in place, and your mates will protect you, and you have me and Xena, and I have some more protections in place as well."

He started to pace, and I was lost in my thoughts, so I guess the guys took this as their opportunity to ask their questions.

"Can't we use concealment spells to cover the marks?" Asked Ryder.

"Yes, except those won't stop a Fae from seeing the marks, only magic users. So there are enemies out there for whom you'll all be an easy target for." Ryder nodded in understanding.

"You mentioned lineage. But both of Hudson's parents are magic users, so how does that tie into her being of a strong Fae lineage?" Asked Grayson.

"Ah, well that's a great question," he looked a little nervous. "The chancellor is not her biological father, that honor would go to a Fae prince who met her mom during a missionary trip to gather allies that live beyond our Veil." *Wait, what?*

"How long has he known?" Growled Zane. I was still stuck.

Kalen scratched his neck, his muscles bulging, and his dark look a complete contrast to the nervous look on his face, "the Chancellor was made aware when Hudson was around ten, it's when whispers of her existence being real made their way to the Dark Fae and we had to be more proactive about her protection. I had no choice at that point but to approach him." My jaw dropped.

"Okay stop, all this influx of information. I need a break." I stood to my feet and went to the kitchen to rummage for a snack. Chocolate solves everything. Ugh, Father. Was that why he went from the man I loved to the man I barely knew? I couldn't know my real father, but did I have to lose the only one I knew too? My chest hurt. Looking around the kitchen, I snagged my phone from the counter, where I must have left it when I walked into the house, took my chocolate and stepped outside. I took a deep breath and sat on the edge of the pool, leaving my feet in the water.

I remember how good it felt the first day I was here, how incredible the pool was, how everything was so picturesque. It didn't seem as pretty and calming out here as it did a few days ago though; it felt oppressive and ominous. I wasn't sure if it was because of what happened earlier, or what was to come, or if it was the information I was just punched in the face with, or even the likelihood of another attack soon. I think what was truly bothering me was that it all fit somehow- it made sense. I felt someone come up behind me and didn't have to look to know Zane had come outside to check on me. Sitting down, he tugged me on to his lap, and wrapped his arms around me.

I sighed and sunk into him, "You know, the craziest thing about this entire thing is? It somehow fits, doesn't it?"

"The connection between us all? Or the circumstances? I don't think finding out you're a little overgrown tinker-bell is fitting." I felt his warm voice caress my neck as his deep voice cocooned me with its sensuality, I suppressed a shiver and turned to look up at him.

"Haha," I deadpanned, taking in the laughter in his eyes, and rolled my eyes. "I guess so," I continued. "I felt it more after our first time together, like a pull in your direction, but after I came here, and I was near you all? It unraveled and happened fast, but it felt right. Beyond that, I have always been faster, stronger, and smarter than anyone in my age group." I paused, absentmindedly running my fingers up and down his arm. "I always felt like I was...more? I can't explain it, but nothing like this is surprising to me. Shock value, sure. Like, 'hey, you're an abandoned Faerie warrior Queen that needs to save the day', is going to hit anyone over the head pretty hard." He chuckled.

"You're rambling," he hugged me tighter and sighed, "I don't know what to say, other than I always knew you and I were more than we were. It just felt like a missing piece being put into place, and I know the guys feel the same way. So, hearing that it's because of a mystical bond or some shit doesn't change that, and if anything it makes us feel more permanent. I like the idea that you're stuck with me, with us, forever. You can't even run, he said we can find you." He looked at me seriously, despite his eyes twinkling. I laughed.

"Please, like I couldn't get away if I wanted to," I teased.

He scoffed, "Like you would want to anyway. What else is on your mind?"

I sighed and kicked the water, "I'm angry at the circumstances when I think about how I was left here by a father who didn't want me, even if it was for my protection or whatever, and then Father finds out and shuts me out, and then you randomly come into the picture right around the time he finds out, which I guess to him was a good distraction to the fact that I wasn't really his. I came out here to call him," I whisper, holding the phone in my hand, "but I don't even know what I would say, or if I should let him know that I know now." I bite my lip right before he picks me up and turns me around on his lap and hits me with his full gaze. I take in his sharp jaw, soft lips and the new marks on his body. Wrapping my arms around his neck, I give him a soft kiss before leaning into the crook of his neck, while he rubs circles on my back.

"It's okay to be angry, it's a lot to take in at once, but he loves you. He just didn't know how to show it properly. It's a lot more than what most people have- remember that before you call him and get angry. Give yourself a few days to process before you do that. You also have Kalen, who you said yourself was like a father figure. Again, not something to take for granted. It's okay to be angry; I didn't expect you to feel any differently." I stay quiet, mulling over his words. Sigh, I know he is right, but it didn't sit right with me. I guess I should take a few days to think it over.

"I guess, I should put on my sexy, big girl thong and go handle this shit, right?" His lips twitched.

"Yeah, that sounds like a good idea, come on let's go grill the great Kalen some more," he stood up and pulled me into a hug. "No matter what, we got this, all of us. Okay?" I nodded, breathing in his scent, taking comfort in knowing that I may be a badass, but I have a team of badasses behind me too.

Chapter Twenty-Two

We settled back on the couch, this time with me on Zane's lap and the guys sitting next to us. Remi sat across the room with a pensive look on her face and it sparked another question. Looks like I was full of those.

"I'm curious. What did you mean before about Remi's age?" I asked, I looked between Kalen and Remi. Kalen leaned back and crossed his arms over his chest, looking over at Remi.

"Do you want to do the honors, Remi?" Kalen growled. I looked at him curiously and realized I wasn't going to enjoy what I was going to hear.

Remi

Fuck, this wasn't supposed to happen so fast. Yes, I was drawn to her, and I figured we were maybe destined to be mated in the back of my head, as our connection happened too quickly, our passion too intense. Seeing the marks appear filled me with such love and joy, I felt like my soul was complete. At the same time, I was filled with trepidation for this reason alone.

"Hudson." I squared my shoulders and looked her right in her eyes. "Alvor and I were sent here to retrieve you by our crown prince when you turned 21. Your powers were supposed to manifest by then and it would have been too unsafe for you to remain in the mortal world." I sighed and stood up from my spot. Her eyes sharpened and she sat up straighter. She was beautiful, even if she was going to hate me. I sighed and rubbed my face.

"I was going to meet you at that party with or without Reed, because that was the plan. I was supposed to get close, become your friend, and blend in. I'm not really a people person, so that actually worked in my favor. We are very similar." I smiled softly. She nodded.

"And that night?" she said softly, her tone laced with anger.

"If you are asking if I planned to have sex with you to get close to you, then you must think very low of me," I spit out, glaring at her. She didn't move, her eyes meeting mine straight on, not giving an inch.

"That night was unexpected. I felt drawn to you. What we felt was real. Every moment was real. The circumstances that led me there may have been false, but since then, I have never been anyone other than myself."

She scoffed. "Except pretending to be human, but please, continue! You were at the part where you were "sent" here to retrieve me like I was property. Kidnap is the proper term by the way." She pointed at me. "Then take me to some random land because I was of age to be powerful and useful, am I right?"

"Yes and no. We were to bring you back, but not because you were only useful. Powerful, yes, as your lineage would have made you so by blood, but because of the prophecy given about 100 years ago, after the murder of our last matriarch. Beyond the Veil that separates the mortal realm from ours, home is ruled by the females of our line. In fact, it is unheard of for the males to take over unless it is for a grave reason, and even then, it's temporary. The prophecy suggested a female of great blood, hidden away with mortals, was destined to come back and return the balance in two hundred years, just like Kalen has described. These past three hundred years have been filled with strife, deception, and torture. The prophecy gave hope, and people started sneaking out, and the Seelie built a home heavily warded from the Queen's influence. I have yet to go, as I knew I wouldn't exactly be welcome.

"Why not?" she asked. I continued as if I didn't hear her. I would get to that part.

"The prince of the second leading family went out for about a year, going on an expedition to the mortal realm. At the time, he met a mortal woman and they conceived a child. He asked for her to come back with him, but she refused. The prince was a kind Fae. He never forced her to come, but he did watch over her. He sent missives to those loyal to the original rule in order to protect his baby girl."

"Tell her who you are, Remi," demanded Kalen. I blew out a breath and glared at him. My uncle's mate always thought badly of me, but I did what I had to do because I thought I was right at the time. I came to see sense way too late and have regretted it every day since then.

"About 320 years ago, I was still young, by our standards, only 85 years of age, and I thought that the idea of a female matriarch, who was to have a child to carry on the line, was outdated. I was next in line for the throne. The Queen at the time was my mother. I was urged to marry, and I refused countless times." I growled and began to pace. "Why does a female have to be able to bear children in order to lead? I was angry. I have never been interested in men. I knew I wouldn't bear my own child unless it was by doing something I was against, physically and emotionally. I just couldn't do it. So, I became friends with people who I believed thought similarly, but they ended up being Dark Fae who had infiltrated the kingdom, who wanted to get closer to the lesbian princess," I sneered, "of the Fae to try to kill the Queen. They used it to their advantage, and I fell in love, well, I thought I did, with the leader of the group. Her name was Nicnevin. I called her Nici, but at the time, I didn't realize the significance of her name. I admit I was rebellious and neglected some of the things I really should have known. She was a Queen of old, moreso known as Gyre-Carling. A strong witch, a strong Fae, with her own following of Fae, she just wanted another Throne. She wanted to rule over both the Seelie and Unseelie. Our people are great; widely spread throughout several countries and every location has its own form rule. Our home is part of the Greater Realm of the North. Our realm is closer to the human realm. The way the Veil works is a bit complicated, and this closeness made it easier to hide you, and just as dangerous as well. Regardless," I waved my hand and tried to get back to the point.

"My mother was fair, just, and kind. She was loved by many; however, she was very stuck in her beliefs of tradition and it didn't allow for much flexibility. The Fae are an old race, older than most as we were born from pure energy and magic when Gaia was first born into existence. I can respect sticking to who we are as a people, connecting to our origins. However, after thousands of years, you can imagine that it wasn't the most accepting of situations. Traditions can stifle. My uncle and his mate couldn't even be together freely because of judgement." I gestured at Kalen and Hudson gasped.

"Like I said, I was angry. I let myself be fooled by people I thought were my friends, someone I thought loved me. I'm a loner for a reason, Hudson. You are the only person, beyond duty, I ever connected with."

"That is where you are wrong, Remi," she interrupted. "I was, and still am, your duty. The marks don't change that." I felt my heart break a little, I needed her to understand. I spent these years not understanding what love really was, and now I knew I did.

I shook my head softly. "Yes, I came because of duty, to fulfill a prophecy, and to bring greatness back to a land that I help destroy. A land now split in two, with people now split into two; no balance in the Realm. I was given a gift for my birthday by Nici; the gift of loving without judgement. It was supposed to be a powerful dream draft that would allow me to manipulate my consciousness and live within my fantasies, even for a night. Except that night, they snuck into the castle, my mother having dismissed the guards for a night off, thinking herself safe between her and I for protection... they... they overwhelmed her, and they killed her while I slept. I woke up several days later to funeral preparations and an interim monarch. Nici had taken the throne. The implications of that were great. She is very powerful; known to bring the winter where she goes... destruction. To fight her was to die. She was cunning. I regret being taken advantage of. I wanted to love, but it was my downfall. I realized then that my emotions were truly frivolous, and I should have tried to be more understanding of my mother's wishes instead of being a brat." I sighed.

"The next leading family with no female to take over had to sit on the side, while a false Queen stood on the throne for those days, causing descent. I wasn't expected to wake up, but I did. However, I was weakened by the potion. It worked more like a poison, which should have killed me, knowing afterwards, it is what Nici was known for. But it didn't, and the other family had hidden and protected me. The Prince and I became close friends. Nici led with cruelty. But tradition was female monarchs and with me in hiding, sick and weak, and the other family only having sons, we were stuck. That prophecy gave me hope. I continued to lead with the Prince from the sidelines the best that I could, as a rebel. I was inclusive, encouraging our people to embrace beyond their norm and give people a chance to love who they loved, despite gender roles. The Fae always lived equally, for the most part. Everyone had large homes, food, jobs, and childcare, but a few trivial things like love were problematic. It was disgusting. However, the new Queen was the opposite of what she had preached to me and undid the little I was able to do, behind the scenes.

She thirsted for power and reform and she changed the status quo. She started castes and Fae were being reduced to squalor. I tried to remain positive, but when the time for the prophecy came around, the Prince confided in me that he had conceived a child with a magic female, meaning that the chances of her being Fae were more than 80 percent. I heard whispers that she wanted the child killed. The timing was right. It was perfect. The Prince begged me to bring back the child to the realm in order for her to take her rightful place as Queen. He expected someone weak, someone without training. But there were spies sent out and the tales of your strength and control surpassed his imagination. He ordered you brought back, in an official capacity, claiming a Fae dissenter was living in the mortal realm and should be brought to justice, as a cover. He sent me and Alvor to do it.

"So, you're the true Queen," Grayson stated. It wasn't a question, but I nodded.

"But instead of protecting your people for the past hundred years, you've been aiding and acting like a rebel and working with the second possible ruling family in the realm," continued Ryder.

"So, your plan was to bring Hudson into a realm full of war and strife, and proclaim her Queen? So now, when you're clearly standing next to her as her mate, how do you think that would work?" growled Hunter.

"I would abdicate the throne in an official capacity."

Hudson blew out a breath and visibly shook with anger, her eyes swirling. "So, then people would lay witness to the mating of two powerful families taking over after being subjected to disregard for three hundred and twenty years, assuming I even survived even entering the kingdom, because the previous Queen was a pussy - is that correct?" Hudson stood up angrily. "I would suddenly come in, fight my way to the top, with Queen Remi at my side. How the fuck would that have even worked, Remi? Thinking like a damn Queen here, you would be a dissenter, a rebel and an abandoner who suddenly brought the prophesized Queen back, and you confidently abdicate and then I'm to take control? Nici would what? Just back away after planning a coop and holding her position for so long? Let's add that now I'm marked everywhere because I'm more powerful than anyone in history, apparently. Now, add five fully marked mates and all of a sudden I'm supposed to walk in and say, 'Hey, I'm the prophesied Queen here to fix shit and, oh yeah, your old Queen was here the entire time and now she is my mate, but I hope you trust me anyway even though she fucking ignored you all these years. By the way, I am ridiculously powerful, don't be scared. I won't kill you...maybe.' I'm sure that is going to go over great with everyone."

I had nothing to say, so I didn't. This was a risk. A calculated one, but a risk none-the-less, and one that would put her in danger from the current monarch and the powerful enemies who wish to do away with the idea of the monarchy altogether at this point. In effect, I was indeed planning on kidnapping her into a mess, simply because I was too selfish, focused more on my own needs, to want to take the seat myself.

"What confuses me is clearly Kalen has been helping rebuild the Seelie Court with the Prince, who would be Hudson's father, and he was sent to watch, protect, and guide her. But yet, it doesn't seem that you knew about his role in all of this. In fact, it looks like the Prince sent you on a fool's errand while she was guarded and protected the entire time. I wonder why that is?" said Zane, standing up. "Maybe it was because he knew he couldn't trust you with the real information and was sending you out to test your loyalty. Maybe he figured you were a part of Nici's plan all along and wanted to see your next move. I don't believe for a second you were actually sent for retrieval, which is interesting, to say the least, considering he sent both you and Alvor and only recently was Hudson ever attacked," he finished, looking around from Kalen and myself. He was actually making a lot of sense. I ran my hands through my hair, feeling lost, like I was missing something. I looked at Kalen and he gave me a look of indifference.

"Because the only way to test loyalty is to do just that. Overall, it was several decades of misguided actions and if he was protecting Hudson like Kalen said, he wouldn't thrust someone into a position like that. No, if I was him, I would be testing loyalty or finding a viper in the nest. I'm going to go with the latter," Hunter said thoughtfully, a direct contrast to the tangible anger radiating from his body. Silence fell in the room as everyone digested my words, and you could almost see the thoughts floating in the air while they considered what everything meant. I admit, everything made less sense now. What was the Prince trying to do and who was he trying to weed out?

"Remi, get out. Do what you think you need to do to prepare for this cluster fuck, because clearly, we are stuck together, but for a few hours, at least, just go," Hudson whispered after a few moments of silence. I looked at her sadly, in all her glory; beautiful, perfect, and uniquely her. Being mated, for the Fae, was beyond anything that could be explained in human terms. I would go, because I respect her, but we were one now. We would all feel the absence of the other and the guys would grow to be something akin to being my brothers. I sighed and walked up to her and looked at her in her eyes.

"I'm sorry. If there is one thing I have taken from my extensive childhood, all 300 plus years of it, is that if life was going to get any easier it was because you were dead." I shrugged, unapologetically. It was the truth. You couldn't expect life to ever be easy and I learned that lesson several times over. "It took all this time to feel a connection with someone, and me being selfish, leaving home and finding a forbidden prophesied princess to find a mate I can love. I finally have the opportunity to love someone who loves me the same, unapologetically, and I damn sure am going to be here to protect you and fight for you no matter how difficult shit is about to get, both emotionally and physically. War is coming, Hudson, whether we bring it there or they bring it here. Take a few hours. I'll go pack my shit, because effective immediately, I will be staying here with you all. We can talk when I get back because this," I gestured between me and her, "is forever. Get used to it." I grabbed her by the chin and kissed her hard, then pulled away. I walked to leave but turned back and said softly, "Give us the chance to love each other, Hudson. However you may see me now, all this shit has brought me to you, and I can't be sorry for that." I shut the door behind me and drove to the dorms. She may be stubborn, but we were cut from the same cloth and I could be just as difficult. This was going to be a new adventure for all of us, and we would face this shit head on. Fuck the past. We have a future to build.

Chapter Twenty-Three

Hudson

I sighed as the door closed behind her. My mind was in a bit of a whirlwind. I hated it. I truly didn't like not having a handle on shit, and this was just a culmination of, apparently, hundreds of years of bullshit.

My mind was in chaos. She was going to kidnap me to take me back to places I never even knew existed until today. She wants to love me. She was going to put me in danger. She wants to love me. She didn't even know we were going to be mates; I was clueless. She wanted to love me. So how did I feel? Angry. I couldn't think past that emotion right now. I must have been in my head for a few minutes because Kalen grabbed me and brought me into a hug, that itself shocked me back into the present, he was never a big hugger.

"Listen, little minx, I'm going to do a perimeter check and call a few contacts. Ryder, Zane, Hunter, and Grayson will stay here with you until

Remi gets back. Don't kill your mate," he chuckled while tugging at my hair.

"No promises there," I said, rolling my eyes. "Before you go, answer me one thing." He stepped back and nodded.

"You mentioned sentinels?" I asked.

"They are people drawn to you with the innate desire to protect you. They will bond with you magically and have your mark, but will be more of a best friend. Your magic will bolster theirs and your emotions will be an open book to them, and vice versa. They can also help you calm and focus your mind and magic. Their appearance is usually tied to the awakening of your powers as well, so we will have to bide our time and wait to see what the future brings."

I sighed, the waiting game, right... that was sure to be a grand old time. I felt the guys' eyes on me. "What about the whole mate thing? What else does it mean, beyond sex?" His face turned bright red and I laughed.

"Part of the fun is discovering a lot of that on your own terms." He cleared his throat and looked at the guys and then back at me, "just know you'll be drawn to each other a lot more than usual. It may seem overwhelming, but just enjoy it. The mate bond is a wonderful gift." He looked away wistfully, his eyes sad. He gave me one final hug and said his goodbyes as he walked through the house and out the front door, following the path of Remi.

I BLINKED MY EYES AT THE BRIGHTNESS OF THE SUN COMING through my window. I shoved Hunter's heavy arm off me as I tried to get through the tangle of limbs on my bed to use the bathroom. After a few attempts I was finally able to get everyone off of me and jump out of the bed. Shortly after Kalen left for his perimeter checks, I declared that I needed to go to bed and the guys all followed and made themselves comfortable in my room. Do you know how four huge men and a woman all sleep on a king size bed? Not fucking comfortably, and I'm pretty sure I kicked someone in the nuts in the middle of the night, if the groans were any indication. I looked at the tangle of limbs and held back a laugh as I took in Ryder and Zane cuddling. I grabbed my phone and snagged a quick picture before I snatched a bathing suit from my drawer and made my way to the bathroom.

After the door clicked softly behind me, I leaned back against the door and I sighed as I ran my hands through my curls. What a night! I don't know how to feel, but I did know that the pool, some food and liquid whiskey-flavored courage were calling my name. I took a quick shower and brushed my teeth before putting on my bathing suit. The suit was a deep purple and it technically could be classified as a one piece, but it dipped all the way down past my navel, stopping right at the start of my mound. It had thin straps that crisscrossed at the hips which led to a thong bottom, and at my lower back, the string broke apart into eight strings that crossed into an x formation across my back. From my shoulders down, it cupped my breasts, barely, considering each piece of fabric on my breast was about four inches of material. I'd bought this for God knows what reason during one of my secret shopping binges, and I was actually convinced it was lingerie, but the sales lady insisted it wasn't. I said fuck it, it was sexy and downright scandalous; perfect for the new me. I loved how it showed off my new marks. Taking a few pictures and sending them to the group chat, I chuckled, knowing their reactions were going to be epic. I tiptoed back into the room and snagged a long coverup before I snuck out of the room with my phone and left the guys asleep.

I walked downstairs and Kalen was in the kitchen, making himself at home, making some coffee and what looked like protein pancakes.

"Good morning, sunshine," I teased him as I sat down at the kitchen island and he rolled his eyes at me.

"It's early afternoon but I'll take it. I assume you all passed out after the excitement of yesterday." He filled a mug with coffee and slid it across to me as I nodded.

"Yup, it was an interesting day, and the guys are taking this mate thing seriously. They all insisted on sleeping on my bed. I'm glad I was tired," I scowled into my cup, "or else I wouldn't have been able to sleep." He let out a deep laugh and shook his head, flipping some pancakes onto a growing stack on a plate next to the stove. He put a few on a small plate and passed it to me.

"It is going to be that way for a while. They won't want to leave your side. I'm actually surprised they didn't wake up with you," he chuckled, taking a sip of his coffee. I shrugged as I shoveled the pancakes in my mouth, moaning around my fork.

"Did you use some of Tinkerbell's Pixie Dust to make these? They are delicious," I said with a small smile on my face and laughed as he growled at me.

"We are not pixies and no, no magic was used in the making of my famous protein pancakes, you little pain in my ass."

"Aww, you love me," I teased, and he grumbled, turning away to put more pancakes on the side. You would think he was cooking for an army, but then I realized the guys were huge beasts and, adding Kalen, I guess they were a small, bulky ass army. I finished off my stack just as I heard footsteps on the staircase.

"Did Remi ever come back last night?" I asked Kalen and he nodded, gesturing outside with the spatula.

"She's been outside, reading, with Xena. I swear that cat loves to swim more than is normal for a feline." I smiled, yeah, she did. She was pretty much a cat version of me. I loved being in the water.

The guys came up behind me and took turns pressing kisses to my cheeks. I hummed with happiness. "Good morning to you all too, although I'm telling you now, if you want to sleep together again, you're going to have to put the beds together because last night was brutal."

"You're telling me? Someone kicked me in the nuts last night," growled Hunter, and I spit out my coffee, laughing.

"Sorry, I'm pretty sure that was me." He glared at me as he went to pour himself a cup of coffee.

I laughed and got up as they settled in to have breakfast and started to talk to Kalen. I gave them a little wave as I stepped outside and took a deep breath. It didn't seem so sinister outside with the sun out, I thought thankfully, and padded over to the sound system to plug in my phone. I noticed Remi on a lounger with a book in her hand, in a bikini, and she looked like pure temptation. I sighed as I walked over to the lounger next to her. Part of me was still mad, mostly at the overall stupid plan, and then at the idea of her in hiding while people suffered. But after a night's sleep, the other part of me, the part that won, knew that no one should be forced into a lifestyle they didn't choose and that, ultimately, fate brought us together, and I saw how much that meant to her last night. Regardless of the madness of our situation, I didn't want to be mad.

I sighed and took off my cover before sitting down next to her. She put her book down and looked at me, knowing I wanted to say something. I smiled at her. "Although I'm still mad," I started, running my hands down her jaw, taking in her features, "I want to say I understand why you made your initial decisions. We're going to have to deal with so much shit soon-I feel it in my bones-and it should be with all of us on the same page, working together." I leaned over and kissed her lips gently before she tugged on my hair and kissed me. She poured every emotion, every apology, into that kiss. It was almost therapeutic.

After a moment, she looked at me and gave me a small smile. "I'll always be by your side, Hudson, even when I'm not physically there, my heart will always follow. I can spend my entire life making it up to you in every creative way I can think of because the truth is, I'm so damn lucky to have you as my mate. You'll be greater in every aspect than I could've been as Queen." I breathed deeply. *Queen.* That was going to take some getting used to. Regardless, I have five mates and I needed to make it work. If anyone can look at their love life and tell themselves that they didn't have to make compromises and hard decisions, they can eat a dick. Liars.

I laid down and we fell into a comfortable silence. She kept reading and I started to sing along to the music playing in the background. I leaned over to look at my phone and noticed a few messages coming through.

Joshua- Hey, didn't see you today, was looking forward to hanging out at lunch.

Hudson- I'm sorry, looks like I'm on house arrest. Haha.

Joshua- Sorry to hear that. I did get your homework for you though.

Hudson- Oh, thank you! You can drop by and bring it; I'm just hanging out by the pool with Remi.

Joshua- Deal, is it okay if I bring a few of the guys with me?

I bit my lip, considering the damn marks. But I supposed with a concealment charm, we should be fine since we weren't leaving the house.

Hudson- Sure, come on by. You guys cutting the rest of the day?

Joshua- Being a senior has its perks. Haha.

Hudson- *rolls eyes* I'll see you in a few, you can bring whoever you want.

Chapter Twenty-Four

Zane

We watched as Hudson went outside and we turned back to Kalen, who had a smirk on his face.

"So, how have you boys been holding up with her around you?"

"Truthfully?" I shook my head, putting my coffee down. "It's been hell." The guys nodded in agreement. "She's either enticing the hell out of us, driving us crazy, or making us want to punch whoever looks in her direction." I scrubbed my hand across my face.

Ryder laughed, "It's been a very interesting few days is what he means. We knew we wanted to be with her for years..."

"But having it confirmed that she really was our endgame makes everything feel, I don't know..." I murmured.

"As if your entire world is on fire? Like your heart and your mind are racing to catch up to one another every time she is in the same room?" Kalen smirked.

"Exactly," we all said at the same time.

"That is never going to stop. Being Fae means having magic as our core. So, when you are mated to a Fae, it truly is magic; colors seem brighter, touches linger, kisses burn, and every second with your mated is a combination of awe and sweet torture. You will always yearn to have each other close, to remain in constant contact; it is as if every single nerve in your body is alive with an emotion so profound, it is almost tangible." I felt every word he uttered, as if the world would burn before I ever thought of her as anything other than perfection.

"Does it come with the desire to punch everyone in the face if they even look her way? Because I feel a thousand times more volatile than usual, and that is saying something," joked Hunter. We all laughed; he wasn't wrong.

"You will be more protective, but so will she. So, keep that in mind because that means you all will be more volatile towards threats, both emotional and physical." I frowned at that.

"Emotional?" asked Grayson.

Kalen chuckled. "Oh, you'll see. You think an angry Hudson is bad? Imagine a jealous Hudson. We are ridiculously possessive." We all groaned. We can't go back into that school again; she would probably set girls on fire.

KALEN LET OUT A BELLY LAUGH, AND I SHOOK MY HEAD. *FUCKER*. THE doorbell rang and we all looked at each other. Who the hell would be coming by the house? I got up to answer the door and frowned when I saw Joshua with a few of his friends on the doorstep. Technically, if we wouldn't have been on an advanced track, we would be just a year apart, so we were all around the same age and knew each other pretty well. Didn't mean I wanted them hanging out with Hudson. At all.

He cleared his throat and smiled. "Hey, Zane, I texted Hudson and she said it was cool if we came by, dropped off her work, and came to hang out for a few." I frowned and nodded.

"Sure, you guys cut the rest of the day? You are all lucky our asses aren't there today, or we would have dragged your asses back and put you through your paces."

He laughed. "Yeah, we don't doubt it. Why do you think we even bothered leaving? Heads up though, Madison heard us talking about it. I think she and her friends might invite themselves over." He rolled his eyes. I groaned. Fuck. Well, this was going to be a cluster fuck.

Hudson

I turned up the music as Evanescence "Bring Me to Life" started playing. I got up and stretched and walked to the edge of the water fall before diving into the deep end. Remi came to sit at the edge of the pool singing along to the lyrics while I swam around.

"You know that bathing suit is going to drive the guys crazy, right?" she teased, with a heated look in her eye. I swam to where she was sitting and pulled myself slightly out of the water, leaning on the side of the pool.

"Just them?" I flirted. She laughed and leaned over to kiss me.

"You've been driving me crazy since I saw you take the damn cover-up off," she groaned, and I laughed. I jumped up and out the pool and walked back up to the waterfall, dragging her with me.

"We need to have a dive off!" I yelled. She laughed at me and flipped me off. "Poison" by Bell Biv DeVoe started to play and we started doing the Running Man and Cabbage Patch, laughing before we dove in the water. We came back up laughing, pushing our hair off our faces. Well, we laughed until we realized we had an audience. Zane cleared his throat and I looked up to see him, Hunter, Gray, and Ryder looking at me, a combination of lust and anger on their faces, with Joshua and his friends behind them. I grimaced at their expressions. *Well, at least I knew which emotion was clearly going to win this battle.* I sighed and smiled.

"Hey, Josh! Thanks for coming by. You guys can get comfortable; no need to stand there."

My eyes flicked to Remi, who was holding back a laugh at the over-the-top voice, but fuck her, I was trying to cover my ass, which I realized was painfully uncovered. Joshua stepped around the guys as he approached the side of the pool, his friends grabbing loungers and talking while keeping their eyes on us. I rolled my eyes inwardly. Don't let people fool you, guys gossip just as much as girls do.

"Hey, Hudson, Remi, you two look gorgeous. Are you guys playing with body paint?" he said curiously as he looked at me and Remi's marks. Fuck, I looked at her and she opened her mouth before I could.

"We figured since we skipped the day, we could do something fun, but when I bought the paint, I didn't realize it was semi-permanent." Remi frowned as she explained. Way better actress than me, by the way. "We figured we will use magic later to take it off," she shrugged and smiled. "We even convinced those old men to put it on too. You should have seen them bitch and moan, it was priceless." She winked at the guys and the laugh I was holding back busted out of me. The guys frowned and I tried to hold it back, grinning like an idiot instead.

Joshua laughed. "I would have loved to see that. The Untouchable Four, made into canvases? Priceless." I looked at the guys and Joshua curiously.

"Untouchable Four?"

"Yeah," one of Joshua's friends spoke up behind me. I didn't even realize his friends had already gotten in the pool. "It's what everyone on campus calls them after someone uploaded a video of them sparring in the gym after classes." He reached out his hand. "I'm Kenneth, nice to meet you, formally." I quickly shook his hand, my smile slipping when his eyes lingered a bit longer on my marks. "You guys went all out with the details on the body paint. Looks pretty cool."

"Yeah, Remi is into art, something serious," I joked. I heard the doorbell ring again and Kalen must have answered it because I heard a few more voices coming from inside the house. The guys looked at each other nervously and I frowned.

"They were also called the Untouchable Four when they kept winning the Christmas talent shows," Joshua said with a smirk on his face.

"Okay, that's enough story time," jumped in Ryder, I laughed until I froze when I saw Madison step out onto the deck with a few of her friends. *The fuck is she doing here? I will set her ass on fire.*

"Oh, why? Those talent shows made these guys famous. It had, and still has, all of the women on campus staring after them like lost puppies," she jumped into the conversation to add. I rolled my eyes, *yeah, and I guess you know a bitch in heat when you see one.*

Except I must have said that out loud because she scowled, while Remi and Joshua choked back a laugh. She narrowed her eyes, and I smiled sweetly.

"You mind if I take over the music, Hud?" Joshua asked, gaining my attention. I nodded, and he stripped off his shirt while he walked over to plug in his phone. I looked at his physique admiringly. I mean, I'm mated, not blind. Hip-hop blasted over the sound system and I smiled. At least he knew music. Remi pinched my side and I looked over seeing Hunter shooting death glares at every boy around. *Oh boy*, I pulled myself over the edge and got out of the pool, walking up to him, side stepping Madison, who was still hovering, even though her friends had already made their way to sit by the pool, laughing with the guys who splashed them with water. The joking and talking dialed back a notch as my suit was revealed, and Madison's glare intensified. Yes, be mad, frumpy Hudson is gone and enter video vixen.

I walked over to Hunter and got on my tiptoes to wrap my arms around his neck and kiss him, ignoring that everyone from school was there. Fuck it, there were no rules, and we were all of age. These guys were mine, and soon, we'll be off saving Disney. I melted for a few seconds before pulling myself away.

"I'm going to go change, I'll be back in a few." I snagged my phone and covered up before heading to the back staircase to get to my room.

I felt the stares, but I ignored it as I got inside the room and locked the door behind me before making my way to the bathroom. I stripped out of my suit and hung it in by the shower to dry. Truth is, I loved my suit but that one wasn't one I wanted to wear in front of a bunch of people I went to school with. I took a quick shower and washed my hair, going through my quick routine before stepping out into my room to get changed. A slow smile spread on my lips as I noticed Grayson and Hunter leaning against near my door on the opposite side of the room.

"To what do I owe this pleasure?" I walked to my closet to grab something to wear but Grayson walked over to me with a determined stride and my breath hitched in my throat at the look in his eyes. Hunter stayed where he was with a fixed smirk on his face, his sweats hung low on his hips, V on full display. My mouth watered at the look on their faces. Fuck me, they were going to fucking kill me with all this sex appeal.

"I loved the suit, but the fact that other people saw you in it doesn't sit well with me," Grayson whispered, his voice coming out like a thick growl, as he reached me and tugged the towel off of me. I bit back a moan as he grabbed me roughly and pulled me up against him. He pressed against me and I shivered at his size as he leaned over and captured my lips with his. This wasn't a teasing kiss; it was a punishing one. He bit my lip and thrust his tongue into my mouth, running his tongue along mine and taking full control as he wrapped one hand in my hair roughly, his other hand holding my ass tightly against his in an almost too painful grip. I gasped into his mouth as he pulled my hair harder, kissing me fiercely.

He pulled away and looked into my hooded gaze. "You are ours, Hudson. I don't like anyone looking at you but us." My knees touched the bed as his hand wrapped around my neck and he tossed me down. I didn't even realize we were moving until we got there, and I blinked up at the look in his eyes. Gone was my gentle giant and I had a feeling the classroom was child's play compared to what he had planned right now. A shiver ran up my spine. Fuck.

Grayson

Seeing her in that suit and being witness to the look of lust on the faces of boys there set something off in me. I made my way to her room with Hunter on my heels after she walked away and closed the back door to her room. A glimpse at her ass when she turned around and I felt my cock weeping at the sight. I nodded at Zane and Ryder, who stayed back to watch the people in the house, but I knew they would get to her later.

The fury and lust I felt coursing through my body was intense. She needed to be punished for that little display, and she was going to learn just how rough I can get. That class act was nothing. On our way to her room, we made a quick detour to grab the things we bought when we went into town. Hunter had mentioned she liked it rough when they were together, so we had gone to a sex store and he got a little carried away and got everything from ropes, nipple clamps, a whip, and a shit ton of toys, flavored lubes, and whipped frostings. It was all going to come in handy right now, as I looked into her face right before I wrapped my hand around her neck and tossed her onto the bed.

I quickly shed my sweats and leaned over her luscious body as she crawled to the middle of the bed. Hunter was quickly on the other side and leaned over to grab her hands, holding them over her head, and tying her wrists up with a soft silk rope. She gasped and I smiled darkly.

"This body is ours, Hudson, don't ever forget that." Running my hands down her body, I squeezed her breasts before I caressed the almost exaggerated flare of her hips. I sucked one of her nipples into my mouth right as my hands reached the inside of her thighs and I smiled as I found her soaked already. Good, I wasted no time tugging her legs apart and sliding inside in one thrust. I groaned as her tightness pulsed around me and she moaned loudly.

"Shh, baby, if you're going to open your mouth, you're going to put it to good use," Hunter growled as he positioned himself to her side, grabbing her head and shoving his dick down her throat. They both moaned as he started to fuck her mouth. I gripped her hips and wrapped her ankles round my neck, driving my dick inside her roughly. Her eyes popped open and she groaned around Hunter's dick, making him jerk in her mouth. He cursed, "Hudson, just like that. Suck and hum around my dick," he bit out.

I reached over and grabbed one of the vibrators we bought before I clicked it on and placed it on her clit. Her pussy clenched around my dick, squeezing me tightly as she started to cum, coating my dick even more as I fucked her harder. She tried to move away from the vibrator, but I kept it in place as she bucked her hips, eyes rolling to the back of her head.

"You're not going to stop coming on my dick, Hudson; you are ours," I growled. She hummed in response as she continued to work Hunter over with her mouth. I moved her legs and turned her slightly, so she was on her side, one leg on my chest, the other pinned beneath me, never letting up my pace. She felt so fucking good and I cursed as she just got tighter and tighter on my dick; almost painful. I smacked her ass and she moaned as Hunter cursed, gripped her head, and came down her throat. The sight had my eyes cross as I came inside of her right after.

"Fuck yes, Hudson, milk this dick," I moaned as I fucked her harder.

Hudson

"... milk this dick," Gray groaned as he fucked me even harder, smacking my ass. I swallowed Hunter down and he stayed hard as he continued to fuck my mouth. *Fuck, if this was punishment, I was going to be bad all the fucking time.*

"Get on your fucking knees, Hudson," Hunter growled and I got to my knees as Grayson leaned over and grabbed something else from the bed. I felt something cold drip down my ass as Hunter grabbed my face and guided his dick back in my mouth. He had such a fucking pretty dick, I wanted it all the time. I swallowed him down, teasing him with my tongue rings before I took him all the way in and hallowed out my cheeks.

"Fuck yes, baby girl, this mouth is going to fucking kill me," he ground out, and I jerked in surprise as Grayson pressed a vibrator into my ass and started to fuck me at the same time. My eyes fluttered closed as the sensations rocked through my body. Grayson was fucking huge and having the double feeling was intense. I moaned around Hunter's dick as Grayson started to pound into me, smacking my ass at the same time. My hands were still tied, so they balanced me between them, and the loss of control was just as erotic as the sex. I cursed as my orgasm ripped through me, my eyes rolling behind my head.

"Yes, cum on my dick again; good girl. You know who owns this pussy," Grayson smacked my ass and pulled the toy out and the loss of sensation made me whimper. He and Hunter laughed as they both pulled out of me before Grayson laid down and told me to sit down on his dick. He gripped my waist roughly shoving himself inside of me just as I had settled over him.

"Fuck, yes," I screamed and Grayson smiled reaching over to pull me in for a kiss while I ground against him, both of us moaning into each other's mouth. I felt Hunter settle himself behind me and Grayson opened his legs to accommodate him while Hunter opened my ass and worked himself inside of me. Bigger than the vibrator, but fuck, it was so damn good. I closed my eyes and moaned as they started to fuck me at the same time.

All this time, I was a shameless hussy, and I was going to fucking revel in it.

CHAPTER TWENTY-FIVE

Grayson and Hunter went to their room to shower and I washed the sweat off my body, still basking in the afterglow. It sounded like while we were upstairs everyone moved inside the house, the music thumping throughout the house. I pulled on a long-sleeved black onesie bodysuit before I tugged and hopped into some tight blue jeans. The bodysuit had a small V-cut to show cleavage, but not fall out of my top. The sides were high, showing off my sides and abs. Putting on a pair of black, high heeled boots, I cast a concealment charm to cover my marks from everyone downstairs. Leaving my hair down, I threw on some light make up and bright red lipstick and snapped a quick picture to send to the group chat with the guys and one to Remi. Stepping out of the room to make my way downstairs, my phone dinged as Remi replied quickly with a picture of what she was wearing too; jeans and heels with a low-cut top.

Hudson- Great minds think alike! ;-)

Remi- You mean sexy bitches think alike. LOL

Hudson- LOL, sexy Faerie Queenly Bitches?

Remi- YES! "Queenly Fae-itches" is going to be the name of our chat.

Hudson- LMAO, I'm coming downstairs now Fae-itch.

Remi- Yes, hurry up because if I have to run interference on Madison and Zane one more time, I'm going to punch her in the face and smack her with a wing.

My eyebrow raises and I back track to go out the back door of my room to see this shit show before Madison has a chance to see me. I go downstairs and see Kalen outside with Xena. I smile at them. "Doing perimeter checks?"

He grunted, "More like avoiding a house full of horny students. But sure, same thing." I laughed. "Good work on the concealment charm, but remember what I said, they won't block you from a real Fae," he continued.

Something in the air is not okay, tell Kalen we must do rounds. I frowned at Xena and relayed the message. His eyebrows shot up, his face hardened, and he grabbed a sword that I didn't even see from next to him, before nodding and striding into the woods with Xena, all without a further word. I stared after him and sighed. Honestly, if we are attacked again, we will really have no choice but to head to the Faerie Realm before students are hurt. More alert, I head inside. I looked down at my phone and replied to Remi.

Hudson- I totally forgot that we get wings! I want mine!

Remi- Yes, but they come soon after you gain your powers. Yours should come out soon. Anyways, did you miss the part about Madison?

I don't answer as I come up behind her in the kitchen.

"No, I didn't. Which is why I was coming through the back so I can see this shit for myself." She looked back and laughed at me. "I should have known; he keeps shutting her down, but she is like a freaking octopus. You can tell he is trying hard to not hit a girl. It's admirable, really." She chuckled and I scowled. Remembering my brief conversation with Kalen, I let her know what Xena said and she frowned and sighed.

"Yeah, the longer we are here, the worse the attacks will get. Eventually, she will attack humans. She doesn't really have a moral compass."

"Yeah, I figured as much. We can talk about that as a group. Until then, let's try to have a decent night before it all blows up in our faces... again." I shook my head and grabbed a beer from the fridge and looked around. The house had a few more people, but it wasn't as crazy as the party from a few days ago. I see Jensi and Luca and wave them over.

"How was your day without us?"

Jensi scowled. "Ridiculously lame and nowhere near as adventurous. We did get a chance to punch Derrick in the face last night though." My eyes widened.

"We will tell you more later, but yeah, it was well deserved," Luca added. I took a swig of my beer, fighting my smile, and Madison comes into my direct line of vision along with Zane.

"I'll take your word for it, and yes, I want more details. I gotta go put a grabby asshole in her place." I stride off toward them and I heard Jensi laugh about life being more exciting with me around. The guys had all changed and they looked incredible, as usual, in jeans, combat boots and varying Breaking Benjamin band tees.

"You keep saying you're taken, Zane, but I don't see this mystery woman. You really should stop playing hard to get," Madison giggles and it grates on my nerves. Zane pinches the bridge of his nose and breathes deeply. I almost laugh... almost. Hunter, Gray, and Ryder were doing enough of that as it was, and they didn't even look convincing as they tried to hold it back. I rolled my eyes. Leave it to them to take perverse pleasure in Zane's personal torture.

"I'm not exactly sure what you need to see, Mackenzie. If Zane says he isn't available, then he isn't," I said brightly coming around them and standing at Zane's side, arms crossed. Her flirtatious smile dropped, and she scowled. Like that scowl is more threatening than a fucking Faerie Queen. Check the prophecy, honey. I kept my smile in place. The smile was saving her from being smacked. No means no, for both sexes.

"Why don't you mind your business? This has nothing to do with you." She flips her hair. "Zane and I were having an adult conversation." She put her hand on Zane's arm and he looked like wanted to be anywhere but between us right now.

I shook my head in mock sadness. "See, that is where you're wrong. Zane is my business," I sighed and moved her hand off of him. "He is taken, because he is my boyfriend." I smirked as I leaned into Zane and he wrapped his arms around me. Her eyes about popped out of her skull, before she sneered.

"Weren't you just making out with Hunter?" she said loudly, drawing the gaze of several of her friends. I smiled at her and nodded.

"Absolutely, I'm glad you caught that. See," I start in a mock whisper, "I'm fucking all of them." I straightened, pointing at the guys and smiled. "Perks of being the only female roommate. You really should have applied before I got here. Unfortunately, the housing office is closed now for new roommates. Sucks for you-oh, wait, no. That's me doing the sucking! Sorry, I get confused, you know, being the newbie and all." I shrugged as she sputtered and stomped away. Two Hudson, Zero *Mad*ison, get it? Mad? My inner Fae-itch cackled. Ryder was just outright laughing now, Grayson just shook his head and drank his beer, Hunter smiling devilishly. I turned around, wrapping my arms around Zane and pulled him down for a kiss.

"Did I ever tell you how ridiculously sexy you are?" His heated gazed traveled from the boots up to my eyes before he leaned over and kissed my neck.

"Mmm, maybe but I can hear it a few hundred times more, mate," I whispered. He grinned at me and winked, giving me a final kiss before making his way to the guys to look over the party. I winked at them, laughing when Zane punched Ryder, who was still laughing, before making my way to the sound system to put my music on. Remi, Jensi, and Luca joined me with a smirk on their faces.

"Well, you declaring that you are fucking the hottest professors on campus is certainly the highlight of my entire life," she laughed.

"I'm nothing if not a people pleaser, Remi." I smiled as I changed the music, bopping my head to the beat. I took a drink from my forgotten beer as I looked around, watching everyone start to sway to the music. Well, everyone but Madison, who was pouting in a corner while her friends danced with Joshua and his friends. I smiled when the doorbell rang, and King walked through the front door. I waved and walked over to give him a hug. "Squishy!" He groaned and hugged me back. I chuckled at the pained look on his face. "Don't be like that, squishy."

"Is she sleeping with him too?" I heard from somewhere behind me, King raised his eyebrow at me, and I shook my head.

"Don't ask," I said and he shrugged and walked over to the boys. I turned around and addressed whoever she was with a smile on my face. "No, I am not, but I promise you'll be the first to know if I suck his dick next." I heard Ryder and Remi start laughing as I made my way to the kitchen to grab another drink.

The house was filling with students and the guys were leaning against the wall watching the room. I laughed under my breath at their serious faces and took a swig of the new drink in my hand. Remi was walking around the room, looking at everyone under the guise of mingling. Everyone was a suspect after what I said in the kitchen and the professor fucker story ebbed away in the favor of more drinks. I entertained myself by changing the music and hanging with Jensi and Luca. The sounds of "Hold You," by Gyptian serenaded the room and I smiled as I started swaying to the music, rolling my hips. I closed my eyes as I felt a warm body come up behind me, recognizing Hunter's scent and overall feel of restrained energy. He grabbed my hips and started to dance with me, right after taking the drink out of my hands and putting it on the mantle. I ground myself against him and he ran his hands up and down my sides, grabbing my hands and tugging my arms up and around his neck, my heels giving me the perfect height to do so. I hummed to the song, my breath catching, as Grayson suddenly pressed himself to my front, running his lips along my collarbone, dancing with us. *Yes, yes, my little mate minions, grind on me.* My inner Fae-itch was a little too turned on.

"You're a fucking temptation, sweetheart, and seeing you dancing is like foreplay to us," Gray whispered into my ear, biting down on my lobe. I gasped and opened my eyes, taking in his eyes darkening as he brushed my inner thigh. I bit my lip and he groaned.

"She is going to kill us," he said, eyes flicking to Hunter.

"She might, but fuck, if it won't be death by orgasm. I'm okay with that," his voice deeper than usual, sending shivers down my spine. We lost ourselves for a few minutes and I was ready for a replay of earlier.

The song switched to "Dude," by Beenie Man and I chuckled when Zane and Ryder took Hunter and Gray's places, dancing to the quicker tempo. Zane wrapped his hands in my hair and tugged my head back, kissing me deeply and I moaned as his tongue teased mine.

"I don't think I told you how sexy it is when you claim me in front of other people either."

"You haven't, but you all better get used to it," I responded. Both he and Ryder's gruff laugh trailed over me. I was going to need several cold showers after this. Maybe not, I thought to myself when I felt them both growing hard against me. *Fuck.* A few songs later and I totally needed everyone to get out so I could do this dance without any clothes.

Yeah, that didn't happen.

Chapter Twenty-Six

After everyone left, we took showers and settled ourselves downstairs for a little nightcap and some movies. We had nowhere to go and it wasn't like we should be going out anyway, with a bunch of murdering winged people on the loose and all. Kalen and Xena were still doing rounds and I figured if I could still feel Xena, then everything was fine.

I was sitting down, wrapped up in Remi, with her kissing my neck and making me giggle and Zane kept rolling his eyes. I laughed when I saw his face.

"Oh, Zane, honey, sweetie, pumpkin pie drizzle, are you jealous?"

"What the fuck is a pumpkin drizzle? And no, I'm never jealous of anyone here, but I'll be lying if I said I didn't want to be inside of you. Especially when I saw you in that bathing suit earlier," he joked but his eyes were full of promise.

"What's my pet name?!" demanded Ryder. I rolled my eyes.

"I should call your ass woodpecker." I laughed so hard, I started to choke, and Remi started to tap my back.

"Fuck your mate against a tree one time..." he grumbled and smiled at me, grabbing me away from Remi, pulling me on to his lap, and giving me a kiss. I hugged him, cuddling into his arms. I sighed in contentment.

"One time is all it takes, but no, I always call you my jolly giant or my jokester. Grayson is a gentle giant, except he damn sure wasn't gentle with my vagina, come to think of it. I think my gentle giant has a dark side."

Ryder groaned and kissed the side of my head, and Grayson chuckled and grabbed me, pulling me into his lap. It was like a game of mate Hot Potato.

"Anyone else get a little chill when Ryder said mate?" Grayson asked. He looked down at me and kissed my forehead, his eyes swirling with so much emotion.

The guys and Remi nodded. I beamed at them. "I'm your mate, mate, mate, mate, mate."

"I always knew you were mine, princess. It was just all a matter of time, mate bond or not," Zane gloated. I rolled my eyes. "By the way, what's my nickname? And Hunters?" I giggled nervously, they totally did not want to know Hunter's nickname, they weren't ready for that daddy bomb.

"I usually just call you 'fuck em and leave em,' but I actually really liked pumpkin pie drizzle. I'm going to have to stick with that one." I nodded as if in deep thought and he growled.

"I will not be a drizzled dessert. It sounds like I'm a cheap hooker at a Walmart-themed strip club," he grumbled. Everyone laughed. I walked over and straddled his lap, and he wrapped his arms around me, palming my ass. I sucked in a sharp breath.

"I'm disturbed that you think there would be a Walmart-themed strip club, yet oddly intrigued at twerking in the ice cream aisles." I smiled. He shook his head at me with a smile.

"Or pole dancing in the disinfectant section, for obvious reasons," chimed in Ryder. I chortled.

"Wait! Or lap dances by the cashiers," I added, Ryder and I high-fived.

"Except in the self-service aisles... well, that one is self-explanatory," he added while laughing and I lost it. I leaned against Ryder and chuckled like a mad woman; they were keeping me in good spirits. I needed this normalcy for a little longer before letting it go. The weight of something about to go wrong was weighing omnipresent.

"Ohh ohh!! Guys!" I stood up and put my hands on my hips. They groaned at the look on my face, I'm sure. "Let's have a dance off!" They groaned and Remi giggled.

"Count me out, but I'll play judge!" Remi threw in. I flipped her off. *Guess I was going to win this shit for all the Fae-itches.*

"The men first!" When no one jumped up and just stared, I pouted. Ryder rolled his eyes and got up and came to stand next to me in the middle of the living room. With no shirt, his muscles rippled even as he stood still with his arm crossed on his chest. His eyes were full of laughter. Ryder would probably do anything to make me laugh, I loved how they were all different. Hunter was what his name indicated, and he was brutal. Grayson was the one you didn't see coming. Zane though? I loved his intensity, like a general they all deferred to him, but while Grayson led with his brain, Zane led with his heart. They complimented each other well. Remi? She was passionate and a smart ass. A blue-haired version of me.

"Hudson? What's wrong? I lost you there for a second. I'm supposed to be beating your ass at a dance competition," Ryder teased, I smiled.

"Nothing, just comparing my awesome mates." I reached up and gave him a kiss.

"Okay, guys." I clapped. "You all have to figure this out and do something together. I'll give you ten minutes to come up with a plan." They all groaned but got up and went to stand next to Ryder and put their heads together. I sat down and laughed with Remi, as Zane and Hunter let out a bunch of 'absolutely not's, and Grayson just nodded his head at whatever Ryder said.

"What do you think they will do?" Remi asked.

"No idea honestly, but I want to see if they live up to the hype of the 'Untouchables'." I giggled.

"Times running out! If we have to win by default, I guess I'll take it, but I won't dance," I yelled.

"The hell will we concede this battle. We have to go change again though. Be right back," Ryder said. Good point; I can't dance and win in pajamas.

"Great call, we will be back too. Five minutes and then living room!" I yelled as Remi and I ran upstairs giggling. We each threw on leggings and a tight tank top before running downstairs. The guys weren't there yet, so we pushed the couch back and made space like it was for the party. We sat down crossed legged on the couch as the guys came downstairs in jeans that hung low showing off their V's, with combat boots on.

"Yummy, all mine," I whispered as I leered at them. Remi rolled her eyes and laughed, and Zane looked at me and winked, and my heart melted. God, he was so handsome. I needed a redo of two years ago. His eyes met mine and he turned his head and smiled, as if he knew what I was thinking. I stuck out my tongue at him and he laughed.

My phone buzzed and I noticed several missed texts from Jensi and Luca. I'll answer those later. *I gotta eye fuck my men.*

I scowled as they stood around in some type of actual formation and Ryder walked over and passed me the stereo remote.

"Press play in a few seconds, and the music will play. Hope we do a good job for you, baby girl."

I rolled my eyes. Grayson stood at one end, then Hunter and Zane in the middle with Ryder at the other end. I pressed the play button and my jaw dropped as they grinned. "Earned It" by The Weekend started playing through the speakers and I almost lost my panties.

Hunter and Zane stepped forward when the beat dropped, rocked their hips back and forth, stepping to the right and left while they dipped low, thrusting to the beat. They lifted their arms, bent them at the elbow, and grinded into the air, knees bent. Grayson and Ryder walked up following suit, and they weaved through each other and took turns pointing at me and winking as they stepped to the right, kneeled on the floor and spun on their knees. Then they fucking leaned back on one arm popping their legs up, planting their feet on the floor, and thrusted and rolled their hips up in tandem. I felt the room get hotter as they jumped up, but not before Hunter balanced on his hands only, while pretending to fuck the floor. Holy shit. As he fucked the floor, lucky bitch, Grayson and Ryder danced in the back, bending their knees, while their feet were moving, crossing quickly to the beat that dropped again and Zane flipped over Hunter and landed in the same position as Hunter. This was just cruel and evil torture, and they did this on a fucking stage? I wanted to claw out the eyes of whoever saw them. They worked their hips on the floor before jumping up and finishing the song by bending their arms again and rolling their hips.

"Holy fucking shit. That was not only ridiculously unfair, but I think the floor is pregnant, and shit, so am I." I fanned myself and pretended to swoon. They laughed.

"Yeah, we may have used that one to win the talent competition last year," Hunter grinned.

"Assholes. Well fine, I gotta go change my outfit! There was one dance I made myself learn that will win this shit, but it involves heels and I'm not going to be outdone." I jumped off the couch and ran to the room, ignoring their laughter. I stripped quickly putting on a strapless bra and a tight tube top with some stretchy medium dark jeans that looked painted on and my sexy black heels. I was having so much fun.

There were a bunch of dance videos where gorgeous women stood in front of mirrors and learned dances and then performed them in heels. The confidence they had was insane and I learned a few from Instagram stalking, but there was one I was really good at. I was going to fuck this shit up.

I went downstairs, and the boys were joking on the couch. I walked to the sound system and connected my phone. I tossed the remote to Ryder and I faced away from them. In a second, "Wild Thoughts" by DJ Khalid comes out of the system. I turned and started walking to them, and I rocked my hips from left to right quickly, before I dropped low, holding my knees while my feet were firmly planted on the floor, and I rolled my hips from left and right. I turned, staying low, while I came up halfway and dropped back down three times until I was facing away from them. I dropped to my knees, my feet behind me as I put my hands in front of me and slid my knees on the floor, bringing my legs together and back out again, sensually, before opening my knees, leaning forward and working my hips low to the floor.

I leaned up and kicked my legs out into a split, popping my hips up and down, moving my arms to swipe my hair back in tune to the music, bending at the knees on the floor and coming back up to my feet. I crossed my feet in front of the other, moving my hips and torso in smooth motions, using my hands to draw from my chest to my belly before I popped my feet apart, bending over at my waist and moving my hips so my ass swayed, before bending back quickly and spinning on the ball of my foot, facing the guys. I didn't make eye contact, lost in the song. I bent back at the waist dropping down to the floor arching my back and kicking my legs open all the way, toes pointed to the ceiling, before closing them and planting my feet on the floor. I put my hands on the floor on my side, while I worked only my hips up and down off the floor. I dropped my hips to the floor, and I moved my legs to the side coming back up to my knees and tossed my hair back and ending the song on the floor. Yup, I won.

Zane

We sat back and relaxed while Hudson ran upstairs to put on what she needed to beat us. We joked that if she thought heels were going to help her win, then we need to wear heels for the next competition.

"Yeah okay, we practiced that shit for weeks. Even the moms of the students were shoving numbers in my pockets," Hunter jokes.

"You had no problem taking the numbers though," Grayson pointed out.

"Like you did? You think those piercings you got on your dick were for a warm grapefruit?" joked Ryder and we busted out laughing.

"Good point, asshole," Grayson said smiling. "They still call me too, asking what we are performing this year." He rolled his eyes.

"You better change your number. Hudson is liable to kill a mom or two," Remi tossed in.

"She is a violent little thing, isn't she? I wouldn't have it any other way. Can you believe we are mated to her? Like an honest to God, in the movies type of mating? Knowing she is ours... damn," Grayson said.

We nodded in agreement. Ryder leaned forward, his arms on his knees. "Guys, we are in Seattle, and we are fucking mated. Who else thinks we need to go hunt down Edward and Bella and tell her she chose the wrong one? I mean, now that we know shit like this is real." Hunter smacked him on the head, and we laughed as we saw Hudson coming down the stairs in body paint. Well, no, they were jeans, but still, they needed to be classified as body paint the way they fit her perfectly. My mouth went dry as she tossed Ryder the remote. She looks too damn perfect, it's just sinful.

When the music started and she turned towards us and dropped it like it was fucking hot, my dick was hard immediately. No need to wait for blood to pump, nope, just boom, hard. Every jerk of her hips, every sensual move of her entire body in perfect beat to the music was downright captivating. We all leaned forward like magnets when she opened her legs into a split and popped her pussy up and down. Then at the end, when she opened her legs, her toes pointed, it took everything in my power to not knock out the other three and jump in between her thighs and fuck her right there. She tossed her head back as the song ended and she smiled.

Our jaws were still stuck, and we were half off the couch. I knew we mind fucked her with the fact that we could dance, but she fucking practiced from videos and learned that?! Honestly, I felt like checking all the doors and windows to make sure no one saw what we just saw. The way she dipped and swayed; she was like a fucking hip-hop video come to life.

"Holy shit," groaned Grayson. Yeah, her gentle giant wasn't going to be gentle for much longer.

"Yeah, um, this was a great idea. Next time, how about lap dances?" joked Ryder. Well, maybe he was joking, because that was actually a great idea.

"How about her face in my lap, choking on my dick instead?" Hunter growled, and I rolled my eyes as Hudson winked at him and laughed.

"Ugh too much information, Hunter," scowled Remi, her eyes bright with her mirth. "Safe to say Hudson won that."

"What?!" we all said, *totally biased.*

"Well, I'm not voting for the sausage fest. I'm into the peaches." She winked at Hudson and laughed. We groaned.

"While those sound like really good ideas, I'm thinking it's 1 am, but I'm not tired... umm can we actually..." she said hesitantly, "maybe all sleep down here? Bring the mattresses down? Like a giant slumber party? That way no one gets their balls kicked tonight.

I laughed and Hunter growled, and I laughed harder.

"Baby, that's a great idea. We should be good with just three mattresses. Why don't you put pajamas back on and we will set it up?" I reached to grab her for a hug and kissed her temple.

"Mmm, you guys are my giant sex teddy bears with abs. I love hugging you all so much," she teased. I laughed at her and smacked her on the ass to get her to go up the stairs. She smiled mischievously and while Ryder had his back turned, she jumped on him.

"Onward, my trusty steed. You have been commandeered to safely get the queen to her chambers in search of pajamas for our cuddle party!" she yelled and laughed when Ryder started to run up the stairs. "Help, my steed is on speed," she cried, and we burst out laughing. She was fucking perfect.

Chapter Twenty-Seven

Hudson

"Ryder, those aren't pajamas, it is a thong," I laughed.

"I still don't see the difference, they are pajamas for your vagina. There were no specifications," he laughed, running away as I tried to snatch my underwear back. I threw my hands in the air and went into my drawer to pick out an actual pair of panties, a tank top, and fluffy socks.

"I sleep in just my boxers, so you don't even need a tank top, I'm all for equality," he said seriously.

"Oh, my goodness. I sleep naked. Doesn't mean I'm sleeping naked in the living room." I started to change in front of him, totally comfortable, while he stared.

"I love that," he whispered. I smiled at him. I loved it too; this ease between us

I gave him a kiss. "Yes, it feels like we have always been like this, so comfortable and perfect." I put on some shorts and tugged him out the door and back to the living room. The guys had set up the beds and comforters quickly and Grayson and Hunter were in the kitchen arguing about the correct way to make popcorn, Remi eventually stepping in and snatching the bag of kernels from them. I rolled my eyes and got in the middle of the beds next to Zane and snatched the remote from Zane's hands. He tried to snatch it back and I screamed in laughter as Ryder started to tickle me. I curled into a ball, holding the remote next to my chest, until Zane picked me up and tossed me and I let go of the remote to catch myself.

"Hey! Using sexy man strength and tag teaming is totally illegal." I stuck out my tongue. I crawled back to my claimed spot and elbowed Zane and Ryder in the ribs, they grunted and chuckled. Out of nowhere, Hunter jumped on the bed and pulled my leg, and suddenly, he was on top of me, caging me in. He had nothing on but his boxer briefs; he needed to be in a fucking commercial because holy shit. He smirked at me and leaned down to catch my nipple through my tee shirt. I squirmed and moaned. "Also not fair to summon your friends to help, this is total horse shit." I pushed Hunter off of me with a huff and he winked at me while I settled in on Zane's other side.

"Oh, angel, there is absolutely nothing fair in a sleepover, this is just the start. We looked it up, tickle parties, pillow fights, but there was nothing about sex, so we will need to write our own shit," Grayson chimed in, holding a big bowl of popcorn. I reached for it and he blew me a kiss and passed it to me.

"Grayson, I can always count on you to be the good guy. It's why I love you the most. Actually, I'm sure our markings are the same, and these assholes don't match ours." I laughed when the other three glared at me. Grayson laughed and crawled up to lay between my legs holding the popcorn on his chest, my hands in his hair. While Zane and Hunter argued over a movie, Remi brought out another bowl and sat down behind me on the couch while I laid my head on Ryder's shoulder. I grabbed my phone from behind me, suddenly remembering the text messages.

Jensi- Okay so yesterday.

Luca- Yes! It was epic.

Jensi- We met up with Derrick and his assholes during swim and they were talking shit in the locker room about drugging you and running a train on you.

I growled and Ryder and Grayson leaned over to read the messages.

Luca- We may or may not have beat the shit out of them with a few of the other seniors.

Jensi- I broke Derrick's jaw. Then his hands when he tried to use magic instead of fists. Pussy.

Luca- Point is, they won't be talking shit anymore and we spread the word that if they fuck with Hudson, they fuck with us too.

Hudson- I love you guys, you're amazing. And you're a lot nicer than I would have been, I would have ripped off his dick and fucked him with it.

Jensi- Jeez, thanks for the visual. I'm sure my dreams will be super sweet. Goodnight babe! Love ya! Tell your boyfriends/husbands that babe doesn't mean what they think it means. LMAO

Hudson- LOL goodnight

Ryder and Grayson tensed when they read his message, so I laughed hard at their reaction.

"They are some pretty awesome friends. See, you guys kept me away from guys my whole life and I could have had friends like this," I joked, peeved about what Derrick and his friends were saying but grateful for people like Jensi and Luca. It wasn't like I couldn't handle myself, but still it was nice for someone else to have my best interests at heart.

"What are you talking about? I heard the word guys and you in the same sentence and I wanna kill someone now," Hunter growled.

"I'm with him. You didn't need any other guy. You had the perfect ones the entire time, and their leader took your virginity," Zane added. I rolled my eyes and passed them my phone so they could see the chat messages. Hunter tossed back my phone and was taking deep breaths while Zane pinched the bridge of his nose. I knew how they felt, fucking scum bags.

Ryder and Grayson were whispering. "Who told him he was the leader? Did we draw straws or something? This is total bullshit. I want to be Batman," Ryder said.

"Batman is shit; I'm totally Nacho Libre," Grayson said, Ryder laughed.

"You guys are ridiculous. Everyone know that Deadpool is where the fuck it's at. I'm the female Deadpool. You guys are my minions," I scoffed and Remi laughed.

"I'll just stick to being Fae, that way I can cast spells on the minions," she chortled.

"That's the wrong fucking movie. Deadpool doesn't even have minions. That's the guy from Despicable Me," Ryder pointed out.

"I don't care! You'll be my minions and I'm the female Deadpool, I decided. You pussies wouldn't last a day being a superhero!" I laughed. Grayson put the popcorn to the side and turned to face me. Ryder got up on his knees and crossed his arms. It would look menacing, if it wasn't so sexy.

"Take it back, little girl," Gray rumbled, seriously sounding like a pack of rocks falling.

"Nope!" I squealed and jumped up when Gray went to grab me. I tried to escape over Zane's lap.

"Protect me! You're my first love. That's, like, your job isn't it?!" I demanded as Grayson started to tug on my legs.

"First love, huh? I know I love you, so when were you going to tell me you loved me?" Zane smirked. I stuck out my tongue and screamed as Grayson and Ryder both tried to wrestle me off of Zane. I mean seriously, no loyalty. We fought and wrestled, Hunter playing referee since he tried to peoples' elbow Ryder and was put on time out. So, he pouted on the couch while Remi recorded this for what she called, "Faerie Prime-time TV".

We fell into a gasping heap on the bed. I laughed as Hunter picked me up and settled me between his thighs, and Zane settled between mine, with Gray and Ryder on the other side, all of them rubbing some part of me. It felt amazing and I sighed.

After a few quiet moments, curiosity burned, and I figured we should talk about everything we learned. "You know what I don't understand in all of this? How was I even going to be put into power with this Nici bitch having had power over the Seelie for three hundred years and God knows how long with her own court?"

"The thing is, she isn't technically the current Unseelie Queen. There is a queen presiding there in an official capacity; Nici just had a lot of followers. Anyone who dissented and crossed back over to official Unseelie territory is killed. She is pretty much now going to be fighting two battles on that front. The distraction was useful for us," Remi responded.

"So, wouldn't that mean the enemy of my enemy is my friend? Couldn't we combine forces or something?" Remi frowned as she mulled that over.

"Not exactly..." she said hesitantly. "Realistically, fighting with them would look as bad as what I did, except it would make you look as if you are taking power to have an alliance. I don't think it would be looked on favorably."

"Well, that is just stupid, you would think people with that ridiculous amount of knowledge and power would understand the need for alliances. I'm sure Nici has made alliances in all this time. We are literally two hundred years behind her if we consider when she found out about the prophecy. I'm sure she planned it well. I'm walking into what's supposed to be the last movie and adding a few more; I'm essentially the Faerie personification of the Fast and the Furious movies, just adding shit and confusing everyone," I grumbled.

"Fae and the Furious," Ryder laughed, and the guys rolled their eyes.

"What's bugging me is where the hell does the dean come into play here? He was sent to help bring you back, right? So why was he so interested in your strength or display of powers?" asked Grayson.

I frowned. "What do you mean? If I'm supposed to be queen, wouldn't it make sense to see how strong I am?"

Grayson thought for a few. "Yes, in theory. Regardless, there were too many variables. It would have been a major move to rely on two people. Remi and Alvor would have needed help, trusted people to be able to bring you back safely and avoid discovery and fend off possible attacks. Call it a hunch, and no offense, Remi," she nodded her head in understanding and he continued, "but I don't think that the Prince, having kept you safe and secret all these years, would suddenly trust Remi, Alvor, and a bunch of foot soldiers. Friendship or not. So there had to be another angle. Maybe to draw someone out?"

Hunter and Remi sat up a little straighter. "I mean, logically, anyone they sent or trusted could be used to double cross the Prince and kill Hudson for this Nici bitch." Hunter tapped his chin, deep in thought. "Maybe he planted a few people here to watch over and make sure shit was done right?"

"Yeah, but who the hell could be planted? Realistically, Hudson just got here. She couldn't have gotten close to anyone that fast, especially not someone new like the freshman," Ryder said, catching on.

"So, they would have had to be here for a while, which means she hasn't been too much of a secret for too long. Maybe something was intercepted? Someone overhearing? Someone close? There are too many questions, but it all leads up to someone having more knowledge than they were supposed to. Someone that has to be at this school that wasn't Remi or Alvor," Grayson mused.

"Here's the problem with that. Me or Alvor would have recognized someone we knew right away or had known previously," Remi tossed in.

Hunter rubbed his head. "I hate to say it, but Logan has been going on and on about the origins of magic, and he wasn't wrong. So, wouldn't someone like the evil bitch of the west use her knowledge to infiltrate? You said it yourself, Gray, anything could've been intercepted or overheard. It's been two hundred years; she must've been planning."

"I can ask Kalen?" I picked up my phone and shot him a quick text. He responded back quickly.

Kalen- Yes, technically. That will take an extraordinary amount of dark magic, not only to change a person but to be able to get by Alvor and Remi undetected. It would mean you are in more danger than I thought. I'm coming back from my perimeter check.

I sighed. "Kalen said that not only is it possible but would involve dark magic. Great; more danger. This is giving me a headache. Kalen is coming back. I think this is going to be a long night. I'm going to go to my room and grab a notebook. I need to take notes." I went to my room, but when I opened the door to my room, something seemed... off. I quickly tossed on a pair of sweats and walked around the room trying to figure it out.

I walked up to my bed seeing a piece of paper and something I couldn't place before I tensed as I felt someone come up behind me. I didn't recognize the scent right away but the voice, the voice was unmistakable.

"Well, well, well, Ms. Jacobs. I admit it is certainly a pleasure. Although, I admit, it is certainly more of a pleasure for me than it may be for you. If you fight me, that is." Then I felt a plunge of a needle in my neck.

Chapter Twenty-Eight

Other than the fucking annoying pain of a needle in my neck, whatever he tried to use had no effect on me and I was seriously pissed.

"You know, Blair, you really chose a bad moment. Can you pretend that you're actually a threat to me a little later?" I'm not sure what he thought he was doing in my room, stabbing me like some mad scientist, but I was so done with this daily dose of fuckery.

"What the hell? That should have knocked you out for hours," he muttered. I sighed and ripped the damn, still hanging in my neck, needle from its spot and threw it across the room. I turned and planted my elbow in his gut, and he grunted before I fully turned and punched him in his nose. Now the fucking floor was covered in blood. Fucking bullshit.

"Hudson..." Zane trailed off as he saw Blair bleeding all over the floor. It took him about two point three seconds to put shit together before he flipped his shit. He let out a roar, yeah, like a sexy protective bear, and walked in two strides to pick Blair up off his feet and slammed him into the wall.

"What the fuck are you doing here, Blair?"

Everyone else ran in confused, but something immediately set off alarm bells in my head.

"Wait, what is he doing here and how did he bypass the wards, Kalen, and Xena? Kalen's wards should be unbreakable."

"They are..." came a dark gravelly voice from the door. We all turned to look to Kalen who had arrived at a record pace with Xena on his heels.

"So, I'm going to ask again. What the fuck are you doing here and answer Hudson's question?" Zane punctuated every word with a shake. We looked on at the pair, and for the first time in a long time, I was calm and everyone else was pissed. It was a nice turn of events.

"You think you are all unstoppable but you're not, you know. That may not have worked on Hudson now, but the Queen will come up with something stronger next time." We blinked.

"Repeat that. Slowly." Kalen approached. Blair laughed, until Zane wrapped his hand around his neck and pressed tightly, then he flailed while his face turned purple; purple was such a nice color.

"I was promised Hudson, for being loyal. I was promised any female I wanted but Hudson is supposed to be my Queen, just mine!" His face contorted into something dark and Kalen looked at him a little closely and cursed.

"You don't belong on this side of the Veil do you, who..." Before Kalen finished, we heard a loud crash from downstairs and my room door facing the pool burst open with Fae warriors. Tall and handsome warriors, but instead of white hair, these Fae had inky black hair, dark eyes, evil sneers, and a feeling of twisted evil. I couldn't put my finger on it, but they looked and felt wrong; unnatural. Hunter, Grayson, Ryder, and Kalen sprang into action despite not having weapons and started fighting the Fae pouring through the door.

"Come out, come out, little princess queen, we know you are here. We smell you," a high pitched, voice echoed through the house. I rolled my eyes.

Fuck me, can't just unwind with my mates, I gotta fucking deal with attacks from what must be the Unseelie Fae. I swear, I was going to tear their wings off and eat them with hot sauce.

I heard Ryder's laugh in my head and my eyes popped open. I quickly looked at him.

HUDSON- *You can hear me?*

RYDER- *Holy shit. I thought you said that out loud.*

HUNTER- *I hear you both. Now, shut the fuck up. We at war!*

GRAYSON- *This is perfect.*

"They are here and you're coming home to be my little queenly bitch, and I'm going to love every moment of hearing you scream," Blair choked out right before Zane positioned his hands around Blair's head and broke his neck, pulling his head from his body. Well damn, that was new. Dancing, mind reading, and head ripping. It's a perfect date night.

"They aren't getting near Hudson, period," Zane said with a finality.

"Yes, baby, but I'm damn sure getting near them. Take care of shit up here. I'm going down before we're all pinned."

"Like hell, go with her Zane. We got this here," Hunter yelled, letting all his anger out on two Fae warriors.

I didn't wait for a response as I bolted downstairs with Zane hot on my heels.

"Oh yes, we smell you little one. Why won't you come out? We only want to talk to you. Our queen has a few questions for you," a masculine voice chimed in as I reached the end of the stairs. Fuck that, I wasn't going to be ambushed in my own home.

Hudson- *Shield now. I'm pissing them off, then attacking.*

Hunter- *Like hell you will.*

Hudson- *Shut the fuck up and bow to your queen, motherfucker.*

No fucking way were they going to stop me; I'll kill these unnatural looking fuckers.

I walked out to stand in the center of the room and as much as I wanted my face to show my shock, I reigned it in.

"Megan, nice to see you." How long has this bitch been on this campus, four years? Fuck, Grayson was right. Nici had planned way ahead. I sighed. "That's interesting, you dumb Fae fuckers, because last time I checked, I was Queen and your little bitch on the throne is an imposter." They growled and walked into the room. I counted about eight sets of pointy eared fuckers. I wonder when mine would be pointy. I wanna pierce them.

"Our queen would tear you apart," one of them hissed, I rolled my eyes.

"I'm sure that is why she is here herself. Since you are unfamiliar with me, let me introduce myself." With an ease that rivaled my previous skill level, I pulled energy from around me and blasted the four closest, knocking them back into the others. Without stopping, I walked forward, Zane backed me every step.

Zane growled, *"by the way, shut up, don't piss them off more, we are outnumbered.*

I scoffed, *"I'm not outnumbered, I'm a fucking boss."*

The front door blasted open and Zane covered my back, suddenly bombarded with three dark Fae. Xena bounded down the stairs and started ripping into one of them.

"You fucking bitch." My head snapped back to my group of 'warriors'.

"Let me guess, you'll pay, right? Yeah, I'm not in the mood for that. So, fuck you and fuck your queen." One of them threw a dagger across the room straight to my heart, which rebounded off my shield. I rolled my eyes. I'm going to need a new pair of eyes to roll soon. Feeling a spike of anger take over, my vision turned hazy and I was done playing nice. I continued my stride, held up my hands, picturing a rope before sending out my magic with a force that broke the glasses in the kitchen. Five of the eight were now tightly stuck together as if wrapped around by rope, their faces changing colors as the rope tightened. The panic in their eyes made me laugh. I was made for this shit. You want a Queen, I'll give you a fucking queen. I looked down and smiled, bent over and picked up two of the dropped weapons; my personal favorites, a short sword and a hand scythe. I approached the other three who had fallen out into the patio. I looked around but I could no longer see Megan. Putting her in the back of my mind I focused on the three in front of me, my magic taking control.

"Nothing to say now?" My voice sounded like nails on a chalkboard and they three looked back and forth at each other. I smiled and cracked my neck and crouched down low as they loosely surrounded me and charged at me at the same time. I laughed. It was surreal for a moment. My senses were heightened, and I felt every molecule of water in the air. I was no longer just a magic user, no. I *was* magic, and this magic was done being caged. I screamed as I spun on the ball of my foot, using the scythe to hack into the leg of one of the assholes on my right, and as I got up from my position, the sword in my other hand came up with me and cut through the man on my left. I didn't spare them a glance as the Fae in front of me approached me, fear in his gaze. I sent out a pulse of magic and I felt my weapons heat before I crossed them in front of my chest and spun, using the scythe to take his head clean off of his body and using the sword to disembowel him. You can never be too dead, my magic whispered through my head. I looked at the other two who attacked me, one cut in half and the other must have died from the blood loss. But I stood over his body and cut his head off his neck.

I grabbed the two heads in my hands and walked back inside the house covered in blood, and loving every moment, power fueling me, bringing me everything I needed. My marks started to glow, and I ignored the gasps of the 5 who were tied up. The men and Remi were now downstairs, covered in blood. Except for these five and the missing Megan, we were winning.

I breathed in. Magic was energy. I control the energy... I control the magic.

I let out a pulse of power, the Fae screaming as their insides heated and boiled. I stopped, feeling benevolent, leaving the Fae barely alive. However, I was delighted at the smell of burnt bodies filling the room. I faced the boiled bitches; the two heads still in my hands.

"Anyone want to speak, or do they want to be the next head for my fucking wall?" I turned and walked around them.

"We were sent to kill you; we didn't know you were mated. Seems like we were working on outdated information," the guy from earlier seethed. He looked a lot angrier than normal for that tidbit, which means he knows more.

"Outdated, huh? No, no, more like someone told you where I was but left them out. Which is interesting but regardless, we just mated so that's a moot point, I suppose." I pointed at them with the heads in my hands.

"Welp, you have lived out your usefulness and you'll die next. Anyone else?"

"How did you take us all on? You can't be that powerful. You're not even of age nor have even crossed the Veil," one of them spat out. *What does crossing the Veil have to do with me being more powerful?*

"Oh, Tinkerbell, *I am power*. You will all see that soon. Well, maybe not you exactly, considering you're going to die." My eyes glowed as my magic spoke for me, my voice dark and my body started to glow. I heard a phone ring and pointed at the female who spoke. "You have a phone," I clapped, gleefully. "I'll take that," I summoned it from her pocket. Oh, nifty trick.

I picked up and Megan's voice came through the phone. "Did you kill her?"

"Hmm, I must say this is a fucking surprise, Megs. I did not expect that you would be this bold. The meek little girl who needed friends. Smart. This must have been a long end game, and you must be fucking pissed that you couldn't take me down. I will fucking dance in your blood like a motherfucking ballerina. You messed with the wrong Fae-itch. So, tell the imposter queen, that I'm happy to report that not only did they not kill me, but all of her rebel cunt lickers are dead, you stupid, pathetic, pointy-eared, little bitch, and you'll be next." I hung up the phone and set it on fire in my hand, admiring how it didn't hurt me and just burned and burned. I laughed and laughed, the group in front of me looking at me in fear.

"Hudson, come back to yourself. It's okay," Ryder whispered. I looked back and Gray, Hunter, and Zane were still visibly restraining themselves.

"I'll come back, sure, but first..." I turned back and waved my hand over the five left, surrounding them with fire, laughing while they burned. "Fuck you, they are mine and no one hurts what's mine." I took a deep breath and slowly let the magic recede.

Chapter Twenty-Nine

I looked around the house and it was a total disaster. I groaned.

"Totally not cleaning this shit up. We are also going to need new beds and to call for someone who picks up bodies or some shit," I stopped rambling as Zane came and wrapped me in a big hug, then Hunter, then Grayson, then Ryder. Kalen and Remi leaned against the side of the kitchen island, looking thoughtful.

"Guys, I'm okay, this isn't hot potato." I chuckled. They all looked at me with a firm look on their faces, expecting me to break down. I mean, yes, this was some unexpected bullshit and fuck if I wasn't ready to go to bed, but strangely, I felt okay for the most part. The mess though? I could do without. I sighed.

"Okay, first things first, there is glass everywhere, and we also need to set up wards again. Maybe if we do it together it will be stronger, Kalen?" He nodded, and we held hands and let out pulses of magic, warding the surrounding area.

I sighed and headed up the stairs to go to my room. They followed close behind.

I'm not going to break, guys. I just want to shower the blood off and put on clothes. This mind connection was going to come in handy.

Zane- *How about we get you your clothes, baby, and you can take a shower in my room?*

Ah fuck, I took a quick peak into the room and swore. The dead bodies; Blair, blood. Sigh. He made a good point. I walked right back around and headed into Zane's room to shower instead.

Fucking shit. I wanted to kill them all over again. I turned on the shower and stripped before getting in and leaning against the wall. My room was reduced to a mess of feathers, blood, and memory foam.

Ryder walked into the bathroom, whistling a happy tune. "Fuck off, Ryder."

"Well, I didn't but it looked like Blair fucked off all over your bed and left you a little note too." He laughed and I shrieked.

"There was fucking psychopathic cum all over my bed?! He came up here, jerked off all over my fucking bed, then tried to drug me, then said I was his. What type of sick shit is this?" I groaned as I angrily soaped my body, with Ryder still in the bathroom, now leaning against the sink staring at me while I showered. It was comforting how he just wanted to watch me and make sure I was good, but I wanted to fucking stab someone.

Zane stomped into the bathroom with the cum note in his hand. Fucking gross.

"Hudson, when I came up and smelled your scent, I had no choice but to touch myself. I may have gotten a little excited. I can't wait until I sink inside of you and create a new generation of Fae. I can't wait for the moment I take that sweet cunt over and over until you bleed. Your Fae Prince," Zane finished the letter with his eyebrows raised.

"Fae prince, what the fuck is this now? I need a fucking drink." Hunter threw his hand out and punched a hole in Zane's bathroom. I didn't even hear him come in.

"Okay, Blair didn't plan on being here for the attack, so clearly he just got excited and tried to take me out before he really thought it through, got caught in the crossfire, and died. One problem solved, I guess. Megan working with the Queen was not expected. She put on a good show, so I couldn't get a read on it. Ugh. This is a cluster fuck." I groaned. Stepping out of the shower, Ryder wrapped me in a towel, and I gave him a quick kiss.

"Okay so, the kidnapping scheme... looks like we were right," said Ryder. He started stripping and got in the shower after me. I looked at him and grinned. Kalen said the bond was stronger than marriage or soulmates. I wonder if it meant it intertwined our hearts together even more than before?

"If they came as a team, it is fair to expect that someone with malintent came with them, or at the very least, they led them straight toward you too," Grayson tossed in.

"What the fuck are we missing? Kalen even said he warded the house more."

"So, someone with knowledge of his wards, or old enough to know which ones he may have used, or..." Ryder trailed off, his eyes wide.

Hunter stood up, wiping blood from his face. "Or someone who knows him and understands him," Hunter growled and screamed. "Someone we thought we knew was going to try and drug our girl, and then we get attacked, the house is wrecked. And all signs point to Alvor being a sneaky fuck. I know you are all thinking it." He angrily stripped and got in the shower with Ryder.

"I swear, Ryder, you better not touch me with your fucking dick, I'm not in the mood," Hunter grumbled, and I busted out laughing. I laughed, and I laughed, and I laughed until I was on the floor of the bathroom rocking back and forth. They stood there, letting me feel without interrupting. It was perfect; I was alone in my head but not in my heart, and not physically. They knew what I needed and right now, that meant the world to me. Right now, despite a long couple of days filled with mating bonds, betrayal, kidnappings, dance competitions, Tinkerbell fights, and the murdered jerker, I had my mates. *I'll never get tired of saying that.*

I felt arms pick me up and cradle me and take me into, I guess, whatever room was left that didn't have cum or blood on it and curl around me. I breathed in Zane and burrowed into his arms, my face in his chest. I felt the bed dip and the guys all touch me and soothe me in ways that my soul just felt relieved. Zane pulled me close and grabbed my chin to look at him before he brought his lips down and kissed me. I moaned softly as he caressed my mouth with his tongue.

He looked down at me and ran his hands through my soaked hair. "Baby, you know if you need to talk, just let it out. You don't have to hide how you feel with us," he whispered. I wasn't ready to talk yet. I just wanted to kill everyone bad, save the world, and skip happily away with my mates. I drifted off to sleep with deep murmurs around me. I felt safe.

Chapter Thirty

I woke up to the sounds of grown ass juvenile men yelling and I groaned. *Fuck, I am not a morning person, but I don't wake up and start screaming like a crazy bitch.* One of the guys had dressed me in a pair of my leggings and one of their shirts, and despite the yelling, I smiled. I felt such an overwhelming feeling of love, lust, and comfort it was staggering. I grabbed a pair of Zane's socks and made my way downstairs to find there was no more glass, bodies, or blood. The mattresses had been tossed out and despite the fuckery and the lack of glass on the windows or doors, it all looked pretty normal.

"What the fuck is going on down here? Jesus, don't you guys know how to let a bitchy queen sleep?"

Grayson- Uh sweetie, we have company. Keep the Queen talks to a minimum. We have some slightly interesting developments.

Hunter- Slight? More like I'm going to fucking kill someone else today.

Ryder- People, let me tell you about my best friends.

Zane/Remi- Ugh, stop with the singing, Ryder.

Hudson- Guys? I really fucking love you. That is all.

I walked into the kitchen and was surprised to see Jensi, Luca, Kalen, and fucking Squishy? Remi was sitting in a corner, looking like someone tried to kidnap her and take her back to a different world... Oh wait, that was me. I walked in and jumped on the kitchen island.

"This is such a nice team meeting, what did I miss? All the screaming sounded very, very productive. Actually, I'm sure you guys were able to make some pretty big decisions." They all looked away. "Ah, okay, maybe plans?" They all stayed quiet. "Oh, so the yelling had absolutely no effect whatsoever. Cool. Well, now that that is out of the way, anyone want to tell me what is going on?" They all started talking at once and I pinched the bridge of my nose and lifted my hand and did a little 'zip-it' motions, and they all stopped talking. I looked up carefully and realized that, holy shit, I totally fucking made them shut up. There was magic and then there was *magic*. I liked this version better. It made men shut up.

"Kalen, since you tend to be more level-headed, usually, you may go." I waved my hand and he glared at me. "I'll also need my royal scepter," I sniggered and the guys shook their head at me.

"Hudson, don't start. Let's not cut corners here. You remember how I said you were pretty much the daughter of my heart?" I nodded and beamed at him. "Okay, remember that just for a moment." I frowned just as fast. "Okay, so when I knew you were coming to DeLorean, I wanted to make sure that you had some protection in place in case I wasn't here. You're a beautiful girl with a hot temper." I looked at him and glared at Zane when he choked back a laugh. "Okay, a volatile temper at the best of times."

"Okay... I'm not sure why this needs to be brought up now though?" I tossed my hair over my shoulder.

"Well, because of last night and because of those." He gestured at my ears. I went to grab them, and they were pointed. Fucking awesome! I clapped gleefully and pumped my fists. I had fucking pointy ears. All I had to do was fucking fry some fuckers up. I started dancing in my seat.

"So, uh, Jensi and Luca... I sent them here." Wait what?

"What do you mean you "sent them"? That's an interesting way to say you hired a couple of magic babysitters, Kalen," I said with a smile, picking up a knife from the counter and flipping it from hand to hand.

"Well, actually, Jensi and Luca are..."

"We are from Kalen's Fae rebel camp. We have been for over two hundred years, since the imposter queen took the throne. Except we don't work like the other rebel camp. We don't live in secrecy through covert ops and murder," Jensi said softly, interrupting Kalen. I nodded, wanting more information, so I stayed quiet; *life was getting juicy! I was in a Fae telenovela; I wonder who I end up slapping dramatically down a set of stairs.* Someone snapped their fingers in front of my face. I growled.

"Can't a bitch daydream, shit," I grumbled. I deserved a mental break.

"So anyways," Luca picked up, "we live within the Veil of Fae, but within our own heavily warded area, where women and children, as little as we do have, are able to live safely. For years, we facilitated getting our people safely across, into our side of the Veil."

"Okay, so you said Veil twice, and I get it's pretty much like a separator between worlds, and the wards keep out not only humans but bad guys." They nodded and smiled. "Got it, so why is your Veil within the Veil special?"

"Well, anyone who tries to cross it with a dark soul or malintent dies instantly and their magic, which is pure in nature, their souls were just stained, fortifies the wall. It is what has made it so strong over the years," Kalen explained.

"Well, in the words of Lucifer Morningstar, my British virginity buddy, that's bloody brilliant." I chortled and the guys groaned.

Zane- *Best sex ever.*

Hudson- *Yeah, we really must do it again. And again. The other guys can join or watch.*

Zane- *Once I have you all to myself for a few, we can make that happen. I love you, princess.*

Hudson- *I love you too.*

His eyes opened wide and I winked at him, I haven't said it straight out like this without a joke laced with it, and I meant it too. He had my heart the day he had my body.

"Okay, cool, so Luca and Jensi are the good guys who came down to protect me. That explains them being so protective... what?" Kalen's face changed briefly then went blank. "Kalen, what? Your face did that weird flickering shit when you don't want to explain something to me."

"Not now, we can discuss all this shit later," he growled and rubbed his face. Oh yeah, there is going to be a fucking later alright.

"Okay, later, I'm serious. Now what the hell does all of this have to do with Squishy?"

"Who the fuck is Squishy?" Hunter growled, hanging on by a thread. Angry baby. But I was in good spirits today.

"King is my squishy, he is mine, and he shall be my squishy." King groaned and smacked his head, and I saw a mark on his hand similar to my swirls.

"I'll get to you handing out nicknames to men like candy and skip to the important part." Zane glared, and Ryder chuckled. Grayson just stood there like a floating cloud of muscle, observing. I'm sure he was taking mental notes and making observations.

"Sure, pumpkin pie drizzle, whatcha got?" I said solemnly. He glared at me and continued.

"Well, this morning King knocked on the door and proceeded to tell us he felt like he needed to be with you all night and that this morning he couldn't take it and came over. Kalen let him in after he noticed some markings on his hand and called him a sentinel.

"Except he didn't have those markings during the party?" King shook his head.

"No, it's weird, they just popped up and I knew I had to come here."

I rubbed my head. Okay, I needed a notebook here. Jensi and Luca equal Fae, King equals sentinel, and Kalen hires Fae babysitter. Sounds about right.

"What does that mean? For Squishy. You said they are normally Fae, but in this case, he isn't, right? Unless Mr. My Squishy-wishy is hiding something from his Queenie-weenie." Hunter threw his hands up in the air and said something about making coffee before beating someone's ass and I laughed and laughed.

"Okay, okay, I'm sorry. Kalen, please, explain and then wrap this up because I'm sure you're going to shock me and piss me off. So, let's get to it." I sighed, kicking my legs and looking around the room at the people here. I guess my new makeshift family.

"Well, yes, typically, but you're not normal. I'm also not sure he has Fae blood directly, but what he does have is the mark, the magic, and the innate desire to protect you, which you are going to need."

"Will not." I stuck my tongue out and him.

"You will so, and not another word or I'll take you out and give you a training you'll never forget."

"Did you just Faerie threaten to spank me?" I looked at him like he lost his mind. Then he started laughing and I started laughing. I jumped off the counter and gave him a hug. "I'm happy you're here, Kalen. Last night was crazy and there are so many theories buzzing around our heads. Between the clear infiltration and now other people tacked on to this merry band of fucktwats... and their queen, that's me by the way, the guys were freaking out over new information." He pushed me off awkwardly, I was going to make him a fucking hugger one day.

"Little girl, I'm going to choke you," Hunter said exasperatedly, stomping to me. I just ran around the island.

Kalen chuckled and shook his head, "Yes, well, the dark Fae know where you are. That's two attacks in as many days. I was going to stay here and just deal, but you can't learn everything you need to learn with so many distractions. Even if no one had left here alive, you would no longer be safe here; it is a death sentence. I need you all to pack your things and then we need to leave within the next few hours." He looked at King. "King, I'm sorry, but with those marks, you are in danger and will have to come too."

He nodded and then looked at me. "This is like when Harry, Ron, and Hermione had to go into hiding from place to place. We are going to have an adventure, Dory!" He grabbed and hugged me and started jumping up and down. We stopped when everyone was silent and looking at us.

Kalen coughed back a laugh. "I should also mention that sentinels pretty much become their chosen's best friend. It's how they are able to sense their emotions so keenly and help ground them, and also how they are able to pick up any malintent near their chosen, so that they can escape accordingly."

"Fuck that, Squishy, we aren't running from shit." We fist bumped and hip bumped.

"They sense with their power, innately first, emotions second," Kalen finished, smirking as the guys looked ready to beat King's ass. Psssh, as if he wasn't built himself, and now part of me. King was absolutely gorgeous. No one was going to hurt his pretty face.

"Close your damn mind, Hudson," growled Grayson, oops. I blew him a kiss then the middle finger.

"Ah, mind reading? Anything else manifest yet?" Kalen asked.

"I don't know yet, but last night I glowed and made heads explode and catch fire, but you saw that part. I was also able to use a short sword to cut the Fae fuckers in half in one swipe and decapitate them with a just swing of my hand scythe."

Luca- "Holy."

Jensi- "Fucking."

King- "Shit."

"Yup, that covers that pretty well." I nodded with a smirk. There was something else nagging me though.

"You know, Blair jerking off on my sheets and proclaiming himself prince, got me thinking. Before he tried to poison me and shit, he mentioned a concoction that was supposed to knock me out. Which, I admit, sucks as a wedding gift, but if they are developing something to take me out or any of the good Fae, we need to start thinking bigger than magic, we need to start looking into science as well." I nodded to King. "King, any chance you can sneak in and get your collection of potions and books? Luca, Jensi, maybe go with him as a cover?" They nodded. "Great, so I must pack all my stuff. Remi, can you help me, please?"

"I already packed a lot of it. We just have to spell the other shit to shrink because I know you want to bring more stuff," Remi sighed. She was right. I needed my books.

"You all have two hours. You'll need clothes for warmth. There are pools, and you'll have your own mating quarters. Also, we will have to trek through the forest, so boots are necessary. It's about a ten-hour drive. The Veil works in strange ways, but I'll explain more on the way. We should all fit in two trucks, Hudson and Jensi's. Jensi and Luca are already packed and ready to go. King, wear a glove, move quickly, pack, and do not let anyone see you. That is imperative, and I mean anyone." We all started moving quickly after that, the sense of necessity pressing on all of us. Some things are not worth arguing about. We didn't ask for a length of time. We needed to pack, and something told me it would be for more than a while, and closer to forever. War was coming, and of course, I found myself in the middle of it. Hell, I found myself the reason for it.

Chapter Thirty-One

We were ready and packed in record time. We each had a few suitcases, and I made sure I packed my bags perfectly by shrinking all my clothes and books and shoes between three suitcases. Yelling over the banister to make sure everyone had their chargers, wallets, money, cards, and emergency cash, I double checked I had everything down to the last lingerie piece. I took a long-ass shower, knowing that my clothes for the next day and forest trek were pretty much it. Tossing on a pair of leggings, crop top, and combat boots, I was ready to go. I made my way downstairs, using my magic to carry my bags down and started packing the cars. Zane, Hunter, and Ryder were going up and down from the gym with all the weapons. I grabbed my own weapons to have near me before I tossed them into the driver's seat and was ready to go. King had already made it back and since I had an eight-seater, he was going to sit with me, the guys, and Remi.

When everyone was ready, the boys and I held hands and put our strength to the test, and we closed our eyes and sent out an extension of our magic toward the home. I felt Remi's connection twine with ours and a purple glow surrounded the home before disappearing.

I had a strong feeling that that ward was going to be completely foolproof.

We jumped in the car and drove silently through campus, tension high, until we got on the road. We were supposed to just follow the good Fae fuckers in front of us. So, I relaxed and turned on my music. The boys sat in the back and Remi sat in the passenger side.

"Which one of you fuckers wanna have a singing competition?!" I yelled. They fake groaned and smiled.

"I'm down," said King, I smiled at him through the rear-view mirror.

"Well, then you get first pick!"

"Oh yeah! Okay, so I'm thinking a little smooth lullaby type of song. The type of song that really soothes the soul." I laughed and passed him my phone.

Queen's "Fat Bottomed Girls," blasted through the radio and I laughed and bopped my head to the song as he sang and played the air guitar and the guys joined in pretending to be his backup band. I drummed on the steering wheel while they finished their air guitar performances and King sang with an exaggerated voice.

"Okay, okay. That was awesome. But please, remind me that you are not allowed to sing lullabies to Rayne and Xavier."

"Who are Rayne and Xavier?" King asked.

"My future kids. I already have them planned out in my head. They will be gorgeous," I said wistfully. "Can you imagine just how hot I'll look in a thong bikini, nine months pregnant?" I started laughing and the guys rolled their eyes.

"Like hell you'll have my babies in a thong," grumbled Hunter.

"Not them, me, and they will be my babies, you are all just the donation sperm banks." I stuck out my tongue.

"I'm calling in my promise the moment we get to where we have to go, for that smart ass mouth," Hunter whispered through my mind. I tossed him a wink.

"I'm next! I have the perfect lullabies for my babies! Pass me the phone." Ryder snatched the phone and started playing "Cold Beer Drinker" by Luke Bryan and the guys all sang along and pretended to have cowboy hats and danced back and forth on beat to the song. *They will definitely not be singing lullabies to the kids.*

"Wooooo, I'm about to start throwing dollars back there!" I joked.

Grayson snagged the phone next and put "Body Like a Back Road" by Sam Hunt and actually carried the tune very well. I cheered for him. "Aww, baby, I'll be your back road." I laughed.

"Angel, you're my everything," his deep voice made me shiver and I blushed. Fuck, I'm becoming a blushing bitch... these guys, I swear.

"Who's next? I will sing Baby Shark unless someone goes next!" Hunter threw himself pretty much across the car to catch the phone. That song is the devil, I admit.

"Over my dead body." He flicked through and found a song and smiled and tapped Zane. The notes of "Tell Me It's Real" by KC and JoJo played softly but when Hunter and Zane started to sing, I realized it was the karaoke version. Holy shit, they can dance, fuck, sing, fight, fuck, not to mention fuck. I won the jackpot.

"Well shit, now I feel like I have to fuck this shit up and make you all cry," I teased.

"Remi, your turn! What are you singing? And no isn't an option!" She grabbed the phone and then started rapping along to "Lollipop" by Lil Wayne.

When she finished, I jabbed her. "Really? The one girl in here that doesn't lick lollipops and you pick that song?" She rolled her eyes and the guys groaned.

"You motherfuckers wish I had hundreds of years of experience with lollipops, I would have had the Fae world under my spell," she giggled.

"You Fae whore!" I teased.

"Oh, I don't know, Remi, YouTube has some pretty good tricks. I know firsthand," Hunter laughed.

"TMI, bro, TMI. I don't need to know about the cum guzzling," Remi quipped. I choked back a laugh and the guys shook their heads. I admit, this type of camaraderie is exactly what I expected when I thought about having my little family.

For the next few hours, we sang and joked in between rest stops, and the tension in the car eased considerably.

Zane

For fucks sake, I thought for the 56th time since we parked the cars in some west bumble fuck part of the woods. How long was this fucking trek? Hunter whistled as he skipped through the woods. He loved being in this shit. I didn't hate it, but I damn sure didn't want to walk in the forest for hours. Bad enough it was getting dark now, with the caws of birds slowly turning into the soothing sounds of insects and owls. Kalen, Luca, Jensi, and Grayson were in the front, discussing security measures. I smiled softly; Grayson was the thinker. The theoretical and practice of his job was a bonus. However, he always thought things through before acting on them, only acting out if pressed, and recently his only trigger was protecting Hudson.

Ryder and King were in front of me, giggling with Hudson, making jokes and movie references. Watching her walk and enjoy her time, okay, despite the shit that has gone down in such a short period of time, was incredible. She left home, finally ready to settle down and go to school, and ended up mated, attacked and was now moving to a safe location. I sighed, I would do anything to keep her safe, so if this was just another way for me to do that, I didn't care.

I observed Remi standing in the back, observing her surroundings, not letting anything miss her gaze. She may have made some pretty shitty decisions, but I knew firsthand how Hudson can make you see stars even in the sunshine. I felt shame and sadness coming from her- it must be the bond between us. I felt the urge to just help her in any way I could. Hanging back, I walked at her pace. Her eyes flicked my way and she sighed.

"Remi," I said softly. "Part of me understands."

She looked at me a little confused, and I chuckled. "The bond. I can feel your guilt, apparently. But yeah, I get parts of it. I wouldn't want anyone telling me to love someone or be with someone I didn't want to be with out of duty. I can't imagine the pressure you were under, but I'll go ahead and say that it was a shitty way of going about it all."

"You don't think I know that..." she whispered angrily, "now." Quickly deflating. "I justified it for years, you know. I kept saying that the prince's daughter would be the best idea, that she needed to take her place and I would just let the throne go. It sounded like a good idea. Alvor was always against it, urging me to take the throne. We got into a few fights about it actually. I just kept telling him no until he just let it go. I just... I just couldn't do it. It wasn't the power that scared me. It was the idea of having to do something that was emotionally, mentally, and physically abhorrent to me..." She sighed, and looked at Hudson laughing, wistfully. I looked at her too; it hurt me for two years, knowing I fucked up. I can't compare years of planning a kidnapping to my choices, but who am I kidding, they were pretty much on the same level of awful.

"She's my mate, Zane, our mate, but beyond that, she is my friend. We are so much alike." She smiles. "In all my years, and I wish I could say it wasn't true, I have not had a true friend. I don't trust anyone, and I met Hudson and it was immediate. I know it was part of my duty, but it didn't feel that way. It just felt right. I know she is not really upset about it anymore, but I feel like I have to make it up to her somehow, you know?" I thought about it for a few minutes.

"You could let her nut punch you. Or rather clit punch you," I teased, and she laughed. "No, but I'm serious, she hurts hard. It's how she's been wired since she was younger. But she loves harder. She started to fall for you, and usually, she is comfortable in her anger because it helps anchor her. But she isn't angry and that's saying something. I think you are pretty much out of the woods. We just have to be here together and help her move past what comes next."

"Yeah, you are right..." She nodded. I bumped her shoulder lightly.

"If you still feel the need to do something extra, we will talk to the guys and we can come up with a plan."

Thinking quietly for a few I realized something, "you know, you mentioned Alvor. I would have thought he would have come along, being part of the entire plan and all." She looked at for me for a moment and sighed.

"I don't know, I told him we were leaving for safety reasons, and he said he still needed to hang back and make sure the students were safe from attacks. It was... strange... he didn't want to come, but if the school board can replace five professors on a short notice, I don't see how they couldn't have done the same for him. I honestly think he is still a little pissed about me not being queen and then meeting Hudson was just a bit of shock. He will get over it and come eventually." She shrugged.

"It's been several years, and I'm not sure why that matters if the plan was supposed to bring her back so she can be put into place as queen..." I hesitated. "You know, one thing that has bothered us was how Kalen's wards were brought down and how she was attacked so quickly after her being mated; there are too many loose ends."

"Except if Megan was there the entire time as a spy, then it explains the wards and the attacks, but I admit I didn't recognize her, not even her mannerisms. Even if she had a powerful spell, it couldn't have changed everything. But then Nici had been planning this for years, apparently." She rubbed her head. "Honestly, just even trying to put this into place is giving me a headache."

I nodded but shelved the conversation for later. I was more confused than ever, truth be told. Why would Megan just leave? If she was older and worked with Nici, she had years on Hudson. She should have decimated her if she attacked. Same goes for the Dark Fae that attacked; they said were working on outdated information and were pretty much cannon fodder, Hudson was strong, and by extension, so were we, but when things are too easy, they put me on edge. Were these the dummy distractions? Were our skills being weighed? And where was Alvor during this entire time? I had to agree that he must have been up to something. So many questions, and time felt pressing.

We joked a little bit more and I realized how much like Hudson she truly was. She joked and laughed with her whole heart and she was indecent, but everything she said was stated with purpose, she didn't cut corners. I loved Hudson, but Remi? Remi is the little sister that I think I was always missing. These two together? Joining forces to torture us? We were all fucked. I smiled at the thought. I loved that idea.

Then suddenly, the wind started to blow around us, making it hard to walk.

Remi cursed. "The Si Gaiothe."

"What?!" I had to yell. She tapped her head.

Remi- *Fairy wind, we are about to be attacked by Slua, some malicious ass Fae creatures. They work for the Unseelie.*

Zane- *Well, fuck.*

HUDSON

ZANE- *WE ARE UNDER ATTACK, OR ABOUT TO BE. HUDSON LET KING know and Gray let Kalen, Luca, and Jensi know.*

Hunter- *Fucking great, everyone strapped? It's getting dark. We will need to pretend we are setting camp, everyone continues to talk and act normal. We need the advantage.*

Ryder- *Will do, I'm good. How many are we thinking?*

Grayson- *Kalen said we aren't far from his part of the Veil; however, we were planning on camping, so we aren't walking in the darkness. So, the time to attack would be best now, which means whoever is following us knows that.*

Hunter- *I literally just said that shit.*

Hudson- *Shut up, I feel a clearing out the right near a lake. Everyone goes right, set your things down, pretend to get things out of our bags and grab weapons.*

Zane- *Feel?*

Hudson- *Full fucking Fae now, baby, I'm part of the earth. And as for how many, I feel about fifteen disturbances on the floor and six in the trees. So, twenty-one against ten, pretty even odds.*

Grayson- *Only you would think that was even.*

Hunter- *She's right, I'm ready for someone to bleed.*

We went to the right and found a nice spot near the nearby lake. I would have loved to admire it under other circumstances. I put our bags down, grabbed my scythe and short sword, and a few daggers while everyone else did the same. Kalen looked over at me approvingly and I gave him a thumbs up.

I put my arms up in the air and announced loudly, "Hear ye, hear ye, the court of the honorable Hudson Morningstar is now in fucking session. We know you are out there, so stop wasting time so I can kill you and then take a nap." Ryder snorted a laugh and Kalen scowled and shook his head at me. Everyone else just smiled. Well, if they thought queen meant boring, they were sadly confused.

Three figures walked, well rather blew in, out of the forest and one of them started to speak, "You know, most people would..." I threw a dagger straight through his head and it cleaved his head in half. Fucking awesome.

"That was a boring speech; mine was better. Who's next?" I threw the two other daggers through his companions before they were able to advance, one going straight through the neck of one and the other through the nose. Damn, that had to hurt.

Okay, now it's eighteen to ten. I totally had more points... they attacked full force after a slight pause.

"Keep one alive, I need to question that Fae fucker." I didn't bother to see if anyone agreed as it seemed the majority were coming towards me and my mates. That pissed me off and my magic responded to the anger too quickly for me to control it. Fucking shit. Shut up, you insolent fool, we are to work together, accept the anger and let it fuel us. They threaten what is ours.

Scowling, I ignored the fact that my magic called me a fool, dumb bitch, and I stepped forward, infusing my blades and got to fucking work. I used the scythe to decapitate one of the attackers while pivoting on my foot to the right to use the short sword to cut through the chest of another. Blood coated in my hands and I relished the feeling. Two down. Xena bounded up, her muzzle bloody, and broke the neck of another right as they started to melt back into the wind.

"Oh no, don't leave now, the party is just starting," I growled, stepping forward. I spun low, cutting off the legs of three attackers and then stabbing them through the heart in quick succession. Five down.

I flipped into the air and ran at those retreating. No survivors. I agreed with my magic there. I ran after five retreating backs and the wind started to blow as they divided and surrounded me. Smirking, I jumped on the nearest fucker and slit his throat, before flipping off and pressing my attack, slashing as if my weapons were paint brushes and I was enjoying a night out at a paint night. Take that, Picasso. I observed the blood dripping from my hands in a daze.

"You know," I murmured softly to the dead assholes, "I like you all so much better when you are dripping from my fingers and my blades." I paused to collect my thoughts. "Much better when you can't speak either. I can't fucking wait to destroy all you fuckers." I whistled, walking around, admiring my handiwork and chunks of evil Fae fuckers, when I heard a sound coming from the forest. Xena perked her head up. No danger. Her eyes glowed as she sat down and observed.

I had to agree, I didn't feel threatened, so I looked around and found the culprit, sitting in the tree like some type of acrobatic bird. The fuck? Someone tell Tuscan Sam his job is being stolen. Something told me this guy was dangerous, but not to me, no. My head quirked to the side, and I observed him as he approached me. He seemed to be doing the same, although the longer he looked, a warm shiver worked its way up my spine and my vagina punched me in the face. Woah, down Bessie, you have more dicks and clits than you can manage right now.

He eyed me too keenly, a little obsessive maybe. I guess the creepiness factor was doing it for me. Still, I have a feeling this guy could put up a fight that would be worthy of a challenge. My magic jumped at the opportunity.

He jumped down from the trees and walked towards me, clapping, a hood with jewels covering his face, a bow slung on his back. I stayed still, comfortable in my blood chunks.

"Well, well, well, little mouse, I thought Kalen was exaggerating about your skill level, but I must admit, I'm very impressed, intrigued, and very turned on at the moment," his voice said darkly smooth, like a favorite cold beer, and I twitched in excitement. I imagined ripping of his cloak and discovering the magic underneath. I frowned, and he smiled at my visible reaction.

"Um, I'm glad you came to my performance. I admit I always get a little bit of stage fright right before the first act." I shrugged nonchalantly, as if I didn't just have sex with him in my head. "Want to explain who you are, other than Katniss Everdeen in a bedazzled cloak, and how do you know Kalen?"

He laughed. Fuck, I needed to start spouting some poetry; let me count the ways thou... I shook my head inwardly. Who the fuck was this guy?

"Ah well, I can answer both of those in time. I do enjoy a good movie, except I really hated Peta. Anyways, tell Kalen the Scail sends his regards and that the path is clear for now. However, camping is not in his best interest and the faster he gets to the Veil, the better. I'll watch your back and dispatch any lurkers. Although, you killed thirteen yourself and you're not even winded." He turned his head and looked me over. "My, my, you are absolutely delicious. I look forward to seeing you soon, Queen." At that, he jumped back into the trees and disappeared.

I SHOOK OFF THE WEIRD ENCOUNTER AND WENT BACK TO CAMP. I took note of the one little present kept alive and being held by Remi and smiled.

Everyone looked fine, just a little bloody, but a little irritated that I left alone.

"Why the fuck did you run off by yourself?" Hunter yelled while I walked over to the prisoner. I scoffed; he had no confidence in me.

"You're hot when you yell, baby, but because I knew I could kill them and Xena was also there. Also, umm because my magic told me to?" Well, that part was also true.

"Your magic told you to? C'mon, love, that's my line," Ryder teased, tense and looking me over for injuries. I batted him off.

I walked over to the prisoner being held by Remi's knee and her sword and grinned when my magic spiked. "Hello, little windy fucker. Want to tell me how you knew where we were and where we were going?" King came to stand next to me, feeling my magic spike, if what Kalen said was true.

"Chan innis mi dad dhut, banrigh meallta," he said scathingly. Sigh, you know it now makes sense why Kalen encouraged I took Gaelic in school as an extracurricular, sneaky fuck.

"Oh, false queen? Well, you're wrong, not only will you tell me, but I'm not a false anything." I waved my hand dismissing the thought. Kalen came close and sighed, "you can't force anything from a Fae... it has to be willingly given. If he doesn't want to talk, he won't. It's one of our oldest parts of us. We are a proud folk. No, if he won't talk, then he's useless." I turned my head in thought.

"Oh, I saw something on Google." He looked at me scathingly. "Do not start, Kalen, everyone knows the internet does not lie. Anyways, doesn't that typically apply to humans who summon Fae? Wouldn't it be the opposite if the Queen demanded it of her subjects?" I asked.

He shrugged. "Theoretically, but although you are prophesied, you are not seen as their queen yet. You are powerful, yet you are not on the throne or gained it through force or abdication. Also, considering you would be a Seelie Queen, not Unseelie." I thought about that for a second and smiled.

"But we do have a rightful queen here; Remi technically never abdicated, she just avoided the responsibility and wasn't killed. So technically, by those laws, he has to recognize Remi. It's worth a shot. Even if she's not technically his Queen, he resides in the territory of the Seelie, subject to our rules?" By the panicked look in the prisoner's eyes, I was right, score for us. He didn't realize who was holding him down. I clapped gleefully. "Okay Remi, your turn. AND SCENE!" I chuckled.

"Gee, I didn't practice my lines." She rolled her eyes, "Subject, how did you find us? We've been traveling for quite some time by motor and by foot, yet you attack us now, why? Oh, and in English so everyone understands." He struggled and spat at me, Remi adjusted her knee and he groaned.

"We were told where you were going by a friend of yours. Well, not really a friend, now is he?" He tried to laugh, but it sounded like a choked meat grinder. Don't ask. "We attacked now because on the way, we were besieged and most of our numbers were decimated, before we could have overtaken you. We chose to attack quickly; fortunate you have a strong ally or else you wouldn't be breathing. Your luck will run out though." He spat and Remi frowned.

"What friend? And who attacked you?" she asked.

"I know who attacked them, but we can get to that in a bit," I muttered. Ignoring the raised eyebrows in my direction, I turned back to the prisoner.

"As for the friend, Queen Remi," he said scornfully, "I believe you call him uncail," and he cackled.

"Uncle... Alvor," I whispered and low gasps echoed in the silence.

Kalen cursed and walked away and roared at the top of his lungs. I couldn't imagine how he was feeling, bad enough to suspect, but to have it confirmed? I shook my head sadly.

"For how long, how long has Alvor been working for you..."

"You can stop with the questions. Nici and Alvor have been lovers since before you were even a Fae cub. This has been long in motion. You just were a pawn. You thought you were attacked by Nici's real army at your pitiful little cottage back there? You would have been dust. You soon will be. I may not be there to see it, but I relish the idea of the idea of your death. Once we find the missing half of the prophecy..." Remi's neck snapped up and Kalen froze.

"What do you mean missing? We have the entire prophecy," Remi growled softly. We were so fucked if this shit is the truth. We have been operating on half batteries if this is the case.

"Oh, no, no, no." He laughed and laughed. "The other half was taken by Oberon, the crone killed by his hand as well, so she couldn't repeat it." Our eyes widened.

"Kill him, we don't need him anymore." My heart was in my throat. I walked away, ignoring the sounds of Remi hacking off his head. I bit my lip while my mind whirled. We were missing a part of the prophecy, and Alvor was indeed a traitor, which means he knows about my growth, my mates, and by playing both sides. He knew way too much to make me remotely comfortable.

I walked up to Kalen. "Hey, old man." He smiled softly, but it didn't reach his eyes.

He looked at me and shook his head, "You're a pain in my ass, Hudson. You're fortunate I trained you or else you'd be dead."

"Yes, yes, I love you too. Before all this information overload, someone named Scail was clapping at me and was admiring how awesome I was; he appreciates my talents clearly. But he also said camping is not a good idea, to keep moving and he'll watch our back. That we need to cross the Veil as soon as possible. After all of this, I'm afraid he's right." He cursed.

"Everyone pick your stuff up and let's go, we can follow the river, but if Scail says go, he means it." Everyone was pretty much ready considering we didn't have anything to really fix, since we threw it down to fight, add in the fact that we were now overly jittery and hyper focused and we moved quickly and efficiently.

"So, who is Scail and why is he right?" I asked Kalen, my guys echoing my sentiments through our connection, as we started walking again. King looked a little tired, so I pulled energy from around me and transferred it to him so he wouldn't have to do it himself. He looked at me gratefully and winked.

"Scail is one of the deadliest warriors and trackers of our time. I've been around many years and besides me, and you, which is because of me by the way," he smirked, and I rolled my eyes before he continued, "Scail is a very disciplined warrior. He also has built a network of underground spies. If there is something you need done or information you need, he would be the one to go to, although he is as cunning as he is helpful, so making a deal with him could easily break you, and he doesn't leave loose ends. He is as great of a person to have by your side as he is the worst."

"How is that possible?" Ryder wondered out loud.

"Well, he has his network and as such, knows where tides are turning and at the drop of the dime, can go either way. If anyone were to ever gain his fealty, it would mean certain destruction for whatever side he abandons. He has made many enemies over the years, in name only, as they are all too chicken shit to actually do anything," he chuckled. "He's a good man; resourceful and intelligent. He reminds me much of you actually - very interested in human relations and making sure whatever new age is brought in is aware of the importance of those relations."

I pondered for a while. He sounds like a dangerous person to get on the wrong side of, which means I would naturally end up there because quite frankly, I always ended up pissing someone off. I sighed. "He said he realized that everything you said about me was true and that he looked forward to seeing me very soon. Does that mean he lives in the Veil?" He frowned at that.

"Not really... he visits but doesn't spend long, if he is as intrigued by you as you say and is coming, it's anyone's guess how long he will stay. He has his own quarters there," he shrugged.

Hmm, well. I guess I'll see Mr. Chocolate, vaginal-punch inducing, mysterious Fae soon. I turned back and the guys and Remi were all in deep conversation. I'm sure I was the topic, so I rolled my eyes and ignored them. Kalen caught my look and laughed. "They are worried about you, you know. I have known you longer and I know how you tick a bit more. You are protective and you are fierce, Hudson, and I love that about you, but they are your mates now; you are a part of them. If anything happened to you, they wouldn't survive and vice versa. If you stay close, you can defend better. In your heart, you know it's a brotherhood of sorts. I taught you strategy, so realistically, you should have thought about that, but you let your magic take over. Your magic is your connection to Gaia and nature, which is a strength, however, with tides having turned... Alvor," he choked up a bit, "with Alvor having always been on the other side, we now know he has been gauging your strengths and weaknesses and he knows more now than we ever wanted him to. We are at a disadvantage; something I do not like. Knowing that, I realize we never went over the importance of fighting with your team, which, in a war, a coordinated team can mean the difference between winning and losing. I look forward to teaching you all I can. We will have to pick up training again soon." I groaned jokingly and he laughed. We walked in silence for about an hour more and we reached... a tree? I looked at Kalen and he laughed.

"Well, it's not going to have a sign that says 'Welcome to the Good Side of the Fae Kingdom'." He chuckled as he cut his palm and placed it against the tree and dropped to one knee. "As blood grounds, I offer my essence to the essence of which we came." Once he said the words, a tightness appeared in my chest, and we were suddenly in a resort-like city with twinkling, floating lights. Holy shit, I fucking entered Disney World. There was even a white horse!

I spun around, taking in the homes and stores carved into trees and beautiful little cabins all around. Surrounded by the greenest of grass and foliage, I couldn't help but picture all of this destroyed, and the white horse covered in blood.

Chapter Thirty-Two

Shaking the bad thoughts from my head, I tried to take in as much as possible, but it looked like everyone was pretty much asleep, and to be honest I could use some serious sleep too. But it all looked so pretty! Luca and Jensi waved at us and went to a cabin to the right of a huge, gorgeous cabin. I wondered who it belonged to until Kalen led us straight to it. I gaped. It was a gorgeous three-story cabin, in front of a still lake and a campfire area. The cabin was all dark wood and the front door was hidden, as you needed to walk down three steps down in order to reach it. When he opened the door, I was taken aback by the open-concept plan that led you into an expansive foyer with a perfect view of a rustic kitchen, and a smooth marble double island. The living room was decorated out of a magazine and the walls were painted a soft green, giving more to the overall earth tones of the home.

"Wow," I whispered. Kalen blushed.

"I started building this for you the moment I knew of your existence. I didn't know how close we would become, but every time I look at this place, I knew in my heart that it was perfect for you and I couldn't wait to have you here." He cleared his throat when he saw my face and I looked away so

I wouldn't get emotional. There was Father and then there was someone like Kalen who truly cared about me and my happiness; that meant the world to me.

He cleared his throat. "Anyways, there are ten rooms, and each room has its own bathroom. Also, the lowest level has a gym, but in the next few days, we'll be moving training to the courtyard. It's how we all train here. Hunter, Ryder, Zane, Grayson, King, and I need to gauge your level of skill and tailor it accordingly." They all nodded. "We have quite a bit to go over, but we can worry about that tomorrow after some rest. Oh, there is also a pool outside and a large bathroom that leads off it. There's also a half-bath in the gym and in the living area near the mudroom. I'll let you explore it. I'm going to bed; my cabin is directly across from yours. The one to your left belongs to Scail, believe it or not. That should be interesting."

Kalen said his goodbyes and we all wandered upstairs to the bedrooms. I laughed when I saw the room that was clearly mine.

Hudson- Guys, my room has like a triple king bed, a huge television, and posters of Lucifer Morningstar, and fuck yeah, direct access to the pool area again. Totally tanning tomorrow.

Zane- Yeah that's your room, I chose an all-black one, its fucking huge. The bed is ridiculous. I'll be watching you tan tomorrow.

Hunter- Fuck yes, I chose the red room, for obvious reasons. Matches all I bought that day we went shopping, all of which I brought with me. I'll be rubbing the tanning lotion.

Hudson- Fucking perv, I love it. Wait, what the fuck did you buy that needs a red room?

Hunter- You better, the only reason I'm not deep in you right now is because we need to shower and sleep, but tomorrow, all bets are off.

Remi- Guys, I can hear you now. Fucking gross. My room is such a pretty autumn gold. I love it.

Grayson- Rolling my eyes right now, my room is green and it is tastefully done for sure. I have to wonder if Kalen knew about our preferences.

Ryder- Maybe. I chose a room with blue. Holy fuck, have you guys been in the bathrooms yet? Also, I'm using the tanning lotion as lube, I hear perineal sunning is good for your health.

Hudson- I am now. Fuck. I didn't even know they made showers this big and I have my own jacuzzi. Ryder, you're a dweeb. Stay off buzz feed.

Hunter- Okay, so we're all sleeping with Hudson tonight?

Hudson- No sir, we need to come up with some rotations and then nights we are all together. I want to be able to love up to all of you individually. Also, I'm going to need to talk to Remi before that. It would be wrong to exclude her in cuddles, even though I'm sure she'll always want to be excluded from sex. Haha

Remi- You're absolutely fucking right. I'll cuddle, but someone is getting punched in the nuts.

Zane- I agree with all of that, except the nut punching. We'll come by for our nightly kisses after we shower.

Smiling, I stripped off my sweaty, bloody clothes and jumped into my gorgeous shower. Holy fuck, it was incredible. Purple glitter tiles and color changing rain shower features, and there was already shampoo in here. I was in Heaven as I finished up, brushed my teeth, and put curling cream in my hair that I snagged out of my bag. I skipped to my room happily, butt ass naked, and unpacked my bags. I hated clutter. Twenty minutes later, all my clothes, shoes, cosmetics, and lotions were put away. The best part? My room had shelves! I started to put my books away when the guys walked in, in only gray sweats; fuck me. Hunter whistled and they all stood there staring at me. I rolled my eyes and put my hands on my hips.

"You've seen it before. Do I really need clothes in here?!"

"Um, sweetie, if King walked in here..." Grayson said tightly.

"Oh, was my gentle giant a little possessive? That was sexy. I like when you get possessive, Gray." His eyes flashed and he chuckled.

"Fair point, just close the door behind you and come get your kisses. Only kisses though." I stood on my tippy toes as they all stood around me and one by one gave me kisses and lingering caresses that set my blood on fire. Okay, maybe not just kisses then.

With every kiss, I was slowly moved further back towards the bed. I wasn't fighting it though; after what we found out today, every moment together counted. I sat down for a few moments, while they kissed me. When I had a chance, I had to let them know something that was on my mind. "You know I will always protect you guys, right? I can't let anything happen to you; I love you all so much" I whispered.

"It should be us saying that, sweetheart," murmured Gray, and they all nodded,

"Everyone will die before they hurt you, Hudson, I promise," swore Hunter.

"Hey, we still have a Kindle and chill date. Let's enjoy all we can, train hard and pray that Gaia choosing you means we have more than a chance we will win," Ryder said while he kissed my neck. Gaia may have chosen me, but I know enough about Gods that they have a funny way of letting things play out, and the chances of her coming down to fight with us was pretty much zero. Otherwise, they would always be down here and there would be no suffering. I sighed.

Zane grabbed my face. "I love you, baby girl. We got this. I told you, you needed to wait for the right person? Well, now you have more than that, you have five. We will figure it out." He kissed me deeply and fuck me, after a long ass day that kiss wiped away every worry on my mind.

I moaned into his mouth and teased his tongue with mine. He ran his hands down my body, lightly tracing my curves with the tips of his fingers. I groaned as I felt someone open my legs, pressing kisses to my thighs. I whimpered as whoever it was, licked a path right to my clit. I gasped sharply and arched my back. I felt the bed dip and Zane adjusted himself because then I felt my nipples being taken into two warm mouths. Both bit down sharply and I squealed as they chuckled darkly, before they swirled their tongues, easing the pain. Zane pulled back to look at my face before wrapping his hands around my hair and tugging my neck back, kissing a trail from my neck to my ears, "I love how your whole body blushes for us, baby girl. That's the way it always should be." I moaned and writhed in pleasure when Grayson wrapped his hands around my neck.

"Don't fucking move, Hudson. We got this, you just lay the fuck back... for now," he finished off with a smirk and laid a possessive kiss on my lips. I was faintly aware of them stripping their pants off and someone turning on some soft music. Very faint because Ryder was fucking my pussy with his tongue like he was savoring his favorite candy. "Trip" by Ella Mai filled the room. Well, fuck they were setting the mood.

I shook and moaned as Ryder wrapped my legs around his head, running his tongue softly up my slit before settling on my clit, sucking it between his lips. I moaned, lost in the overwhelming sensations, oblivious to the fact that Hunter had grabbed my hands and held them over my head, tying them with a red silk rope. It wasn't until he gave the rope a sharp tug, making me gasp in both pleasure and pain, that I realized I was effectively at their mercy.

"You don't touch unless we say so, baby girl. You're not a queen here. We own you when it comes to all things sex. Now, what do you say?" I whimpered, not able to speak as his demanding voice and Ryder sucking my clit into his mouth brought me to the edge.

Grayson growled, "Stop, Ryder." Ryder chuckled and leaned away from where I needed him the most right now. His voice darker, downright demonic. "Did we say you could come, Hudson? You also didn't answer Hunter and we can't have that, can we? Ryder, I think she owes you for denying you her orgasm, by not following directions."

Ryder stepped away and smirked.

"Turn around on your knees, Hudson, and take Ryder into your mouth," Hunter said sharply as he adjusted my hands so I could turn around.

I tossed my hair back and arched my back. "Yes, sir." They cursed low as I took Ryder into my mouth, "Pillowtalk" by Zayn started to play and I worked him into my throat to the beat. He cursed as I gently worked my tongue on the sensitive underside of his dick. Fuck, these guys were fucking blessed. I hummed in pleasure as he tugged my head, shoving himself further into my mouth.

"Fuck, Hudson," he groaned. I hollow my cheeks, sucked and swallowed while turning my head left and right as I worked every angle of his dick. I grew wet every time he moaned, feeling the rush of cockiness as I made him lose control. Someone pressed against me and worked themselves inside. I groaned, eyes rolling back. Not feeling any piercings, I knew it had to be Zane. Fuck, I missed having him inside of me. He scratched down my back before he wrapped his hands around my waist and worked his hips to the song playing. He smacked my ass hard and I moaned, taking Ryder deeper inside of me. Gray was pinching my nipples and Hunter was having too good of a time observing and stroking his dick. Zane fucked me with precision, always needing to be in absolute control. He was taking his time, hitting every spot I had, speeding up and slowing down, keeping me on edge.

I started to work my hips in time with his thrusts, and he swore as I clenched and unclenched my walls. I used the same rhythm with my throat, tongue, and cheeks, swallowing, tightening, and swirling my tongue. After a few minutes, both of them cursed as they lost control, and I greedily took every drop, moaning at Ryder's taste. I winked at him as he slid his still hard dick out of my mouth.

"Good girl, you can cum next time," whispered Hunter in my ear. I moaned as he smacked my ass. He then wrapped my eyes with a silk scarf and laid me down on the bed. They took turns alternating between worshiping me with their lips and tongue and running a feather across my body. It was a sensation overload. Someone covered my mouth with their hand right before one of them lifted one of my legs and slid inside of me in one thrust. I screamed at the pleasure and pain combination.

Had to be Grayson, fuck. My suspicions were confirmed as he laughed darkly, working himself in and out of me, my eyes rolled to the back of my head. His Jacob's ladder? Fuck! It was a Jacob's escalator. His confession was false advertisement, by the way. I moaned loudly, as he tossed both of my legs on his shoulders and fucked me unmercifully. I lost it; I came so hard, I screamed. Someone laughed before covering my mouth with theirs, kissing me into silence. I saw the fucking planets; fuck seeing stars. He groaned as I tightened around him, cursing as he came.

"Shit, Hudson, you're going to fucking kill me," Grayson growled as he leaned over and choked me, as he kept fucking me, staying hard. What the fuck was it with these guys and their dicks? Don't they ever stay soft?! Shit.

"I think she's ready, guys," said Hunter quietly. I didn't ask what he meant. Grayson held my hips tightly and leaned back, switching positions, so I was on top of him. I moaned as he settled himself, he was way too big for this angle. I bit my lip. "Nice and Slow" by Usher started to play but I had a feeling this was all about it be anything but that.

Hunter ripped the sash off my face and kissed me roughly, grabbing my hair in his fist. "I told you that ass was going to be mine again, right?" he said as he rubbed my ass, and I groaned. Well, I guess this is the way I die, two huge dicks inside of me.

I leaned over as Hunter pushed me down and I placed my hands on Grayson's chest. He dripped oil all over my ass, rubbed my ass, and slid a vibrating toy in and out of me a few times, to make sure I was ready. I moaned as Grayson gripped my hips and started to urge me to glide across his dick. Hunter adjusted himself and moved himself inside of me. "Wetter" by Twista started to play and I would have laughed if the sensation of being so full wasn't so intense. We all groaned as we worked into a rhythm.

"FUCK," I groaned. I tossed my head back into Hunters shoulder as they both gripped my hips and worked themselves inside of me slowly on beat to the music. Fuck, it was like they were making love to me. Zane poured more oil on me and Hunter grabbed my neck with one hand while using his other hand to glide his hands across my breasts and abs. Grayson reached between us and started to play with my clit. I was completely zoned out, my body shaking.

"Turn your head, baby girl, take Zane into that perfect mouth, and I want you to work Ryder over with your hand." He nipped my ear, and I turned my head sucking Zane down my throat. I reached over to my left to stroke Ryder, not that I could get my hand completely around him.

Zane cursed and grabbed my head, his eyes rolling back as I took him into my throat, almost gagging, but I adjusted myself and relaxed my throat. Ryder covered my hand with his and I caressed him.

I have to admit, I moaned into our connection, *I love being your little plaything. You all feel so damn good inside me.*

"Fuck," they all cursed. Hunter bit my neck lightly. "You can cum now, angel, I don't think we are going to last much longer." Grayson worked my clit faster and I felt the orgasm wash over me, from the tips of my toes to the crown of my head. I groaned and clenched, and they came. Zane in my throat, Hunter and Gray inside of me, and Ryder on my side. Time stood still for a second as we came down from our high.

I smiled lazily, as I sat up and they disengaged myself from all the organ appliances. I giggled at their faces as I made my way to the shower. I cleaned myself up, letting the water work over my muscles, my body feeling like Jell-o. Honestly, these books I read have the right idea. There definitely needs to be more harems out there.

Chapter Thirty-Three

I walked into my room and saw they had changed my sheets; they were so sweet. I laid down, still strangely wired. They went to take a shower and came out of the bathroom, giving me puppy dog looks. I laughed. Romance books are cool and all, but after a ten-hour drive, a four-hour walk in the woods, a fight against some D-grade Halloween movie actors, and some mind-blowing sex, I needed to go to bed. So, I shooed them all away, despite their grumbling, and laid down in my bed, in my now new room. Sigh, a new room for the second time in a week. I just hope I stay longer here; you know, as I train to be Queen and all. I used some magic to fix the slight soreness I was feeling from earlier and I smiled as I tried to relax.

After about forty minutes of listening to the quiet sounds of the breeze and insects, I just couldn't help but think myself into a frenzy. With a maddening tick in my jaw, I kicked the sheets off and went back to rearranging my books, so I can think. Fucking bullshit, if you ask me. I didn't fight the entire prophecy idea for several reasons. It wouldn't make it less true, and the look in Kalen's face pretty much sealed the deal. I had always been more powerful than most, and a lot of that was because of Kalen's brutal training, but the connection I felt with nature did not need much prodding; it felt as if it was a part of me.

After all my books were put away, my drawers were organized, and my clothes and bathing suit were set out for tomorrow, it was already about two a.m. I was still restless though, my exhaustion forgotten in my sudden maddening urge to run and feel the earth under my feet, the wind in my hair and heart pumping. Without a second thought, I threw on my running shorts, trainers, and a sports bra, threw my hair up, and shot the guys a quick text to let them know where I was. Granted, I didn't know if technology worked the same beyond this Veil thing, it didn't occur to me to ask, so I also left a note on my door.

I didn't know the area well enough to really go exploring, but I couldn't go wrong with maybe a quick run along the river; can't really get lost doing that. I left through the back door of my room and warded it as I ran down the stairs. I stretched briefly, taking in the pool lit up by underwater lights as well as beautiful glowing floating lights all around. There were two mini waterfall grottos, and the entire pool was encased in light and dark stones on three sides. It was set up with a few lounge chairs and even some in-pool seating as well. From what I was able to see, it was fantastic! I couldn't wait for later today.

I sighed and walked around the pool area and started to jog. I tried to empty my mind but, realistically, I had so many questions I needed to ask. What were my duties, what was expected of me? Because if there was one thing I wasn't going to be, it was a false queen with false idols and some forced expectations. I was a fighter; I learned from my father to play the part of phony politics. I would deal with pomp and circumstance, even if I didn't want to, but just as my father learned quickly, I was no one's pawn. Prophecy or not, if, for one second, they thought they could use me as one, I would take them all down with me. If my mates were harmed for any reason, I would make sure that every last one who did us harm was bleeding and begging for mercy. That thought fueled my anger and I ran faster, my arms pumping and my legs working on overdrive.

The wind whipped past, hair flying as I picked up speed. If anything, I was punishing the wind instead of clearing my mind. With a sigh, I slowed down and walked closer to the shore, deciding to sit down and take off my shoes and dip my toes in the water. As I did that, I heard a sound of someone approaching behind me, I sighed and ignored them, dipping my toes in the surprisingly warm water. If anyone was really going to hurt me here, they would not have been silly enough to let themselves be heard, and as I breathed in the air around me, I felt no sense of malintent.

I wrapped my arms loosely around my knees. The breeze played with the tendrils of my hair and whistled a song in my ears. It felt as if my recent connection opened more within me than I realized, and I felt a pang of sadness. How amazing it would have been to grow up and always feel as if I was carried by the beauty, and sometimes devastating power, that came from nature. It was certainly one of the questions I had for Kalen; why not just bring me home? I truly feel that destiny would have eventually brought my boys and Remi. However, I guess that is the interesting thing about destiny. You could never truly understand it. The power would probably drive you mad. I had enough to worry about now to throw in a mystical power.

I sighed and listened to the breeze, compelled to sing with the melody whispering around me. Well, I guess if Disney princesses can break into song and dance, I might as well embrace my inner Tink and sing too.

"Tis there the fairy-court is holden,
Hush-a-by baby, babe not mine,
And there flow beor and ale so olden,
Hush-a-by baby, babe not mine,
And there are combs of honey golden,
Hush-a-by baby, babe not mine,
And there lie men in bonds enfolden,
Hush-a-by baby, babe not mine.
Shoheen sho, ulolo,
Shoheen sho, strange baby O!
Shoheen sho, ulolo,
You're not my own sweet baby O!

How many are there of fairest faces,
Hush-a-by baby, babe not mine,
Bright-eyed boys with manly graces,
Hush-a-by baby, babe not mine.
Gold-haired girls with curling tresses,
Hush-a-by baby, babe not mine,
And mothers who nurse - with sad caresses,
Hush-a-by baby, babe not mine,
Shoheen sho, ulolo,
Shoheen sho, strange baby O!
Shoheen sho, ulolo,
You're not my own sweet baby O!"

"You have a beautiful voice, My Queen. I wonder why the breeze brought you that song to sing this moonlit night?" a familiar voice whispered smoothly, like melted chocolate.

"I'm not sure, Scail, but step back. You never know if I'll start singing and dancing to 'We're All in This Together'. Disney has taken control of my life." His sudden laughter made me smile and peeked at him from the corner of my eye. His hood was still on and I had to suppress a chuckle myself. This guy was either too beautiful or too hideous. Either way, he was hiding. Whether that was for self-preservation or to avoid murdering those who saw him and could identify him, I didn't know. Although, I guess all options were plausible for self-preservation in a sense; fear, vanity, saving the soul, one could only guess. I have a feeling you would only know as much as he wanted you to know.

He chuckled. "I have an inkling, I'll never really expect what will come out of your mouth next," he paused. "High School Musical was certainly not one of those things I would have expected." My eyes widened, a fucking Fae, other than me, who knew his movies. I'm impressed, I told him as such and he chuckled. *Damn, I'm tired of people laughing sexy. It's seriously distracting.*

"No, one thing about me is that I'll constantly keep you on your toes, or wings in your case," I paused. "My case too now, I suppose." I sighed. "Tell me, Scail, did the breeze tell you to stalk me today?"

"Good point, but no. I question if the breeze brought me your way to protect you from the lack of self-preservation you have already exhibited twice since I have known you."

I looked at him, raised my eyebrow and pointed at him. "A. You don't really know me. You technically just show up randomly and B. Why would you feel the need to protect me anyway? The way I see it, I'll either defend myself and win, which is much more likely, or I'll die. I admit, I don't look forward to dying. I have a lot more smartass remarks in my repertoire before I'm gone." I laughed and wiggled my toes. He stayed silent for a moment, and it was a comfortable silence. Then again, I was rarely ever not comfortable.

"You know," he said after a while, "there are a lot of stories of Fae stealing children because they weren't able to have any. We are an old race, yet our numbers are small. That song was sung by sad mothers who would often punish themselves by watching mortal children and lament that they weren't able to have them. Likewise, it was sung by angry mothers who resented that they couldn't have children. Those women would steal children and raise them as their own and grow mad when the child would live its mortal life and perish. More likely, the child went mad, for it is an old tale that those who come across the Fae die, become mad, or become a poet."

I thought about that for a while, *the breeze was a sick bitch making me sing that.* Looking away briefly, I asked, "Which do you believe would happen?"

"All, of course. They would go mad; often the craziest of people create the most amazing masterpieces. Eventually, though, they would die, for even that ability is too much for them to handle," he finished sadly.

"Sounds like you may have witnessed this firsthand," I said gently.

He scoffed, his voice switching to a harder tone. "Possibly, I've been around many years and the mind forgets sometimes." I doubted that he forgot very much of anything. Every moment with him, though, left me more intrigued.

"I would ask why the Fae have trouble conceiving, but I guess it makes sense. Nature has a way of balancing itself, and since we are so deeply entrenched with nature, it would make sense it would balance us first. I feel badly for those mothers who wish to have children; my own mother would rather sing a lullaby to a bottle of liquor than to hold me goodnight. I spent a lot of my younger years wondering if there was something wrong with me until I just gave up. I didn't think I wanted children when I was younger, but I admit, I would probably be a great mother with the support I would have." I smiled gently, picturing the guys trying to decide who was changing diapers next.

"Hmm, you would be a much better mother, my Queen. In fact, I can feel it in my bones. However, you would be right, my Queen, on both accounts. Nature does have a way of fixing what is wrong. Also, there is indeed something wrong with you..." I laughed at that; I didn't disagree. Often what one classifies as normal is simply based on their version of normal; my normal meant flaws, challenges, and inner strength.

"You got me there, so tell me. If there is something wrong with me, why did you choose to sit with me tonight? I mean, there must be dozens of shadows you can find yourself sneaking through, like a giant cloaked creep, yet you came out here instead. Why?" I was genuinely curious. He didn't seem like a very social person, and from what Kalen told me, he wasn't someone who ever tried to get close to anyone unless it was for information or secrets, which I have neither. I leaned back in the soft grass and looked at the sky, feeling his eyes on me like the flicker of a fire, warm yet almost uncomfortable.

"I have yet to come to that conclusion, although, I have been asking myself that question since I came out here. However, we have been cautioned about dwelling in the shadows. Maybe I came to warn you. Mayhap it was the way your hands were coated in blood that attracted my darker nature, or mayhap it was the way you ran with the breeze that attracted my... baser nature."

"Hmmm, sounds confusing," I teased. "Although, I do not believe you have a darker nature. Darkness, perhaps... we all have some inside of us, but a separate portion of you that's just dark? No." I turned my head to look at his hooded figure. "Something tells me you are more than that. Nature tells us every day, as if it flows through us, we are a balance. The facets of it do not matter in the grand scheme of things, do they? Essentially, our actions determine who we will be, just as our actions can determine how we shape our future." He was silent for a few.

I felt so comfortable next to him. Usually, I never feel so attuned to someone to this degree so quickly. Perhaps it was how, in the quiet of the night, your soul can talk more freely; perhaps his loneliness and his desire to hide away matched the part of me that felt the same, growing up.

Suddenly, I felt his warm hand trace the inside of my thigh, so briefly that even though my breath hitched, I might have imagined it.

"The balance has been off for several years, maybe you'll put it right. In all the years living with the Fae, I have been stuck in what I guess humans would call a time warp. Traditions never changed and it took one silly decision, opportunity, and a dark time for change to occur. The same can be said for the prophecy that brought about the hope for change, where we started to build this side of the Fae world. Many like to separate the two sides, Dark and Light. The truth is we all came from the same base. Circumstances just change who we are. Those same circumstances have made me feared, revered, and yet so well connected, I find myself alone, not knowing if those connections are wanted for gain, or if I'm wanted simply for me. It's as complicated as explaining the voice of the breeze, although, I admit you mimicked it quite beautifully."

My heart jumped and I frowned at my reaction to his compliment. "Thank you," I said slowly and he laughed. I sighed. "I'm sorry, that does sound lonely. Maybe you came my way because something in you recognizes that I don't covet the things others do. Or," feeling the need to break the solemness in the air, "it could be that your inner asshole finally recognizes someone who can kick his ass and *he* feels challenged." He laughed loudly at that. I felt the itch to prove myself to him. I didn't know why, and it bothered me a bit. The only person a woman needs to prove herself to is herself, and no one else. I leaned forward, took my toes out of the water, slipped on my socks and trainers, and stood up slowly.

"Why did you come find me, Scail?" I said softly.

He looked me up and down and hummed. "Why, indeed?" He stood up abruptly, grabbed me tightly, and kissed me like his life depended on it. I felt his tongue tangle with mine, his hands gently tugging my hair back to gain a better angle to explore my mouth, and I gave as good as I got. Suddenly, he pulled back, turned on his heel and walked into the forest near the lake path.

My hands to my lips, I still felt him there. I shook my head at the cobwebs there, he was very confusing, and yet, I found myself way more intrigued than I should have been. Sighing, I slowly made my way back to the house, lost in my thoughts, and imagining his kisses in other places, and I walked up the stairs to my room. I looked back at the house that was supposed to belong to Scail and saw him facing my direction as well, hood still on. He was an interesting one. I wonder the things he has seen in his life to be so jaded. I stripped, took a quick shower, and fell into bed. Falling into a sleep filled with dreams of a beautiful woman warning me of something, but I couldn't quite hear what it was. After a while, I just slept.

Chapter Thirty-Four

I woke up to the sound of splashing in the pool and the guys laughing, and I smiled. I stretched and headed to my bathroom to take a quick shower, pee, brush my teeth, and wash my face before coming back to put on a bathing suit. In true Hudson new fashion, it wasn't really a bathing suit but more of a 'who am I going to piss off first' suit. My money was on Zane, then Hunter, then Grayson, then Ryder, who never really got mad. Besides my mating marks were everywhere and they totally counted as a cover up. I tied my small purple bikini top, that held up my breasts with little triangles, around my neck and again around my back, then I slid into the matching purple glitter thong bikini bottom. I looked into the mirror and cackled as my abs were perfectly displayed with the low slung, tight bottoms. I was on a mission to tan today before Kalen lived up to his promise and started training, which I'm sure he meant later today and not in a couple days like he said. He doesn't really operate that way.

I looked out the window and it looked like Remi and the guys, including King, Luca, and Jensi, were out there wrestling the shit out of each other. Actually, all things considered, it looked like a fucking remake of Jaws. I did hear music playing, so there was definitely a system out there.

I flicked on my phone and turned on my Bluetooth, seeing the only one system available as VeilThisBitches, and I laughed. That had to be Jensi's doing. I put my music to play instead. I needed some pool party music, I thought to myself as I opened the door to head outside. My eyes flicked towards where I saw Scail last night, watching me, and I saw the curtains move. Hmmm.

I walked down the stairs as "Too Close" by Next started blasting on the radio. I felt eyes on me, and I smiled at everyone and waved. King looked like his eyes were going to pop out of his head and he blushed before he looked away. Luca and Jensi admired but they always had more of the big brother type of vibe, so nothing in their look was lustful. It was sweet; they just always wanted to protect my honor.

Zane- Go and change, now.

Hudson- Yes, I win.

Zane- What?

Hudson- I bet myself that you would get pissed first, then Hunter, then Gray, and Ryder wouldn't get mad at all.

Hunter- Right, I'm pissed too, now go change.

Grayson- I swear, I'll punch a Fae in the face, Hudson.

Ryder- I see what you did there, Gray, Fae-ce. Good one! You guys get mad; I get to put the tanning lotion on her.

I laughed, my eyes landing on Remi, who was dressed, or undressed, in a similar bathing suit, and I swallowed thickly. I lost my train of thought, and I must have stared too long because she threw a cocky smile my way and I rolled my eyes and looked away before she could see me smile.

I walked up to her and smacked her ass. "You and I are in need some alone time, but right now, let's fuck shit up," I giggled.

She winked. "You got it." She smacked my ass, walked away and grabbed a bottle of some type of alcohol and opened it. "Faerie wine. This will fuck you up. Are you ready?" she asked. I scoffed at her silly question. I opened my mouth and she poured it in. The fruity taste exploded on my taste buds and a few seconds later, the buzz punched me right in the face.

"Fuck, what is that? A magic version of Devil's Springs 151 Proof?" I laughed as I swayed. She laughed at me and winked, chugging from the bottle. Show off.

The song changed to "Bring it Back" by Travis Porter and we started to dance, ignoring the growling from the Neanderthals. There was no one here but us and after this shit storm, we needed to have some fun, jealousy be damned.

We finished off the first bottle and jumped into the pool with the guys. I had to avoid five pairs of hands but then I swam under the water and hid under one of the waterfall grotto's while Jensi and Luca laughed, and played stupid to my whereabouts.

"That's cheating, angel!" yelled Hunter and I giggled. *If you are't cheating, you aren't trying.*

King swam up and sat next to me in the little grotto with a small smile on his face.

"How are you holding up with all this change?" I asked.

"Honestly? Since I met you, I felt that you were a little different. I didn't guess this damn different, but we had so much in common," he shrugged, "I knew we would become friends eventually. This was just like a fast forward, plus a cool, "hey, you, calm your tits" type of power." I giggled and he smiled.

"DON'T SAY THAT SHIT IN FRONT OF YOUR BEST FRIENDS. THE LAST thing I need is them repeating that shit." I fake groaned. He laughed and leaned back and reached over to hold my hand. I felt a sense of peace, as if I was floating between consciousness; it was pleasant.

"I just want you to know that I always got your back. Of course, I got to learn a little bit more about my powers and what the fuck I can do, but I admit, King the Sentinel sounds badass. Who knows, maybe I'll find myself a nice Fae lady of my own, since the only one I wanted squishy-zoned me." He laughed, but I felt his sadness. I guess the connection worked both ways. I smiled at his use of his nickname. Isn't it incredible how the smallest of things can bring people together as friends? Just a few movie references and genuine connections.

"King, if I could, I would snatch you up in a second, but the connection I feel with those five on an emotional level is beyond something I can explain." I sighed. "You and I are going to be the best friends who play pranks on those assholes. We are going to get you all the Fae girls, the good ones anyway, and I'm going to kick their asses to make sure they treat you right." He laughed; I wasn't joking. Women empowerment and all that, but I'll empower the hell out of a mallet if they hurt my squishy.

"Strange thing is, King, I felt something similar last night too." He looked at me and nodded.

"The scaley dude, right? I could totally sense a Ron and Hermione connection there when he followed you last night during your run. It's why I didn't say anything." I laughed and then frowned.

"Yeah, with the guys, we have history, kind off; a magnetic attraction the moment we got closer, just like with Remi. With him, I felt the similar connection. What if me finally transitioning is causing all of this? I really would like to not be mated to anyone else. It's scary, splitting your heart into five, and then I gotta split it again to thousands for the people I'm supposed to protect and help according to some damn prophecy. How much space can a heart hold?" He smiled gently and gave me a hug.

"Didn't Dumbledore always tell Harry that love protects? That it was ancient magic? I dare say, you are part of a people who have been around longer than almost anything; almost ancient. The more you love, the better protected you are, Hudson. It is how you wield that love that will make the difference. Keep opening your heart, and you have more than enough space. And stop worrying about fearing love and be happy that you have the ability to feel it." I choked up a little; love. Was that how I felt about Hunter's consistent chasing, Grayson's need to protect, Ryder's ability to make me laugh, Remi's way to go from lover to best friend in 1.2 seconds? Zane, I loved, and I knew that his quiet intensity, him putting aside his alpha tendencies to make me happy, were unique to him.

"You're right," I sighed, "I'll have to remember that when I want to kill a few people and dance in a pool of their blood, but yes, love and all that jazz." He laughed and bopped my nose.

"That's my blood thirsty girl, and by the way, I may not always be right, but I'm never wrong." At that, he picked me up and tossed me out of the grotto and flung me into the deep end of the pool. Asshole.

I swam up to the top and propelled myself out of the water and landed at the end of the pool in a crouch. Well, that was new, and fucking awesome. "Guys, I'm a dolphin-mermaid-Fae hybrid," I laughed. They rolled their eyes. Jealous much?

I wrung out my hair and went to lay down at the edge of the pool on a chair to live up to my promise and tan. Before I even laid down, Ryder was laughing as he rubbed the tanning lotion all over me.

"Enough tanning lotion, Ryder, I'm going to fucking turn into a stone." He laughed as I swatted him, and he ran inside with the rest of the guys, who were on a mission to make lunch.

REMI JOINED ME AND WE HELD HANDS BETWEEN THE LOUNGERS.

Remi- You know, you five are a sexual mess in my head. You all need to stop that sausage talk. You're making me nauseous.

I laughed.

Hudson- It never crossed my mind to be honest, sorry. Don't need you picturing licking lollipops. I'm able to block out who I want and talk privately, which is pretty cool, like texting, so we could just do that. Which reminds me, I see the music works, but can you text here, and get Netflix?

Remi- Haha, you and Lucifer. Yes and no, what we get is because we use magic to tap into a nearby satellite.

Hudson- Oh you guys are some pirating-ass thieves... I like it, it speaks to my darkness.

Remi- Oh God, insert eye roll here. By the way, I felt the need to mention that I know you went out to run last night. I didn't want to stop you, but even though this is a safe zone, you need to know that not everyone is excited about a new queen. They are afraid of another crazy leader all over again. They also, um, don't know I'm here yet. They know who I am. They won't be too excited about you being mated to me either.

Hudson- Well, what's a proper uprising without a little dissent? All the great books have it!

Remi- I'm serious, Hudson. War and death is coming. We need to try to unify everyone as much as possible.

Hudson- Can I roll my eyes now? War and death, you say? Honestly, that fucking sounds fascinating. Way better than a movie. I have one question. Can I wear pink? Oh, and can I totally collect the skulls of thine enemies? They are so pretty to make cups from. Imagine all the Fae wine served in authentic Fae skulls.

Remi- You are ridiculous.

Hudson- I know but seriously, you sound like Scail.

She sat up at that and stared down at me.

"What do you mean I sound like him?"

"Sounds like who?" Zane said, and I popped one eye open in time to see him setting down a tray of sandwiches, crossing his arms, and leaning against the outdoor wall. Fucking yum, but fucking shit. I stayed in my prime tanning position and closed my eyes again.

"I said... she sounds like Scail." I felt Hunter, Gray, Ryder, King, Luca, Jensi, and now Kalen walked out of the kitchen. Shit, there were so many people for my head to keep track of.

"Explain," said Zane, evenly.

"Well, I went running last night." I held my hand up as they started to complain. "Shut the fuck up. I'm a grown ass woman who can literally beat the shit out of almost all of you. Anyways, I the grown ass Fae woman, went running and I sat down for a bit and Scail joined me, and we spoke for a while."

"A while? He never says more than a handful of words and even then, it's all with a purpose," Kalen looked startled.

I shrugged. "He is a genuinely nice guy, maybe he is misunderstood. He seems lonely. Anyway, he mentioned that I lacked self-preservation and needed to stop running off by myself. I told him he could shove it too. And he laughed. I wasn't joking though. You all say the same shit. You should have tee shirts made."

"He... He... laughed? Are you sure you are talking about the same person who is known and feared throughout the Fae kingdom?" said Luca. I opened my eyes just to roll them.

"You guys are so dramatic. So he has an underground network of spies, thieves, and murderers, and people fear him. How many people do you know would follow a girl they don't even know, sit with her in the darkness, by a dark lake, shoot the breeze, and share Fae stories with her?"

"Plenty. They are called serial killers, love," muttered Ryder. I rolled my eyes. Good fucking point though. Still, I felt myself and my magic get irritated. It didn't like the way they were talking about Scail. King came up beside me and put his hand on my neck and I relaxed. I looked at him gratefully, reveling in the peace, but quizzically.

"I don't know, Dory, your magic told me it was annoyed, and it bitched slapped me to calm you." His handsome face looked down at me and I laughed. He was just a genuinely nice guy, and I love it.

Kalen looked at me. "Interesting, you are just always so damn interesting, Hudson. To be honest, if there is anyone that can make a serial killer laugh, it would be you. Gaia knows I hadn't cracked a smile in a long time until you told me to shove my sword up my ass. You are special." He shook his head with a smile. "Anyways, eat up. You have forty-five minutes to get your asses in the training combat area. Wear something that shows off your marks and stay armed. Hudson, try not to hurt anyone outside of the ring. I know asking you to not piss someone off is asking way too much. Jensi and Luca will guide you all to the combat area."

"I love when people tell me to be naked. You hear that everyone? Show off my marks. Ha!" Grayson picked me up and threw me into the pool. Motherfucker.

Chapter Thirty-Five

Forty-five minutes later, we were entering the combat area and, as demanded, I was dressed in my tight training shorts and black sports bra with combat boots. I had found a leather weapons belt that fit snuggly, as it clipped to a back holster that you slid on like a backpack, where you can put in your swords. I had daggers in the belt and two short swords in the holsters, and I palmed my scythe in my hands. Remi was dressed similarly, and I guessed she was the one that put it on my bed while I showered. My guys had combat boots and black cargo pants with no shirt on and similar arming setups that had me drooling. King, Luca, and Jensi were the only ones in our group with shirts on, but fuck it. We were a good-looking group of badasses. I took in the large domed building with various combat zones being used for various exercises. I noticed the weights and the weapons wall and took note of all possible exits and faces. One can never be too cautious.

When we walked through the town, despite some of the hostile stares aimed in Remi's direction and a few fearful ones aimed at me, I saw plenty of hopeful and friendly faces. There were little shops, barely any children, and there were more warriors out than anyone else. If it weren't for the lush greenery and beautiful flowers everywhere, you could almost, almost ignore that this was a place readying for a serious Fae-agaedon.

Kalen was standing in the middle of the area with a group of massive looking Fae Warriors. On the side lines were quite a few people and judging by the irritated looks Kalen was tossing that way, it wasn't a usual occurrence. I smiled at those who glared at me and blew a kiss to one particularly angry person who was red faced. Guess he didn't think the prophecy was a good thing. Well, fuck you, buddy! I would rather be in a plaid skirt right about now, in class, having regular college issues too.

"Hey, grandpa Kalen, are these the sorry fuckers I'm going to make cry today?"

They all turned my way and, fuck, they were tall as hell, growled. My mates stood behind me and stared them down, but let me do my thing. I loved that.

"Fucking men and their growling. Don't you fuckers know any other sound?" I mumbled. Luca choked back a laugh. The warriors flicked their eyes in his direction and then back to me.

"Show some respect, little girl; the great Kalen will take a lip from no one," some guy grumbled. I rolled my eyes at the great Kalen comment, like he needed to have his head made bigger. It's why he needed me, I brought him down a few notches. I waved him off, which pissed him off and he took a step towards me until one of his friends put an arm out.

"Not yet." I looked at him and he smiled ferally. Oh yeah, I'm going to love fucking that one up.

"Yeah, listen to your master, fucker," I scoffed, more growling. "Kalen has been training me for years, so spare me the theatrics. The only thing Kalen is good at is getting on my damn nerves with his drills. He never gets tired of making you fucking die until you come back to life just to die again."

A few of them laughed and Kalen smiled and shook his head. "Right, well, after that great introduction, men, this is Hudson and her mates. I'm interested to see how she fares against at least one of my top soldiers." I scoffed and peered around the room, taking in the bright walls full of weapons I previously missed from when I walked in. Punching bags and gym equipment took over the other side of the huge area and the now spectator area that just kept filling with people. I felt the burn of eyes on me and I couldn't pinpoint them, but there were a shit ton of eyes on me right now.

"Cool, sounds like fun. So, who is first? And am I allowed to kill them?" They laughed like it was the funniest joke, but I was not joking. Why did everyone always think I was joking? Kalen rolled his eyes and shook his head very subtly.

"Zane, Ryder, Grayson, Hunter, and Remi, grab a ring and," he pointed at the warriors, "you all, grab an opponent. They will choose the form of combat; nothing more, nothing less." My mates each took a spot, their faces blank.

Hudson- *Quick theory, we are all connected, two Fae and four not, so we share the same base of power now, right? Pull on it and fight, no fucking mercy. No weakness.*

They subtly nodded, too focused to speak, with their opponents already talking shit. They smiled in return. I loved them. Ha.

"Talon, since you seem so eager, you and Hudson, front and center." He nodded his head at us before continuing, "everyone, listen up! First to a knock-out, blood doesn't count." Kalen's voice echoed over a now quiet room. My group stayed near the rings. "Talon, you choose this time. Magic, weapons, or hand to hand?"

Talon smiled. "Weapons, sir." I laughed and I took off my belt and shoulder holster and threw it to the side, but I kept my scythe and short sword. I'll switch it up next time. No patterns. He laughed like I was an idiot, keeping his belt with several daggers. Something in my gut told me this Talon would be quick to get the draw on you if you have extra weapons. I needed to be fast and there was no need to weigh yourself down, unless necessary.

Kalen nodded and the room grew quieter as opponents advanced. I focused on mine. He advanced slowly like a cat chasing his prey. I pulled from my core and blocked everything but all possible situations out. I have never fought a Fae until I fought Remi, and we were evenly matched, but that was before I got my full power.

He took a deep breath then grabbed and shot several daggers in quick succession at varying heights. Everything went slow in my eyes as I knocked each dagger to the side with a spin of my short sword, one hand behind my back in case of an incoming attack. He pressed forward, trying to stay on the offensive, arching a broad sword straight down with enough speed and strength to cleave me in half. No idea what possessed me, but my magic shot me towards him, faster than his swing. Crouching before swinging myself between his legs, I turned, catching his ankle with my right leg before jumping back on my feet.

Right before he hit the ground, he was able to catch himself and turn on one knee but as he pivoted, I was already in front of him, straddling his neck, using my momentum to flip him on to his back as I rained blow after blow to his temple. I smiled as he reached up to dislodge an arm from my position to grab my neck. I let him pull it out and I grabbed the arm and spun, breaking it. He grunted, and I admired that, because that must have hurt like a bitch. I backed up from his now broken arm and smiled at him. He had a bit more respect in his eyes, and I cut that look short because when he went to get up from the floor, I threw all my weight into an uppercut and followed with a combination to his face; I spun and round-house kicked him in the collar bone, which cracked, and then kicked him in the middle of his chest. He fell back and didn't get back up. One down, who is next, bitches?

Scail

When I walked into the combat zone and settled myself into the shadows, I expected to see Hudson. I just wasn't prepared to *see* her. Watching her walking in, in that outfit, all her marks on display, I was completely blown away. Her head held high, she walked up to men who all towered over her, coupled with hundreds of years of experience, and she barely gave them any consideration. She was either very stupid, or very confident, but after last night, I knew she was far from stupid. I still felt her lips on mine. I had no idea what came over me, but it just felt right. After so long, I finally felt more peace within myself than I had in centuries.

That day in the forest, I recognized her recklessness, her desire to protect above her own self-preservation. I had been there, trailing the attackers, a little birdie telling me the new Queen was crossing into the Veil. I couldn't miss that. But what an opportunity that turned out to be. I didn't have to take care of them myself at that point, even though I killed several before they reached their group. I saw how they noticed the winds change, the quick way they deviated from the path, the snarky way she challenged and then killed them. I found myself chuckling during the attack, surprising myself. The prophecy was clear. However, I don't think the Veil leaders quite understood who would be walking into their camp when informed of their arrival. Hell, they didn't bother to show up to the training facility to see her in action, although they will soon catch whispers of it through the winds and through the chatter of the Fae. *Hudson was not just a Queen, no, she was change.*

The fight had begun in the middle of my musings. I was enraptured, just like that day in the forest. She moved like something I have never seen. No words had a comparison that held a candle to her speed and her prowess. Yet, I felt like she was holding back, she was toying with Talon and despite all of that, she bested him each time. When she broke his arm and followed up with a combination, rather a flurry, of punches, my mouth dropped.

Holy fucking shit. This five-foot five-inch girl just took down Talon without a fucking scratch. She was incredible! Every hit, every pivot, every move, beautifully executed with a flex of her abs and keen intellect. It's like she knew exactly what would happen and how it would happen. I shook my head from the shadows, I knew she felt me looking at her earlier. It was something I couldn't stop, looking at her, that is. She was beautiful. Last night, just hearing her voice was soothing. A balm to the soul of someone who has been so lonely for so many years. Even this morning, I heard her defend me to her mates and friends, and for the first time in a long time, I felt something other than emptiness. I felt warmth and true acceptance. After hundreds of years, maybe it was time to stop hiding in the shadows.

But before anyone can gain that respect, even the girl who sang with the breeze, they needed to do a bit more to earn it.

Without realizing what I was doing, I stepped out of the shadows, something telling me that with Hudson, my time hidden in the shadows was long over.

Hudson

I looked over as my mates traded hits with their opponents; Remi and Grayson already standing to the side, their men passed out. Zane and Hunter used this time to get out their frustrations and anger and toyed with the warriors. Although I admit, they were fortunate they had the connection; Kalen didn't train these men for years without serious advancement. They just wanted to feel blood on their hands. Remi and Grayson must have finished because they used magic fighting and they were damn good at it. Ryder, having infused his weapons, was giving and taking hits at dazzling speeds. Fuck, who knew my jokester could move like that? It was fucking impressive. Then Hunter exploded and picked up his opponent and slammed him into the floor while Zane stomped on his opponent's chest. Well, they coordinated that, and I shook my head. All eyes were on Ryder, who was moving with a grace that belied his magical upbringing. Finally, there must have been an opening because Ryder brutally cut down his opponent, drawing blood and shocking his opponent at the same time. The room was silent. Five newcomers, Remi not being counted, came in and kicked the ass of warriors trained for years. These same people were mated and connected to the most marked Queen ever seen. If this wasn't a testament to our abilities, I'm not sure what could be.

Interesting words. Because, of course, then I heard clapping. Yet, I recognized that clap. I turned around and smiled widely. "Scail, we have to stop meeting like this. What would our guardians say? I am but a chaste maiden!" He started laughing and the crowd gasped low and started whispering, goodness he wasn't fucking Jensen Ackles coming back from hell for the 29th time, people.

"A chaste maiden indeed, Queen, but I find myself intrigued. Talon hasn't been bested in a long time. Yet, you have not even a scratch. That's not even touching your mates' abilities."

"What can I say? There is something to be said about underestimating a woman. It's always going to be my advantage. Something tells me you wouldn't do that."

"No, I wouldn't. Those worthy of my time are my equals. Want to know who is worthy of my time? No one... yet..." The way he finished that last part, like a promise, I swear I felt my body catch on fire. My magic liked him; my magic loved my mates, but my magic liked him. This was going to be interesting; I clearly needed a heart-to-heart with King again.

"Hmm, sounds like a challenge..." I teased.

"No, it's... a warning wrapped in a promise," he whispered. I shivered, fucking sex voice. He started to take off his hood and cloak, and my breath caught. Holy suffocating vagina. This man was a fucking specimen. How? Oh Gods, I'm going to faint, and I'll need him to perform vaginal CPR. He stood to his full height and he had to be a good foot taller than me. Much like my men, his muscles bulged with every move. All golden skin and long white hair and ice blue eyes. I have no idea where this pale Fae shit humans came up with, but his skin looked like warm melted sugar. How a cloak can hide the lethal gait he possessed as he continued to walk towards me was astounding, let alone that body. Wow. Guess Harry wasn't the only one with a magic cloak.

I cleared my throat. "Well, I don't make it a habit to turn down worthy opponents." He raised an eyebrow. "Okay, okay, I don't turn down anyone, alright?! I'm a bloody gore whore, okay?!"

He shook his head in awe. "I literally have no idea what is going to come out of your mouth next."

"Join the club," my guys and even Kalen chorus behind me. I flung up my middle finger and they chuckled. How dare they? I was clearly a gem. They didn't realize my worth. No sex for them. I scoffed.

"Okay, Scail, which I'm almost positive isn't your name, what are your terms? Weapons? Magic? Rock, paper, scissors? I'm flexible. Ever heard of Kama sutra? Yeah, I'm an expert at that too." Kalen groaned and the guys choked a laugh, Remi straight up laughed along with King, Jensi, and Luca. The warriors were staring at Scail in awe, eyes flitting back and forth between us. They really weren't kidding; he didn't often show his face, nor did he interact or speak to many. *Aww, my poor Scailsnugglekins, he needs cuddles.*

"All variations of combat are fine, Hudson, which isn't your real name either." I smiled and brushed by him to collect my weapons. No patterns, but damn it, I really wanted my pretty scythe. I took a gander at all the pretty sharp weapons and I closed my eyes and let my magic decide; it just felt like the right thing to do at the time, let the first guide me and shit. I settled on two battle axes and tested their weight in my hands. They were certainly well made and incredibly light for being such brutal weapons to wield during battle. I walked to the center of the combat zone area where Scail was already waiting with two short swords. He liked to get close. I like that.

I didn't wait for a nod, and I infused my weapons and crossed my axes in front of me before gathering enough magic to blow up a building, but he spun and crossed his swords behind his back, deflecting. I smiled, *show off.* I reabsorbed the magic and my skin started to glow as I spun one of the axes in my hand like a parlor trick, however, the faster I spun, the more magic I fused into the ax, like a wind-up toy of sorts. I threw the ax straight at him, but he was able to move out of the way. He smiled, thinking I was down a weapon, and pressed his advantage and attacked with a speed that took my breath away. I parried each of his strikes with my remaining ax, then I pivoted to the left, then quickly to the right. Using my instincts, I found myself summoning the magic I had infused into the ax, bringing the thrown ax back into my waiting hand, which I then used to strike down, with the blunt edge, on the left side of his ribs. I was Thor, motherfuckers. Fae-or? Tho-ae? Whatever.

He grunted but used that moment of closeness to swipe at my neck with the short sword, drawing blood before I launched myself back, kicking my legs forward, planting my feet on his chest, pushing him back. Instead of the one step I expected of someone of his size, he took several steps back.

My blood spilling filled me with a primal urge to destroy, and despite my magic liking him, she also recognized weakness was unacceptable. I threw my weapons to the side, ignoring the gasps of the crowd. I crouched on the floor, one hand on the training mat, and my eyes focused on Scail. He smiled at me and I licked my lips and winked. I briefly registered his surprise, he didn't hide quickly enough, before I pushed off and ran straight towards him, faster than I could track, before I wrapped my legs around his waist, took the swords out of his hands and crossed them over his neck.

"Yield," a dark voice came from me.

He smiled ferally. "Never, my Queen." He shoved his thick arms into the openings of my arms from where I held the swords and flung them to the side. Grabbing me, he flipped me as he came to his knees and used his upper body to press me down onto the mat. I vaguely heard the crowd becoming more agitated.

I looked him in his gorgeous eyes and whispered, "I am magic, and my magic recognizes you." My body heated and started to glow in swirling colors. I jerked my hips, and I wrapped my legs tighter around him, using my magic to twist him beneath me and pin his arms over his head.

"You made me bleed, now you bleed too." I leaned forward and bit into his chest, drawing blood. On pure instinct, I swiped the blood from my neck and rubbed it into his fresh bite. It felt dirty... sick... right. He arched his body as a red glow lit him from the inside and wrapped around me. A brief, but searing, pain, left us out of breath. I finally opened my eyes and I looked down at him, cursed and scrambled off him.

Fuck, fuck, double fuck. He laid there in a daze and I bowed to the crowd that must have been the entire village at this point, as a giant fuck you to them and hastily made my way out. I ignored the calls of my men and my friends. Nope, fuck that. I ignored everyone until I made my way back into the cabin and stripped off my clothes and took a shower. I tried not to look at myself as I showered but I felt it; the new and fresh sensations all over again. I marked him, and he marked me.

Chapter Thirty-Six

I heard the guys come into the house a few hours later and snuggled deeper into my bed with Xena, who had gone God knows where all this time and wouldn't tell me, watching Lucifer. I used these past few hours alone to go back and forth over every possible situation I have ever put myself in. I couldn't figure it out. I was just marking people willy nilly, left and right, back and forth.

I mean, come the fuck on, I already had four dicks and a clit to suck, flick, and lick. Now, I also apparently had a Scail to shine. I groaned into my pillow and punched into it like a shit load of feather punching bags. I didn't hear the door open, but I recognized the glare coming my way, even if I was hidden underneath the covers assaulting shit.

"Kalen, go away, I'm a filthy whore and you shouldn't see me this way."

He chuckled softly and I heard him move across the room to the closet before he closed it and sat down on the edge of the bed. "Hudson," he sighed, and his gruff voice filled the room without him even trying. "Look, I understand this is a lot for you at once. Hell, it is a lot for most people over a span of time, but in all the years I have known you, little girl, running is not something you ever did. You face problems head on. Even when Zane broke your heart." I made a small sound of shock. "Yes, I knew it was him. I'm not stupid, you know. You are strong, Hudson. Stronger than I think the prophecy ever truly described. Not because of something as stupid as destiny, we are the masters of our fate. But because your mouth, your kindness hidden under layers of snark, your inability to watch other people treated badly, or to let them feel badly even though they warranted it." I laughed, knowing he was thinking about Remi, and I poked my head out from underneath the covers, sat up, and sighed.

"Kalen, I can deal with changes, challenges, fights, and battles. All of that is in what you taught me. How to find patterns and yet never have a pattern. Those things prepared me for more things than just combat, I started thinking that way for almost everything. I guess in a way, you conditioned me to always be fluid and be ready to move and countermove. I see life that way. Does being part of a prophecy suck? Sure, but that's just a strike of a sword I had to parry before I made my next move." He gazed at me warmly, but fleetingly.

"I guess I never thought about it that way. You are very wise, daughter of my heart, and I'm proud to love you every day of my life." He sounded a little emotional, but a quick peek and his face was a stoic as ever. I rolled my eyes. "I told them all to give you some space, and I think they needed some as well. They grew up with the idea of loving you by themselves, then Remi came along and now Scail. It is going to be a very rough transition and I would wish you luck, but, in all honesty, I wish them luck," he chuckled. Of course, they would probably piss me off and I would kill one of them. I looked at the time and sighed at the hour, it was totally dinner time.

"By the way, Hudson, usually I would push this back until you had more time to acclimate in the Veil, but after this afternoon, well, you are to attend a little dinner in your honor." He rolled his eyes, meaning it was probably all a farce. "Well, you met the warriors, but you have yet to be introduced to the Guardians of the Veil, and they tend to be more traditional."

"The guardians of what? Isn't that copyright infringement?" He rolled his eyes, it's true though. That was just a terrible name.

"They are the ones that make the decisions and help the people here. Think of it as a counsel of sorts. They lead fairly, yet I warn you to be on your best behavior. There are those who would rather not see a Queen of Fae ever again." I frowned and sighed. I was good with this political stuff; I just didn't like it.

"I brought you a dress and hung it in your closet, and there are shoes there too. Everyone should already be there, but I knew you needed some time. So, get on up and I'll meet you downstairs in ten minutes."

"Twenty minutes and if you insist." He sighed and shook his head and made his way to the door and out of the room. I jumped out of the bed, brushed my teeth, and washed the feathers off my face. Grumbling, I wet my hair, put in some curling cream and called it a day. When I opened the closet door, I gasped. It was a beautiful green dress with gold straps that crisscross in the back. I excitedly pulled it on, and it fit me like a glove but with just enough give that the gathering of the soft fabric would blow in the breeze. The dress fell about two inches below my ass and I had a feeling it was done intentionally to show off my marks as much as possible.

I sighed, the marks. Knowing that, I quickly ran to the bathroom to comb my hair into an upsweep to show off my new marks that went up my entire neck, upper back, and my pointed ears. I took the chance to spray on gold body glitter and then made my way to grab the pair of matching peep-toe see-through, gold stiletto Louboutin heels that Kalen also left. If his intention was to make me look like nature dressed me herself, he hit it right on the nose. I looked delicate, like the breeze, my curves in this dress calling animals in, like the anticipation of a storm, and the marks representing the deadly power nature can wield. Overall, he gave them a Fae Queen.

Ryder

Kalen asked that we gave her space and I respected that, not because he said it, but simply because I respected Hudson. Hudson was strong and faced everything head on. To feel that she needed to leave instead of face what happened with her magic and a new bond, made my anger spike. Scail disappeared shortly after, more than likely to make sure Hudson wasn't unguarded at the house. As much as I wanted to be the one to do that, I knew she wouldn't appreciate my intrusion and she couldn't keep Scail out of his own house.

We spent that rest of that time fighting and training with the warriors. Despite the various insults and challenges that left us all pretty much fueled with nothing but blood lust, we gave as good as we got. Whether it was the marks shared between us or not, something here just felt right. We felt whole, our magic untapped, and we pressed our advantages and felt our power respond in kind. It was exhilarating, to be honest. Grayson observed and picked up on small things and while we all fought, we stayed connected, mind to mind, and were nigh on another level than we ever have been. Remi had an internal battle all her own, but with every snide remark, she hit back in kind with a power and force that was indicative of her inability to back down, much like Hudson.

On our way back to the cabin, Kalen let us know about an introductory dinner to meet the counsel here. I'm sure that was going to go over great with Hudson. I smiled at the thought of her all dressed up, having to deal with the pomp and circumstance she left behind. I laughed as I showered and got dressed. At least she will be dressed better this time. I thought of those dresses she used to have to wear. She was adorable, even then.

I met Hunter, Zane, Grayson, King, and Remi downstairs, all dressed in varying shades of green and white. If we didn't look so much like moss and seafoam come to life, I would say we cleaned up well. As it was, we looked like we were ready to play hide and go seek in the woods. Sigh, at least we would look damn good doing it.

We made our way as Luca and Jensi knocked and led the way to an outdoor pavilion area with a dance floor, vines with flowers hanging down, and glowing lights giving it a magical look. There was soft music playing a combination of flutes and harps, and there were tables around the dance floor decorated with flowers and champagne flutes, and the effect was beautiful. A little higher than the dance floor was a longer table with seven seats, which I'm assuming that was where the counsel would sit, and Luca and Jensi were explaining their role here. It was going to be interesting to see them interact with Hudson. A little blood thirsty; I couldn't wait.

Hudson

I walked down to meet Kalen, and he looked at me and nodded his head and took my arm. He was dressed in a black and green suit and it was the first time I saw him dressed up. I felt like my dad was taking me on a daddy/daughter date and I felt so special. We arrived at the Pavilion and it looked gorgeous. I took note of the higher dais and my eyes flicked to it, noting the people sitting there, before turning away and looking for my group. I sensed irritation but ignored it as I saw my handsome group, and, to my surprise, Scail was also with them. Looks like we were also a group of seven, fuckers.

"I'm going to take you to their table first, your mates will stand behind you. I'll present you and you'll take your seats, and for the love of Gaia, mind your tongue." I smiled and nodded, but I let go of his arm, to his shock and dismay.

My group took one look at me and stood up and followed my lead. We stood before the dais and all eyes flew to us, I inclined my head in a show of respect, but if we were to play the politics right, I needed to establish myself and my position from the beginning, otherwise they would always have a leg up. I looked at the table and met the eyes of a Fae with green eyes who looked startling familiar. He had an empty seat next to him that was quickly taken by... Kalen. I kept the surprise off my face and smiled. They looked alike, but I swear the Fae, there was something about him.

"Ah, if it isn't another imposter Queen and her trope," said a shrill sounding female. I kept my face blank of any emotion and laughed a dainty laugh.

"Oh, it is indeed a pleasure to meet you..." I waved my hand, "doesn't matter what your name is." The curious male in the middle, and two other women and Kalen and another male hid a smile behind their drink, while another looked furious at the slight.

"Excuse me, you will address us with respect," said the red-faced Fae while the woman sputtered.

"Apologies, decency requires respect to be given so that it is earned. Otherwise, we all stand in a precarious situation."

"Pray tell, young one," said a female, not unkindly, "what precarious situation would that be."

I smiled genuinely, knocking everyone back a bit. "Well, the kind that isn't appropriate for polite conversation. Am I correct to say this is supposed to be a polite conversation and meeting?"

"Indeed, it is, indeed it is. Kalen, you failed to mention that she was as quick witted as she was charming."

I inclined my head. "Many thanks, I'm afraid Kalen likes to keep his protégée's skills to himself; makes him a tad more mysterious." I winked, and a few of them laughed.

"I apologize for the slight in manners, let me start with introductions. We are the seven. Here, on the right are me, Brighid Alvin, and then Dana Alston, and next to us is Kalen Fheall, who you know. On the other end is Radella Oren, Ealdon Warren, Bran Eitri, and in the center is Shea Fheall."

"It is a pleasure. This is Zane, Hunter, Ryder, Grayson, and I'm sure you are familiar with Scail, and Remi."

Radella smiled evilly. I had a feeling I wasn't going to like what she was going to say. "Oh, we know who they all are, pray tell. We actually know them better than you do." I frowned. What the fuck did that mean? Kalen glared at her before she laughed. "But those are stories for later! Let's all enjoy our meal in your honor." She inclined her head and we turned to sit down at our table. A Fae filled up a few flutes with wine that tasted of cherries and sunshine.

"Holy... this is amazing," I whispered, admiring the drink.

Remi laughed. "Just wait until you try the food; it will blow you away." I smiled and looked around the space as dishes were being set out. My eyes kept shifting toward the man now leaning in to talk to Kalen, and his resemblance was setting me on edge.

"So." Ryder cleared his throat. Oh, here we go. "Are we going to just ignore the ele-Fae in the room? Get it?" He cackled; Zane smacked him upside the head. Dinner was placed in front of us and I took a bite, hiding my response.

"I'm not necessarily ignoring it, just not something I want to discuss in this setting. If there is one thing I have learned, is that there are ears everywhere," I whispered. Scail nodded in my direction and his eyes lingered on my face, before he looked away. He stood out in a way that was just different. He exuded a confidence, yet an air of power, fragility, and tenderness. As if all he was waiting for was the opportunity to show the world that he could be more than he was painted to be, but still burn the world down when needed. It was an interesting way to describe him, sure, however, like attracts like. For someone who preaches self-preservation, I have a feeling that for me, he wouldn't have any, and that could either be dangerous or downright terrifying.

He wore a tailored black suit with a green shirt underneath that stretched across his expansive chest. My men looked good tonight, and Remi was a vision, with her blue hair in an updo, slightly curled around her ears, her pale green dress not clashing. To be honest, as much of an honor this was supposed to be for me, as the "Queen", the honor was mine, to have such an amazing group of people by my side that would do anything for me.

After several moments, we ate in silence, all of us enjoying the food. Soon, the food was taken away and our drinks were refilled, and I felt lighter and more carefree. Couples were standing to get on the dance floor and Kalen approached me and took my hand.

"I know all your men want a turn, but you would do me a great honor to be my partner." I nodded and blushed as I walked around our table and stepped onto the floor. It looked like a fast waltz, so I basically just followed Kalen's speed with my knowledge of the dance from all the parties I had to attend with my father.

"I should have known that a girl who fights with so much finesse would dance with it too," he teased as he spun me around. Suddenly, I was in the arms of another man and smiled when I saw Zane twirling with me instead, the song having slowed down just a tad.

"Oh, who knew you could dance so well?" He stuck out his tongue and I laughed.

"I used to have to go to the same functions as you, you know. I just was better dressed when I went." He laughed but before I could swat him, and he dipped me and passed me along to Hunter. Goodness, Hunter danced just like he fought, with an intensity that was borderline violent as he turned me faster and brought me up against his body.

"You look beautiful tonight, Hudson. It looks like I'm going to have to call in that promise you made," he growled low and licked his lips.

"You don't have to call it, handsome. It was already in my plans." He pulled me in for a kiss, biting my lip before stepping aside for Gray to take his place.

"It's amazing, sweetheart," he murmured, looking deep into my eyes, making my breath catch and heat pool low. "All these people here looking at you, admiring you, and yet, you only have eyes for us. It is intoxicating." I smiled up at him, taking in his dark blonde hair and blue eyes, admiring just how devilish he looked, yet was just so kind. I wrapped my arms around his neck as picked me up and twirled me, making me laugh. "Gray, there is no one else but my mates. Nothing will ever change that." I reached up for a kiss and then giggled when Ryder snatched me up, making Gray growl at him.

"Nope, everyone gets five minutes with this beauty." I don't think I stopped laughing the entire time he was whispering secrets about the guys and what they used to do when they were younger. He kissed my cheek and winked at me before Scail took me into his arms. A zing of electricity shot up my spine when he tugged me closer, one hand in his and the other firmly pressed against my back. Of course, the song slowed down to a snail's pace and we danced and stared at each other.

"Staring is rude, Scail," I said, and he smiled.

"Not when you are looking at the most amazing person in this room."

"Hey, I resent that!" whisper-yelled Ryder, who was dancing with Remi next to us. I rolled my eyes and we moved away from them.

"Mmm, with the compliments, I admit I like them. You look very dapper tonight, Scail. I can't decide if I enjoy the hood more or not; you look dangerous in both."

"Dangerous in what way, my Queen?" His hoarse whisper drives me insane.

"Well in the hood, you are aloof; the unknown is always a bit dangerous. But this? This is dangerous to just me."

"Is that so?" He smirked, taking my hands and doing a turn that left my back to his front, while he hugged me. He leaned down and kissed my neck and I shuddered. "Hudson, I don't think I knew I was waiting for you, but when you ran off today, I wanted to go to you with such an intensity that I felt like I was burning up all over again," he whispered into my ear and then turned me back around. He cupped my chin and looked into my eyes; I was transfixed. "So, the only danger here is you... to me," At that, he grabbed my lips with his and kissed me feverishly until I was dizzy. When he pulled away, he winked at me. "By the way, my name is Oberon, I look forward to hearing it on your lips." He sauntered away and I was in a slight daze when Remi pressed a flute into my hand. That name sounded familiar, but the stupid Fae wine was messing with my memory.

"Well, that looked intense," she teased. I nodded, not being able to speak still, and I watched them all to the side, talking and smiling with each other.

I danced and giggled with Remi between refills of wine, sharing kisses despite the looks of anger from the bitch Radella. Speaking of...

"I would like to propose a toast, to the future and all it holds. May the prophecy," she sneered, "live up to all that it was supposed to be." The disapproving looks from the rest of the table didn't seem to faze her as she continued to prattle on. "One would only hope we keep traditions alive and prosper, despite a few hiccups down the road." I laughed, genuinely busting out laughing. The look on her face made me laugh even harder.

I stood up a little straighter and took a good look at everyone in the crowd, before settling on those at the table, specifically the Fae bitch. "The future will be bright, simply because it will be completely different." A few people gasped. "The old ways did not lead to a hiccup, as so callously put by Radella. It led to murder and an uprising for those who wanted to leave tradition behind, but were conned instead. That is not my intention, nor my goal. Simply put, tradition can be enlightening, beautiful, and magical in many ways. However, in the ways that count, it will lead to more issues. I have studied history, and I have learned a great deal. I see that the Fae are a noble people who truly wish to bring balance back to their world despite the unfortunate situation we are currently in. Understand, that doesn't mean I'll live in the past, nor will I lead with the intention of keeping traditions that should have died a long time ago, alive. We will prosper, because I will it and because I will make it so. Let's make one thing perfectly clear." I smiled at the people, some who nodded emphatically, others who looked wary, some furious. "I'm not a pawn, I will not be moved until I wish it so. I am a Queen, I have six mates, and we will do what we need to do for nature to restore itself back to the way it was intended. It was never my goal to be here. However, you'll be hard pressed to have me back down from any challenge thrown my way." I looked directly at Radella. "Those who challenge may dissent to the Dark Fae." The crowd gasped. "But make no mistake, you will die." I lifted my glass and took a drink.

Holding Remi's hand, we walked back to the guys, ready to go. It's been enough for one night. I can declare more shit tomorrow. We started walking when I felt an icy hand on my arm. I raised one eyebrow, looking back at Radella's right hand bitch, Ealdon.

"Nice speech, little girl. I wonder if you'll feel the same way about all your little friends and family when you read this." He shoved two envelopes into my hand and walked away whistling. I looked over the letters in golden envelopes, wondering if there was poison laced into it. I wouldn't put it past the slimy fuckers. I let the guys walk into the cabin in front of me, and even Oberon was with them, joking and settling into the living room. I waved them off and sat on the front porch while I carefully opened the letter, until the sound of laughter and joking reached me and I smiled. I stood up and went inside instead, throwing the letters on the side table, I'd get to them later.

Chapter Thirty-Seven

We made our way to the backyard and settled around the pool loungers. Remi and I took off our shoes and put our feet in the water and I set up my music to play on the speakers. We passed a bottle of the Fae wine around and we fell into a comfortable silence. Scail kept looking at me and I met his gaze head on. He smirked at me slowly and my heart started to beat faster.

If you keep eye fucking him, your eyes are going to get pregnant. Remi's voice floated through my head and I burst out laughing and I pushed her into the pool. She came back up sputtering before using magic to pull me in after her. We laughed and splashed each other while the guys shook their heads at us. While the guys entertained themselves, I pulled Remi into the waterfall grotto and kissed her. When our lips touched, it may have been the wine, or the fact that we haven't had time alone in a few days, but fuck if I didn't see stars. I groaned as I pushed her back onto the seating inside.

She sat in front of me, my head right in front of her thighs. Before she could react, I reached up and pulled her dress over her head, leaving her in her underwear, before I pulled my dress off the same way. I ran my hands over her breasts and caressed her sides and abs, following the path of the new patterns on her skin. She took in a shuddering breath and let out a low moan, her skin as sensitive as mine. Tugging her thong off and throwing it to the side, I brought my face up front to her freshly waxed center. I didn't know what to do really, but I figured I knew what I liked, so I'll just do that to her. So, I grabbed her ass and brought her closer to the edge and pressed a kiss to her clit as I opened her legs wide, putting them on my shoulders. Her hands wrapped around my hair as she let out a long moan, while I sucked her clit between my lips and swirled my tongue around, occasionally flicking it while gently nibbling on it. She tasted like the wine we had been drinking. I moaned and she gripped my head harder as I took my hands and wrapped them around her waist, settling in closer, completely taken in by her sounds of pleasure.

"Fuck, Hudson, yes, baby, yes, right there. Fuck, that's so good, yes!"

I dragged my tongue from the bottom to the top, continuously dipping my tongue inside of her tasting her. Damn, she was amazing. Groaning, I came back up and sucked on her clit, alternating between light and hard pressure until I felt her thighs tighten around my head. She screamed when I wrapped my lips around her clit and picked up my pace, as she came.

"HUDSON, FUCK!"

I licked and tasted her until she stopped shaking before I unwrapped her legs and licked my way up the dips in her abs and swirled around her nipples, taking them in my mouth, her breath hitching before I came up and pressed a kiss against her lips, our tongues rubbing against each other, tongue rings teasing. Our hands roamed and caressed each other, bringing each other to the brink and falling over the edge a few more times before we left our little cocoon of paradise.

When we finally came out, the guys were gone, and we went back to my room and lost ourselves in our shared pleasure for the rest of the night.

I WOKE UP TO XENA PAWING ME. *WAKE UP. YOU MUST EAT AND TRAIN. Cerberus told me he feels danger coming. We must be strong.*

I groaned and rolled over to look at her. "Your speech is a lot better now. You think it's because we are across the Veil?"

"Yes," Remi said, yawning and pulling the covers over her head. I chuckled. "She is going to get stronger too. When you are across the Veil, you are closer to the core of your magic; no longer dampened by being on the mortal side, you both should be stronger and more in-tune with your magic and your connection." She sounded muffled under the cover, but I heard her just fine. That must be what that Unseelie guy was talking about, that I hadn't crossed the Veil but I was already stronger than he anticipated.

"Wait, what do you mean danger is coming?" I asked Xena, and Remi sat up and looked at her curiously.

Something doesn't feel right. We must train, we must be strong. I frowned.

"She said Cerberus told her danger was coming and she said something doesn't feel right and that we have to train and get stronger."

"Familiars tend to be more connected to everything around them, and, being animals, they pick up on things that we may have missed." Seconds later, there was a giant fucking snake in our bed, and I had to stop myself from screaming. Remi laughed while she had her private conversation with her familiar.

It was too early for this madness, but I got up and trudged into the bathroom to shower and handle my morning routine before I came back and threw on my workout gear. When I came back out, Remi was in the room, dressed in her gear too, her hair still wet.

We made our way downstairs to the kitchen, "Ceri told me the same. It would make sense. I'm sure Nici knows that you crossed the Veil, which means she is probably prepping herself to attack in whatever capacity. I let the guys know. Ceri and Xena are right, we need to train harder and be prepared for everything possible." I nodded, knowing that if I opened my mouth, I would have nothing constructive to say other than that bitch needs to die.

I busied myself making protein shakes, eggs, and bacon for everyone. Remi and I hummed along to the music I had playing in the background while we filled plates and took them to the table. The guys were already on their way down the stairs and I put cups of coffee down next to their plates. I set the table for seven, feeling Scail close. Right as I was coming back with the last cup, I felt arms wrap around me.

"Someone needs to really go into your closet and replace all of these fake workout clothes that can double as lingerie to something that covers you up head to toe," Zane grumbled into my neck. I laughed at him.

"I agree," Hunter yelled from the table. I shook my head.

"Fuck you, fucking fucks. You touch my shit, I'm closing up shop and you will never get some again."

"Woah, woah, let's not threaten diabolical shit here! Baby girl, blame them, I'm but an innocent bystander in this brotherhood," pleaded Ryder with a note of laughter in his voice.

"Suck up," Zane and Hunter grumbled at the same time.

Ryder scoffed at them. "I'll be a suck up, who's getting sucked off. I can be happy with that." I laughed and went to the table and gave him a kiss.

"Because of that, you can get your Kindle and chill date tonight." I winked at him and laughed when he flipped off the guys at the table. Scail observed the dynamics at the table with a smirk on his face. I wonder where his personality will fall in this group. He was sarcastic, funny, endearing, dangerous, quick, and lethal. He was pretty much a combination of all of us in one sexy ass Fae body, and I wanted to lick him. As if he knew what I was thinking, he caught my gaze and licked his lips. I squirmed in my seat, trying to avoid the urge to jump over the table and fuck him senseless. *Stupid horny, vaginal bond.*

Everyone settled in and ate quickly before we headed to the training area. We walked in just after dawn and the area was filled with warriors in various states of training. I smiled at the dedication and I walked in there owning the place and headed to the punching bags and equipment to warm up. I wrapped my hands and turned on some punk rock music on my headphones and started to stretch. In my own world, I took a step back, took a deep breath and did a front flip without using my hands and started to punch the bags in a series of combinations. I crouched and swept my leg out low, pivoting on the ball of my foot before moving around the bags. I loved when the bags were formed in a circle to mimic multiple opponents. It works out every muscle when practicing and helps to sharpen your peripheral vision.

I breathed deep as I round-housed one bag while flipping and using my other leg to kick the bag next to it. I did a series of kicks and punches before stepping over to the weapons wall next to the bags and grabbing two sparring sticks. I was completely obvious while I worked; nothing else mattered but making sure I was in the optimal training condition. Xena's warning ringing in my head, I twirled the sticks in the air, gauging their balance before spinning one behind my back while using the other to hit the punching dummy in front of me.

I brought the stick from around my back, crossing both across the rib cage of the punching dummy in a strong hit that echoed. Had it been a real person, it would have broken ribs. Not all moves are about showing off. I spun the sticks behind my back because it helped with the dexterity of my wrists and I needed to make sure I was able to fight if I was down one hand. I tossed the sticks in the air, flipped, and kicked the dummy before catching the sticks and using them to knock down their opponent. My speed increased since I mated, and sometimes I used to miss the catch completely. I had to drill it into my head, the timing. Testing my speed, I dropped both the sticks and ran at the dummy, wrapping my legs around its head flipping the dummy over my head. Those shits were heavy, so I was proud of my hips, thighs, and core right about now. I stood up and kicked the closest dummy and knocked it down as well.

I'm not sure at which point I lost myself to the training completely, but I found myself moving to the weapons wall, infusing two blades, and slashing at the air, kicking out while stabbing and cutting into my imaginary opponent. I started to let my mind wander. We have yet to really speak of it, but now knowing that Alvor had been watching my skill set the entire time we were in the school really pissed me off. He was the enemy and was in my grasp, but realistically, knowing he had been planning this, would I have even had a chance against him? I was cocky, but he had been working for years with someone who was able to use magic to infiltrate a magic school… I yelled as I did a backflip and stabbed a fake opponent behind me, stepping forward, bending my knee, and using an upsweep to cut through someone in front of me. Stupid fucking Alvor. *What type of stupid name is Alvor anyways?*

Another thing that plagued me was that my magic must have recognized his treachery. I remember, through the haze, calling him a rabbit, a predator recognizing its prey. My magic thought it would have ripped Alvor apart, but, logically, magic isn't the only way to have combat, so I may have been setting myself up for a quick downfall. I need to be able to hone my new strengths and use them to their full capacity. I wanted to scream. It wasn't like there was a magic measuring stick. How the hell did I know I was magically ready?

Then there was Nici. How can you beat an opponent you knew nothing about? Sure, there was a history, there is knowledge of what she was then and is now, however, her plans are what is important. She has spent two hundred years preparing for a war; that's about 180 more than me, so how the fuck do I possibly gain an advantage on that? There had to be a way to gain information. Whispers... and as I spun and threw the blades in quick succession into the nearest dummies, the idea hit me... Scail. The king of whispers. It excited me, but then something else hit me, a mind not clouded by fairy wine or sex. His real name. Oberon. Motherfucker had the prophecy.

Chapter Thirty-Eight

My eyes narrowed and my mind whirled a tad. I wasn't upset, he literally had just met me, found out he was my mate, and I expected what? For him to break down into a Shakespearian scene and offer the missing prophecy in exchange for my hand in marriage? I scoffed. We are going to need to figure out what it said, which meant we needed to have a team powwow. The entire prophecy, and not the cliff notes version, either.

I forced myself to stop, close my eyes, and take a deep breath, releasing my magic into the ground, and grounding myself back to nature and into reality. When I opened my eyes and looked around the room, everyone was staring at me, jaws open.

"What?!" I asked, and Remi smirked and pointed behind me, I looked, and I winced at the dummies that resembled pulverized plastic and the punching bags which fell over at some point.

I walked away with my head held high and confidently said, "well, they started it."

Ryder snorted and rolled his eyes, everyone else had a small smile on their faces, "They have been starting it for over an hour, baby girl. Those poor things never stood a chance." Over an hour? Looking at my phone, my eyes bugged out. Holy shit, I have been going at this for over an hour, and it didn't feel like it. Well, I guess that's why it looks like Barbie found all her Ken dolls cheating. I grimaced at the extent of the plastic everywhere.

"Ah well, what is next?" I looked at Kalen, and he rolled his eyes and gestured for me to come closer.

"We need to start laying groundwork and start getting you to learn how to fight as a team, instead of rushing in and doing things without help. Scail has graciously volunteered to help train you all to get a better grasp on it." I nodded, pushing the thoughts of the prophecy away until lunch, so we can at least focus on the task at hand. Scail stepped up and started talking about the importance of working together seamlessly, while part of my brain took it all in. The other part admired how strong and compelling he looked. It made me wonder if we had that same telepathy powers so I can rattle him a bit.

Testing, testing. One, two, three... Earth to Scaly fucker. I hid my smirk when his eyes shot to mine and he continued to speak to the group.

Scail- *I'm going to turn you over my knee, people fear me... and I'm not scaly, my skin is quite soft.*

I snorted a laugh, and everyone turned to look at me. I shrugged my shoulders and rocked back on my heels, pretending to be the best student.

Hudson- *I highly doubt 'quite soft' is remotely correct. You know, swinging from trees and shit. Makes me wonder why they call you Scail and not Tarzan. Or at least Toucan Sam.*

I smirked when he barked my name to come forward.

"Hudson, I know you are more than capable of defending yourself and others, but in the heat of the battle, where there are thousands of enemies and we are going in full force, it will be hard to tell, after a while, who is who. In a matter of minutes, everyone will be covered in blood and indiscernible from the other; there isn't going to be a sign that indicates who is on your team or not. The one thing you must have over your enemies is focus." His voice is hypnotizing but he makes a valid point.

"Makes sense, so, fine. Who are we taking on first? I'm more of a hands-on learner." I pointed at the thick crowd of tall, gorgeous, Fae warriors.

Goodness gracious, I just registered all of the men around me, but when I'm looking a bit further, I notice a few women are geared up and training as well. I don't know why it shocks me, but I guess with the inability to have children as often as they would like, I thought that the women would have taken a back seat. I guess that is a pretty stupid outlook, now that I think about it. I mean, I'm not backing down because of some bitch ass ovaries, so why should they? Do Fae women call them ovaries? Do they call them like seedlings since they are closer to nature? I startled as Ryder started laughing and Zane groaned. Scail just looked at me with his eyebrow raised, completely confused. Oops, I guess I was projecting my thoughts.

My mind was a bit scattered, but I focused back on the task at hand and we spent the rest of the morning trying to fight like a team. Scail was definitely holding back the day before because he put me on my ass way too many fucking times, which pissed me off. I learned a few more maneuvers, but I hate being taken out so easily.

"Focus, Hudson," he said for the 45th time that damn morning I was on my back.

"Easy for you to say. You're over 900 years old, you fucking cradle robbing fucker," I swore angrily, wiping the sweat from my face. He laughed, reaching down to help me to my feet.

We worked well past lunch and it was time to take a break and have a prophecy-sized talk. Teamwork was fine and all but fighting with a crowd of people next to me confused the fuck outta me. When we are all covered in blood, how do I know who is good and who isn't? It will all just meld into a giant cluster fuck of meat. I growled in frustration. Kalen and Scail kept telling me to center myself and to let the magic and the breeze guide me. I felt like telling both Mr. Myagi's to fuck off so many times, but I tried to listen to them, I really did. At one point, I ended up smacking Zane with a stick and almost stabbing Grayson, confusing him for the other team in my haze.

I stuck my tongue out at him. "It is time for lunch. If I'm going to keep letting a grandpa put me on my ass, I'm going to need to fuel up." He laughed and I rolled my eyes. I started to walk away from the training area, stretching as I walked along. Everyone nodded at me as I walked away, and

I realized all these people are going into battle essentially as my people and I knew nothing about them. I sighed and turned back, clapping my hands and let loose magic sparks to get their attention. I'm a savage, classy, flashy... okay, not the words but you get the point.

When they all looked my way, I smiled kindly. "I don't know how things were done in the past, but I made a promise to be different and I plan to be. So, I would like to extend an invite to everyone here, as well as their family and friends, to come over to my cabin later for a little party. It will be a good way for you all to get to know me and I you." They looked a little surprised at my request. "Don't go getting soft on me, besides, it's a good chance to see me fall into the pool after my mates give me too much Fae wine," I tease, and they chuckle. I tell them to be there around five, giving everyone a chance to have lunch and get ready to come over, and more importantly, giving me time to talk to the guys because we all needed to be on the same page.

We made our way out into the forest path that leads to the cabins. I paused to look into the heavy foliage and smile, it truly is beautiful out here. Just walking around filled me with an energy that made me feel like I was vibrating with power. The guys are joking around with Remi and I rolled my eyes when Scail, Oberon, Obscailian? *Whatever!* The scaily fucker, grabbed my elbow softly. "That was a very kind thing to do."

I shrugged. "I mean, I don't know how else I'm going to get to know the people I'm supposed to protect and simultaneously lead into battle to die. How did other Queens do it? How does the Council do it?" I put quotations around council and sighed.

"They don't." He shrugged and paused for a bit. "They typically hold court where there are parties, but only the notable warriors get any notice, and that is after a battle or if they have proven themselves in other ways. You would be the first to actually actively want to get to know anyone." I stopped walking and my eyebrows shot up.

"How is that possible? No, wrong question. How is that remotely okay? We are expected to sit on a throne and hang back? That doesn't seem okay." I frowned and started walking a bit more slowly, pensive. I'll have to make this a lot more special then. These people didn't deserve that; everyone needs to be taken care of, sure, but they deserve to know that they matter beyond what they can bring to table.

"In that case, we need to make this a monthly thing." Oberon's eyes popped open, but a smile was fixed on his face that took my breath away and made my stomach do back flips. I pushed that thought away and smiled back. "Don't look so surprised. I came in with fresh ideas and I damn sure plan to live up to my promise." We got to the cabin and paused outside the front door.

"I don't think anyone is really ready for the Reign of Hudson," teased Zane, planting a kiss on my lips on his way inside. I laughed and stuck my tongue out at him.

Zane- Careful, Hudson, I'll happily put that tongue to good use, his voice whispered through my head. I smiled and headed inside. Yeah, I'm going to have that happen soon.

Chapter Thirty-Nine

Oberon

I WENT TO GET DRESSED AFTER HUDSON INDICATED IT WOULD BE AN indoor and outdoor get together. I threw on a pair of swim trunks and a button down, left open, and braided my hair before I made my way next door. I let myself in through the back door and was met with Zane, Hunter, Grayson, and Ryder sitting at the kitchen island, dressed similarly.

"Gentlemen." I nodded at them, and Hunter smiled ferally. Zane may be the leader of their friendship group, but Hunter was definitely the protector of the group, always ready for a fight. When I first saw them, they looked familiar, but I haven't been able to place exactly why I felt that way.

"You know, now that you are part of the 'I love Hudson Crew', you're going to have to start pulling your weight around here," Ryder started, his eyes twinkling, belying his heavy tone and I frowned.

"Okay, I'll bite. In what way?" The rest of the guys smirked, and

Hunter made his way around the island to stand in front of me and crossed his arms.

"Talent. We were made to put on a talent show. We decided, just now, that it is a rite of passage and you will have to do something too." My head snapped around when I heard laughter come from the staircase and my breath caught in my throat. Hudson and Remi were walking towards us in bathing suits and a long see-through skirt that I guess was supposed to be a cover up, but I'm not exactly sure what it was supposed to cover up if it was see-through. Humans are weird and I keep having to remind myself that she grew up on the other side of the Veil.

Her green bathing suit was supposed to be a one piece, but her stomach was exposed and there was just enough to cover her breasts, which had me salivating, and barely enough material to cover her ample behind. I cleared my throat and swallowed thickly. Over nine hundred years old and I'm reacting like a Fae pup at the sight of her.

"You guys are full of shit, that is not a rite of passage." Remi pointed at them making her way to the fridge to grab a bottle of water.

"That's not fair, we totally had to perform. It's the new guys turn." Ryder playfully stomped his feet, crossed his arms and pouted. Hudson laughed and walked up to him, wrapping her arms around his neck and kissed him. I looked away while he wrapped his arms around waist and caressed her back side, eliciting a moan from her.

That is the only way to shut Ryder up, Remi's voice projected through our heads. I laughed and the guys smirked.

Ryder pulled away and laughed. "I'll take it." I shook my head at the easy feel of their group dynamics.

Hunter scoffed. "Yeah only because we aren't going to be kissing your ass to shut you up. I'll just punch you in the face."

"Well, I guess I'll consider that the foreplay," Ryder retorted and Hunter rolled his eyes.

"Okay, deal. I'll perform something tonight," I said seriously, and Hunter laughed and clapped my shoulder.

"Oh, I'm looking forward to this," Zane murmured, pushing Ryder away and hugging Hudson close. My jaw ticked, wanting to be in his place.

It is certainly a strange feeling to come in last when they have already built a history over the years. Remi even seemed to fit in like a puzzle piece, despite just meeting them as well, but it could be because Remi was a blue haired version of Hudson, so it made sense. I would earn my place soon, in the meantime, being around so much affection was comforting.

Hudson

"Where is Kalen? We really need to discuss this entire prophecy thing. I want the entire thing plainly put out in front of us; we have a slight advantage now, considering that we now have Scail."

Everyone frowned but Grayson sighed. "I'm afraid to even ask why, considering every time we get an answer, it leads to fifty more questions, but I'll go ahead and ask. Why is having Scail a deal breaker?"

I smirked at Oberon. "Well, Scail, which I looked up your name and I have no idea what the fuck that means." I looked at him and shook my head. "Scail's real name is Oberon." I waited for a second before everyone started talking at once.

"Wait, the guy who has the prophecy?" Hunter's voice came out through the cacophony of voices. I smiled at his expression.

"Yup, the one and only. Now, I know what you are all thinking, literally it's distracting, and Ryder, I don't think that position is even possible," I said, giggling as he projected a bunch of images to me. "Anyways, it wasn't like he was going to meet us and be like 'hey here's the other part of the prophecy, I totally trust that you are who you say you are, you definitely won't fuck us over or anything'," I imitated Oberon's sexy chocolate voice.

"Do I really sound..." I waved him off before he finished and sat down on top of the kitchen island.

"Like you are trying to solicit sex from every female within a thousand mile radius?" He choked back a laugh. "Yeah, not funny, it is seriously befuddling, and you should really work on not sounding like that. I mean, it's bad enough these four," I pointed at the boys, "sound like a wet dream, but now I get a fifth male mate and he sounds like an orgasm?" I shook my head. "It is not even fair to my ovaries." He shook his head at me, and the guys rolled their eyes.

"She is right, you know," Remi added. "If I liked your vaginal stabbing packages, it would be tempting. I thank Gaia every day I don't have the 'scramble my insides' gene." I about fell off the counter as we burst out laughing. Kalen, Jensi, Luca, and King had chosen that time to walk in and their faces were priceless, and I couldn't stop laughing.

"Great timing," Kalen deadpanned. I giggled as he pulled up a chair and settled down next to us.

Finally calming down, I took a deep breath, winked at Obi and turned to Kalen. "Right, so now that the laughs are out of the way, we were discussing how Scail's real name is Oberon. Yes, we already went through the shock phase, moving on." Noting their faces. "Kalen, you need to give up the entire prophecy and Obi needs to add the last part so we can figure this all out."

Kalen sighed and took a piece of worn paper out of his pocket and handed it to us. King and the guys crowded around as we read what was on the paper. I frowned and looked at Oberon.

"This is what you meant when you mentioned staying away from shadows and the breeze bringing me that song to sing that night." He nodded.

"Mystical brotherhood, that must be referring to the mate bond," added Grayson.

"Humanity being your greatest weapon, makes sense seeing how you see things a lot differently than everyone here and want to rule differently," Ryder murmured, reading the paper over and over again.

"People keeping more secrets, fucking great," Hunter huffed angrily, and I absent-mindedly grabbed his hand and rubbed small circles to soothe him.

"It sounds like the secrets were necessary so that Hudson would become stronger through the deception. I mean, firsthand, I can see how betrayal can make Hudson stronger," Zane winced as he said it, and I grabbed his hand too and winked at him. The past is the past, we needed to move forward. I sighed and jumped off the counter and walked to the living room, wrapped my arms around myself and started to pace back and forth. Everyone else followed and stood around awkwardly. Most of this shit was just as confusing.

"It definitely said twenty years old, so the idea that you guys had about being twenty-one until I came into my powers doesn't make sense unless you figure twenty years of fun before a shit show. The real question is what secrets do I need to discover?" I paused, suddenly thrown back to the party where I saw Kalen sitting with the counsel, and the introductions. "Faell," I whispered and spun to look at Kalen, who looked uncomfortable. I narrowed my eyes.

"You said my name is actually Riona Fheall, and during the dinner two other people were introduced with the same last name, you and the man named Shea." I rubbed my temples. "Shea was also the name of the prince. So, for the sake of pretending I'm at least semi-intelligent," I scoffed, "it's safe to say Shea is my father, who saw me for the first time in person and didn't bother to say anything, which would make you related to him in some way." Everyone fell quiet as we stared at Kalen.

"Shea is my older brother," he finally sighed after several moments of silence. I stepped back and bumped into Hunter who wrapped his arms around me, steadying me. Brother. So, Kalen was my uncle.

Is everyone around me someone more than what they seem? This is becoming a real-life game of Clue.

"Nice. Awesome, anything else you want to say to me now, Kalen? Because I seriously will fucking lose it if you keep popping up like some Faerie popcorn version of Ms. Cleo to tell me random shit that I should already know." He shook his head but looked away, so yeah there is something missing here. I sighed and looked at Oberon.

"Your turn, what does the other part of the prophecy say?" I demanded. At this point, I was going to get all my answers, or someone was going to get their ass beat.

"Well, it isn't another half, but there was a part that I felt would put the future Queen in danger. All it read was Queen be wary, Níl aon ghrá ann go dtí go mbeidh teaghlach ann. Níl aon anró anam ann go dtí go mbeidh leanaí ag duine," he said silkily, as I shook my head out of the trance of him speaking another language and asked him to repeat the words.

"There's no love until there's family. There is no anguish of the soul until one has children," I said shakily. *Well then, talk about a fucking life plot twist.*

Chapter Forty

"Right. We can dissect that in a bit, after I don't feel like I'm choking on this informational deep throat." The guys chuckled low and Remi came to stand next to me and started to rub my back. They started to talk about what the prophecy can mean and how it could be interpreted, and I noticed the letters given to me by that annoying Fae guy at the entry table and picked them up. I sat quietly at the edge of the couch and started to sift through them. One of them was the prophecy, well a little too late, although I appreciate being given a copy, but I don't see why he felt like I needed to have it.

Frustrated, I threw the prophecy to the side and picked up the other letter. Except three pieces of papers fell out. I blinked and I read them over and over again. This... this was just wrong.

Shea,

Your daughter is simply beautiful. I would send a picture, but it isn't safe. I wish you could see how amazing Hudson is doing. She is taking every training I'm throwing her way and absorbing it all like a sponge. Even when she falls, she gets right back up and keeps going. Her dickhead of a fake father is making her take extra training with me at five a.m. and again after school. If she comes home with a mark, he increases her training. He wants her to be the best, but his methods are questionable, to say the least. I often wonder if he has a sixth sense about her future. Today, she made me laugh; she told me to shove my sword up my ass. I never thought I would like kids, but this one, Shea, she is a combination of the good things in both of us. Hell, a combination of all the good things in our world. She is a force of nature; I'll be shocked if she wasn't from Gaia herself. As promised, I will watch over her. I love her like she was my own, she is the daughter of my heart.

Kalen

Shea,

The father has found out that Hudson isn't his. Do not worry though, he still loves her in his own way, but he is a lot more callous now. Just makes her work harder, drags her to these ridiculous council events, dressing her up like a pink potato sack. She is learning a lot of socialite policies and decorum though, so I guess there is that. It was time, though, that I brought in some additional back up. I chose four boys that are best friends. They will serve to deviate Jacob's attention so he isn't so hard on her. I know he cares, but I still think the knowledge has rocked him to his core. At least now we will have extra eyes on

Hudson as she continues to grow; she is drawing the eyes of young men despite her pink potato clothes.

Anyways, the boys have had their memories thoroughly wiped; they were given the barest of memories and their power tampered down. You are fortunate that the old crone in our old home owed me a favor. I cannot imagine what she needed to perform that type of unnatural magic, but it worked. Their hair color is even permanent. It is amazing. The breeze pushed me towards these boys, believe it or not. I shouldn't be surprised though; the breeze has its way of getting Gaia's message across. They were already best friends, working within the rebellion. Their new names are Zane, Ryder, Hunter, and Grayson, instead of their given names, Caer, Aiwel, Arallu, and O'Donoghue. The crone promised the spell would be in effect for a long time. I asked what would break the spell she cast, and she mentioned a great loss; we can only hope it isn't a death sentence. Caer is now living in the Jacob's home and seems to be getting on well. The things we do for love.

Your brother, Kalen

The letter shook in my hand. It was hard to catch my breath. I read the next letter out of sheer anger.

Shea,
It's been a while, but I trust your little messengers have updated you. Quick rundown, I didn't count on them going to university, but I damn sure didn't count on her losing her virginity to Caer. Their connection seems to

run deep. She was changing and I had to train her harder than ever. She will be more than you ever dreamed of Shea. It is a scary thing, letting someone with her fire out into the world. I pity whoever she comes in contact with. She's not only beautiful; she is all things right in the world.

The reason I am writing now is that she will be going to the university with the boys living in the same home. However, I caught wind that Alvor, that piece of shit, and his niece will be there as well. She gave up the throne to steal the one thing we have strived to protect. Why do I feel like you had a hand in this? If you're trying to make someone slip up, I caution you. If there is one thing we have learned is that not everyone is as they seem. I have a feeling there is something else going on here. I don't believe in coincidences, Shea, and he brought on too many to help secure her.

I'll keep an eye out but I have a feeling I'll be seeing you soon; prepare. Things are going to get ugly fast.
Kalen

The words were there, I could probably repeat them verbatim right now, but they were also not there. My mind wouldn't register the lies, the deception, the years of having my life infiltrated. In a few seconds, I questioned everything. Nature told me my mates were mine, regardless of the circumstances that brought them to me. Thank goodness the breeze guided Kalen, or I could have taken years to meet my mates. *No, no, no. I had them, that's all that mattered.*

. . .

I took a few calming breaths and I stood up shakily and tossed the letters on the living room table, effectively stopping everyone's conversation.

"Kalen, I asked you if you had anything else to tell me. I highly suggest you do. I may respect you, but I'm extremely close to losing my shit." King stepped closer to me as my magic spiked repeatedly. The guys picked up the letters and passed them around, varying degrees of anger fleeting across their faces.

"Certain things needed to be kept secret in order to protect you, Hudson. We did what we could to ensure that you were trained well and were well protected. I can't apologize for that." I nodded, in my head though I stabbed him with a branch.

"How about kidnapping four men from their home and making them believe they were human, in order to thrust them into a new place?" He looked away and I laughed humorlessly. I turned around and went upstairs.

"Let me know when people start to arrive. I just need some time to process and possibly not punch anyone in the face, and you owe my mates an explanation, seeing as you not only kidnapped these four but also knew Alvor was into some shady shit, effectively putting Remi in danger." I looked at Kalen as I said the last part and made my way upstairs, but not before snagging a bottle of the Faerie wine we had on the kitchen counter.

I threw myself on my bed and looked up at the ceiling. I knew shit sucked for me to find out I was being watched my entire life, but I knew things were even worse for the guys to find out they were effectively Fae-napped, just to come and play babysitter. I bit my lip. The only way for the guys to get their memories back would be to suffer a great loss. I don't even know how to touch that with a ten-foot pole. You would think the loss of their memories and who they were as people would be a loss, but when dealing with blood magic, the loss must be equal or greater than what was lost in the first place. Kalen was stupid to do something so damn costly, four times over.

I laid there for at least a half hour, halfway through my Fae wine, until I heard my door open. Looking up, I saw Oberon at the door. I gave him a small smile. "Hey there, handsome. To what do I owe this pleasure?" I smiled, the Faerie wine still flowing through my system.

"Just thought I would come check on you and see how you were doing. Kalen and the guys are all discussing things quite loudly, so I figured I can hide out up here." I laughed.

"The great Oberon, hiding behind the skirts of his woman."

He scoffed. "I don't need to hide, but I do know when to gracefully bow out and let other people fight their own battles." He walked closer to me and sat on the edge of the bed before laying down. "You would think the ceiling had all the answers to your future, the way you're staring at it," he teased.

"If it did, I would have saved the world already," I sighed. "You know, I have been thinking." He turned to look at me. "The only way we are going to win this thing is to get allies. I mean, I don't know how that councilman got copies of those letters, but think about it. If he has them, what makes you think that Nici doesn't have them? In fact, in all the information overload, we didn't stop to think about why the council fucker gave them to me to begin with? To sow discord? I can't imagine it was for a good reason, which makes him look suspicious as fuck. Makes me want to go throat punch him actually."

He hummed his agreement. "I would have to agree with that. It doesn't make sense; it wouldn't be the first time Ealdon has caused trouble. He has a strange superiority complex when it comes to Fae. He truly believes we should be run by a council instead of a Reign." I paused to consider my answer to that.

"I mean it's not a bad idea." He raised his eyebrow. "Think of it as a Queen at the helm, but a board of advisors that she can actually trust. I imagine it would be difficult to find advisors that aren't interested in their own gain but there are always truth spells." I shrug.

He turns over, leaning on his elbow to look at me. After a few minutes, I feel awkward and turn to face him too. Damn, why is he so freaking perfect? I take in his crystal blue eyes, sharp jaw, and his long, braided hair, and I just want to eat him.

His eyes heat when they meet mine but like a champ, he clears his throat and returns to the conversation at hand. I'm not sure if I like his restraint or not. Kind of want him to show me how forest creatures fuck. I smile despite myself and he raises an eyebrow.

"I don't think you meant that nefariously, but casting a spell on your subjects wouldn't be the best way to gain their trust when you are trying to start something based on loyalty, faith, and trust." I frowned. He makes sense, but fuck, the weight of change is on my shoulders and how the hell do I figure out how to lead without making the same mistakes from the past, build a strong foundation and yet still have people I can trust? I groan and toss myself back.

Chuckling, he adds, "The fact that you care is important, Hudson. Remember that, but we can come up with better ideas to determine loyalty. Starting with the ones closest to you." I bite my lip and sigh. He's right, but then I have to consider leading with a counsel of just my mates and how that would look. I really shouldn't give a flying pixie shit, but the severity of my new future just hit me like a freight train.

My thoughts scatter as his warm mouth covers mine. I moan, arching my back, leaning into his warmth. My mind flies back to that night in the woods and he was certainly holding back then.

Leaning back, he searches my eyes for what I assume may be hesitation, and, finding none, he groans and pushes himself so that he is over me instead of beside me. The delicious weight of his body sends me into a frenzy, and I reach to drag him closer.

"Hudson, I don't think I can stop if we keep going," he pants, pulling away. *Why the fuck do they say that shit, do you see me stopping you?* In response, I lean up and tug my bikini top off and his eyes darken, and he stands up to slowly to take off his clothes. I tug off my bottoms and cover up and I stand up to meet him, pulling him closer. He smirks and I wrap my arms around his neck and pull him down for a kiss. We both groan as our lips connect, my tongue teasing his mouth. Grabbing my ass, he spins me around and slams me into the wall near my bed. Well, well, the winged man has claws.

Wrapping my hands in his hair, I pull hard and he hisses, biting my lip, drawing blood. I tug my mouth away and running my lips down his neck and bite down before I'm licking his slightly marred skin, fucking up his perfection.

This wasn't passion, this was two souls finally breaking through and finding each other, he waited too long for this and I didn't realize how much I was missing another part of me. From five to six mates, and it feels like the final puzzle piece was fixed into place.

I push him onto the bed, letting my hands and tongue roam all over his body. He quickly turns me around, pinning me on to the bed, grabbing my jaw roughly and catching my lips in a bruising kiss. I moaned, and I knew I was dripping from the pleasure. Fuck, yes. He tangles one hand in my hair, using the other to choke me, cutting off my air supply, and making me come off the bed in excitement.

He groans, pulling back, and looking me over. "Fuck you are perfection..." he growls, turning me over, grabbing my ass, and sliding into me in one thrust. I bit my lip to stop from screaming, my hands grabbing the sheets underneath me as he fucks me with abandon.

Oberon- *Fuck, Hudson you are so fucking tight. So, fucking perfect.*

Hudson- *Shut the fuck up and fuck me until I can't breathe.*

Oberon- *Deal.*

He pulls out quickly, flipping me, before slamming back into me, laying me down, never losing his pace. Impressive. Grabbing my waist, he leans over to take one of my nipples in his mouth and bites down, hard.

"Fuck yes!"

I arch my back and scratch my nails down his back. I silently urge him to go faster, my head thrashing as I felt myself on the edge. Reaching one hand between us, he pinches my clit, and my eyes roll as my orgasm sweeps through me. He curses and flips me over to all fours, slamming back inside of me, reaching over to play with my clit, making me shudder with pleasure, and drawing another orgasm out of me.

"Mmm, is that all you got, Scail?" He laughs and he wraps one hand around my hair, smacking my ass over and over with the other. I clench and moan with each smack, getting wetter with each hit.

"Fuck, Hudson," he shudders out, bottoming out and hitting my cervix with each stroke. Flipping me over again, he settles me on top of him, facing away, and I ride him. He reaches around to grab my breasts, rubbing and pinching my nipples, eliciting another moan. I smile when he says my name as a curse, as I alternate between sliding and bouncing on his dick. Grabbing my waist roughly, Oberon takes control pounding into me before I feel him swell and fill me.

I feel a rush of satisfaction as our souls collide. This was more than just sex; this was a craving, a need. This was him accepting and fucking his mate. This was me making me his and me making him mine.

After a few moments, I get up and grab his hand, leading him into the shower. I bite my lip, looking at him while he lathers himself, never letting his gaze leave mine. Fuck this, he looks like a fucking sex symbol. Pushing him against the wall, I lean over and take him into my mouth, and he tosses his head back. I fucking loved the way they all responded to my mouth pleasuring them. Anyone can fuck, but can you give head? I could and I damn sure was going to show it when I could. I urged his hands around my head, none of that gentle shit. *Fuck my mouth, just as hard, baby,* I whispered into his head. Groaning, his eyes roll back as I work him over as fast as he fucked my mouth. Sucking, swallowing, and humming, working my tongue rings around his dick just enough to drive him crazy. I reach down to play with myself and his eyes snap open as he looks down at me.

"Don't touch yourself. That is my job," he grinds out. I raise my eyebrow and hum around his dick, making him curse as he fills my throat with his cum. He bucked into my mouth and groaned, and I stay until I swallow every drop.

"Fuck, Hudson, your mouth. Holy shit." He leaned his head back in a daze and I laughed. I finished showering while he composed himself and he soon followed and showed me what hundreds of years of experience truly meant when he laid me down and settled himself between my legs. Holy shit, how the fuck was I getting my ass downstairs now?

Chapter Fourty-One

We did eventually make it downstairs. The guys still looked angry after their conversation with Kalen and I wondered what else was said. Putting it in the back of my mind, I focused on the purpose for the evening and I spent the evening talking to everyone who made their way to the cabin. The house was filled with Fae and even a few of the Council members were there. Remi and the guys made their way around the home, talking to people as well, and it was amazing to see how receptive people were to us. I was even fortunate enough that the mothers in the village felt comfortable enough to bring their children to play as well.

I was in the middle of talking to a few soldiers when a little girl walked up to me and tugged at my hand. Smiling, I crouched to one knee, aware of everyone staring with a bemused expression. "Hello, what's your name?" She was adorable; green eyes and long white hair that touched her feet, she must be around four or five. I hid my frown, remembering that Kalen mentioned that kids don't typically gain white hair until they are a bit older, making me wonder if this child was strong magically or if it was an anomaly.

Looking at me curiously from under her eyelashes she gives me a hesitant smile. "I'm Li'Ella but my mommy and daddy call me Lili." She paused for a second. "But you can call me Li'Ella since you're not my mom." I laughed at her firm tone and nodded.

"Li'Ella it is, although I would love it if I had a nickname for you that was only for us to share too," I said seriously.

Li'Ella looked to consider what I said before responding, "Is it true you're the new Queen?" I nodded. "Well, then I guess it's okay. I don't want you to smite me." Her little voice echoed in the now quiet living room and I bust out in laughter.

A woman came rushing to grab her hand. "I am so sorry, your majesty." She grimaced.

"Oh, no, don't apologize," I reply, looking up at her, "My mates can tell you I don't hold my tongue either. In fact, they have known me since I was a little girl and I don't think I ever held back my thoughts." I looked at the guys, who came closer and they smiled.

Grayson crouched down. "Li'Ella, you want to know a secret about the Queen?" Stage whispering, he continued, "she used to threaten to kick our butts all the time and you know what she did when she got older?" Li'Ella shook her head, eyes wide looking between her mom and us.

"She actually did it," Hunter threw in. "In fact, you see that guy right there?" He pointed at Zane. "She kicked his butt first. He cried like a baby." Li'Ella started to laugh and Zane growled.

"I did not cry. Don't let these vagrants lie to you, Li'Ella, but I did run away. She's a feisty one, but I deserved it."

Li'Ella nodded sagely before looking at us. "Well, if you deserved it, then I guess you had it coming." We laughed and Ryder reached down to give her a high five, which she returned with a smile on her face.

"Li'Ella, do you mind if my mates and I call you Ella? It will be a special nickname between just us. That is how important you are to the Crown." Her eyes lit up and her mom's eyes filled with tears.

"Thank you so much, can I give you a nickname too?"

"Of course, you can. When you think of one, let me know and that will be our special nickname." Throwing herself into my arms, I sigh as her little arms tighten around my neck and I hug her back.

"You're going to be the best Queen ever and me and your babies are going to be the best of friends ever. I can see it." The way she whispered the last part for only my ears had a chill run down my spine.

As her mother led her away, I stopped to think, *how long has it been since we had a Seer?* I projected the question to Oberon, who looked at Ella curiously, as her mother led her away.

Three hundred years.

Well, fuck.

Once everyone had left, I felt a boost in my confidence. I beamed at the guys and Remi. "I think tonight was very successful!"

"I think everyone loved you," Zane says from the couch where he is leaning his head back with his eyes closed.

"As if they had a choice. You are probably the most genuine and equally feral person ever," teased Remi, leaning over to kiss my cheek. I playfully push her and roll my eyes.

"What the fuck ever, I'm an angel." I stomp my foot. They had the nerve to roll their eyes.

"Yeah sure, an angel." Grayson walks over and gives me a kiss on the cheek before sitting down on the couch next to Zane. How can a kiss be sarcastic? I scowl at him.

You guys don't appreciate my amazingness. You'll be sorry when I punch you right in your faces.

Zane scoffs. *That right there, is why you're no angel.*

We appreciate you plenty, especially when you're naked, teased Ryder. I set his pants on fire.

Yelling, he runs and jumps into the pool. I smirk at the guys faces and Hunter just backs up.

"Oh man, why don't we have surveillance cameras? That would have been gold to have on tape," Remi laughs, holding her stomach. Oberon smirks and I stick my tongue out at him.

Ryder stomps back into the house and throws me over his shoulder, I squeal with laughter and he carries me up the stairs.

"Where are we going?!"

"We are going to Kindle and chill, and I'll show you how much I appreciate your Queenly ass." He smacks my ass and I giggle as we get to my room and he throws me on the bed. Walking over to the bookcase, he grabs my Kindle and settles on the bed.

While he goes through it, I lean forward. "How did the talk with Kalen go?" I finally am asking the question that has been burning through my head all night.

Grimacing, he looks up briefly before looking back down. "Honestly, not well. I think we were all too pissed to really take anything in. We all agree that we are happy we met you, but not knowing our past is a tough pill to swallow. Hunter is taking it the hardest because his memories were suppressed the most. Apparently, the Fae-witch had started on him first and used too much of her potion, which is why he feels the loss the most." Sighing, he runs his fingers through his hair, which has gotten longer while we have been here. I recall how Hunter said he didn't remember his childhood and I frown at how sad that made him and I feel another wave of anger start low in my belly. The prophecy clearly said I would meet my mates; it isn't fair that Kalen essentially Fae-napped the guys.

I sigh and we push the conversation away to enjoy our night together. I was going to enjoy all the time I could get with my mates individually before everything exploded in our faces and we had to fight for the survival of the people I got to know today. Ella's eyes flash in my mind and I make a promise to do whatever I can to protect everyone, even if it means I have to sacrifice myself.

Chapter Fourty-Two

A sense of urgency falls over me and at my insistence, we spend the next several days training for over twelve hours a day, from dawn to dusk, with only breaks for lunch and dinner. I don't pause to wonder where Xena went during the day, as she always popped up at random times to remind me to train more because the danger was closer. She annoyingly would pop out of the room when I asked her why, and I'd just grit my teeth and keep pushing myself.

During training, I found myself getting more and more exhausted and I was barely able to hold down the protein drinks I was forcing down my throat. I knew I was pushing myself harder than anyone else because I felt that it was my duty to protect everyone, but I didn't care. I would spend my days training, my nights rotating with my mates, giving them all the individual time that I knew they craved, and I would be lying if I said I didn't crave it too.

Kalen avoided being alone with us beyond training and I wanted to throat punch him and ask him what his deal was. I also wanted to ask him why my father had yet to introduce himself, and that pissed me off more than I wanted to admit.

It was one evening, coming back from training, when shit hit the fan. Walking into the cabin, I ran upstairs and barely made it to the toilet when my stomach heaved and expelled everything I had eaten during the day. I groaned and leaned my head against the cold tile on the floor.

"Fuck," I whispered, nausea rolling through me, my head starting to pound. Sighing, I crawled into the shower and shed my clothes, trying to shake off the feeling. A few seconds later, I look up as six faces stand in the bathroom, staring at me with concern.

"You are pushing yourself too hard, baby girl," Ryder says, coming closer and passing me my toothbrush. I smile gratefully and start to brush my teeth until I smell the mint and start to heave again. I see them looking back and forth at each other and I sigh.

I'll be fine. Go get cleaned up, I'll be out in a few. They scoff at the same time, and the guys start to strip, and they get in the shower and help me get cleaned up. I laugh when Remi raises her eyebrows and looks away.

"I'm going to avoid the hanging sausages and go take a quick shower. I'll also go make you some tea, babe."

"Thank you, Remi." She makes her way out of the bathroom and the guys make quick work of getting me cleaned up, nothing sexual, just comfort, and I find myself ridiculously happy as Zane carries me out and dries me off while Grayson grabs me some pajamas. Remi comes back upstairs with a cup of tea just as the bell rings. I frown and the guys dress while she goes to answer the door. Seconds later, Ella's little face bursts into the room, her mother hot on her heels.

"I'm so sorry, your majesty. She took off and came straight here," her mom apologizes.

"It's okay," I assure her. Ella was suddenly at my bedside and she reaches her hands up and touches my belly and her hands start to glow. I gasp and we all look at each other in a panic.

"My best friends are coming, but you have to be careful or they will die during battle," Ella whispers softly. We stare at her, dumbstruck.

"Ella, honey, what do you mean?" I ask stupidly, making sure we all heard her right.

She giggles and leans her head on my stomach. "My best friends are in your belly. You're going to be a Queen mommy."

Yeah, that's what I thought she said, I think to myself and even though I'm laying down my head drops back, and I faint from shock, the last thought in my head I projected.

You fuckers knocked me up.

Oberon

We all sat on Hudson's bed after Ella and her mom had left. Ella clapping her hands happily, talking about her best friends and how awesome they were. I hid a lot over the years I have been alive; some of these secrets were for the good of the people, or so I felt, others were for my own selfish reasons. The moment I ripped the prophecy, I couldn't tell you why at the time, I just knew that if there is one thing the Fae revered was the ability to have children. I couldn't bear to see that portion of the prophecy used to hurt the one who was to save us all. I always felt pulled towards that prophecy, to someone who hadn't even been born yet, but I'm glad I did; to protect her. Our bond was sealed, and now the final part of the prophecy was true.

"Well, that is an unexpected end to our day," Ryder says, trying to lighten the mood.

"That sounds about right," Grayson says low, holding Hudson's hand in his. Grayson is usually the quietest of the bunch, always thinking and observing. His eyes haven't left Hudson in all this time. At some point, King had walked into the room and settled himself next to the bed. Xena also popped in out of thin air, pacing back and forth across the room.

"It is amazing," whispered Hunter almost reverently. He was rubbing Hudson's belly and whispering to her belly the entire time she was passed out, the guys and I exchanged smiles watching the tough Hunter, who was always spoiling for a fight, completely taken down at finding out he was going to be a father. Zane looked at her with so much tenderness, it was almost too intimate to watch, and Remi pulled up a computer and started looking for something Hudson could take for her nausea. Love filled the room and it felt incredible to be a part of this. After so many years, it was a blessing.

After a few more moments, Hudson stirred and slowly sat up blinking at us.

"Tell me I just dreamt that I found out I was pregnant, and that Ellie did not say best friends as in multiple little uterine hostages?" she groaned and rubbed her head.

"Vaginal destroyers, as in plural? Yes. Yes, she did," Ryder jokes. She laughed and shook her head.

"Fuck," she whispered. "I made little versions of myself that are going to drive you all bat shit fucking crazy," she tried to joke, but the nervous look in her eye didn't fool us. She was scared and I didn't blame her. We had more to protect, more to value. We just had to survive what was coming. And as that thought crossed my mind, an alarm sounded; the Veil had been breached.

Hudson

"Tell me, I just dreamt that I found out I was pregnant, and that Ellie did not say best friends as in multiple little uterine hostages?"

It hit me like a fucking freight train.

I'm pregnant.

"Fuck... I made little versions of myself that are going to drive you all bat shit fucking crazy," I tried to joke. Pregnant. A baby. Babies, I corrected. I had been joking in the car, but this was insane. Damn that car ride seemed like months ago instead of just weeks. I had a battle to fight, several of them, what was I going to say, *oh I'm sorry, I'm having morning sickness and throwing up glitter dust. I can't make it to the ides of March, try me in the ides of next February*. It just didn't make any sense. There was a prophecy damn it. At least it should have gone in order and let me have babies last, after I kicked some ass. What was I supposed to go into battle with a stroller wrapped in knives?

No sooner than the thought crossed my mind, an alarm blared throughout the village. I jumped up and, even without knowing we had an alarm, I knew what that meant. We were under attack. Well, new moms were made of tough shit, but I was about to bring that full fucking circle. Let's fucking go.

THE START OF A WAR

"I am ... the first-born of Her light
Who ushers ... forth the day from night
Bear witness to my starry might
And join my grand seduction!
Now hearken you unto my song
Of life within destruction ...
I am ... the serpent in the well
Who rises ... up to conquer hell
Calling heaven down upon the earth
And as the stars do fall ...
My precious jewels reside in thee
Rise and hear my call!
I am ...
Mine is ... the path of sacred love
The serpent ... twining with the dove
And as below so is above
All life in your reflection!
For each of you I'm in your heart
Your beauty-flawed perfection!

I am … the lust that rises high
Into the heavens beyond the sky,
Who dares to stand proud without shame?
And as the sun does rise …
A new day dawns in paradise
And met with joyous cry …
I am …
I am beauty, I am pride!
I am the light that never hides!
I am the power without shame!
Holy power, yours to claim!
As we sing the universe
In concert with us now affirms
This sacred light within our hearts
Never dies, never departs
So we sing together now
To call that love and power down
Within our blood, within our bones
The song that's calling us … home …
I am …"
STORM FAERYWOLF

Chapter Fourty-Three

"We can do this later," I say as I rush to don all my thick leather that would be hard to cut through and the chain metal I used to use for training. The guys all run to do the same and as I strap on my weapons belt with all my daggers and short swords, the window in my room is thrown open and the breeze wraps around me and whispers, "It's time, daughter, the start is here. We have a war to win and babies to bring into a world, clear from the dark. Restore the balance."

Frowning, I pause. I don't know how but I recognize the voice and I think Gaia is talking to me directly. Pushing that golden nugget from my head, I seethe as I finish quickly donning my combat boots. I have no idea how the Veil could have fallen, other than the simple age-old answer, a traitor. That traitor's ass was mine. Voice or no voice, Gaia can warn, but Gods do not interfere. It was up to us and this was only the beginning. I felt it in my bones. The imposter wouldn't come so soon, so these were some of her actual soldiers. Now, it was time to prove myself as a Queen and as a protector. Before I stepped out of my room, I wrote a note to my mates and to my friends, leaving it on my dresser. I paused and touched my belly, praying that we could overcome this battle with more of our men then

Nici's. Praying for anything else would be a wish, and a wish is a dream your heart makes, according to Disney, and look how wrong they were about fucking Faeries.

Palming two of my scythes in my hand, I no longer felt like myself. I felt grounded. I feel like power. Problem was I now had more than just myself or my mates, I had a part of all of us to protect.

I STEPPED OUTSIDE WITH THE GUYS AND SAW KALEN AND SHEA, AND I nodded in their direction, internally rolling my eyes at Shea's convenient timing to fucking be around me. Father of the year, folks. Looks like I have two. I make a mental note to contact my father outside of the Veil after we survive this shit.

"I assume there is a safe house where people are going?" Kalen nodded. "Good, I want no soldiers outside of it." They looked shocked. "Don't look so shocked, it's simple logic. I'll ward it. Soldiers there will draw them to the safe house. It will be a weakness that will be exploited and to these filthy fuckers, we don't have a weakness, understood?" They both agree with small smiles on their faces. Don't fucking smile at me.

"Point me to the direction of the building. I'm assuming you ran drills. How long does it take for everyone to fill the building after an alarm?"

"Two minutes, Queen," Kalen responded, pride in his eyes. I wanted to roll mine, but it's been a long day. I just wanted to make people to bleed and take my ass right back to bed where I can start buying onesies that say, "My moms and dads will punch you in the Fae-ce."

"It's been two and half minutes." Letting instinct guide me, I put my hand to the ground and found the safe house by using the vines under the ground to guide me, I warded the house with everything nature had. If the traitor was in there, they will be hard pressed to get the fuck out. My wards were different; they were wrapped in anger and power. Sometimes traditions end up breaking a society, and I plan to rebuild this one.

I looked at Xena and smiled softly. "I know you want to be in battle, but please, pop into the safe house and keep everyone safe from the inside. Let me know if it is breached."

I will not let you down. Stay safe. She bounded away and disappeared, and I focused on breathing deeply and opening my senses. We are energy and elements, and right now, the energy in me sensed hundreds of tainted entities. I cursed.

"We have several hundred soldiers here, and I don't fucking think it's a damn welcoming committee." We jogged to the center of the village where the edge of the Veil was breached.

"I don't know, maybe they heard of the party and brought cupcakes," joked Ryder, always trying to lighten the moment, even now. I shook my head and laughed.

The smile quickly faded from my face when I saw who was standing front and center of the breach, surrounded by Dark Fae. Dean Motherfucking, Twat-waffle, Alvor, that son of a bitchy Fae.

Our soldiers have already started to engage the fighting masses. Kalen and Shea ran forward and, back-to-back, started cutting down everyone in their way. It would have been poetic to watch, if we weren't about to jump into the fray. My mates surrounded me, Oberon with his face in shadows again. I palmed my scythes and started forward. I ducked as a dagger was thrown at my head. I sent out a pulse of magic and the creature who threw the dagger was incinerated. I crossed my weapons and infused them, going low as I cut through the legs of two incoming Unseelie and Hunter followed through and cut their heads off. His eyes glowed as he breathed deep and the fire of battle filled him with excitement.

Hunter and Grayson took my left flank, and Zane and Ryder took my right, while Remi and Oberon covered my back. Knowing they had me covered was hard to swallow, I wanted to shelter them and keep them safe, but I focused on what was in front of me. Several Fae approached us at once, and to my left, Hunter and Grayson were engaged with five opponents. I'm not sure what they were considered, but they were black from head to toe and were able to disappear and appear at will. It was as if they could pop in and out of reality.

I growled when I saw a blade stab into Grayson's side. His wound was pouring blood and he had to divert his attention in order to heal and attack. Hunter spun on the ball of his foot and continued the fight for both, parrying and slashing, his feral smile coated in blood and glowing from the magic imbued into his weapons. Although I knew from our connection that Grayson was okay, the idea of anyone hurting my mates was too much for my magic to handle, controlling ass bitch. She rushed to the front, seeking control, but I held her at bay until it was necessary.

Everyone was holding their own, Oberon and Remi glowing from the sheer strength of their age and power, tearing down anyone who came close. Zane was fired up from the idea of anyone getting close enough to hurt me, and Ryder's weapons were damn near indestructible as he cleaved opponents and their weapons in two.

"Hello, fake queen." One of the disappearing fuckers popped up in front of me and I narrowly avoided being beheaded. King came out of nowhere and kicked out, catching the shadow fucker unaware and I slashed upwards, cutting through its stomach. I smiled at King and he jumped back into the fray. However, no matter what we did or how much we fought, no matter how much blood coated our hands and body, the counts were increasing, and the battle didn't seem to be letting up.

I felt, rather than saw, our warriors pressed back. Despite all we did, it was as if an invisible force was feeding us more to fight. In the center of the battle, Alvor stood untouched, smirking, while seeming to be unbothered. But why? It was as if he thought he had this battle already won. There is no way the fake queen would possibly send all her forces here for a battle to take me out so soon. No, no one spends years of planning for a quick destruction. She would want to draw this out, and torture those who oppose her. Torture. A light went off in my head.

I wiped the blood of some ugly looking goblin from my eyes and, despite the mental concerns from my mates, I moved forward without them and fought my way towards Alvor. I let my magic take control. This fucking asshole was not only in the middle, untouched, but his bitch-ass was literally floating on a fucking pedestal, as if he was fucking king. No. Not happening. I let loose a pulse of magic, and those protecting Alvor boiled and busted. I loved that little trick, even if hot blood wasn't the most therapeutic of experiences.

"My dear, you can kill everyone around me, but you'll never get through my shield to get to me. I'm merely here to view your destruction. It's quite entertaining, is it not, to know that after all this time of hiding and practicing, that your little blip of an existence will be nothing in our vast timeline," he said scathingly. It was like he was talking right in front of me, even though we had a few feet of space. I smiled.

"Wow, and here I thought that you would actually participate. Or are you going to leave everyone else to die and fight your battle for you? Tsk, tsk, what a shame. You are a fucking pussy. You couldn't even get through the Veil by yourself, old man. You had to have a traitor do it for you. Tell me, Alvor, what did you promise them? Fortune? A spinning wheel?" I laughed as he narrowed his eyes.

"Oh yeah, I did a little research on your imposter queen, except she's past her time, isn't she? The old crone who spins her wheel and works in dark magic, yet is known for her Faerie rule as a ruthless cunt. Interesting really. Except Nicnevin sends a little bitch boy instead of coming to face me herself." I laughed mockingly as his eyes light up with anger.

"You are wrong, she sent me because I am to be her King, you insolent child. She trusts me to carry out her wishes and win." He stepped off his pedestal and came closer. Yes, come to me, just a bit more fucker.

"Really? Because it seems to me that she sent you off to slaughter. I mean, here you are, surrounded in a bubble, not even fighting. What King doesn't fight with his people? What Queen doesn't, for that matter? She's a punk and so are you." He growled and brought down the extended shield around him.

"You think you can beat me?" He laughed and I rolled my eyes. "I'm as old as Kalen, trained just the same. I observed you, and yet, you still lack understanding of the basic history of our people. Maybe you should have studied that instead." Two swords appeared in his hands and he held them out, knees bent. I mimicked his stance. What the fuck is he talking about, history? Was he the fucking Dean of battle? He confused me but I refused to show it. What basic history did I possibly need to know to beat him into a fucking bloody pulp?

"Ahh, you didn't know, did you? Laughable, really. You all so readily accepted Gaia as the Goddess of All but never questioned her husband?"

He moved faster than I could see and sliced down my arm, drawing blood. Blocking out the pain, I parried his next blow and used my scythe to draw blood from his neck, except he healed almost immediately. *What the fuck?*

He pressed his attack, every spin and blow coming at faster intervals as he spoke. "We come from Gods; our history is steeped in our connection with them. Uranus also had some consorts. Did you know that part?" I studied mythology; I understood the connection of the Gods to each other, but I didn't understand what he was getting at. All I knew was every pulse of magic, every swing of my scythes, ended up absorbed by him as if he was drinking my power. I understood absorbing energy, I would do it often, except despite every hit I got on him, I couldn't absorb anything in return.

He stepped forward and almost cleaved me in two, I spun on the ball of my foot and hooked his ankle, making him crash to the ground, before I leaned in and sliced across his stomach, too far to reach his neck. I cursed internally.

"Thanks for the history lesson, pops, I know who you are referring to, but what the fuck does that have to do with your bitch ass?" I pressed out, trying to focus on his handwork. He had no pattern, this was simply a determination of who was better, and for the first time, I do not think it was me. He stepped forward and sliced across my stomach, and my magic rebelling at the idea of the babies being harmed, pushed back. I leaned to the side and countered his attack by digging my scythe into his back. He swore and stepped back.

"You fool. His consort was Nyx, the daughter of chaos, the mother of sleep, death, fates, and even Nemesis. She gave that power to Uranus as well. Your prophecy is a joke, as those who control the Gods control the Fates." He laughed, delivering a blow to my other arm, weakening my hold on my weapons. The only thing keeping me up was my deep connection to the earth itself. I needed him distracted. I needed him to slip up, so he needed to keep talking because at this rate, every time he drew blood, he sapped my energy. I had no idea how he was doing that, but holy shit, it was effective.

"You can't control the Gods. You are a fucking idiot." I stepped back, circling him, moving forward, and throwing a dagger right into his leg. He pulled it out and laughed. I don't know what is so fucking funny, you little shit.

"Perhaps, perhaps not. Except when you work with the God who hates his wife and all she stands for, we will always have an edge." He laughed and swung, knocking one of my weapons down. I mentally cursed myself for being shocked. He was working with Uranus. Gods can't interfere. What the fuck could they possibly have that a God would have use for? Our history may start with the Gods. Heck, it's why the Fae were so strong and pure. We have unique powers and abilities, but we were not Gods ourselves.

"Want to know what the best part in all of this is, Hudson? That darling husband stole his wife's sword made by her consort, Hephaestus, that draws power from every drop of blood it collects from the enemy of the person wielding the sword." I cursed, that explains why every hit made me weaker. The God of all weapons?! I mean, seriously? Stealing a fucking throne, stealing a fucking sword, and duping a God into helping them. This bitch is either seriously stupid or ridiculously cunning; my bet is on both, because all those decisions will backfire.

"I can understand you being a good warrior, Alvor. You have age and the experience. But I'll always be better and stronger, because I am blessed by Gaia. I protect my people in battle, and I don't summon a God and have dealings with things way beyond my understanding, just to win a war you are literally prophesied to lose. You stand behind a queen who won't fight herself, sends her errand boy with a God to protect him because she knows he can't do it himself. The sad part is, you are with her because you hate who you are. You have a mate, yet you reject your sexuality-the one man who was put here to be yours-just for power and because you have been brainwashed by traditions that do not carry on in this century. You are a sham. A disgrace and I'm glad Kalen will have the opportunity to find someone else once I kill you," I yell angrily as I unsettle the ground beneath him, making him lose his footing. As he falls back, I notice he is holding on tighter to one blade more than the other, even though the swords were identical. He finally had a tell, and something told me that was the sword he needed the most. I take advantage of his position, swiping out and cutting his hand off. Blade still clutched in his missing hand, I kicked the hand and sword away from him.

He laughed. I admit, not the reaction I was expecting, but the sword started to glow and switched over to his other hand. I cursed. What the fuck was that? You would think that shit is the Sword of Gryffindor. I needed that fucking sword away from him. I breathed slowly, I felt my chest tight, and I felt the flutters in my stomach getting weaker. As he stood up, I took note of the battle still raging. Just how many people did this bitch have to sacrifice?! I had no idea, but all of these people couldn't be here because they believed in her cause.

I suddenly remembered that part of the prophecy noted that I had the ability to save those whose hearts had been frozen over time. I wonder if that meant... I wouldn't put it past her... from the corner of my eye, I saw Alvor advancing, I parried his attack and split my attention realizing that this bitch must have manipulated these people to fight, regardless of their wishes. Fuck my golden heart. I couldn't let innocent people die because of her selfishness.

I breathed in deep, hoping I was right. As it was, I was too weak to keep fighting, but maybe I could save enough people so they could carry on the war without me. *Fucking morbid, but what else could I do?* The thought saddened me. I mean, for fuck's sake, this was only book one of my story! The prophecy said I would be the rightful Queen; it didn't say for how long, but it said plenty about blood and death. However, it said nothing about me surviving to see it through. If I could sacrifice myself for the greater good, then that part was true. My humanity was my greatest strength.

I just hope I knew what the fuck I was doing, other than going off magical theory. I collected my thoughts quickly. Magic was pure, nature was pure, and it fought to balance itself, no matter what. Therefore, what corrupts nature may destroy aspects of it, but can't destroy all of it. Eventually, it comes back stronger, like a rose and concrete. So, while half of me fought with Alvor, every one of my hits getting two or more from him, my magic pulled from the energies around me, the trees miles away, the rivers across seas. I pulled energy and spoke to the nature around me. I embraced it and I used it as it was intended; to protect, to guide, to grow, and not to be perverted or abused. Knowing my intent, the magic of nature flowed through me, and like a net, I extended it across those attacking our soldiers and our lands. I willed it to capture the essence of corruption. I was a fucking Faerie catcher.

Except this queen was very fucking powerful, and whatever she used as a spell was beyond anything I could have ever presumed. Nature fought hard to overcome the darkness, but it was being blocked, presumably by Uranus. Stupid interfering asshole. Any time here, Gaia, would be a fucking great time to jump in and smack your bitch ass husband.

Suddenly, there was a flash of light, and the sounds of clashing, as a light and dark force fought in the Heavens above us. Well, thanks.

However, with the Goddess now fighting, nature was left without its protector. The net started to drain me, and I felt like I couldn't breathe as I fell to my knees. Alvor took advantage of my position and as he went to swing his sword across my neck, suddenly Kalen found his way from the battle to my side. My face splattered warm with his blood and I cried out. After what seemed like hours, everything moving slowly. He dropped to his knees and his head separated from his neck. I felt the concern of my mates at my despair, felt them weakening in battle, and I refused to let them die.

I took a deeper breath. My magic spiked so hard at my grief, that the ground shook, the sky slamming her bolts of lightning on the ground. The breeze no longer moved gently, no, she whipped around me, filling me with another song. One where she told me she was understanding my anger, fueling my anger, letting me rage and she raged with me. Her daughter hurt. The sky opened and rain poured, weeping, as the breeze raged, mourning. A soul was now fully unleashed, accepting the loss of the only innocence she had left. I'm tired of this stupid bitch controlling every aspect of my life.

Breathing deep, I poured my energy into the net I was casting, and I sent a pulse of power that knocked Alvor back. The sword flew out of his hand and King caught it. Xena appeared and grabbed the sword and disappeared again.

But the damage was done, my energy, my powers had been sapped by a weapon forged by a God, and there was no way to come back from that without another God to help.

Taking a final look at my mates, I felt grief overwhelm me as I slammed down on our connection, cutting us off. Vaguely, I heard a dark laugh, followed by a boom and then silence.

"You stupid girl, you think you could really do anything to stop Nici? You are nothing. Just a joke." Alvor gasped as he crawled on the floor, with his protector gone, it looks like I was the better warrior after all.

"It looks like your God is gone, Alvor, your people dead or retreating, and those forced to defend your bitch ass are no longer trapped." I projected as much as I could, my body draining, the fluttering in my stomach, becoming further and further apart.

"He'll be back." He stumbled to his feet and backed away, disintegrating into thin air. All I heard was his voice. "Uranus hates you, his wife's precious Seelies, just as much as we do." He and that fake queen were idiots. I groaned. Even I paid attention in fucking mythology, this idiot called down a God to a realm they weren't supposed to be in so they could be stronger? There was using Gaia's natural gifts and then there was asking favors from a God. We were so fucked if we couldn't figure out what favors they asked for. More questions. Always more questions, and I had no time to get them answered.

"He hates you too, you fucking idiot," I moaned out, using the last of my strength to take one more breath and pray that my mates will be okay, then the fluttering in my stomach stopped, but so did my breathing. So did my light.

"Empty your heart of its mortal dream.
The winds awaken, the leaves whirl round,
Cheeks pale, hair is unbound,
Breasts heaving, eyes agleam.
Spirit wavering, lips apart in a silent scream.
If eyes befall the rush of emotions,
Let the breeze come between and the hope in their hearts,
The soul, has spilled and is rushing 'twixt night and day and 'twixt the in-between,
And where is there hope when no deed was as fair as the purity of the Seelie Queen?
My soul is now one with the breeze, no longer an instrument.
The only instrument played will be those that echo the screams of the unloyal."

Zane

Everything was drifting in and out as it has been for the past several days while we collected our fallen dead. Thankfully, there weren't many. Grayson and Ryder helped question those who were saved by Hudson's net. In truth, what saved us was the knowledge that Uranus was helping the imposter queen and once Gaia realized he was there, they waged a battle above us. It was true what the stories say, 'Gods don't interfere unless other Gods do'.

I'm glad she interfered or wouldn't be here at all. I sighed, well some of us.

I rubbed my face as Remi brought me another cup of tea. She was going around making sure everyone had what they needed. I think she needed to keep moving to stop herself from thinking.

In the end, nothing, and I mean nothing, affected everyone as hard as seeing Hudson laying on the floor, Kalen stretched out beside her, headless. Her body, despite the armor, had just felt so weightless. We carried her to the cabin to clean her up, her breath barely there, her skin changed from golden to yellow. That day, as we cleaned her up, Remi lost it when we saw the blood pour from between her legs. We cried as we lifted her up and laid her down in her bed. We showered and all laid down next to her, hoping she would wake up, but she didn't.

After a day, we had to have her hooked up to an IV. After a week, her curves started to disappear. We stood around her bed for hours, praying, holding hands, crying, trying so hard to just be together as a family without our one guiding force, the one that brought us all together. For days after, we played her favorite music, and we read to her. Ryder would lay down at night and read as many books as he could to her before falling asleep himself. I would smile as he would argue with her as if she was there, ranting about some characters in a series; yelling about how he was right about the serial killer in something he called the Harkwright Trilogy by BC Morgan. He even went as far as to have shirts made that said, "I was Wright all along." He made us laugh, despite the sadness, but even with Ryder trying, if it wasn't for Remi, I don't think any of us would have been eating.

After some time, Oberon took off, saying he needed to watch out for whispers or whatever the fuck that meant. It was right after we finally noticed a written note from Hudson none of us had noticed before. In truth, I just don't think he was able to be around. His grief almost too great, too palpable. But so was ours.

Hunter spent his time reading the prophecy and her letter over and over again. He would rage and cry, kissing Hudson's pale hands, apologizing over and over again for not being enough. Between all of us, Hunter was always so close to the edge, that his emotions went from that of anger to enraged in a second. Except that the snake coiled so tightly within him went from anger to that of despair in less time than that; I didn't recognize him.

After all the chaos, when Alvor retreated and we had yet to find two of the council members, Raedella and Eldon, no surprise there, we figured out they were the moles but that was nothing in the grand scheme of things, the damage was already done.

Kalen gave the last of his strength and his breath to try to keep her alive. I think it is exactly the way he pictured himself dying, next to Hudson, his life for hers, because despite just being her trainer, he was her uncle and he loved her just as much as we did. We buried him near the house, after having a ceremony with the village and remaining council members. Shea made his presence felt by constantly coming over to check on Hudson while dealing with his guilt and grief. What made it tougher was that we had to bury Kalen without her there and it really set Hunter off. He threw himself into helping the town and was barely home unless it was to kiss her good morning and goodnight, his face always tracking tears.

Grayson went back to training and Ryder helped. Nothing felt like it was going to be normal again. Two weeks later, despite the IV, and healers, she didn't wake up. Tears wouldn't work, reading didn't work, music didn't work.

I spent my spare time at her bedside, reading the note she left out loud. It was a little poem she must have read, that much was clear. Try as I might, it was hard for me to make sense of it.

"Find what you love and let it kill you.
Let it drain you of your all. Let it cling onto your back and weigh
you down into eventual nothingness.
Let it kill you and let it devour your remains.
For all things will kill you, both slowly and fast, but it's even
better to be killed by a lover." Charles Bukowski

We would sometimes pass it between us in whispers. All we can figure was that for such a short time knowing she was Queen, she took it all in stride. She took her responsibilities and thought about solutions rather than complain about more changes or challenges. In truth, the world would never deserve a person like Hudson, but we did. She was our light, and we knew it, so it hit us harder every time we saw her in that bed. It seemed that in that time, she fell in love with her responsibilities as well, seeing them more as a gift. Maybe she realized that dying for her people was for a better cause, a greater one. We took that passion, and we made our presence known to the village, getting to know everyone and building relationships and talking to the council members about our next course of action.

In all of this, there was the last part of the prophecy. It pissed me off to no end. I read it repeatedly. "There's no love until there's family. There is no anguish of the soul until one has children." Except, I think it was wrong, there was love within our family. There is no anguish of the soul until one loses their children. Even if they had been just a flutter, I truly think Hudson's soul just didn't want to come back to her body, to a world without the possibility of those flutters becoming kicks, becoming smiles, speaking the words 'mom and dad'.

I don't think her soul wanted to come back at all, and I don't think that the number of tears I have cried could ever bring her back to me or Rayne and Xavier, the babies we should have had but didn't.

Our love should be forever. I don't care to hear that love transcends death. I can't hug a ghost, I can't kiss a ghost, I can't make love to a ghost. What's worse? I cannot pick up a ghost and kiss their boo boo's, I can't check a closet for monsters and for ghosts. It hurt. It all hurt so much.

I prayed, I hoped, and for brief moments when I couldn't stay awake, I dreamt. Unfortunately, the dreams were so sweet and so perfect, everything hurt even more when I woke up.

So, I wrote my own note to her, in response to hers and I encouraged the others to do the same.

Hudson,
My first love, my first heartbeat may not have been with you, but my last will always be.
Zane

Baby girl,

I could read you a thousand words, but no combination of those words will be able to describe the way I have felt for you since we were kids. The way you made me laugh when I first saw you in that pink potato sack. The way you would scowl at us and tell us to leave you alone. The way you grew up and became an amazing woman. The way my heart flew out of my chest the moment I saw you that day in the pool (even if you ruined my favorite shoes.)

For every moment of my life, I have already known you.

We may have been put here to protect you, but I know that fate put us here for eachother. You are my mate, you are my heart beat, you are my laughter.

Hudson, you have taken my laughter with you and you have taken my heart. You can borrow them, it is okay, I look forward to getting them back when you open your eyes.

Just, please. Open your eyes.

Ryder

Angel,

You protected me even when I didn't need protecting, I could have kicked Hunter's ass. Hudson, you are so special. I don't think you understand how important you are to me. But I will explain. I am always the quiet one but since you have come into our lives, you have made me laugh. You have snapped me back to reality when I was stuck in my head coming up with some theory or another. In truth, you brought me out of my shell and you made me see things that I didn't think I could see.

But I have also always been the observant one. So I used so many moments in our short time to observe you. The way your eyebrows would come together right before you said something snarky to Zane when he was trying to tell you what to do. The way, you would pop your hip out when people challenged you. The way your eyes would light up like green stars the moment anyone challenged you in combat, that blood thirsty look spoke to my inner demons like nothing else could.

Most of all I noticed how your eyes would soften when you looked at any one of us, the way you would wet your lips whenever we drew close, the way you clenched your thighs when we sat near you.

You may have been great in battle, but when it came to us, you were just the way you were supposed to be, weak, but strong willed. Just know, every touch had meaning, every caress meant something to me, and as I write this, I feel those touches still.

For I may be quiet, but I love loudly.

Your Gentle Giant.

Hudson,

It took years to meet you.

In those years I have dreamt about my mate thousands of times.

No dream could have come close to you. Your smell, your taste, your smile, your body, your warmth. So as your mate I will say; You are everything I could want and I will spend my entire life being your best friend, your lover, your mate, your wife, your confidant, your protector, your guide.

As your best friend I will say; I have hope you will come back to us because I hid a classic aged bottle of Faerie wine under your bed, I'm sure that will wake you up bitch.

I love you.

Mimi

My love.

It is an interesting feeling saying that after such a short time, but it doesn't make it any less true.

My love, from the moment I saw you fight, from the moment I heard your voice in the breeze, I knew you were everything.

I am one of the oldest of my kind, have seen many atrocities, so much pain. But unlike others I grew and I understood that with time comes growth and understanding. I would like to think that these years have taught me everything this is to know, but it isn't true.

These years have not taught me how to meet my true mate and lose her so quickly. I cannot imagine the fates would be so cruel. Hudson, if there is one thing I have learned about you is that you are more than a fighter, you are a survivor. I don't see you leaving us. Everyday you sleep, I think about you, our children, our future, our dreams that will come to fruition.

Faerie has always been said to have a balance;

I am darkness, you are my light.

If there is to be a balance, you cannot go,

for I will cease to exist.

Your Obi (yes I heard you call me that)

SWEETHEART,
I SPENT DAYS WRITING THIS LETTER BECAUSE I JUST CANNOT SEE THROUGH MY TEARS.
I CANNOT BREATHE KNOWING I'M NOT HEARING YOUR SASS, YOUR ANGER, YOUR SWEET LAUGHS OR SEEING YOUR SMILES OR DEALING WITH YOUR CHALLENGES TO MY MANHOOD. REMEMBER THAT DAY YOU BOPPED MY NOSE? I THINK THATS THE DAY I REALLY FELL FOR YOU. I KNEW I LOVED YOU ALREADY, HOW COULD ANY MAN NOT? BUT FELL HARD FOR YOU? YEAH IT WAS RIGHT AT THAT MOMENT.
OUR FIRST TIME TOGETHER? WHEN I HELD YOU? I SWEAR MY HEART STARTED BEATING IN TIME WITH YOURS.
I CAN DO EVERYTHING IN THIS WORLD HUDSON, BUT WITHOUT YOU IN IT, ALL THOSE THINGS WOULD MEAN NOTHING.
I REALIZE, NOW, WHAT LOVE TRULY IS AND THE MATE BOND DIDN'T DO THIS; WE DID.
I MADE A PROMISE TO YOU BABYGIRL, YOU MAY NOT HAVE HEARD IT BUT I PROMISED THAT I WOULD PROTECT YOU AND THAT ANYONE WHO TRIED TO HURT YOU WOULD SUFFER FOR IT. I FAILED TO DO THE FIRST, BUT THE WORLD WILL BURN WITH MY FURY, JUST LIKE THE TEARS BURN HOT DOWN MY FACE.
FOREVER YOURS AND ONLY YOURS,
HUNTER

Oberon's Remarks

Sit down and learn a bit of our history.

There are thousands of old tales revered by our people about those who, instead of being born of Gaia and her offspring, can be created. *Changed into Faerie.* There are many variations to the tales, but one of those versions highlights the need for a particular person to already have a talent for magic. It is why those magic users beyond the veil often make wishes or deals with the Fae, although those are typically Unseelie, the Dark Fae, to gain more power or be changed. Problem with the overall concept, despite the obvious, is that the Unseelie never truly keep their end of the bargain, often stealing children instead, playing cruel jokes or leaving people mad.

A change from human to Fae can be complicated and often the person is barely recognizable. While there are various creatures who reside in the large world of Fae; from goblins to brownies, to nymphs we often find ourselves completely enamored by the idea of "other." To humans, nothing is ever good enough, concrete enough; there is always more to find, more to discover and more ways to grow. Some of these journeys have led to hundreds of revelations and scientific discoveries. Some have changed the world.

However, there were some of these journeys that have led to the decimation of the human soul. Humans, who rot from the inside out, not from evil, although there is plenty of that in the world, but from the attempts to tamper in things that are beyond this world, beyond simple understanding. The Dark Fae, the Unseelie, take advantage of these weak individuals. For it is the weak who fall prey to the temptation of being stronger; it is the weak who fall prey to simple temptation of power. In their thirst, they fail to realize that the strong already have the power. In their hunger, they pick up scraps, and they grow unstable. They take thrones, they hurt others, and in the Veil, that makes you a threat. In the Veil, that makes you vulnerable to the true force that governs, Gaia; and *Gaia has already chosen. Those who oppose Rhiona of Faell will fail, shatter, and plead for forgiveness.* For those who have reveled too long in their scraps, will now learn the true pangs of hunger.

For it is during this time that we will see true destruction, so that we can soon rebuild.

LI'ELL

I had to sneak out of my bedroom while Momma was in the garden to go see Hudson and my best friends. Momma says that I should let her rest because she's been through a big battle and isn't doing too well, but she doesn't get it. Hudson is my friend, she even gave me a nickname! So, of course I have to go see her, *parents don't understand anything*.

I ran my hands through the flowers as I followed the trail to her cabin and jumped when Xena appeared next to me. "Xena, you silly kitty! You scared me. Are you going to walk me the rest of the way?" I asked.

Yes, I will keep you safe. I felt you coming, little one. I giggled, I could speak to all the familiars here; it was one of my gifts and it was so much fun.

"Okay, I won't be dying for another six hundred and thirty-two years, Xena. Don't you worry," I said calmly. She raised her fuzzy eyebrows and growled.

Not if I can help it.

I released a heavy sigh. Not too many people understand me. It's okay though, I think it will always be that way, except for my best friends. I didn't bother knocking on the door when I got to the cabin; everyone was too sad to answer. I went straight upstairs and saw all her mates sitting around her while she napped. That's all it was to me, a long nap. I didn't like naps, but I knew Hudson would wake up soon, only something big would change my visions.

"Hi, guys, I'm back for a visit." I clapped and jumped on the bed, laying my head on her tummy, they looked so sad before they tried to smile at me.

"Hey, little one," Ryder started. "Hudson isn't feeling too well and ermmm," he looked around the room to the other guys there. I look a closer look at them. From the last time I saw them, it looked like they finally changed back into what they were. Now all six of them had white hair and pointy ears. They looked like me!

"That's okay. It won't be for long. I just wanted to tell my best friends I was here!" I giggled and started telling a story to her belly. For a few minutes, everyone was quiet.

"The thing is Ella, I don't think your best friends are ready to come quite yet, it may be a few more years," Zane said sadly. I jumped off the bed and walked closer to him, putting my hand on his cheek. It was so weird being around my best friend's parents when they weren't here, but I knew that I would be a part of their family soon.

Looking into his eyes and glancing around the room I smiled. "You know, just because I'm little doesn't mean I don't understand," I giggled, grownups were so funny. "My best friends will be here soon, all four of them."

Their eyes popped open and I skipped out of the room and then out of the house. I didn't want Momma to get worried.

ALSO BY RUBY SMOKE

For **Maximum Enjoyment** Read Infiltrated **BEFORE** Within the Veil and pay special attention to the forward 😈

ACKNOWLEDGMENTS

For several fucking years, I have dreamed of writing a book. For all those years I read instead, and I grew inspired. I have survived suicide attempts, bullies, assholes on I-95 and motherhood (Okay, I am barely surviving that.)

Point is, I was pushed by my husband, Julian, to write and then I was tossed over the cliff by my best friends, Anna and Marjolein. I found my confidence and I waded through some interesting waters until I found an amazing team of people who helped me grow as a writer and as a person.

Julian, thank you for being everything you are and serving for the inspiration for all my steamy scenes. I love you hot stuff, always and forever.

Anna and Marjolein, thank you for simply being everything you are. I can't wait to move to the UK and take it by storm with you two bad bitches by my side.

Savannah, thank you for quite possibly being the best PR team ever, understanding my vision, hearing me rant while still guiding me. To Bibi and Ash, you both understood that same vision and gave me some of the best advice. (Even when Bibi would message me and start with "So feel free to tell me to fuck off but..." or "lube up, shit is about to get real..." I knew she did it with the best of intentions.)

Savannah, Bibi, and Ash- being a supportive and guiding force is not just a job, it is a talent, and you ladies have it in spades; I can't thank you enough.

Jess, despite going through some seriously trying times, you came out on top and helped me edit and re-edit and you are one amazing woman; your grandmother is so proud of you.

Dani, you came in at the last minute and saved the fucking day. This book wouldn't be nearly as amazing without you.

BC, you truly are a gem... not only have you inspired me to be a better writer, but you have also given me the strength to help talk to the damn voices in my head asking for one more chapter.

To my amazing beta team, thank you for everything you have done. This book wouldn't be here without you all either. Shannon, Melinda...you freaking ROCK!

Finally, to my four little girls, this is just the beginning of my journey. I waited long enough, and I'll always be the mom that encourages you to push until you embark on your dream. Nothing is out of your reach because your dad and I will always be there to lift you up to reach them. I love you. (Eventually, you'll be old enough to read this book, but until you're ninety-six years, just know I mentioned you here.)

CHAPTER 1

INFILTRATED SNEAK PEAK

Nici, Imposter Queen

I SAT IN MY WAR-DARKEN CHAMBERS, CONSOLED BY THE SOUNDS OF the screams coming from the dungeons behind me. The dark gray walls, the worn brown table, lack of windows, and the opium wafting from the corner of the room, adding to the overall ambiance. *It's good to be a twisted bitch.* After all this time, people still chose to rebel against my rule, still chose to believe the silly little prophecy that would give someone else back the power to the Seelie. *Not if i can help it.* I scoffed, staring at the chess board in front of me, trying to make better sense of my next move.

My gaze flicked up to the historian at the right of my table. "Tell me, how divided are these Magickal Communities, again?" I didn't really need to ask twice. I knew there were two very separate worlds of magick users; two factions, if you will, separated by their levels of thirst for power. It was a fair assessment that one of these factions was ruled by intelligence, and the other by sheer stupidity. That stupidity, I might as well use to my advantage.

"Very. It's as if they no longer have any knowledge of each other. However, we know the individual councils per community are aware of one another, but the people, for the most part, are kept unaware. Factions are completely apart and warded accordingly." My historian remarks, his fierce blue eyes pulling me in, his voice captivating me. I bit back a smirk and ignored the jolt of pleasure from having him here. *I loved the sounds of take-overs, in the morning.*

"Well then," I started, coming to my final decision. "What better way to gain allies against this...threat." I rolled my eyes at that. The idea that this prophecy was any more than a joke, but I didn't get this far from underestimating possibilities. I accounted for everything and moved my pieces accordingly.

"How do you mean?" I looked over to my left, my war advisor, Ren, sitting up intrigued. If there is anyone as bloodthirsty as I, it was him.

"The faction that seeks power wants something I can provide, and they have something to provide me." I paused, leaning back against my chair and propping my bloody feet up on the table. No one at the table flinched. At this point, from the dungeon and back to planning, what was the point of keeping the blood off my body until the end of the night.

"Another army," I added, looking away from my chess board. Humans can be quite droll, but this game was an excellent way to calm the mind. So was murder, but I was fresh out of desire to do that, and was filled with the fury to destroy the chances of this prophecy, coming to fruition as we get closer to the end of my timeline.

"So, what do you propose?" Ren inquired.

I looked at him closely, a slow smile stretching my face. "Make contact with the Council that represents the ones who are the most divided—who thirsts for power. We will start there and work our way in." I smiled, the bloodthirsty smiles in the room bringing me a sick pleasure. *These are my people.* The Fae were so steeped in tradition that it led to the ultimate lack of awareness; those who have deserted and are in hiding would hardly find the merit in looking for outside sources for allies in the upcoming war. Me? I will use everything at my disposal to make sure the enemy is destroyed; I will sow the seeds of discord. Failure wasn't an option. Time was ticking, *forty years left.*

My attention snapped to my historian as he looked down at his list. "I'll make contact with the Darnika Council immediately." He nodded and made his way to leave my planning chambers, striding out with a gleeful look of determination.

I sat back and looked at Ren. "Any news on the Seelie's new location?"

He looked at me, slightly irritated. "They are warded well, and we haven't been able to pin down the secret keepers from Scail," he said scathingly. "The Seelie rebels are proving hard to find and right when we think we are close... they disappear." He stood up angrily, approaching my chair. I breathed in, trying to control the spike of anger that flowed through me. This *Scail* was proving to be problematic for several years now. He had a network of spies that was downright impossible to penetrate, and I hated being taken for a fool.

I sighed as Ren stood behind me and started to unbutton my dress, his hands skimming my neck, the smell of dried blood from his hands an aphrodisiac. "Any news from the infiltrator?" I asked, moaning softly as his hand wandered right to where I was now aching.

He pressed an openmouthed kiss to my neck, his sharpened teeth drawing a piercing, satisfying, pain. "Mmm, yes, he will be back later, and will be the best fae to carry out this new plan of yours," he answered.

A sliver of doubt ran rampant, but I bit back the possibility that this infiltrator may actually be against me, but he has proven his loyalty too many times. Although I had to wonder... *never mind*, I thought, shaking my head. *I had a contingency plan.*

I smiled as Ren picked me up and set me on the table. "We can discuss this later, for now, please your Queen."

He smirked wickedly. "As you wish."

Chapter One

"When life hits you hard, get up and say you hit like a bitch," - ***Unknown***
"Assuming that bitch lands the first punch. Right? Right?"- ***Charlie***

Charlie

I wiped the blood from my favorite blade. *Sigh.* Nothing better than serving justice to some sick motherfucker who thinks he can get away with whatever he wants. Granted, in this case, I was killing three birds with one stone, is that even a thing? Never mind. I looked down at the serial killer/gargoyle shifter—a shady, stupid motherfucker—and waved my hand over his body, summoning my fire, burning the body, before using air manipulation to scatter the ashes into the water, surrounding the abandoned boating dock. I found him feasting on one of the gifted kids who had been reported missing. I am just pissed it took three dead children for me in order to finally pick up his trail. I have no idea why he had been fascinated with killing the children, and to be honest, I didn't give a flying fuck; he needed to die, I had an itch to kill something, and everything worked out. At least, I was able to fortify my blade with the blood of a gargoyle.

Using magick had its perks, one of them being that every creature I killed imbued my blade with their particular powers or quirks, and transferred some of that power to me, whatever power I don't already have, anyway; which is to say, barely any. Nonetheless, this blade has become an extension of my arm if I am out on patrol, like tonight. I paid a lot of money, a few years ago, before I learned how to spell properly or this shit to be spelled by some hidden witch in West bumble-fuck Pajila, another magickal community, but larger, north of Darnika, which was my home, in a sense. We were a decent-sized community made up of three castes: low, middle, and high; and yes you guessed it, the castes were named and placed for the level of power of the people in those communities. Same applies for the socio-economic status of those castes as well. I hated it, and my plan was to get everyone on the same playing field instead of the division instilled by the Council of Magick over the past few years. I did my research, albeit illegally, but not all communities were set up the way ours was. But for now, Darnica was my responsibility to fix.

We also had a decent outer-lying communities made of shifters, vampires, demons, and a few otherworldly creatures, although they weren't policed by us unless they attacked us outright; then all bets were off. No, they pretty much handled themselves, just stayed within the ward to avoid human interaction. Not that that always controlled the Vampires who had their ways to make it into the human world undetected. But I had an understanding with that community. Stay the fuck out of my way and live. Simple.

But first I had to protect and serve, and more importantly take out murderous sons of bitches. Gargoyles are hard to kill. Although, rogue shifters in general, are. But gargoyles? They are just some big assholes and it took a lot more than just magick to take care of them. You had to be quick and efficient enough to strike right under the wing where they are the most vulnerable. It didn't take any chance of turning human but as I went out of my way to find this shifter and to kill this slimy-child-thieving murderer, the look of shock on its face when I won, was particularly delicious. My blade is stronger, a serial killer is dead, and my blood lust is satisfied—for now.

I looked around as I tucked my blade into my holster. Slightly glowing, it sent a delicious shiver up my spine and I took a brief second to acclimate to the powers transferred to me. Grinning wickedly, I gave another brief look around as I tested my new powers. I have never killed a gargoyle so I didn't know what to expect. In truth, they were strong, they could fly, had a tendency to have harder hides, and were heavy as fuck, so being pinned by one was surely death. My philosophy? Never be fucking pinned by someone bigger than you. My back started to itch through my new leather jacket and I felt it rip as wings sprouted on my back.

I groaned. *Fuck me. My new riding jacket. I just got this shit.* Looks like the perk for this particular murder was wings! I may have lost my jacket, but fuck it.

I wonder if I could fly? I put the idea in the back of my head to try later as I heard a small sound coming from my right. I ignored all the thoughts that flitted through my head as I headed over to the child, now cowering on the floor. The child. *It had to be a rough time for her as it is, especially now that she saw me go all murder and mayhem.* Well, that doesn't exactly set the stage for trust.

"Hey honey, my name is Charlie, you can call me Ellie. What's your name and how old are you?" I attempted to ask in my best motherly tone. Which means my voice probably came out as more of a husky growl, and judging by her flinch, I was right. She wasn't convinced by my attempted motherly nature. Well, I wouldn't blame her. I don't really have one, but still I tried.

"Hi, Ellie, I...I'm Ambrosia, thank you for kil...helping me." I smirked at her attempt to cover up what I did, but the truth was, I did kill him, so I shrugged.

"Don't mention it," I said as softly as I could. I took a casual once over and realized her leg was at an odd angle and she was bleeding from her neck, where the gargoyle was trying to hold her down. A fury rose deep within me and I'm sure my eyes were glowing red, a nifty trick I got for killing a murderous vampire, a year ago. Ambrosia looked at my face and whimpered, for sure trying to figure out what I was at this point. *You and me both, kid.* I shoved the anger down after a few seconds of breathing and tried to focus. I killed him, she's safe, and I will make sure she stays safe.

"I see you have some nasty injuries there, but guess what? I have pretty strong healing powers to help you but since your leg seems to be broken, this may hurt." Who was I kidding, it was going to hurt like a bitch but the child seemed to be a little bit more comfortable as I spoke quietly, so I didn't want to freak her out.

"S-sure, it hurts so much."

Without waiting or any prior warning, I put my hands over her body and pulled on my healing powers from deep within the recesses of my soul. Sounds strange, but that is where anyone's power comes from. Their soul. People forget that the soul is a constant energy that cannot be easily destroyed.

When my power finally peaked, I put my hands over Ambrosia and let my power work slowly, trying to at least alleviate some of the pain. When healing, a typical healer needs to focus and touch their patient, for me, I didn't have to touch, but it was always good practice to make myself look as inconspicuous as possible in this world. So overtime, I mentally developed what I would call a power condom; it didn't feel good but I had to fuck with the constrictions of it.

Ambrosia took a deep breath and made a small sound in the back of her throat but continued keeping a brave face. Impressive. Most people would flip their shit. I wanted to wrap her up in a hug, but that was more Pixie's thing, not mine.

While my power worked, Ambrosia seemed determined to keep the pain from her voice, and said, "I'm eleven by the way," answering my previous question.

I cursed under my breath. Eleven years old, kidnapped, hurt, and having to deal with a Gargoyle and whatever the fuck I am (again, later.)

Ambrosia looked at me. "You curse a lot. My foster mother never lets me curse. She believes it is beneath me." She looks at me speculatively. "But you curse a lot and you're saving my life, so it can't be a good way to judge someone's character." She takes a deep breath as her leg adjusts. I let out a surprised laugh. I admit she is a strong kid if she can take that level of pain. I have had to reset my legs quite a bit over the past six years since I have been on my own and it was not pleasant.

"There, all done. Would you like me to take you home now?" I cursed inwardly as I realized I brought my beautiful cherry-red and black motor cycle, and it was no place for a child. *Sigh.* As much I hated giving away all my secrets, there was no way I could take a kid back home on a bike, when every magickal law enforcement was out looking for this particular child, *that I have already saved, useless fuckers.*

"Please, I know my mom must be worried and I just want to be home," Ambrosia said softly, looking exhausted. Being healed, especially after such injuries, takes a toll.

"Ambrosia, I need you to keep what you saw me do tonight a secret, can you do that for me?" Something about this girl told me she would, but I don't trust anyone. Not anymore. Not after...no, I ignore that memory trying to rise, and focus on the little girl in front of me. She nodded gently.

"Thank you. I will take you home now. What does your home look like, picture it in your mind." I picked her up gently and surprisingly, she was lighter than I expected, but again, thanks to my badass abilities, I am stronger than your average magick user. She gave me a tired smile, and projected a quick picture of her home. I picked up the image of her home from her head, right before she passed out in my arms. Thank goodness, I was able to ask her before she fell asleep. I needed it to create the portal, and while I could have taken it while she was sleeping, without consent, she would have had a heck of a headache, not to mention I don't do anything without consent. Period.

I quickly threw an illusion, hiding my beautiful bike, Beast. I wasn't Belle, but we could share; he looks like a motherfucker with some serious stamina.

I opened a portal, then quickly and quietly stepped through, sighing in relief as I looked down and saw that Ambrosia was still sleeping. Portals tend to make you feel as if someone is stretching you to make you into a human Laffy Taffy. Not fun. I don't let people know the extent of my powers. Hell, I don't even know the full extent of my powers. I keep learning more every day. *Being this badass was a process.* Anyway, what I did know is that with every kill of a depraved Druko, I was stronger and took on a little of their powers, rather perks, as well. For example, I couldn't kill an elemental with fire and take their power because I already had elemental fire. Also, killing a shifter doesn't give me power to go through a full shift, but I can still create an impenetrable illusion of that person, that even mimicked certain personality traits. Learning. Process.

Unlike the other children who have to go through the Surge—our magickal awakening that gave us our powers—I was born with it. It had never happened before as far as I knew, or at least it was never documented, I should know, I have done the research. My parents kept my unusual birth a secret, and kept me hidden, so even despite their resources and connections, they couldn't make waves to alert anyone on the Magick Council—the Council that controlled the magick population for our community pocket anyway. Sigh. When I was born, I let out a burst of fire magick and damaged my mother from being able to carry children in the future. Although, according to my parents, they had intervention to have me, and chances are I was a one-off without more help.

Regardless, they always loved me and never made me feel bad about it.

My parents were strong elementals and well-known; while my mom could control water better than anyone, my dad could control fire and heat. So opposite, but for magick, it wasn't about what power you had, it was more so about how your magick called to one another. Once that bond tugged, you blended into one another. Some call it the bond, others referred to it as the Call. Their love for each other was just perfect and well-balanced, it made me who I am, and I will always be grateful to them.

I smiled sadly, I missed them. I missed their smiles when I manipulated my bath water to make water balls when I was two, I even missed their anger when I set the backyard on fire when I was practicing my fire magick when I was four. I missed their shocked faces when I did something extraordinary like regrowing the grass, trees, and my mother's flowers, shortly after the fire without breaking a sweat. I have always been different, my power was vast, and unlike most Magicks I did not seem to have a refractory period. I scoffed, like men who need thirty minutes just to get it up for two minutes of grunting. I liked being different. But often times, different meant lonely and I had always been lonely, my parents couldn't allow me to be around other children to avoid anyone learning of my power. I was tutored at home and my parents did everything they could to make me laugh and happy. Still I was alone. I wanted to go out, I wanted to play, hell, I just wanted to be normal.

Lost in my thoughts, I blinked as I suddenly found myself in front of a gorgeous southern style home with a wraparound porch and swings right in front of the door. Magickal Law Enforcement, I scowl, also known as a pain in my sweet round ass, must have left earlier after asking their questions. Useless if you ask me. I heard the alert on the app I illegally had installed into my phone, *don't judge me*, as I was patrolling the city from the shadows and was able to find her pretty quickly. Granted, it took me three days to figure out the gargoyle's patterns, three children who will never see their friends and families again, who will constantly be mourned. I may not have been able to save those other children, but I was able to save one and any future victims by killing the filthy, fucking, murdering garbage.

I quickly created an illusion—another perk of my powers—of a stout officer with a heavy mustache. I made sure the green and yellow uniform that I had worn, indicating I was from the MLE, was perfect and crisp. Yuck, definitely not my colors, and quite frankly if they were going to suck at their jobs, at least they could dress better and try to look badass. Anyways, I knocked on the door, and a frantic woman in her bathrobe opened the door, and screamed and started sobbing. *Ouch. Why do women scream?!* I hid my wince. I held in the urge to shuffle my feet as she quickly grabbed Ambrosia and called out for her husband.

"Chad...Chad, she's home!" she yelled.

A blond man, with permanent laugh wrinkles in his eyes, came to the door, and sighed in relief. He was wearing a college jersey and sweats, and looked just as rough and emotional as his wife.

"Hello ma'am, we were able to find your daughter near the docks before any harm was done, and we caught the Druko responsible." I schooled my features into a look of relief and happiness, which to be honest wasn't hard to do because I was feeling both.

Even though I do not do well with emotions, I smiled. In the Magickal Communities, foster parents were a lot different than those in the human world, on the other side of the magical border. We valued our children and did not tolerate abuse of any kind. These kids were fortunate enough to be able to be loved and taken care of by another magickal family who understood their coming powers. I'm not sure how Ambrosia lost her parents, but I'm not one to pry.

I sighed, a lot of these foster parents have lost a child of their own when those children came into their power; it's a grueling process and can take a toll on the body because some kids just don't survive the Surge. Most kids came into their power when they turn twelve. I didn't sense any power on Ambrosia, so she has yet to go through the transition. I hope she survives. I can feel that she has a fortitude in her that reminds me of myself when I was younger.

Ambrosia's parents thanked me for saving their child, and finally I made my way from their porch and further down the road before I was able to use my hacked phone, to send an encrypted message that the missing child was found and to call off the search. The MLE wouldn't be able to tell who sent the message but knowing them, they wouldn't even give a fuck.

The MLE was just a front, the real people who protected the city, protected in shadows. Hell, they were called the Shadows, pretentious fuckers. They were primarily made up of men, and as my dad once eloquently put, they were little bitches of the Magick Council. Ten users that helped contain and use paranormal beings who have special abilities for whatever the Council needed them for. My mother and father were on the Council for years, being the strongest elementals with their perspective power, and being one of the five founding families, they were voices of reason on that corrupt ass-fucking board. For hundreds of years, the Elimentis were known to be very affluent, strong, and level-headed. *Our surname turned heads, used to anyway,* I thought sadly. Then suddenly on my thirteenth birthday, they didn't come home. My parents never missed a birthday and they always came home every night. After two days, I put forth our emergency plan, but I knew they were gone. Not just gone, but murdered, because my parents would never leave me. Not willingly.

I didn't mourn, logically, there was no time. I opened my heart, said goodbye, cleared my mind and focused on finding the truth. I had no proof...yet. I used that time to continue my magickal training and abilities through the vast amounts of information in my childhood home.

I made illusions to go over the border into the human world and underwent intense training in all forms of martial arts to hone my body and mind even further. Why the human side? Because the council fuckers didn't believe in their people learning to defend themselves, if we had the Shadows. What was the purpose, right? Fuck that. So for six years, I trained. After about a year, I felt the pull of my magick to a beautiful girl marred in bruises in one of my classes. I smiled at the thought of Pixie. She was perfect.

At the time I was confused why there was another magick in the same place, but like I said, the process is like a pull. A pull so young was rare, but when have I ever been normal. Pixie had been in the human realm with her dick-head human foster parents, and had wanted to learn how to fight. She snuck out, and the gym gave her free lessons once they picked up on her injuries. Why they didn't help her was beyond me, regardless she was tenacious then, and even more so now.

She didn't know about Darnika, hell, she didn't even know about her powers, and that I felt some of the strongest mental abilities emanating from her, other than me. I was cocky as fuck, but truth was truth. After a few weeks and sessions, the bruises started getting worse. I asked her if she would want to come home with me to my world instead. She wasn't the most trusting individual, from what I had observed, over the weeks. Always looking around, keeping to herself, unless it was time to train. She always gravitated toward me, even with seemingly no knowledge of Magick; she couldn't help the pull of the bond. The night I asked, she left the human realm and never looked back. We continued to train, our bodies becoming weapons and our magick becoming one. While we felt the pull young, we never crossed the line to fully bond until we were much older. We focused on hard work and knowledge.

We took it a step further, and learned every form of hacking and data encryption, there was to learn, and used that knowledge to hack into the Council's database, waiting for a slip-up on information via email, files, or chats. I was a ghost, a hungry one. After several years of searching, nothing popped up about my parents, just very small details about the new Council members that replaced them. Two weak elementals. I scoffed as the thought crossed my mind. No one on that Council was weak, they couldn't afford to be because they needed to maintain power. No. Someone is hiding something and I'm going to fucking find it. And I had the perfect plan. I needed to get closer. Pixie and I are going to infiltrate the motherfucking Shadows. Not just the Shadows, but we were going to get into their Elite Squad, closer to the Council, closer to the truth.

ABOUT THE AUTHOR

Ruby curses a bit too much, moms a bit too hard, and loves her husband with everything she is. Even more so, she loves all her characters because, in some aspects, they are a small representation of who Ruby is; bold, unapologetic, and accepting of her sexuality and all of her desires. She has never been able to do anything without being considered a bit TOO MUCH. But that is okay because there is never such a thing as too much love (for oneself or others), too much sex, or too much support for her friends and family.

Oh, Ruby is also a bit of a smut enthusiast and proud of it.

So, if you found me, don't hide, enter my World of Smoke and Shadows and find your forbidden desires. (AND some super forbidden ones as well, hey who the fuck am I to judge 😉)

Join Me!

Follow me on Instagram @RubySmokeAuthor

Join my Facebook group-
https://www.facebook.com/groups/rubysinfulreveries

www.ingramcontent.com/pod-product-compliance
Lightning Source LLC
Chambersburg PA
CBHW070644310726
48982CB00001B/412
9781916521698